When Christmas Bells Ring

Katie Flynn

When Christmas Bells Ring

CENTURY

1 3 5 7 9 10 8 6 4 2

Century
20 Vauxhall Bridge Road
London SW1V 2SA

Century is part of the Penguin Random House group of companies
whose addresses can be found at global.penguinrandomhouse.com.

Copyright © Katie Flynn 2015

Katie Flynn has asserted her right to be identified as the author of this
Work in accordance with the Copyright, Designs and Patents Act 1988.

First published in the UK by Century in 2015

www.randomhouse.co.uk

A CIP catalogue record for this book is
available from the British Library.

ISBN 9781780892313

Printed and bound by Clays Ltd, St Ives Plc

Penguin Random House is committed to a sustainable future
for our business, our readers and our planet. This book is
made from Forest Stewardship Council® certified paper.

For Amelie and Mia Turner with lots of love,
Grandma.

Letter to the Reader

Dear Reader,

I've always been fascinated by twins, ever since researching into the studies done on identical twins parted at birth and then brought together. The results of these studies were absolutely fascinating; twins who had never met and did not know they even had a sibling would turn up for the first interview in identical clothes and with identical hairstyles, sometimes with identical Christian names; weird. Unfortunately, several of the twins in the study fell for each other's husbands, though the said husbands' feelings are not mentioned!

But of course none of this had anything to do with April and May, the twins in *When Christmas Bells Ring*, because on this occasion I wanted to write about the more human side of twins as children. April and May infuriate each other and are by nature naughty and, alas, extremely selfish. But when things go wrong for one of them the other can be seen in her true colours, being as supportive and loving as any sister can be. They are born as the story starts and it ends when they are sixteen and seeing, possibly for the first time, someone else's point of view.

And before I leave you to find out what happens to Rosheen and her daughters, I'd like to add a personal experience of twinhood. My second son was eighteen and going through the interviews to see which university might offer him a place. His best friend, a twin, was examining the same universities so on one occasion we took twin A to Bangor University whilst his brother, twin B, went to Edinburgh. During the night twin A developed a bad stomach ache which had us worried; other people's children . . .

Next day we rang our twin's home to say that their son had been suffering from stomach ache but it had now cleared and he felt fine.

His father was not in the least surprised because the other twin had been rushed into a hospital in Edinburgh the previous night and had his appendix removed.

So in my opinion there is a link between identical twins, even if, like April and May, they occasionally fight like cat and dog!

All best wishes

Katie Flynn

Chapter One

Spring 1932

Staff Nurse MacIntyre took the corner of the corridor at something perilously close to a run, then slowed to a guilty walk as Matron, presumably having heard the rapidly approaching footsteps, opened her door and came out of her office. She was a large woman, probably in her mid-fifties, with greying hair and hard eyes, and she raised her eyebrows enquiringly as the nurse skidded to a stop. 'MacIntyre, you know the rules almost as well as I do myself,' she said. 'Nurses do not run; they proceed, if necessary, at a fast walk, unless of course you've come to report an emergency. *Is* there an emergency, Staff?'

Staff Nurse MacIntyre shook her head, then changed her mind and nodded. 'It's Mrs Clarke; the patient who came in earlier in the day. She's in the delivery room … or was when I left it. Dr Flitwick said to fetch you, Matron.' The girl hesitated, pushing the strands of hair which had escaped from her cap back out of sight. 'She says she's waited long enough and if we can't produce her baby in the next ten minutes she's going home to get her tea.'

Matron's eyebrows shot up, then descended in a scowl. 'So she thinks we can produce a baby on demand, does she?' She swung the nurse round by her shoulder. 'Come with me. I expect Dr Flitwick is afraid to lay hands on her in case she complains to the authorities. I, however, have dealt with worse than a foolish young woman in my time.'

As they entered the delivery room the patient was swinging her legs off the couch, regardless of the cries of anguish from the doctor and the midwife still in attendance. But Matron moved quickly, despite her size, and almost lifted her back on to the sheet. The girl looked startled. 'Gerroff!' she said crossly. 'Why can't you gerra move on? Ain't nobody ever telled you havin' a baby hurts summat rotten?'

'Do you know nothing, young woman?' Matron said in a hectoring tone. 'Your baby will come when it's ready. Have you no patience? I take it this is your first, but you must know that birth has to be controlled for the good of both mother and child. Now let me have no more nonsense about leaving this hospital until I say you may.'

The girl on the bed scowled up into Matron's rubicund face. 'But I've bin 'ere for ages, pushin' away like what the doctor said to do, and nothin' happens 'cept I feel like I'm bein' split in two. I'm sure if I could just gerroff this 'ere bed and walk about, the baby 'ud come in no time.' She began to heave herself into a sitting position, but even as she did so there was a warning cry from the doctor, the midwife rushed forward and the baby was neatly fielded by Matron herself.

'There you are! A fine baby girl,' she said with forced joviality. The waiting midwife whipped up a clean piece of sheeting and wrapped the infant firmly, then handed it to its astonished mother.

'Well, may I be buggered. It's as ugly as a can of worms.' She giggled. 'Not unlike its father, I suppose.'

Staff Nurse MacIntyre tutted. 'It's a beautiful baby,' she said as defensively as though it were her own. 'All babies look like this when they are born, and besides, you said you didn't know who the father was.'

Rosheen Clarke giggled again. 'Well, don't you try and tell me it looks like me; what it looks most like is a squashed tomato.' Looking up from the red and crumpled face of her firstborn, she bestowed a smile upon Matron and another on Nurse MacIntyre. 'Can I go home now?'

'Well, not quite yet. There's—' but Rosheen was putting a hand to her heaving stomach.

'There's summat more in there!' she said fretfully. She peered at the tiny mite in her arm and began to undo its wrappings. 'Feels like there's a leg kickin' in me guts. Is this 'un a leg missin'?'

Wondering whether the patient was tuppence short of a shilling, as the saying went, Staff Nurse MacIntyre cast a quick look at Matron, but even as Matron opened her mouth Rosheen, unasked, gave another terrific heave.

'It's what we call the afterbirth ...' the midwife began, and then stopped. 'Oh, Mrs Clarke, it's another baby! You've had twins; two for the price of one, you might say. Aren't you a clever girl?'

But Rosheen was scowling, not with anger but with puzzlement. '*Two* babies?' she said incredulously. 'Well, I don't want the second one. Me mam's bin naggin' on for weeks about the expense and makin' me knit till me eyes popped out and me fingers was sore. What she'll say if I tell her there's two, God above knows.'

By now the medical staff were gathered around the bed and the second baby, also sheet-wrapped, was being tucked into its mother's reluctant arm. Matron leaned over and patted Rosheen's shaggy head. 'Two little girls. What'll you call them, Mrs Clarke?' she asked tactfully. 'Have you chosen names, or is that a pleasure to come?'

Rosheen began to reply, then gave an enormous yawn and swung her legs off the delivery couch, losing her grip momentarily on the second baby, which was once more seized by the midwife. 'I dunno as I've been ever so tired; can I have a bit of a kip? It's gone midnight,' she said in a sleep-blurred voice. 'I never knew as havin' a baby was so tirin'.'

'As soon as we've cleaned you up we'll get one of the porters to take you along to the ward,' the midwife said. 'Is your mother in the waiting room, or the father, of course?'

Rosheen looked blank, then dropped her gaze to the baby's head. 'Father?' she said, as though she had never heard the word before. 'Do you mean me dad? He's bin gone five or six year, so I dunno who's in the waiting room.'

Staff Nurse MacIntyre decided to give it one more try. 'Do you know who the father of the babies is?' she almost shouted. 'Does he know you're in hospital? Is he waiting for news?' And then, as Rosheen continued to look blank, she added: 'Don't you know his name?'

'Oh, his *name*,' Rosheen said, as though light had just dawned. 'His name's Bert; or was it Andy? But it were a long time ago and I'm rare tired.' She smiled placidly into the circle of interested faces. 'No rush,' she said dreamily. 'No rush, Nurse. After I've had meself some kip you can ask me again.'

Sally Plevin tiptoed down the corridor and paused outside the maternity ward. One of the hospital cleaners, she had tried to visit her friend and next door neighbour, Rosheen Clarke, the previous day but the staff nurse on duty had turned her away.

'Relatives only,' she had said primly. 'You may come on Saturday afternoon.'

'Oh, but Staff, I work here; can't you bend the rules a little? Rosheen lives next door to me in King Edward Court ...' Sally had looked hopefully into Staff's sharp little face and smiled winningly. The hope had been in vain, however; Staff had driven her out like a dog chivvying sheep and Sally had had to admit defeat.

Today, however, in the blue and white chequered uniform dress and enormous all-enveloping apron, she thought she might get away with a visit. She carried her mop in one hand and the bucket in the other, and would claim that she had been called into the maternity ward to clean up some milk which one of the babies had deposited on the gleaming linoleum; she knew Rosheen would back her up.

As soon as she entered the ward she saw her friend sitting on the end of her bed clad only in her nightdress; two things frowned upon by the nursing staff. Sally knew Rosheen had bought the cotton nightdress, along with a worn and patched dressing gown, second hand off Paddy's market, and guessed that her friend had either not noticed the large ironing burn just below the waist of the dressing gown, or had noticed but had obtained it extremely cheaply as a result. She was just wondering how to get Rosheen's attention when her friend swung round and saw her. Immediately, an enormous grin spread across the cheerful pink-cheeked face, and Rosheen lurched to her feet and padded up the ward to give her a breathless hug.

'Oh, Sal, I can't wait to get home,' she announced. 'And they say I can't go under the week! All them rules; don't do this, do do that, no talkin', mustn't go barefoot ...' she waggled her bare toes expressively, '*and* we ain't allowed to pick the babies up when they cry. Have you ever heard of anything so daft? Kids cry 'cos they's hurt or hungry or wet, so I picks mine up and cuddles 'em and puts 'em to the breast, wharrever that nasty old Nurse Soreen says.'

Sally put a finger to her lips: 'Hush. Everyone else is asleep,' she reminded her friend, indicating the humped figures in the other beds. 'Let's have a look at the babies, then?'

Rosheen wobbled back to the end of her bed, where the twins lay head-to-tailing it in the basket the hospital provided, and bent over them, a fond smile spreading across her face. 'Ain't they the prettiest things?' she said as Sally joined her. 'I thought they was hideous when they first come out 'cos they was all red and crumpled, but now they're like two little Dutch dolls. See their black hair and lovely dark eyes? Me mam agrees; she says they'll break hearts one of these days, which is what grandmas always say, I reckon. What d'you think, Sal? Ain't they just beautiful? And I'm goin' to see no one bullies 'em, like my bad dad bullied me when he were alive.

7

And Mam was always strict too, but my little 'uns won't have to fear their mam.'

Sally bent over the cot and peered into the two small faces. 'You musn't spoil them,' she said. 'Have you named them yet? Are they goin' to have Irish names?'

Rosheen giggled. 'They keeps askin' me when their dad's comin' to call. I telled them his name was Bert.'

Sally laughed. 'And I expect they said *which Bert*, didn't they? You do know who the father is, don't you?'

Rosheen shrugged. 'Anyway, I know what I'm goin' to call 'em.' She leaned over and patted one baby's pink cheek. 'She come first so she's April, and she come next, so she's May. Anythin' wrong wi' that?'

Sally stared at her friend; of course it was the best solution. 'You really are clever, Rosheen,' she said admiringly. 'I've been thinking of lots of different names for twins, but you've hit on the very thing. April and May! They're beautiful names and will remind everyone of spring flowers.'

Rosheen beamed. 'Yes, I thought that too,' she admitted. 'April was born at two minutes to midnight on the very last day of the month and May was born on the very first day of May.' She chuckled. 'Good thing they wasn't winter babies; if I'd called 'em January and February it would make folk stare.'

'True,' Sally said, but just at that moment a child began to wail and Rosheen heaved herself to her feet and went and lifted the baby out of its cot. Sally frowned. 'That's not your baby. Ought you to be doing that?'

Rosheen settled herself on the bed once more. 'Why not? This 'un's a feller; blue bootees, see? He's got wind so I brings it up and then I puts him back in his basket. His mam don't mind so long as she ain't disturbed.'

'I see,' Sally said thoughtfully. She and Rosheen had known one another all their lives and now it occurred to her that though they were fifteen Rosheen had never, to Sally's knowledge, been interested in either boys or babies.

Looking back, Sally remembered how astonished everyone had been when Rosheen's figure began to blossom. Mrs Clarke had questioned her daughter closely, as indeed had Sally, but to no avail. Questions as to who had done this to her were either ignored or given a variety of answers. Apart from the fact that she said the man was "nice", Sally thought, the babies might have been born by divine conception.

Sometimes, however, Rosheen had let drop little clues: 'He were grand,' she had once said vaguely. 'He took me to the flicks and bought me an ice cream.' At times, she had told various people that her lover was a seaman, a fisherman, a railway employee, a tram driver and even one of the fairground chaps who brought their fairs to Liverpool at Christmas and Easter, but when Sally, as Rosheen's best friend, had asked her why she was being so secretive, Rosheen had only giggled. 'It's no one's business but mine,' she had said, then had added: 'He don't know there's a baby; if he did he'd probably die of astonishment, and then where would I be?'

Sally had been quite cross. 'You can't be any worse off than you are already,' she had said huffily. 'Keep your wretched secret then, see if I care!'

But now that Rosheen had twin daughters it seemed to Sally that it was her duty as a friend to discover the name of the father. After all, bringing up two babies was going to be an expensive business and Sally saw no reason why the begetter of April and May should get off scot free. Sitting on the end of Rosheen's bed and keeping her voice down so as not to disturb either the babies or their sleeping mothers, she pointed out that Albert, or Cuthbert, or Herbert might be only too delighted to help in the upbringing of what, after all, were his daughters.

Rosheen bent her head over the little boy, who had released his wind and appeared to have gone to sleep. 'I like babies; they don't keep asking stupid questions. Besides, even if I know who he is I still don't know where he might be now, so no help there.' She draped the infant over her shoulder, and took him back to his cot. Then she cast a defiant look at Sally. 'If you want to please me, just tell me how long I have to stay in this place,' she said. 'I've asked and asked, but all they say is I have to be here at least a week, 'cos I have to give the twins a bath and find up a few more nappies afore they'll let me quit. I'd go whether they like it or not, only they've hid me clothes and won't give 'em back. Oh, Sal, I'm that fed up! Mam nags, them perishin' nurses find fault, the other patients talk about nothin' but fellers and babies. I'll go mad if I'm kept here much longer.'

'I guess it's for your own good,' Sally said rather feebly. She stood up and leaned over the basket. 'Which is which?' she asked, hoping to take Rosheen's mind off her grievances. 'Did you know Mrs Hastings at number nine says you can have the use of her old pram for them? As soon as you're out of here you'll be parading up and down the Scottie, showing off your kids. Which one's April, did you say?'

'The one on the right,' Rosheen said briefly. 'I know – they're like as two peas in a pod, but then all babies are. Shove this lot in a playpen or a big bath and no one 'ud know which were their own kid. I'm lucky 'cos I've got the pair of 'em.' She settled back on the end of her bed with a sigh of satisfaction. 'I don't understand me mam,' she went on. 'You'd think she'd be tickled pink to be a grandmother, but not her, ho no. Says I should have warned her that there was two babies but how could I? I didn't know meself.' One of the babies made a hiccuping sound and Rosheen snatched it from its blankets, not noticing that the door at the end of the ward was opening. 'I'll just feed this 'un whilst t'other's quiet ...' she was beginning when Sally jumped to her feet and began mopping vigorously at a clean piece of floor.

The sister, for it was she, jangled a handbell so vigorously that there were mumbles of protest as the sleeping mothers were rudely aroused, and under cover of their complaints Sally, armed with her mop and bucket, walked purposefully up the ward, murmuring: 'Afternoon, Sister,' as she approached the bell ringer.

Sister was just beginning to ask her what she was doing on the ward when Rosheen created a diversion by proclaiming loudly that she would kill for a glass of lemonade. Leaving Sally, Sister hurried up the ward to tell Rosheen that she could have a cup of tea in half an hour but until then she must make do with water, and Sally made good her escape.

Making her way out of the hospital to the nearest tram stop, she presently climbed the curling stair and settled herself comfortably in a front seat. She reflected that Miss Evans, who had taught the girls for their last year at school, had once told Sally that Rosheen was an enigma, and now Sally found herself agreeing fervently with the teacher. Some people said Rosheen was tuppence short of a shilling, but Sally had known for a long time that this was not the case. The truth was that Rosheen went her own way regardless; what she wanted to do she did, and what she didn't want to do, she left.

Yet Rosheen had been popular with the other pupils, both boys and girls. They liked her sweet, undemanding temper, and her sense of fun. Mrs Clarke worked in the bar of the Cuckoo's Nest in the evenings, and at the bakery on Everton Road during the day, and when she made the little cakes which her daughter loved Rosheen always took plenty, packed into her satchel, so she could treat her friends.

Sitting in the front of the tram watching the world go by, Sally wondered whether she might get a clue as to the identity of Rosheen's lover as the twins grew older. Babies are just babies, but by the time they were five or six it might be possible to trace a resemblance. Rosheen herself was not pretty, but she had large hazel eyes, unblemished creamy skin and soft, untidy dark hair, which she was forever impatiently pushing out of her eyes, or tucking behind her ears. Yet she had gone with a man she could not have known well, and made the twins. An enigma indeed!

Before going into hospital Rosheen had been working at the laundry on the corner of Snowdrop Street and Stanley Road. Would she return there? Her mother had said reluctantly that a neighbour would no doubt 'give an eye' to the baby but that had been before the advent of twins, and whether anybody could be found to watch two for the price of one was doubtful.

Sally, who attended evening classes at the Bank Halls Girls Institute on Stanley Road, was learning secretarial skills and proving to be an apt pupil. She had once suggested that Rosheen should join her, but her friend had shaken her head until her hair stood out like a dandelion clock. 'I'm not like you, Sal,' she had said. 'I ain't ambitious, nor I doesn't want to be shut up in an office all day. As soon as I can I'm goin' to get out of that perishin' laundry and find meself an outdoors job – dunno what, so don't ask – or mebbe I'll work on the trains, seein' different parts of the country whizz past every day. Who knows – perhaps I'll even go to America.' *Oh, Lee* . . .

At the time, Sally had been looking into Rosheen's large hazel eyes and for a moment it was as though she, too, saw what Rosheen was seeing; beautiful countryside, wide beaches and rapidly roaring rivers had flashed in her vision, and then it had gone and all she saw was Rosheen's dreamy face. But that had been weeks ago and now she must descend from the tram, return to King Edward Court and tell Mrs Clarke that she had visited her daughter and seen the twins.

When Sally had gone and the mothers began to sit up and rub their eyes, Rosheen bent over the basket and stared at her offspring. Because of the noise of the bell rung with such enthusiasm by that nasty sister, every baby on the ward was bawling its eyes out, and hers were no exception. Eyes screwed up, tiny fists clenched, tears still wet on their cheeks, April and May bawled on. Rosheen clucked indulgently and shuffled her bare feet out of sight under the bed. No point in courting trouble, she told herself; nurses had a thing about wearing slippers but that was one item which she and her mother had failed to agree on in Paddy's market. There had been some carpet slippers which must once have belonged to a very large woman indeed and Mrs Clarke had pounced upon them with a cry of delight, but Rosheen hated the things. When she had them on they slipped and slid, and had twice nearly caused her to fall on the slippery linoleum. She had even been annoyed into the use of bad language, and the nurses disapproved of even a whispered expletive. Rosheen sighed. If only she could get out of here, but Matron had hinted that the twins should really stay in hospital the full fortnight.

'And don't think we don't know that you spend a great deal of time roaming round the hospital and popping in and out of every ward, chattering like a magpie and upsetting *my patients*; an activity which is strictly forbidden,' Matron had said. 'You are a disruptive element, and one I shall be glad to see the back of.'

15

Rosheen had folded her lips tightly over at least half a dozen rude replies. She had not bothered to answer; what was the point? Everything she did in this place was wrong and all she wanted was to escape. For one bad moment, she had actually found herself considering simply marching out of the hospital in her ragged old dressing gown, her feet in the enormous slippers, and making her way back to King Edward Court. But then she had remembered the twins – so little, so dependent – and realised that leaving in the dead of night, by herself, would not be possible with a baby under each arm. She had sat back on her bed – not allowed during the day – and viewed Matron's enormous backside with contempt. The older woman might win for now, but Rosheen knew her time would come. And when it did come, she intended to tell Matron just what she thought of her.

Almost purring with satisfaction, Rosheen planned her farewell speech.

The dream began as soon as Rosheen closed her eyes, or at least so it seemed. She was in his arms, feeling the thunder of his heart against hers, telling him that she loved him, would never love another. He had been so kind, so tender! When she told him about the twins, however, the image of him began to fade and she remembered even in her dream that by now he must be far away, for he had told her that if he could not get a job – he had come to Liverpool to apply for work – then he would take his chance and go to America, that land of opportunity. Rosheen began to weep, and presently awoke to find her pillow damp with tears and an ache in her heart. Reality was painful, and sitting up to glance around the ward of sleeping women she decided that it was about time she forgot the young man who had given her such joy as well as the twins. Their love affair had been brief and magical, but now it was over, and it was time she pulled herself together. She was luckier than most because she had the twins, and all the love that she had lavished on their father she would give to her two little girls.

Rosheen sighed and heaved the blanket up over her shoulders, vowing as she did so that she would be the best mother in the world.

Chapter Two

Summer 1937

'Shan't!' April gazed defiantly up at the older girl, ignoring the hand held out to pull her to her feet, for she and May had been playing at shop, right in the middle of the court and, as it happens, right where the older girls wanted to skip rope.

Ellen Hastings lived three down from the Clarkes and had heard stories about the naughtiness of the Clarke twins, but being six years older she had rarely come into contact with either of the little girls, so now she stared in astonishment as the two children remained where they were, though the smaller and slighter of the two looked a little self-conscious. Ellen glared at them both. 'Don't you know nothin'?' she asked angrily. 'We allus skip rope here, 'cos the boys play footie up t'other end and our mams won't let us skip rope too near the Scottie. Gerrout of it before I land you a slap round the chops.' Ellen glared, then moved away, sure that her command would be obeyed.

The smaller of the two girls, squatting on the dirty paving, got to her feet and tugged at her sister's arm. 'C'mon April; we can play shop just as well if we move nearer to where the boys is,' she said in an urgent undertone. 'That there Ellen, she's a rough 'un, Mam says. If'n she slapped our chops, our chops would know all about it … oh, April, do come on.' As she spoke, little May, being the shopkeeper on this occasion, began hopefully to pick up the pieces of broken china, odd twigs, leaves from a rather drooping plane tree, and other impedimenta which had marked out their game. '*Please* don't argufy; our mam would say "don't start trouble". And don't you dare suggest we skip rope with the big girls else they'll marmalise us; or Ellen will at any rate.'

Reluctantly, April began to help her sister with the move, but just as they got level with the football match the ball, which was made up of rags tied roughly together in a slightly less than perfect sphere, shot across the court and landed squarely on April's chest, causing her to drop everything she held and give a shriek like a train whistle as the air whooshed out of her. The boy who had kicked the ball grinned, but came over to where April lay on the ground, her expression malevolent.

'Sorry, kiddo. I didn't mean to hit you,' he began, but April, struggling to her feet, was now in a blazing temper.

She kicked the bits of broken china she had been

holding and squared up to the boy. 'You did that a'purpose!' she screamed. 'You've wrecked our shop, mine and May's; just you say you're sorry, and build up our shop again, else me and me sister will poke your eyes out, so we will!'

The boy's expression, which had been almost apologetic, promptly changed to one of fury. 'Why, you nasty little toad. If you don't want to play rough then keep up your own end of the court,' he said. 'Go on, gerrout of it.' He turned to another boy who had skidded to a stop beside him. 'It's them kids wi' the mental mam,' he explained. 'I told 'em if they don't want to be hit by the ball they oughter keep to their end of the court.'

The newcomer grinned at the girls. 'You know how it is: boys one end, girls t'other. Why don't you go and skip rope with the big girls?'

April jutted her lower lip and was beginning to argue when a voice they knew well cut across her words. 'April, May, teatime,' came the shout. The voice acted on the twins immediately. They dropped the contents of their 'shop' and ignoring the boys and the lure of the skipping rope made for home at a brisk pace.

All the houses in the courts were back to back, so no one had a yard; no one except Sally Plevin, that was, whose parents lived in No. 1, which was quite different from the other houses. 'More posh, with its own yard and its own privy,' April had said boastfully when describing their next door neighbours' home to school pals. 'Sally Plevin's our mam's bezzie, so we get to use her privy whenever we like, *and* we can feed our scraps to the two hens what lives in the yard and will be our dinners come Christmas.'

But right now, with the sun beating down hotly on the whole of Liverpool which – so far as the twins were concerned – was the whole of the world, no one was thinking of Christmas. April, who had a hearty appetite, was thinking of the scouse her mother had promised to prepare for their tea, whilst May was thinking of the enamel mug of milk which the girls were given when their mother could afford it.

Rosheen herded her small flock through the front door, down the hallway and into the kitchen. On the table, instead of the expected scouse, there were three plates upon each of which reposed a hard-boiled egg, a slice of some unappetising-looking pink meat – luncheon meat, May thought despairingly – and a round of thinly buttered bread. May opened her mouth to voice both a complaint and a question – where was the promised scouse? – but she had no chance to get the words out. April was older, and bigger and stronger than May, and was usually the spokesperson if one were needed. 'I want scouse; you promised,' she said reproachfully. 'I hate luncheon meat. You said—'

'Oh, shurrup,' Rosheen said, but her voice did

not sound annoyed. 'I *telled* you I were goin' for a job interview at Gran's bakery. Don't you remember me sayin' I might be a trifle late? The pair of you was playin' shop and the Hastings girl, can't 'member her first name, said she'd give an eye to you till I got back. Only they was interviewin' a grosh of women, so it took longer'n I expected. No time to make scouse, see?'

'Don't care; you promised,' April said firmly. She half turned in the doorway but her mother propelled her forward, a hand in the small of her daughter's back.

'Sit down and eat up,' she commanded. 'When you goes to school in a few weeks' time d'you think they'll let you pick and choose what you eat and what you don't eat at them school dinners? I'm tellin' you here and now, girls, that you'll sit up to the table ...' as she spoke she lifted first one twin and then the other on to their chairs, 'and eat wharrever's on your plate, or you'll find yourself in deep trouble. Gerrit?'

'I don't like luncheon meat and I won't ...' April began, but May hastily picked up her knife and fork and began stabbing unenthusiastically at the food before her, casting a glance at April as she did so.

'Better eat up; make a sandwich wi' the bread and put the meat in the middle,' she advised. She cut a very small piece off her meat and then shoved bread in her mouth and spoke thickly through it. 'It ain't Mam's fault that the 'view took longer than she thought it would so she had no time to make scouse.'

Unwilling to concede the point, April changed the subject. 'Mam, when we was outside just now one of the boys called you our "mental mam". What's that mean?'

There was a moment's silence, during which April turned in her chair to examine her mother's face. Slightly to her disappointment, Rosheen said airily, 'Mental mam? Oh, it's just an expression for a person who's brighter than the rest. And now gerron wi' that delicious grub wharr I made for you, or you'll find yourselves goin' hungry to bed.'

'I'm tellin' you, Sally, that you could've knocked me down with a feather,' Rosheen said that evening after they had put the twins to bed and were sitting over cups of tea and jam sandwiches in Rosheen's large and extremely untidy kitchen. 'Cheeky little bugger, to call names. I've a good mind to let his mam know I took agin her son's description.

Sally laughed. 'You're too easy-going to object, and the lad's mam probably knows it,' she pointed out. 'But you've got to curb April's tongue or she'll get herself and her sister into every sort of scrape when they start school. Indeed, from what I hear, they're always in trouble already. Did they eat their tea?'

'Well, May did, but April's a cunning little devil,' Rosheen admitted. 'She must've eaten about half, though; the rest went under the cushion I put on their chairs to bring them up to the right height for the table. Indeed, if it hadn't been for Fudge, it could've stayed under that cushion until Doomsday!'

'I didn't know cats liked luncheon meat,' Sally said idly. 'Did you tell her off? April, I mean, not the perishin' cat.'

Rosheen sighed. 'No point. After all, if she wants to go hungry I reckon that's her business. Now, aren't you goin' to ask me what happened at the interview?'

'Oh, I'm sorry, I completely forgot. What did happen? Someone told me there were dozens and dozens of applicants though; any luck?'

Rosheen beamed. 'I gorrit,' she said triumphantly. 'Funny old hours, but I'm that fed up wi' the laundry that hours and pay didn't seem so important. I told 'em I needed a fortnight to work my notice and they agreed to that. 'Course, it ain't no good sayin' I got the job 'cos I were the best; I gorrit because Mam's been workin' for Mr Roberts for a thousand years, so he reckons any daughter of hers would be worth her wage.'

'I bet your mam's pleased as punch,' Sally commented. 'What did she say when you told her?'

'She don't know yet, but she'll be in presently and I'll break the glad news, though I reckon she'll already know.'

Sally laughed. 'Heyworth Street, Everton Road and the Scottie are like a village. They say bush telegraph in remote areas gets the news around; well, that may be true or it may be fiction, but it seems to me that if you tell one person in our area some news, it'll be round the entire district half an hour later.'

'Yeah, I reckon you're right ...' Rosheen was beginning when they both heard the rattle of the front door opening and Mrs Clarke came into the kitchen. She was a small woman, with greying hair pulled back into a tight little bun on the nape of her neck and sharp brown eyes, and usually her expression was somewhat grim, but today as she pushed the door open she was actually smiling.

'Well, Rosheen, I hear as how you got the job,' she said. 'So we's goin' to be fellow workers! 'Course, you wouldn't of got the job 'cept for me, 'cos I put in the good word to Mr Roberts. I told him you was reliable and mentioned as how you'd iced that birthday cake a couple of months back, when the twins were five. Someone took a photy of it, remember?' She was carrying a large oilskin bag and now she delved into it and produced quite three quarters of a Victoria sponge and a number of little fairy cakes.

'Oh, Mam ...' Rosheen began, but her mother shook her head impatiently.

'I know what you're a-goin' to say ... as if I'd prig 'em when Mr Roberts 'as always bin good to me! No, no, they's leftovers which he said I could take to celebrate.' She glanced towards the range which, despite the warmth of the day, still glowed. 'Let's have a nice cuppa. Sally love, go and fetch your mam from next door so's we can all celebrate me daughter's good fortune.' She pointed at the ceiling. 'Kids in bed?'

'And no doubt fast—' Sally was saying even as they heard feet pattering down the flight of stairs at the end of the hallway. Sally, already on her feet and heading for the kitchen door, tutted rather disapprovingly and would have commanded the twins to return to their beds, but Rosheen grinned delightedly.

'They don't miss much, my girls. They've got lug 'oles like donkeys,' she said proudly. 'They can hear a pin drop a mile away.'

Mrs Clarke sniffed. 'It ain't a pin droppin', it's the sound of a cake bein' taken out of its bag. They'll be sure to demand their share,' she said. 'Go you on, Sally, and fetch your mam afore these two gannets gobble the lot.'

As she spoke the twins erupted into the room, squeaking with pleasure as their eyes lit on the cakes which their grandmother was spreading out on the table. Two identical hands reached out and just as Sally disappeared through the doorway she heard Rosheen saying firmly: 'Hands off. You've not washed, though I'm sure there's water in the ewer and a nice piece of soap as well! Don't worry, you'll get your share, but I knows you. You'll handle every cake wi' your grubby paws in the hope that no one else will want what you might call "second-hand goods". Dirty little tykes,' she added fondly. 'Just sit yourselves down and wait while we make a pot of tea.'

Both children obeyed the first instruction, but the moment their bottoms touched the cushions each twin grabbed a fairy cake and proceeded to take an enormous bite. Mrs Clarke frowned reprovingly but Rosheen smiled at her daughters and rumpled their already tangled hair with a caressing hand. 'D'you know why Grandma Clarke bought cakes?' she asked. 'Can you guess?'

April had finished her cake and was reaching for another but May hesitated, thinking back. 'Did you get that job, Mammy?' she said tentatively. 'It were a job in the bakery, weren't it?' She smiled delightedly and reached out to take a second cake. 'If so I reckon we'll have cake *every* day.'

Rosheen's smile widened. 'Not every day, but a bit more often,' she said. 'And broken biscuits an' all. Well, we have them anyway, 'cos Mr Roberts lets Grandma bring home anything what's not perfect.

Ah, kettle's boilin'. But you two had best get back to bed before Auntie Sal and Mrs Plevin come a-callin'.'

May slid off her chair at once but April lingered, clearly trying to take a third cake whilst her grandmother was not watching. Rosheen, however, knew the twins too well to take her eyes off them, though she did object when her mother slapped April's hand so hard that the child gave a surprised squawk.

'Two each is your limit,' Mrs Clarke said firmly. 'Your Auntie Sal thinks your mammy's too soft with you, and there's times when I think she's right. Get up them stairs before she and her mam come back.'

The twins made their way up the stairs and into their own room, where April climbed straight into her small bed, ignoring the washstand despite Rosheen's shouting up the stairs not to forget to wash.

'Mammy doesn't care what we do,' she said comfortably, pulling the bedding up over her shoulders, for although it was a warm night she liked the comfort of a blanket round her ears.

May, however, was not yet ready to settle down. '*I'm* going to wash,' she said defiantly. 'Auntie Sal says people shouldn't carry their dirt into bed with them.'

This behaviour on the part of her meeker sister caused April to sit up abruptly. 'It's only Auntie Sal who said that, not our mammy,' she reminded her sister. 'I do as Mammy tells me – well, I do sometimes – but Auntie Sal isn't even a relation so she shouldn't tell us what to do.' She stared angrily as her sister padded across the room and began to tilt the water from the tall jug into the basin. 'Stop that at once, I say! You do as *I* tell you or you'll get a poke on the snout.' April remembered another grievance. 'It's summer so it won't get dark for ages. Mammy ought to know we can't sleep whilst it's still light, and anyway cakes is indiwhatsit … it means you gets a stomink ache if you lie down when you've had rich food.' She got out of bed. 'I'm goin' downstairs again and I don't mean to wash first either.'

'Oh, *you*! You're all talk an' no trousers,' May said, quoting Eddie who lived further along the court. 'When I go down I'm goin' to show Mammy my nice clean hands and face, but of course if you won't wash …'

She had her hands in the water as she spoke and the temptation was too much; she flicked water at her twin and in two seconds, battle was joined. May might be meek in some ways but she had a temper, and long association with April had taught her how to fight. Indeed, despite her small size she was getting the upper hand when they both heard heavy footsteps ascending the stairs.

By the time the door burst open and Rosheen entered the room both combatants were back in bed, though the bedroom was in considerable disarray. A chair had been knocked over; the blue jug with its garland of poppies lay rocking gently in a puddle of water and the girls' cotton frocks, ancient plimsolls and white cotton knickers were strewn around the room as though they, too, had been involved in the fracas.

Rosheen, mopping her hot face with a handker-chief, looked around the room and then at her children, who gave every appearance of innocence. She sank on to the foot of April's bed. 'Who started it?' she asked, though not as if she expected an answer. The twins might fight furiously – they often did – but they would not tell on one another. After a few minutes, therefore, punishment was handed out to both. 'Gerrout of bed the pair of you and clear up the mess,' Rosheen commanded. 'I stand a lot from you kids but water fights is goin' a step too far. There's more cake in one of the tins downstairs, but it ain't for the likes of you; and I want this room spotless by the time I come up to my own bed. Understand?'

May nodded resignedly but April did not mean to give way without a fight. 'It's too late to work; the light's nearly gone,' she said, her voice perilously close to a whine. 'If we promise to do it before brekky tomorrow, won't that do? Only we's so tired and we does love fairy cakes ...'

As the child talked, Rosheen had been moving

30

about, almost subconsciously it seemed, putting the room to rights, and by the time she had agreed that she supposed the morning would do if they really were so dreadfully tired, both twins had lain down again and were curled up beneath their blankets, feigning sleep.

Downstairs once more Mrs Clarke raised her eyebrows at her daughter. 'Did you give 'em a good slappin'?' she asked hopefully. 'Spare the rod and spoil the child they used to say when I were a girl, and it's God's truth.' She turned to Mrs Plevin and Sally. 'Don't you agree? Rosheen lets 'em get away wi' murder; she's never smacked either of 'em, no matter what they've done. I think all kids need discipline and the twins is no exception; why, when my Matthew were alive he kept a little cane down by his chair and walloped Rosheen whenever she got above herself.'

Rosheen grinned at Sally. 'Yes, and I've still got the scars,' she said with unabated cheerfulness. 'That's why I never hit me girls, ain't I right, our Sally?'

Sally shrugged. 'Your dad was maybe too fond of a quick slap around the ear, but you carry no smacking to extremes,' she said rather reproachfully. 'May is a good little thing but April's getting a bit above herself. She orders May about as though she was ten years older, not ten minutes. Still, it's my belief that school will sort them out. And it might be better if they were put in different classes. They might both work harder if they were separated.'

She expected some sort of objection from Rosheen but her friend merely shrugged. 'That's up to the school and the teachers,' she observed. 'But I wouldn't like to be the one what done it!'

By the time Rosheen had prepared the next day's breakfast, made jam sandwiches for the twins' snap and found up the money which she paid Mrs Bracknell for keeping an eye on them, she was longing for her bed. Nevertheless, she paused at the head of the stairs and gently pushed the twins' door a little wider so that she could look in. She was not surprised to see that May's bed was empty and both twins were sharing April's. It was often the way: the twins would fight or argue or fall out in some manner and get into their own beds shouting abuse, or sometimes icily silent. But when Rosheen came upstairs herself, whether consciously or unconsciously the children would have crawled into one bed and cuddled up to each other, and thus they would remain until it was time to get up next morning. Rosheen never knew who gave in first, because sometimes the pair occupied May's bed and at other times April's. And she did not particularly care, as long as the twins began each new day as fast friends and never let the sun go down on their wrath.

So now she stole into the room and straightened the blankets over the two small bodies, then brushed the dark hair off May's brow and ran her fingers through April's untidy locks. She wondered how they would like their hair done when they started school; they might want it cut shorter still, in a style popular with older girls, and wear it simply held back with an Alice band. But her touch had disturbed April, who muttered a protest, and she stole out of the room as quietly as she had entered it, reflecting that the girls only had another few weeks of freedom before starting school.

She opened her own door, checked that her jug had water in it and that soap and towel stood ready, and then undressed, pulled her white cotton nightie over her head and climbed into bed. What a day it had been, she reflected, as she bunched up her pillow and then flattened it out again. First there had been the interview, then she had called in at the laundry where she had explained that she had got another job and would be leaving them. They had been very nice about it, assuring her that she would be sadly missed, and saying that should she ever wish to return they would be happy to employ someone both cheerful and reliable.

Then she had returned to King Edward Court, collected the family's water bucket and gone to tell Mrs Bracknell that she was home. Mrs Bracknell lived right at the end of the court, where the two communal privies and the water tap were situated, so by filling the bucket at the same time Rosheen saved herself the trouble of a second trip later in the day to collect the water they would need for the night.

It had been a full day but quite a nice one, getting the job being the highlight, of course. Rosheen reflected that no two women could be less alike than she and her mother; in fact the only thing they had in common was their love of cooking and their ability as cooks. Mrs Clarke was one of the best confectioners in Liverpool, and now Rosheen was hoping that Mr Roberts would let her show him what she could do for she, too, could create beauty out of icing sugar, a drop of olive oil and some colouring. Still, until Mr Roberts had seen for himself the results of her skill with an icing bag, he would be happy enough with her ordinary baking, she was sure.

She was about to snuggle down when she remembered her mother's warning. 'When you work with food you have to be clean as a whistle; no matter how tired you are you must scrub up like the nurses in the hospital before you so much as touch any of the ingredients in the bakehouse,' Mrs Clarke had said. 'I know you of old, my girl; you won't get away with your slapdash habits as you did at the laundry, so unless you want to lose your job almost before you've got it ...'

'Ma!' Rosheen had said, cut to the quick by this unfair criticism. 'Mr Manners at the laundry is every bit as fussy about cleanliness as Mr Roberts. Why, you've never set foot inside the laundry, so how do you know what goes on?'

Mrs Clarke had sniffed. 'Who says I've never been inside the laundry?' she had enquired belligerently. 'I worked there as a delivery girl when I first left school. I remember them big ol' sinks and the air near as wet as the water 'cos of the steam, and the women's hands all puffy and swollen. Oh aye, I know all about that laundry.'

'Then you know Mr Manners were right fussy about us bein' clean,' Rosheen had said defiantly. 'Don't you worry, Mam. I'll scrub up before I leave the house and get to the bakery in time to scrub up again.'

She had been half joking, but her mother had given a grim little nod. 'That's right. Keep yourself spotless and don't mind the heat, 'cos you'll be glad of it come the winter, and you'll not go far wrong.'

Chapter Three

December 1938

Rosheen came down the stairs and went straight into the kitchen, where she dumped the bucket of soapy water and scrubbing brush down by the fire and the sheets over her arm on to the kitchen table. 'Mam?' she said tentatively. 'I've done the bedrooms. I'll dry them pots for you and then we can clean ourselves up a bit and do the marketin'. I'll be gettin' in some nuts and fruit and a little gift or two ahead of time, though I'll save buyin' the Christmas bird and that until nearer the day. Are you comin' out? Only I know the cold plays havoc wi' your arthritis.'

Mrs Clarke sighed. 'You're right, o' course; I like to stay by the fire and toast me toes on me day off, but I s'pose I'd best get some of me holiday shoppin' done, so I'll come wi' you.'

'You could give me a list,' Rosheen suggested, but Mrs Clarke shook her head.

'I won't know what I want until I see it,' she said. 'And there's still no sign of the twins, by the way. It might be a good thing, because if we told them we was buyin' a few extras they'd poke their noses into every parcel and not have any surprises come the day, whereas if we don't tell 'em and pretend it's just ordinary marketin' they'll bobby off on their own business rather than have to help carry.'

Rosheen opened her mouth to say that the twins were always helpful, but then closed it again. In her heart she knew her mother was right.

Mrs Clarke turned from the sink and gave her daughter a somewhat wintry smile. 'You're a good girl, and I'm sorry I was cross,' she said. 'But Rosheen, I told you and told you that you ain't doin' the twins no service by makin' up their beds, bringin' down their slop bucket and generally waitin' on them hand and foot. Folks say they're spoiled rotten, and instead of getting better as they get older they're gettin' worse. Why, when you were their age you didn't just make your own bed, you made your dad's and mine. You were a handy little cook an' all; oh, mebbe nothin' fancy but you weren't useless, by any means. I know you say your dad was hard on you but you can't say as I ever raised a hand, and you've turned out pretty well in spite of your dad's bein' a trifle unreliable when he'd had a few bevvies.'

Rosheen heaved a sigh, picked up a tea towel from its hook beside the sink and began to dry the four porridge bowls. Earlier that morning she and her mother had disagreed over the twins' unwillingness to do anything to help in the house. Mrs Clarke had sworn they were lazy and cared nothing for anyone but themselves, whereas Rosheen did not see why any child – or any child of hers, rather – should have to perform household tasks such as bed-making or cooking whilst they were still at school. As for cleaning floors, her mind winced away from the awful things the twins, left to themselves, could do with a scrubbing brush, a bar of yellow soap and a bucket of hot water.

The argument had arisen because the moment Rosheen had said it was time to give the house its pre-Christmas clean the twins had disappeared. Rosheen would have let them get on with it, but for once Mrs Clarke had come out with what she really thought and had insisted that Rosheen should fetch her daughters home in order that they, too, might assist in the grand clean-up. 'At least they could have taken the bed linen along to the washhouse,' she had said in a grumbling tone. 'All they needed to do was put it in a sink to soak, so it wouldn't be so hard to get clean when one of us goes along there to give it a good scrub. But no matter; the linen will have to wait till Monday.'

So Rosheen had agreed and had gone out into the court shouting for April and May, but was in no way surprised when they did not appear. She had just opened her mouth to shout again when her mother had said crossly, 'Don't waste your breath. They'll wait until they see you with your marketin' bag and then they'll pop out from wherever they've been hidin', because they know you just as well as I do. You'll go into Sample's and they'll make eyes at the cook and get a penny bun for a ha'penny. You'll visit the greengrocer's and they'll be after gettin' themselves an apple or an orange with a mark on the skin. And if you go to Paddy's market to buy that new skirt what you say May needs, they'll ask Mrs Harrow if she's any spare hair ribbons. But if we go to places where they won't get treats, they'll suddenly disappear and we shan't see 'em until we put dinner on the table.'

Rosheen had felt a flush creep up her neck and bloom in her cheeks. She had told herself that Mam was being unfair, that the girls were a great help on marketing trips. They carried her bags – well, sometimes they did – and would run errands for stallholders to earn a penny or two. Once, they had carried home a roll of linoleum, for which they had been paid the princely sum of sixpence, and to be fair they had offered Rosheen the sixpence before visiting Kettle's confectioners and buying three penn'orth of toffees each.

Rosheen had opened her mouth to remind her mother of this, and had then closed it again. If she was honest, the twins were likely to carry a heavy marketing bag for two minutes and then put it down on the ground and dash ahead to the next stall. No use to expect old heads on young shoulders; April and May were just thoughtless, not naughty or wicked. Other children might nick fruit or hair ribbons, or a penny bun from the traders on the Scottie, but her children, Rosheen now told herself virtuously, knew right from wrong. She would allow that they were high-spirited, but they took after her.

Having satisfied herself on that score, Rosheen put away the last pot and headed for the stairs. She was wearing a baggy grey skirt, a striped blouse with patches under both arms and a pair of stockings which were more ladder then lisle, and she meant to change into something more presentable. Hurrying up the stairs, she considered her choices, which were few. She had a fawn skirt and cardigan which were quite good, and a beige silk blouse which was at least respectable, having been given a good wash within hours of being brought home from Paddy's market.

Rosheen, struggling out of her scrubbing clothes and into her marketing ones, reflected that she had been extremely fortunate so far as the girls' clothing was concerned. When the twins were two years old she had taken April and May round to Mrs Harrow's stall and explained the difficulty: that she had twin girls of similar sizes and would like to dress them alike. Mrs Harrow had responded that she often bought clothes from other parents of twins, and though Rosheen had to pay a little more April and May were almost always dressed alike as a result. Often Rosheen had to work overtime to afford particular pairs of frocks or skirts, but when she looked at her daughters, so beautifully turned out, pride had simply almost swamped her. So if she had to go short in order that they might present a good appearance, what did it matter? No one looked at Rosheen when she was with April and May, and the admiration of other children and their mothers was reward enough.

Rosheen loosened her hair from its tight bun and began to brush it out. When she went downstairs she would get Mrs Clarke to plait it into a long braid, which she would then wind round into a coronet on top of her head. There was a mirror on the inside of her wardrobe door and as she slipped her feet into her walking shoes she felt a glow of satisfaction at her appearance. Neat but not gaudy, she told herself. I just hope April and May haven't got mucky, because their grandmother would have something to say about that. Deep down, though, I know she is as proud of them as I am.

Satisfied that her appearance would not let her down, Rosheen went down to the kitchen and presently, armed with large canvas marketing bags, mother and daughter left the house, Rosheen looking all round for some sign of the twins. How wonderful it would be if they were doing something useful;

and how unlikely! It was a Saturday, which meant that the streets were full of children, and Rosheen found herself wishing that she had worn her little red beret so that the girls could spot her more easily in the crowd. However, it was too late now. Rosheen tucked her hand into her mother's arm and they set off towards Scotland Road.

As they went Mrs Clarke talked casually about this and that, but Rosheen's thoughts followed their own path, searching for the reason why her daughters were becoming more difficult as they got older. School, of course, had a great deal to do with it. Rosheen sighed. When the twins had first started she had been apprehensive, sure that they would not take to being told what to do. But Miss Rogers, the infant teacher, had assured Rosheen that the girls were model pupils. They were the first in her class to conquer reading and writing and very soon arithmetic too. At home they had quoted Miss Rogers as the source of all knowledge and the words *Miss Rogers says ...* had become their rallying cry.

Almost unable to believe her good luck, for the twins could be both naughty and disruptive when they so wished, Rosheen had arranged her shifts so that she could usually meet the twins out of school, and whenever she did so she brought some little gift for the teacher: a currant bun from the bakery, a rosy apple from one of the stalls on Great Homer Street, or a newly sharpened red pencil.

But those happy times had come to an end when school had reopened in September. April and May had gone up to Standard One: no more sand trays, no nature table, no amusing jigsaw puzzles; nothing, in fact, but work, and hard work at that. The twins were bright but Rosheen could have told anyone that they would only work hard for someone they loved, or at least respected. Miss O'Brien, who taught Standard One, was neither of these things. She was a strict disciplinarian and frequently used a small cane on tingling palms, besides not allowing talking in her class, and ignoring pleasant subjects such as the use of large sheets of paper and powder paints. The twins had been looking forward to airing their artistic abilities, but apparently this was not to be.

When term began the girls had been advised by an older pupil how to keep on the right side of Miss O'Brien. 'Never contradict her even when she's wrong, and always remember not to call her "Miss" but "Miss O'Brien". And don't ask to go to the lavvy, even if you're desperate, 'cos she'll think you just want some time out of her classroom and if there's one thing what makes her mad it's people saggin' off. If you're polite and don't take advantage, stick to the rules and never argue, then you'll gerron fine wi' the old bat. She ain't a bad old stick, 'specially if she takes to you, and though you may not like her just remember her little cane. Ever been whacked on the fingers?' The older girl had chuckled. 'You're supposed to be caned on the palm of your hand, but if you flinch she'll mebbe get you across the fingers, which is worse. I don't think she means to hurt you bad, but it makes her mad if someone giggles when she misses and she'll hit all the harder next time.'

The twins had told Rosheen that they meant to follow this advice, but Rosheen could still remember her own entry into Standard One, many years earlier, and knew with a rising sense of dread that Miss O'Brien would never take to her daughters. Nevertheless, she had done her best to ingratiate both the girls and herself with the elderly teacher. Miss O'Brien had accepted a well-sharpened pencil to 'help you with your marking, Miss O'Brien', but when Rosheen had presented her with an almond slice, neatly wrapped up in one of Mr Roberts's paper napkins, Miss O'Brien had gazed at it as though it were a scorpion waiting to strike. 'If this is a bribe, Miss Clarke, I'm afraid you're giving it to the wrong person,' she had said crossly, thrusting the small parcel back into Rosheen's hand. 'There are some teachers who might accept such behaviour, but I am not one of them. If you cast your mind back, you'll remember how I taught my class when you were in Standard One. You may have changed – I hope you have – but I have not.'

Rosheen had felt so humiliated that she could have wept. She had been a fool to try to get on the teacher's good side, if she had one. Her own mother had never tried to give a teacher anything but a polite 'good morning', but Rosheen had not been at all interested in school, had disliked Miss O'Brien and had, she believed, been caned far too often, though she soon learned not to snatch her hand away but to put up with the pain of it for the sake of peace.

'Rosheen? Stop dreamin', girl, and remind me why we're off to Paddy's market.'

Mrs Clarke's voice was peremptory, but Rosheen answered as vaguely as she usually did. 'I told you, May needs a new skirt. There were a fight in the playground after school yesterday and May got knocked over in the scrimmage. She tore her nice pleated skirt from hem to waistband, as well as scuffing the material summat shocking, so I thought I'd see if Mrs Harrow's got one what'll fit and ain't too pricy.'

Mrs Clarke sighed. 'All right, we'll try Mrs Harrow, but if she's got nowt suitable I'll do me best to mend the old one for you. After all, it can't be *that* bad.'

The two women turned their steps towards Paddy's market and Mrs Clarke's prophecy immediately came true as the twins popped up one on either side of them. 'We'll help you to choose a nice skirt for me,' May said excitedly. 'But must it be grey, Mammy? There's a girl in our class what wears a navy blue one; it's real smart, and she has a navy blue cardigan to go with it.'

45

'Oh does she?' Mrs Clarke said grumpily. 'Her mam must have more money than sense, 'cos grey don't show the dirt the way navy blue does. Besides, near on every kid in your class has some sort of grey skirt and a white blouse, so don't you start, May Clarke.'

May ignored her grandmother and looked hopefully into Rosheen's face. 'Miss O'Brien might like me better if I had a real smart navy skirt. Please, Mam, let's look for a navy one before we give in and buy a grey.'

Despite herself Rosheen grinned at her mother. 'Here we go, tryin' to make me change me mind!' she said. 'Haven't you learned by now, May, that we get what we can afford, not what we want? April, help your sister to choose something which looks as though it'll fit her, and May, just you stop your whinin' 'cos if there's one thing I can't stand, it's a kid what whines.'

At this point they reached Mrs Harrow's stall and all four of them began to rifle through her stock. Mrs Harrow greeted them cheerfully, but slapped the twins' hands when they began to rootle through the piled garments. 'That's enough of that,' she said. 'Tell me what youse is after and I'll see if I can oblige.'

Nothing loth, April described the playground fight with much gusto. 'And when it were over her skirt were torn and there were blood splattered all over it, 'cos she'd scraped her knees summat rotten.

It weren't just a rent either; there were quite a bit of skirt missin' and the elastic had gone and—'

'All right, all right, I get the perishin' picture,' Mrs Harrow assured them. She looked May up and down, then fished a couple of grey skirts out of the mounds of clothing. 'Wharrabout one of these here?' she suggested. 'There ain't a mark on 'em … well, mebbe a tiny mark, but your mam could give 'em a quick run through at the washhouse and you could go off to school on Monday smart as an insurance clerk.'

May slipped the skirt on over her frock, then pirouetted so that her mother could see the back as well as the front of the garment. Then she glanced across at Rosheen. 'Shall we try one or two others?' she asked hopefully.

May loved trying on clothes, but Mrs Harrow had other customers and did not wish to waste her time over a perfectly ordinary skirt for which she could scarcely charge more than a couple of bob. 'Tek it or leave it,' she said briskly. 'As I said, there ain't a mark on it. It's a snip at five bob, but because you're good customers you can have it for a silver dollar; that means half a crown to ignorant kids.'

May stepped out of the skirt and pushed it towards her mother. 'Hem's comin' down, and where it's been mended the mam has used white cotton 'stead of grey,' she announced. 'Don't you buy it, our Mammy. It ain't as good as the last one

47

and we got that for one and tenpence, *and* we didn't have to put the hem up.'

She reached out a hopeful hand towards another grey skirt, but Mrs Clarke shook her head and slapped her fingers, though lightly. 'You buy what your mam says,' she ordered her granddaughter. She turned to the stallholder. 'The kid's right; me daughter'll have to set to and stitch the hem back into place. Ha'n't you got nothin' which don't need no work?'

Another customer had just plucked from the pile the prettiest red dress May had ever seen. It had white cuffs, a white Peter Pan collar and smocking across the chest, and stitched on to the waistband was a matching purse. Both twins sighed with envy. 'Is it *very* expensive?' May asked anxiously. 'I'd like that frock more'n anythin' else on the whole stall. Oh, Mam, please can I have it? And it's my size as well.' She glanced quickly at her sister. 'April's too big for it, she'd split the perishin' seams, but it would fit me like a glove.'

Mrs Clarke, eyeing the little frock with admiration, nevertheless shook her head. 'We come here to buy a skirt for school,' she reminded her granddaughter. 'Besides, a frock like that'd cost a mint of money. And when would you wear it, pray? It's too fine for school and your mam bought you a party dress last year so you don't need another.'

April had lost interest and wandered off to the

next stall, but May had not given up hope and even when she saw her mother handing over the half crown and taking the skirt in exchange she continued to plead. But Rosheen, losing patience at last, told her daughter that she would stand out like a sore thumb if she wore the red dress in Miss O'Brien's class. 'And besides, I can't afford it and wouldn't buy it if I could,' she said, moving away from the stall. 'You know very well I like to dress the pair of you alike and we'd never find another red dress like that 'un.'

This, however, was like a red rag to a bull, for both May and April had begun to object to being clad in identical garments. Only the previous day, coming home from school, April had told her mother that she was fed up with being dressed exactly like her sister. 'It makes us look silly and everyone who looks at us knows we're twins,' she said grumpily. 'We don't mind when school's over and we go out to play in old clothes, but we don't like it other times.'

Rosheen had understood this, for the twins' characters were very different although they looked almost identical, but today she found she was growing annoyed with May's persistence and April's renewed complaints. Taking her mother's arm, she whisked her out of the market without looking back, leaving the twins staring resentfully after them.

*

Left to their own devices, the twins made up their minds, without exchanging a word, that they meant to disappear. Having come as far as Paddy's market, they decided, their mother would not bother to traipse all the way to her usual shops to do the rest of her messages, but would head for the city centre instead. This meant, of course, that the shopkeepers from whom she purchased her wares were unlikely to come across with small free gifts for the twins, since they were not regular customers. Once or twice, in Christmases past, Rosheen had taken them round the shops, noting the objects which the girls admired most. Then, when they were not present, she searched out similar but much cheaper items, buying what she could afford and hiding them away in the homes of friends until they could be wrapped and handed out on Christmas morning.

This year, however, the twins decided they would have more fun if they were not accompanied by an adult. Both girls had loved the glitz and glamour of the big stores – Bunney's, Lewis's and T. J. Hughes – and left to themselves could have spent the entire day examining everything on sale at these vast and popular emporiums. Of course their mother might catch up with them and impose punishment, but they had one cast iron excuse which, again without consultation, they intended to use. And that excuse was Uncle George.

Uncle George was their grandmother's brother

and therefore the twins' great-uncle. He was the commissionaire in the striped trousers and tails who stood outside Lewis's, greeting customers, telling them what was to be found where and handing out a sweet to any respectable child who entered the shop.

Accordingly, the twins made their way towards Ranelagh Street, but when April would have joined the throng of people about to cross the road May clutched her arm, saying, 'You're daft you are, April Clarke. Mam knows about Uncle George's sweets, so she'll guess we've come here, and if she's mad as fire she'll take us straight home without so much as a toffee between us.'

April sniggered. 'We'll tell Uncle George that if he says a word about seein' us we'll go up to his allotment and do summat horrible,' she said. 'You're the stupid one, anyhow. We can sneak in when Uncle George is seein' to a customer, easy peasy.'

'But if we do that we shan't get give any sweets,' May pointed out. 'Or we could play the "our mam's gone ahead and we's just catchin' up" game.' She looked hopefully at April. 'Like we does on the trams.'

April considered. When the trams were crowded the conductor could not always take a fare from every passenger, and if a bright child – bright but not very honest – claimed that her mother had already been given their ticket, then the conductor would simply push his way past her to other standing passengers, unable to check, in the press, whether some adult had parted with the obligatory cash. But having considered the matter, April shook her head. 'You are *so* stupid I can't believe you're my twin,' she said scornfully. 'Trams ain't shops, you halfwit. I suppose you think you could walk into the Red Rose restaurant, swig a cup of their creamy cocoa, claim your mam had paid in advance and walk out without one of them pretty waitresses demandin' your money. Tell you what, though. If Uncle George promises not to tell our mam or Grandma that he's seen us, we might get a chance to spend a really long time in the toy department. Oh, May, if only we was rich! But at least we can look; no one can't charge us for lookin'.'

May looked wistful. 'But they can make you leave,' she pointed out. 'They'll soon know we ain't customers. And we don't want to get Uncle George into trouble, do we? You know they don't allow unaccompanied kids into the store, and he's the one what's supposed to stop them. Don't you remember him once saying he was really and truly just a posh chucker-out?'

By now they had reached Ranelagh Street and could see that Uncle George had quite a little group of would-be shoppers around him, though no children. Excitedly, April grabbed May's hand. 'Come on,' she hissed. 'If we go now whilst he's not lookin' out in the street, we can get past him. Good thing we've got our brown marketin' coats on, not our blue tweed ones with the velvet collars. Tell you what, we won't go together. Oh, if only Mam would *listen* to us when we say we hate wearin' 'dentical clothes! It's a dead giveaway. Now, May! Run for it, and keep your head down!'

Had they been in their best coats, Uncle George would undoubtedly have spotted them, for on top of the velvet collars the girls wore bright little orange berets and could, to Rosheen's satisfaction, be seen half a mile off. As it was, though, it seemed as though their plot to get past Uncle George without his so much as raising an eyebrow was about to be successful. May thought it very odd to be hurrying along the pavement with no one to hold her hand, but she saw the sense of April's strategy. Together, even in their ugly brown coats, they were undoubtedly twins, but apart the deception proved as good as they could have wished. In fact when at last they found themselves among the shoppers outside Lewis's, April was sure, if they kept their hats low on their heads and did not glance at their uncle, he would not be able to tell their mother that they had so much as visited the store.

Unfortunately for the success of their plan, however, May suddenly hissed in her breath and grabbed her twin's arm. 'Of all the awful luck. See that boy edging round the group of women waiting to talk to Uncle George? Isn't he in Standard Two?

Oh, damn and damn and damn. If he recognises us he'll probably call out and Uncle George will notice. What do we do now? Shall we hang around out here until he's gone? I bet he's on his own too – he's edging near the doors already.'

They stared through the crowd at their school-mate, wondering how he would get past Uncle George. It turned out to be simple. He got as close to the nearest adult as he could and said in a low voice, which nevertheless reached the twins' ears: 'Want a hand with that bag, missus? It looks pretty heavy from where I'm standin'.' The woman with the oilskin bag shook her head, but Roy stood so close that an onlooker would have thought at once that the two were together. Brilliant, April thought with much satisfaction. If they could do the same when Uncle George was concentrating on directing another customer ... They chose their moment – and their victim – very carefully and presently they found themselves inside the big store and all set for a wonderful day, free from parents and teachers, and with all the joys of the biggest store in Liverpool at their fingertips.

Determined to see as much of the big store as possible before their mother caught up with them, the twins spent a blissful hour in the toy department examining the various wonders on display. May was particularly taken with a baby dolly in a beautiful painted crib which played 'Rock-a-bye Baby' when one set it in motion, whilst April could not rest until she had had a ride on a dappled rocking horse with scarlet reins. Grabbing her sister by the hand, she dragged her over to join the queue of excited children awaiting their turn, and when she reached the head of it fairly flung herself at the saddle rather than be seen to be in need of a leg up.

After the thrills of the rocking horse, however, everything else seemed rather flat until they went into the clothing department for girls aged ten and under. There, to May's astonished delight, they discovered the very dress for which she had been searching. It was a brand new version of the one their mother had rejected in Paddy's market, and for a moment May stopped in front of the wax figure wearing it and simply yearned to possess it. 'If Mrs Harrow had had two dresses like that I'm sure Mammy would have them,' she said, knowing even as she spoke that Rosheen almost certainly would have done no such thing. 'Wouldn't you have loved a dress like this, April? It's almost the nicest thing we've seen in the whole shop; if only there were two!'

April sniffed. 'You really are the stupidest girl in the world,' she said scornfully. 'Don't you remember we were saying only just now that we didn't like being dressed the same? If we'd been together when we came into the store Uncle George would have spotted us first go off. And anyhow, what good is a pretty dress? You can't wear it for school, Mam would say it was too fancy to wear to church on Sunday, and we've got our party dresses for when we go to Uncle George's on Boxing Day.' She sighed dramatically. 'Your trouble is you leave all the thinkin' to me, 'cos I'm oldest and cleverest.'

As they talked they were making their way towards the Ranelagh Street exit. Suddenly May, who had had enough of her sister's criticisms, saw Uncle George come into the store to point out to a customer where the lifts were situated, and grabbed April's arm just in time to stop her from almost certainly being seen. 'If you're such a big thinker, why don't you think of a way to get past Uncle George?' she asked derisively. 'If I hadn't pulled you back you'd have walked straight into him.'

April promptly took offence. 'I was just testin' you out,' she said untruthfully. 'Keep well behind those glass cases full of china and when I give the word, scuttle. Not that it really matters if we're caught now; in fact it might be a good thing because we don't want to have to walk all the way home and I'm goin' to spend my tram fare on summat to eat 'cos I'm fair starvin'.'

'Me too. I could eat all those sandwiches what Mam tried to make us have for tea the other day,' May said. 'I wish she worked in the bakery on a Saturday; Mr Roberts always give us summat when she's workin' there. Oh, look. There's that boy again; he's askin' Uncle George for summat. Let's skip off whilst they're watchin' each other and not us.'

April was so accustomed to making all the decisions for them both that she opened her mouth to object, then closed it again. May had already broken away from her and darted outside, where Uncle George stood facing the street once more. The boy was nowhere to be seen. April joined her sister and was then struck by what she considered to be a brilliant idea. She ran up to the commissionaire as though she had just that moment arrived outside the store and gave him her sweetest smile.

'Hello, Uncle George. Have you seen our mam and our grandma this mornin'?' she asked. 'We got separated from them in Paddy's market and now we's hungry and wants us dinners and they's nowhere to be seen.'

Uncle George beamed and fished in his pocket, then held out a large palm in which nestled half a dozen sweets, all wrapped in cellophane in order, as he had explained to the girls before, to keep his pocket clean.

'Help yourselves to a sweety,' he said jovially, and pretended to be surprised when the sweets disappeared completely into two little brown pockets. 'Were your mam and your grandma comin' to Lewis's? I haven't seen 'em this mornin'.'

April would have turned away without further

ado but May wanted her dinner. 'If we go back to Paddy's market we might miss them on their way here,' she said. 'We've spent our tram fares, haven't we, April, and if we skip a lecky ...'

Uncle George's eyebrows shot up towards his hairline. 'Little ladies don't skip leckies,' he said reprovingly. 'I'll give you your tram fare if your mam doesn't appear in the next ten minutes, but I'm sure she will. In the meantime you can look at the Christmas displays in the windows, or stay by me if you prefer, but don't interfere when I'm answerin' customers' questions.'

'Righto,' said April, and May suddenly realised how lucky they were to have Uncle George. At first being alone had seemed like a big adventure, but now she remembered that big cities are dangerous places and they had strayed far from their usual haunts. Even following April round the corner and out of sight of Uncle George seemed risky, and when she heard a voice calling her name and turned to see her mother hurrying towards them she ran to greet her with a squeak of joy.

Rosheen grabbed the twins and shook them, but they could tell she wasn't really angry. 'Your grandma said we'd find you here, and Uncle George assured me you've not got up to any mischief,' she said. 'But don't you go runnin' off again or you'll find yourselves in disgrace. Now, your grandma's chatting to Uncle George and looks like being a while yet, so why don't I mug the two of you to a penny bun and then I'll finish me shoppin' and we'll get off home.'

So presently the twins stood outside the bakery gazing wistfully through the window at the delights within whilst their mother joined the short queue waiting to be served. They were wondering which buns were about to be popped into her basket when May said idly: 'I wouldn't be surprised if Mam bought saffron buns for a special Christmas treat – that would be prime, wouldn't it, April?'

April had been gazing hopefully through the glass at her mother, who had reached the head of the queue and was being served by a plump and smiling shop assistant, but at her sister's words she turned away from the window with a snap. 'You're stupid you are, May Clarke. Why should Mam buy buns for Christmas now when she'll be working in the bakery next week?' she said scornfully. 'I don't know how I come to have a twin who can't think straight. Why, next thing I know you'll be sayin' she should buy hot cross buns for Easter ...'

But May had had enough. She swung round and smacked her unsuspecting twin's face so hard that April staggered, and in seconds war was joined and the twins had fallen to the pavement kicking and screaming, whilst each tugged furiously at a handful of the other's hair.

Two older girls who had been looking into the

window at the tempting array of cakes, scones and doughnuts turned as the twins' bodies, now locked in mortal combat, rolled around at their feet. As one, the pair bent and grabbed a twin each, shook her, and bade her sharply to stop using language.

'Because if we start slapping you'll both regret it,' the shorter of the two said threateningly. 'If me and my pal Cassie here let you go, will you behave?'

April scowled, but May nodded eagerly, though this did not stop her from getting in one last kick at her sister's shins. 'We'll be good,' she said. 'Leggo, you! I said we'd be good, so there's no need to grip me arm so tight. Here comes our mam, anyway.'

The girls hastily released the small combatants and straightened up as Rosheen came out of the bakery. The taller of the two – Cassie – turned and smiled at her, and Rosheen grinned back. 'Sorry they've been so bad,' she said apologetically. 'But you know what kids are.'

Cassie laughed. 'I didn't know twins ever fell out,' she admitted. 'I'm an only child, and I've always thought it must be great to have a twin, someone who thought the way I did and enjoyed the same things, but now I'm not so sure.'

Rosheen fished a paper bag from her basket and held it out. 'I reckon I owe you both a bun for coming to my rescue, so help yourselves,' she said comfortably, biting into her own bun and speaking rather thickly as a result. 'As for twins, I dare say some are just as you imagined, but mine aren't like that. One minute bosom friends, the next deadly enemies, that's my girls!'

Chapter Four

Earlier that morning, Cassie Valentine had shot out of her front door, slamming it noisily behind her. She waited for a roar of protest, for her father liked his daughter to behave like the nice little High School girl she was supposed to be, but apparently he had not yet come downstairs.

She reached her garden gate in a couple of bounds and turned on to the pavement. She was a slim girl with dark hair and eyes and she knew she was not pretty – her friend Rebecca Spencer was the pretty one – but Cassie comforted herself with an overheard comment from one of her mother's WVS friends. 'Your daughter's face is full of character,' the older lady had remarked, not realising that Cassie could hear every word she uttered. 'Oh, I don't deny that Rebecca will have every boy for miles around chasing after her in a few years – golden curls, blue eyes and a lovely figure seem to have a magical effect on young males – but it's character that counts, and Cassie has that elusive quality we call charm.

And that will stay with her for the whole of her life, whereas good looks are not so durable.'

But right now Cassie was not concerned with looks or character, but with the forthcoming Christmas shopping trip into Liverpool. 'Makes a change from Chester; the shops are bigger and my mother says some of them are really cheap,' Rebecca had assured her friend. 'Only if we want to make the most of it we really need to catch the earliest possible train.'

So they had agreed that they would meet at five to ten on the station platform, which was why Cassie was flying along the pavement, eyes fixed on a small figure ahead which she hoped might be Rebecca. Consequently, she did not even notice when a large foot was placed between her flying ones and a mocking voice said: 'What's your hurry, Cassie? ... Oh! I say, I'm sorry. I didn't think.'

Cassie sat up and regarded grazed knees and palms, then glared at the boy standing over her and holding out a hand to help her to her feet.

'What did you do that for, you beast?' she said, trying to sound as angry as she felt. But the fall had been a painful one and despite her resolve tears welled in her eyes and trickled down her cheeks. 'Honestly, Andy, I could've broken a leg!'

Her next door neighbour, now holding her hand in a comforting grip, said apologetically, 'I didn't realise you'd not seen me. I thought you'd dodge, only of course you didn't.'

He bent to pull her skirt up to look at the ruin of her stockings, but Cassandra slapped his hand away. 'Don't!' she said sharply. 'I'm on my way to the station to meet Becky, and if we miss the ten o'clock train because of you I'll be very cross indeed. Oh, it's coming; I can see steam! Andy, do run and persuade the driver to wait! Or you could get Becky to do it; she has a way with her, or so my mother always says.'

Andy slid an arm round her waist. 'Pretend it's a three-legged race,' he suggested. 'We'll make it to the train in plenty of time, and knowing Becky she'll save you a seat.'

Sure enough, they reached the station platform before the guard had even started to close the carriage doors. 'There she is, waving from the window,' Cassie said. 'Oh, my knees and hands sting like anything! I wonder if there's a lavatory on the train? If so, I can wet my handkerchief and clean myself up a bit. Oh, crumbs, help me up, there's a good fellow.'

Andy bundled her into the compartment and saw her settled in the seat next to Rebecca's just as the guard came along the platform, slamming doors and waving his green flag.

Rebecca greeted her friend with relief. 'Glad you caught it,' she said. 'I was just wondering what I should do all by myself in the big city.'

'Me too. I've been looking forward to this!' Cassie

said as she examined her wounds, before jumping to her feet again and addressing Andy through the glass. 'Where were you going when you tripped me up?' she bawled. 'I should have thought you'd still be in bed, knowing your usual habits.' She liked to think she had outgrown her childhood crush on him, but she was still well aware that his mother had to practically dig him out of bed at weekends. As the train began to move she repeated her question, causing Andy to wag an admonitory finger at her through the glass.

'Rugger,' he shouted. 'Have you forgotten? You were supposed to be coming to watch the game.'

But the train was gathering speed and Cassie only had time to laugh mockingly and shriek: 'Watch you make a fool of yourself? Ha! Becky and I are going shopping, so we won't even be in the village when you start fooling around …'. But the words were swallowed by the roar of the train and she sank down into her seat once more, noticing for the first time that the compartment was by no means empty, and a number of passengers were looking at her disapprovingly. Good thing I'm not in school uniform, Cassie thought with an inward chuckle, otherwise Miss Bramwell would receive complaints.

She leaned forward on the thought, letting her glance take in everyone in the compartment. 'I'm most awfully sorry; please forgive me for making such a racket,' she said apologetically. She lifted her skirt to reveal her sore and blooded knees. 'When I saw the train was about to leave I tried to run but tripped and fell, and the – er – the young man coming up behind me pulled me to my feet and almost threw me on to the train. So you see I had to thank him, didn't I?'

A fat woman with a marketing bag at her feet snorted. 'From what I can recall you wasn't apologisin',' she said acidly. 'He looked a nice young gentleman, too.'

Cassandra leaned back. 'I don't like rugger; too much mud and too many boots,' she said frankly. 'That young feller is my next door neighbour so I do sometimes go along to the game to give his side a cheer. Anyway, I'm sorry for shouting …' she beamed round and was pleased to notice that most people smiled back, 'but today they will have to do without my friend and me to cheer them on, because we're going Christmas shopping!'

By the time the girls descended from the train at Central Station they had chatted so freely of the day they hoped to enjoy that finally even the fat woman had given them advice on what to do and where to go. 'You go round Lewis's and price every item you're considerin' buyin',' she had said. 'Then go to TJ's, and you'll find the same stuff – more or less the same – for half the price.' She had appealed to the other passengers. 'Ain't that so? Lewis's is a grand shop, but my goodness, the prices! Sky high, my good man says, sky high!'

The other passengers had agreed and Rebecca, who had been listening avidly, had asked in a tentative voice: 'TJ's? Is that what you said? I don't believe I've heard of a store called TJ's. Is that spelled J-a-y?'

Everyone in the compartment, save for the two girls themselves, had looked shocked. 'No, 'course it ain't. Don't you know nothin'?' a skinny husband and wife had said, almost in unison, the man adding: 'It's T. J. Hughes, and it's on London Road. Oh aye, you'll find everything you want there, and when you're looking for somewhere to eat youse dinners you could do worse than Fuller's in Ranelagh Street.' He had sighed reminiscently, licking his lips. 'Their walnut cake is the best thing this side o' paradise.'

But now, as their new friends dispersed, the dark auburn head and the gold drew close together. 'I think we were given some good advice,' Cassie said. 'Lewis's first, 'cos by the sound of it we'll be there all morning, and after that we can go to Fuller's and have our lunch. Then, if we've seen something we really want to buy, we'll go on to T. J. Hughes and get it for half the price. But first we'll explore Lewis's.'

Cassie and Rebecca, as intended, had explored Lewis's from the top floor to the basement, but all afternoon Cassie had found herself hoping for another glimpse of those two little terrors who had started the fight outside the bakery. She thought they had behaved like a couple of little ruffians, despite their neat appearance and the endearing friendliness of their mother, and afterwards Rebecca had laughed at her assumption that twins would always be the best of friends.

'There speaks an only child,' she had said mockingly, for Rebecca was one of a family of six. 'There are times when Cecilia and I don't speak for as long as a week. And we fall out over such silly things. Who took the last ginger biscuit, whose turn is it to have the cat on the bed, whose vest is the one with the pink rose on the chest ... really silly things. And perhaps being a twin makes it worse, not better.' She chuckled again. 'Those little devils were certainly going through an unfriendly patch, wouldn't you say?'

'I suppose so,' Cassie said. 'Oh well, let's forget about them. You bought the book about trains for Jimmy, didn't you? Then let's get on with the rest of our shopping, or Christmas Day will dawn before we've found so much as a holly berry.'

In the train going home Cassie's thoughts returned to the topic of war which her parents had been discussing at dinner the previous night.

'I've been thinking about joining one of the forces,' she said. 'If I do I'd like to go into the Wrens, because they have such lovely uniforms, but when

I sounded Mother out she said I would do better in the WAAF because I wouldn't be sent to sea, and I must admit I'm not a good sailor.' She grinned at her friend. 'I'm sick crossing the Mersey on the ferry, so heaven preserve me from a life on the rolling deep.' The two of them had left the city later than they had intended because the commuter trains were packed, but now they had the compartment to themselves and because the train was a slow one, stopping at every station, they had plenty of time to talk.

'I did consider joining the forces myself, as soon as I'm old enough,' Rebecca admitted, gazing out of the window as the rural landscape jogged slowly past. 'In a way it's just changing one uniform for another – school uniform for forces uniform, I mean – but we'd be fighting for our country and not just plodding on with exams and things. Fact is, Cassie, there's a sort of glamour attached to being in the forces and I'd feel I was doing my bit, if you know what I mean.'

'Is Cecilia going to join up?' Cassie asked idly. 'Goodness, we knew this was a slow train, but not how slow! But of course she's younger than you, so you'll be the one to go or not to go, if you see what I mean. Only she's so tall and – well, mature.'

Rebecca sniffed. 'We're in one of our not speaking moods,' she said. 'If Cecilia goes for the ATS then I'll go for the WAAF, and vice versa, of course.'

Cassie giggled. 'Oh aye? And then next week

you'll be all over each other,' she prophesied. 'But anyway, Mr Chamberlain said there wasn't going to be a war and my father wants me to go to university and I can't do that unless I pass my Higher. I think going to university would be even more exciting than going into the forces.' She sighed rapturously. 'All those gorgeous undergraduates and a beautiful city like Oxford or Cambridge to explore, and when I got my degree I'd be earning a decent salary … you know, the future looks pretty bright, one way and another. Don't you agree?'

'But it's all so far in the future,' Rebecca said mournfully. 'And it depends on so many different things. Do you *really* want to stay on at school, Cassie? Three more years of slogging away in class with increasingly difficult homework. Three more years of being just a couple of schoolgirls.' She sighed, breathed on the window and drew a little miserable face on the glass. 'I know it's wicked to want a war and I don't, not really, it's just the uncertainty. Oh, was that a snowflake? Yes, it was! Do you think we're going to have a white Christmas? It's certainly cold enough!'

'Shouldn't think so,' Cassie said. She rubbed the mist off the window and peered out. 'Can't see a thing; too perishin' dark,' she informed her friend. 'Never mind, it can't be much further.'

'When we get home I vote we both go straight to your bedroom,' Rebecca said, sinking back in her seat. 'I want to wrap my presents before the children clap eyes on the parcels, and hide them in your spare room, if that's okay? The parcels, not the kids. You know what my brothers and sister are like: if I keep the stuff at home they won't have a surprise left when the day arrives, no matter how carefully I wrap it, but they've not got the cheek to invade your house to satisfy their curiosity.'

'Of course it is,' Cassie said readily. 'Don't you always? But of course we've been able to buy much nicer things this year because of having that little bit more money.'

For the rest of the journey they discussed the gifts which they had purchased.

Meanwhile, the twins had had what April described as 'a scrumptious day'. When the snow began to fall – big, gentle flakes – their cup of happiness had overflowed, and they had stood at the tram stop with closed eyes and clasped hands, praying to God for a white Christmas. They were not even unduly miserable when the snow had stopped falling, because Mam had promised them, if it snowed again before school started at the beginning of January, she would take them on a bus out into the country where they might make snowballs and build igloos to their hearts' content.

When Mam and Grandma had herded them on to a tram they clutched each other's grubby and rather sticky little paws, squeezed into a seat on the upper deck and had great difficulty in remaining awake. They had just about been alert enough when they reached their stop to push their way to the front of the departing passengers and jump off the platform, seriously endangering the waiting crowd on the pavement who did not appreciate being landed on by a pair of sturdy six-year-olds with no thought in their heads but that of the 'festive tea' they had been promised if they should by some miracle behave.

Chapter Five

Cassie opened her eyes and lay curled up for a moment in her warm bed, feeling a sudden rush of excitement. It was Christmas Day! Very soon Rebecca would be hammering on the door, come to collect her presents, all neatly labelled and gift-wrapped, to put beneath the Spencer Christmas tree. Cassie had suggested taking them round to the Spencer house around nine o'clock the previous evening, when she assumed the children would be asleep, but Rebecca had shaken her head.

'They'll come sneaking downstairs as soon as they're sure Mum and Dad are soundly off,' she explained. She had smiled a trifle guiltily at her friend. 'I know that's what they'd do because it's what I used to do before I reached the – the age of discretion. So I'll come in the morning, if that's all right?'

Cassie had agreed, and had explained to her mother that they would probably be having a visitor rather earlier than expected. So now as she lay in her bed she glanced at the face of her little alarm clock and saw that its hands were pointing to eight o'clock. She sighed; she could hear sounds of stirring from her parents' room and guessed that her father would be shaving, having just enjoyed the nice hot cup of tea his wife delivered every day of the year. Then, as he made his way downstairs, Frank Valentine would bang on Cassie's bedroom door, ignoring his wife's instructions to let her lie in because she had been up so late the night before helping her mother prepare for the great day. Between them they had baked a couple of dozen mince pies, peeled potatoes and cleaned sprouts, and last of all had iced a magnificent cake and placed little ornaments on the flat white surface – a Father Christmas, a laden sledge and half a dozen reindeer.

By the time Mary Valentine had taken the last tray of mince pies out of the oven and put them on a wire rack to cool, both she and her daughter were ready for bed. Mrs Valentine had brushed the hair off her forehead and smiled at her daughter.

'Phew!' she had said. 'Well, I think that's enough for tonight. I'll tell your father to let you lie in tomorrow – we don't want you falling asleep in the middle of Christmas dinner.'

Naturally, Cassie had laughed this idea to scorn, and now, as her father's crashing knock sounded on her bedroom door, she thought the sooner she could start her own day the better. Although she told herself she was too old to be excited by Christmas she was not too old to enjoy the pleasant thrill of opening a parcel and being surprised and gratified by the contents. Accordingly she shouted, 'Okay, Dad. Any hot water left over?'

Her father laughed. 'Lazy little puss,' he said affectionately. 'Are you decent? Bathroom's free.'

For answer Cassie trotted across the lino, wincing at the cold of it, and flung open the door. 'Thanks, Dad,' she said. 'Tell Mum I'll be down in ten minutes.'

Her father nodded. 'I'll tell her. And don't forget today we have the great Valentine Christmas breakfast!' He smacked his lips. 'Kidneys and bacon, toast and your mother's homemade marmalade, pints of coffee and possibly a sneaky mince pie. Don't be late!' He gave her his cheekiest grin, the one which made his moustache curl up at both ends as though it too were smiling, and turned to the stairs.

Cassie trotted to the bathroom and closed the door on her father's retreating back. Christmas breakfast! They usually had a boiled egg at weekends, or sometimes a rasher of bacon and half a fried tomato, so the Christmas breakfast was a real treat. The last thing Cassie had done the previous night was take out her best dress and the woollen jacket which her mother had knitted and hang them on the door of her wardrobe. Now, after a brief but thorough wash she dressed, made her bed and tidied her room, then made for the stairs. As she descended she felt again the glow of anticipation and remembered something her father had said as he and her mother had watched her icing the cake the previous evening. 'This may be our last Christmas at peace,' he had told them. 'And don't quote Mr Chamberlain to me, because war and peace are not in one man's gift to give or to deny.' He had cocked an eye at his daughter. 'You've only got to watch the newsreels to know that Herr Hitler isn't the sort of man to keep a promise. But there's no point in talking about what might never happen, and having lived through the last lot ...' His voice had tailed away as his wife tutted gently.

'I lived through the last lot too, if you remember, Frank,' she said. 'I can't think that the world will let such a terrible thing happen twice in one lifetime, so no more of your talk of war. Christmas will come next year whatever that dreadful little man does, so let's just get on with our work. My, doesn't that Christmas cake look wonderful! By the way, the Spencers have invited us for Christmas tea so I expect we shall be offered a piece of theirs.' She frowned thoughtfully. 'I think it would be polite to take a tiny piece, but remember the Spencers have four children, not just the one.' She had smiled affectionately at her daughter. 'This is one of the times you should be glad you don't have to share that Christmas cake with anybody but your father and me.'

Mr Valentine snorted. 'And with every friend and

acquaintance of the Valentine family,' he pointed out wryly. 'We'll be lucky to get so much as a sniff of it, if you ask me.'

Mrs Valentine had laughed. 'We shall have to call you Scrooge,' she said mockingly. 'But I know you, Frank! Tiny Tim would get more than his fair share of any cake in this household … which reminds me, we shan't be seeing Andy tomorrow. The O'Learys won't be back from Ireland until the day before school starts again.' She sighed. 'It will seem strange not having them over for a drink on Christmas morning, but Theresa said that Mr O'Leary senior is getting too old to undertake the journey to England. This will be the very first Christmas since they moved in next door that they haven't come round for cocktails and mince pies on Christmas morning. Christmas is celebrated differently over there, apparently. I think they call the sixth of January "little Christmas" and that's the day they have presents and a special dinner. Christmas Day itself is just a religious festival.'

'Trust the Irish to get it right,' Mr Valentine said. 'Well, we'll miss them but we mustn't complain; of course their family comes first.' He had grinned slyly at Cassie. 'No boyfriend for you this Christmas! He'll be flirting with all the pretty Irish girls, not giving a thought to his next door neighbour back home.'

Used to being teased on this subject, Cassie had merely sniffed disdainfully. 'For the nine millionth time, Andy is *not* my boyfriend,' she had said firmly, while her mother tutted disapprovingly.

'Don't be so foolish, Frank,' she had said. 'Cassie and Andy have been good friends since pre-school days. He's like a brother to her and brothers don't marry sisters, so let's change the subject if you please.'

But right now, as Cassie opened the kitchen door the delicious smell of frying bacon met her nostrils, causing them to twitch hopefully. Her mother, standing at the stove, turned and smiled lovingly. 'Happy Christmas, darling. I hope you've brought a good appetite with you,' she said gaily. 'How many rashers can you eat? Your father has just devoured four, two kidneys and two fried eggs ...'

April woke first and looked towards the foot of her bed, where, last night, a bulging stocking had hung until the church clock struck two, at which point both twins had stirred and sat up. They had glanced across at each other in the pale radiance of their nightlights and with one accord had removed the stockings from the bedposts and scrambled back between the sheets, clutching them lovingly to their small bosoms.

They knew, of course, that the contents of the stockings would be identical, and indeed would have been very upset had it been otherwise, and now they set to work immediately to spread everything on their coverlets so that they might be sure nothing had been forgotten. There was an orange in the toe of each stocking, and then a bag of chocolate energy balls. Next came a cartoon book showing the adventures of Sinbad the Sailor, and then a penny whistle. May put hers straight to her lips and was about to blow hard when her twin snatched it from her.

'Mam don't know we're awake and if you blast on that thing she *will* know,' she hissed. 'When it goes light, which ain't for hours yet, then you can blow until you're red as a tomato, but right now shut your gob and save your breath to cool your porridge. Ooh, a Mars bar! I don't remember havin' one of them in our stockings last year.'

'I gorra monkey on a stick,' May said rapturously. 'You'll have one an' all, April, only mine's gorra blue coat so I reckon yours will be red. And I've a packet of cigarette cards, the very ones I were wantin': fillum stars.'

But that had been at two o'clock in the morning, and now April looked at May, still slumbering, then reached across and tugged her blankets off. 'Gerrup!' she said brusquely. 'There's scrambled eggs for brekky; don't you 'member Mammy telling us not to be late? Oh, May Clarke, you are a lazy lump. Gerrup, gerrup, gerrup!'

May, sighing, got out of bed, grabbed her clothes and made for the door. 'I'm goin' to dress in the kitchen, where it's warm,' she said decidedly. 'You stay here, April. No need to do *everything* I do.' On the words she left the room and began to pad down the stairs, but the mere recollection of scrambled eggs had galvanised April into action and in her hurry to be first in the kitchen she tripped on the fourth stair from the bottom and cannoned into May, whose shriek would have done credit to a steam train and brought Rosheen hurrying out to disentangle her daughters.

'It were an accident,' April wailed, fearful lest she might merit a smaller helping of scrambled eggs as a punishment for apparently pushing her sister downstairs, but Rosheen's mood was benevolent. The three of them entered the kitchen together, April still explaining at the top of her voice how she had come to trip and May wailing that she was sure her knees and the palms of her hands must be black and blue, but Rosheen was hurrying to put spoonfuls of fluffy egg on to two rounds of buttered toast and paid no attention. And presently, when the scrambled eggs, toast and mugs of milk had disappeared and the girls were dressed, she fetched out two parcels and handed one to each twin.

'Happy Christmas, you two,' she said. 'I hope you like your gifts. Grandma helped me choose them so if they're wrong you can blame us both.'

For a moment the twins just gazed at the gaily wrapped parcels, then fell on them with squeaks of excitement, ripping the paper off and dropping it on the floor. Rosheen uttered a mild protest, and began to gather up the scraps just as her mother entered the room.

'Aha, I'm in time to see the grand opening,' she remarked. 'What do you think, girls?' She waited expectantly, clearly hoping for cries of joy, but the twins were ominously silent. May's parcel had contained the frock, or one very like it, which she had seen in Paddy's market on the day they now thought of as their great escape, whereas April's had held a pale blue dress with cornflowers embroidered around the hem.

'Well?' Rosheen demanded, unable to keep the hopeful excitement out of her voice. But both girls were glaring at her as though she had done something unforgivable. Rosheen looked from April to May and saw the trembling of her younger daughter's lower lip.

Staring unbelievingly from the little red frock to her mother's face, May stammered: 'It's clothes! People don't give people clothes at Christmas. It's not fair!' She flung the pretty little frock down on the kitchen table. 'I don't want it! I want a skipping rope!'

Rosheen was so disappointed that for a moment she couldn't speak, but then April flung her own frock down on the floor and her sorely tried patience snapped. 'What you both want is a damned good hiding,' she said, her voice hovering on the verge of tears. She turned to May. 'You said you wanted this frock more than anything else, and look how you behave when you're given it! As for you, April, you *said* you wanted to be dressed differently ... or had you forgotten? Grandma said you wouldn't appreciate clothes, but I thought you'd like the blue and you *said* ...' Rosheen slumped into a chair and began to sob.

Mrs Clarke came across the room and gave her daughter a hug. 'They's all talk and no trousers,' she said bracingly. 'They've said and said as how they don't want to keep lookin' alike, yet when you give 'em two beautiful frocks they throws 'em back in your face. I'm surprised they haven't chucked their stockin's out of the winder, 'cos they's ungrateful brats, and in future we'll keep their presents for someone who'll appreciate 'em.' By now both twins were roaring, their faces red and shiny with tears as they bewailed their lot, and at last Mrs Clarke herded them outside and told them not to come back until they were truly sorry for their behaviour.

Ejected from the cosy kitchen with its exciting smells of the dinner to come the twins looked around King Edward Court with jaundiced eyes. There wasn't a soul about, icicles hung from the eaves of a good many of the houses and it was bitterly cold, not at all the sort of day to find yourself outside without so much as a woolly hat or a coat to protect you from the icy blast. April looked at her sister and knew she was feeling equally hard done by, which was enough to make April march back to the door of No. 3, confident that neither Grandma nor Mam would think of locking it. She found she was mistaken. She turned to look at May, sitting on the cobbles snivelling, and was about to raise the knocker and slam it home when she heard the key grate in the lock and the door opened just far enough for Grandma – or possibly Mam – to hurl their outdoor clothing through the gap.

'We doesn't want you to turn into a couple of pillars of ice so you'd best put your coats on,' the voice of the dispenser of winter woollies said, and it was definitely Grandma. 'No, April, I know it's you a-pushin' of the door but you ain't comin' in until you's ready to tell your Mam you're sorry for bein' such wicked, ungrateful girls.'

April had been thinking it might be worth apologising just to get out of the cold, but these words roused all the devilment within her. She grabbed the bundles of clothing and descended the steps, saying haughtily over her shoulder, 'You've ruined our Christmas, you and Mam. We've done nothin' wrong, and when we tell our friends you kicked us out of the house without so much as a pair of gloves between us and we die of the cold you'll be sorry.'

April thought she heard a murmur from Rosheen

begging Mrs Clarke not to be too hard on them but Grandma's reply was cut off by the slamming of the door and April, still furious and without the slightest intention of apologising, stamped back to where her sister sat. The twins struggled into their winter coats, wrapped scarves round their necks and thrust their hands into woolly gloves, and then May looked at her elder sister with a mixture of defiance and regret.

'My feet is cold,' she commented. 'Mam's a cruel woman; feet is the hardest thing to get warm again, and my chilblains is itchin' like anythin'.'

April gave the matter short consideration then headed to the steps once more. 'I'll bang the bloody knocker till they open up and then we'll both rush at the door and push our way inside,' she said. 'And we *won't* apologise, not even if they beats us black and blue. Not that they will; it's only nasty ol' Grandma eggin' Mam on to be mean to us just 'cos we didn't like them fancy frocks.'

May sniffed dolefully. 'I did like the red frock, only it were clothes,' she said, pulling her hat well down to cover her icy ears. 'Oh, look, the door's openin'. Shall we—'

But they were too late. Two pairs of wellington boots and some hand-knitted socks hurtled through the air. One of the boots struck April on the shoulder, making her give a squeal of protest, and for the first time she actually began to feel regret for her behaviour … though what she really felt was regret for the consequences of their behaviour. When they had misbehaved in the house Mam and Grandma had more than once sent them off to play in the court while they made good whatever the twins had spoiled. But this had always happened in the summer; Mam was far too fond a parent to force her children to leave the warmth of the kitchen in winter, especially on Christmas Day. April sat down on the bottom step and began to cram her foot, now sock clad, into the nearest boot, and May followed suit. Once the boots were in position April leaned down and pulled May to her feet. Then she addressed her in ringing tones which she hoped would be clearly audible to the cruel relatives enjoying the comfort of the firelit kitchen.

'We're goin' to run away, 'cos we've an unkind mammy who don't love us,' she announced. 'We'll run away to – to Seaforth Sands, and we'll tell people that our mammy and grandma threw us out into the cold so's they could have Christmas dinner all to themselves, and if a policeman comes and wants to know what we're doin' we'll tell him our names and where we live and ask him to go and throw them into prison for bein' cruel to little children.' Her tone dropped to a more natural one. 'Do get a move on, May, or it'll be dark before we reach the Sands and very likely we'll be drownded by the tide comin' in before we can stop it.'

May gave a smothered giggle. 'You can't stop the tide comin' in, norreven if you're a policeman,' she observed. 'How are we goin' to get to Seaforth, though? I bet you've got no money, for all your talkin' so big.'

Before April could acknowledge that this was true, a neighbour emerged from his house, empty buckets clanking in either hand, and made for the tap at the end of the court. April immediately accosted him.

'Wotcher, Stevie,' she shouted. 'We's runnin' away, me and May; can you lend us our tram fare? We'll pay you back out of our Christmas money, only our mam's chucked us out and locked the door so we can't get in to get it.'

Stevie lived at No. 11 and was well known to the twins, but unfortunately Stevie knew the twins rather well too. He gave a mocking laugh, told April to 'pull the other one' and clanked off down the court, calling over his shoulder that he hoped the water weren't frozen since his mam had neglected to fill the buckets last night and there was grosh of vegetables waiting to be cooked.

'And as for catchin' a tram, or a bus, or the overhead railway, you'll be hard put to it since none of 'em run on Christmas Day,' he told them. 'You'd best go back in, say you're sorry for whatever you've been and gone and done, and help your mam dish up your Christmas dinner. You may be sure your mam will forgive you, no matter how naughty you've been, 'cos it is Christmas after all.'

May stamped her cold feet and longed for the courage to defy her sister and go back in the warm, but she knew that if she did so she would be letting April down, and her sister could be extremely nasty if she thought May was not on her side. Oh, they might fight or argue, but they always stuck up for one another, and for May to give in and tell her mother she was sorry would not only be betraying April, it would be a tacit admission that the twins had been in the wrong and Grandma and Mam had been right to demand an apology.

April looked at May, and May looked at April. Then May had her bright idea. 'You know the Great Homer Street market?' she said. 'If we was to go along there we'd find no end of bits and bobs – clippings of holly, broken flowers, maybe even a bruised apple or a couple of oranges what have got dropped. It will take us a little while to walk there, but ain't that a good thing? Mam and Grandma will think we really have run away, so when we come back with a bunch of flowers for them they'll be so pleased to see us safe and sound that they'll let us back in straight away.'

Secretly, April thought this an excellent plan, but she did not intend to say so aloud. So far as she was concerned she led her twin round by the nose and always treated May's suggestions with suspicion.

But today was the exception. After all, there was something special about Christmas, and anyway she had no desire to be out after dark, a prey to tramps and drunken seamen, so they would have to go back to the house in the end. So instead of laughing May's idea to scorn she nodded grudgingly and headed for the arch and the street beyond.

'We'll give it a go,' she said. 'Mam never lets us be out after dark so she'll be real worried by the time the street lamps come on. Hurry up, May, best foot forward. And when we get inside I vote we just mumble something that sounds like sorry because tomorrow is Uncle George's Christmas party and we wouldn't want to miss that!'

When Mrs Clarke had thrown the twins' winter clothing into the court Rosheen had started forward, wanting to tell them she was sorry for spoiling their Christmas – April's parting shot – but her mother had put a restraining hand on her arm.

'Don't you realise what you're doing?' she demanded. 'You are rearing two of the most spoilt and selfish children I've ever had the misfortune to meet. April throws her weight about and bullies, May whines and weeps until she gets her own way, and between the two of them they're wearing you to a thread. Rosheen, you *must* stand up to them, make them mind you, or you'll regret it for the rest of your life.'

'But Mam, it's Christmas …' Rosheen began, but her mother hushed her with an impatient gesture.

'No, listen to me, my dear. I've kept my tongue between my teeth even though I saw you makin' the same mistakes over and over, givin' way, deferrin' punishment for naughtiness, spendin' all your money on the twins with never a penny to spare for yourself. You think you're doin' them a favour, but I'm here to tell you you aren't. You're like the man in that story – Frankenstein, wasn't it? You're creatin' a monster: two little girls who take, take, take and never even think of givin'. And you are the only person who can turn them round, make them see someone else's point of view as well their own.'

Rosheen, sitting in the fireside chair, hiccuped on a sob and nodded miserably. 'I know you're right. Other people have told me I spoil the twins, but Mam, they're all I've got. If their dad— but he's not and twins are different from other children, or that's what I tell myself anyway; surely as they grow older they'll be easier to handle?'

She looked hopefully across at her mother, who had looked up sharply at the bitten-off words, but that wise woman shook a reproving head. 'Have they got any easier since going to school? I think not. Oh, I'm not denyin' that they're good in class and do well at their lessons, but that's because no teacher would stand for their rudeness and bad behaviour, so they save all that up for when they get home.'

'But it's awful cold out there and the girls don't have their wellingtons or thick socks …' Rosheen began, but her mother only snatched the twins' footwear, marched over to the door, unlocked it and hurled the boots out into the court.

The two women listened intently, one at least of them hoping to hear the word 'sorry', but apparently the twins had not yet even thought of apologising. Instead April shouted a few more threats and then everything went quiet. After a minute or two Rosheen climbed the stairs and looked out of the window of her bedroom, which overlooked the court. When she came down again she was pale and clearly more than a little apprehensive.

'They've gone,' she murmured in a hushed tone. 'Oh, Mam, they can't really have run away, can they? Where would they run to? They know Uncle George spends Christmas Day with his daughter in her smallholding on the Wirral, so they can't have gone to him. Oh, I do hope they're not telling lies about us, or we'll all be in deep trouble.'

Mrs Clarke sighed. 'They won't risk losing their Christmas dinner,' she prophesied. 'They'll be back here on the dot of twelve thirty, and if for the first time in their lives they're unsure of their welcome, all the better. You've made the stuffin', haven't you? The bird will only need basting a couple of times, then we can dish up.' She fixed her daughter with a stern look. 'And don't you go givin' in just because it's Christmas. It's time that precious pair learned a much needed lesson, and I'm tellin' you straight, young woman, that not one mouthful of dinner will pass their lips until you have a genuine apology. Promise me you won't give in?'

Rosheen gave her mother the promise she asked, though with a certain amount of reluctance. Even so, she glanced uneasily at the window some time later as a few snowflakes began to fall, and just as she was about to suggest that she might take a stroll outside, for it was very warm indeed in the kitchen, there came a hesitant little tap on the door.

Rosheen rushed to answer it, yanking the door open with such enthusiasm that May almost fell into the room. She was holding a crushed and frosted bunch of tiny flowers in one hand and a large orange, badly split, in the other. She said nothing but glanced over her shoulder at April; clearly the elder twin was to be the spokesperson once more. The words *Oh, twins, we've been so worried, especially when it started to snow* longed to be said, but old Mrs Clarke dug her daughter warningly in the ribs, though she let the children sidle past her into the warm and welcoming kitchen.

'Well?' she said belligerently. 'Let's have an apology, or you can go to your room without more than a sniff of the best Christmas dinner your mother and I have ever cooked.'

April unwound the scarf which hid the lower

half of her face and smiled ingratiatingly at the two adults. 'We've brung you some flowers,' she said, and then glanced at May, and the two girls spoke in chorus.

'We's sorry for what we said, and we'll wear our new frocks to Uncle George's party and say our mam chose the prettiest she could find.'

April glanced from her mother's face to her grandmother's. 'Is that all right? Can we have us dinners now?'

Rosheen laughed and agreed that they could, but Mrs Clarke sighed and flourished the damaged orange under April's nose. 'You can throw that orange away; it's goin' bad so fast that by the time it were peeled it would be rotten all through,' she said. 'Your mam and me don't need a bribe, just a nice apology.'

Rosheen said equably: 'They have apologised, Mam. Didn't you hear 'em?' But her mother shook her head.

'They learned those words off by heart,' she said reprovingly. 'But I suppose it were none worse for that. Oh, come on, twins, get your coats and boots off and put your slippers on. Then you can go to the sink and have a good wash and after that we can have our Christmas dinner, and about time too.'

Chapter Six

Andy slid off the back of old Mr O'Leary's latest acquisition, a high-spirited chestnut colt, and took a deep breath of the fresh morning air, grinning at his grandfather's manager as he handed him the reins.

'Sure and isn't it a perfect day to be celebratin' Christmas?' he said, imitating Liam's accent. 'Only of course things are different here in Ireland. Back home they'll be opening presents and preparing a huge dinner, whereas here we'll just go to mornin' service. I guess at home they'll pray for peace, but that's a prayer that won't be answered, I fear. What d'you think, Liam, or do you reckon it's no concern of yours because Eire isn't part of the United Kingdom any longer?'

The young man shrugged. 'Sure and what does it matter when it comes to defendin' the king?' he asked. 'Didn't me own daddy volunteer and join the army before war had even been declared in the last lot? It'll be the same this time, so it will. Meself and two of the stable lads were talkin' it over after old

Chamberlain's promise of peace, and Aedan reckons that we'll be at war within a year.'

Andy fished in his pocket for a sugar lump. He felt the colt's soft lips as the two-year-old accepted the titbit, and patted the chestnut's gleaming neck affectionately. 'D'you want to see to him or shall I do it? He's a grand fellow, isn't he? He's scarce broken a sweat and I gave him a good go on the gallops.'

Liam grinned. 'Come wi' me and we'll share the work,' he suggested. As they set off, one on each side of the colt, Liam raised his brows. 'I've been meanin' to ask you. Why've you never come home to Ireland at Christmas before?'

Andy shrugged. 'My mother's a nurse back in England and she usually works right up to Christmas Eve, but she's got a whole ten days off this year. Besides, Gramps is getting a bit old to make the journey over to the Wirral, where my family live.'

By now they had reached the stables and the colt quickened his pace, knowing he would get a carrot or a sweet red apple whilst he was being untacked. 'D'you think your father will take over the stud?' Liam asked as they entered the stall.

Andy grinned. He should have guessed that the staff – or at least the stable staff – would be well aware that old Mr O'Leary hoped to hand over the business to a member of the family he could trust. But Andy's father had his own company and had never been even slightly interested in the stud, and

Andy himself, though keenly interested, was still too young to be considered, he supposed. And if there is a war, Andy thought but did not say aloud, I shall join the air force and nothing on earth will persuade me to abandon that idea, much though I love the horses, the house and Grandfather's acres. But he could say none of this to Liam, whose whole future at the moment was the stud.

They watched as the colt, untacked, plunged his muzzle eagerly into his waiting food bucket, and then Andy slapped Liam on the back and turned away, knowing that a first rate breakfast awaited him in the large kitchen.

Indoors, Andy's mother greeted him cheerfully and thrust an enormous plateful of food into his hands. 'Get outside of that,' she said gaily, and turned to smile at his grandfather, sitting in his favourite chair eating a bacon sandwich. Andy settled himself at the kitchen table.

'Morning, Gramps. Where's Dad?' he asked. 'I took the young colt up on the gallops; he's a grand feller, isn't he? You'll get a good price for him when the next hunting season starts. Liam thinks he wants more flesh on his bones and he's probably right, but as you know I'm no expert. I'm just impressed by the speed and strength of him.'

His grandfather nodded. 'Aye, he's a grand feller so he is,' he agreed. 'But who knows where we will be in a year's time, or six months come to that?'

Andy, in the act of spearing a slice of fried potato, paused to look across at his grandparent. 'Do *you* think there's a war coming, Gramps?' he asked curiously. 'What about Mr Chamberlain's piece of paper?'

Old Mr O'Leary sniffed and suggested a use for the piece of paper which Mr Chamberlain had certainly not considered. 'D'you think I'd have asked your family to come across to the farm if I'd not made up me mind that time's gettin' short?' he asked. 'I've a good business manager in Liam and a good head lad in Terry, young though he is ... in fact the staff could run the place without any outside help at all. But even so I want an O'Leary in charge, someone to overlook the yard, someone to make decisions. Your father can't or won't do it because he's got a thrivin' business of his own. We've discussed the matter and I know he's right when he fears he would run the place into the ground in less than twelve months. He knows nothin' about horses; sure an' me blood runs cold when I t'ink of him tryin' to be what he isn't, a judge of horseflesh. If you'll make your mind up to give it a go when you leave school I'll give you all the help I can. Liam would be at your elbow ready to guide you; what d'you say, lad?'

Andy had been half expecting some kind of offer, but this one was almost irresistible. Almost. Ever since he could remember he and his family had come over to Ireland in the summer and riding had become second nature to him. He had taken his grandfather's magnificent horses for granted and had fearlessly ridden the wild shy ponies brought in by the farmers from all over the back country. Had he secretly hoped that his future would be concerned with the stud? But he knew that if there was a war he wanted to fly. From the moment he could toddle he had collected anything to do with aircraft, but he also owed some loyalty to the old man sitting in the chair opposite his own.

Gramps was beginning to tap his fingers on the table, clearly waiting for his offer to be either accepted or rejected, and Andy wished his father were present to advise him which course to take. His mother cast him a quick glance and a reassuring smile, but he was not sure whether this meant approval of one answer or the other, and in any case it was he who must make the choice.

'Well?' Gramps almost barked the word, whilst beneath his bushy eyebrows his little dark eyes were beginning to sparkle dangerously.

Andy took a deep breath. 'It's an amazing offer, Gramps,' he said slowly. 'But I can't take it up, much though I would like to, just like that. I still have to sit my Higher and of course there's the threat of war, which would mean I'd get called up, but taking all these things into account can I say ask me again when I'll have had my results and the future's a bit clearer?'

He half expected a furious tirade to burst about his ears, for he had heard Gramps in the stable yard letting rip to one of his staff, but to his relief the old man merely nodded slowly. 'You're right; 'tis a big t'ing for a young feller to decide,' he said. 'Shall we give it till June, then?'

Andy was beginning to nod when his mother interrupted. 'Sure and you won't get your results until the end of August at the earliest,' she said quietly, addressing her son. 'The time to make a big decision like this is September. If'n you get your Higher, which is quite likely since you did so well in Matric, then the universities will open their doors to you, whereas your grandfather's offer will stand whether you pass or fail.' She turned to the old man. 'Isn't that so, Gramps?'

There was a perceptible pause before old Mr O'Leary answered, and then Andy felt that he did so grudgingly. 'I saw Dr McLean last week. He says at my age I ought to be tekkin' it easy.' He turned as the door opened and his wife came into the room. 'Well well well. If it isn't like you to leave me to fight me own battles and then to come smilin' into the room! I don't like 'put offs' but this one is fair enough, so it is. We're to leave the big decision until after the lad has got the results of that big examination he's won the right to tek. I've never seen the use of paper qualifications meself – they took me only son away from me – but Andy loves the horses, so he does, so

I'm hopeful, very hopeful, that when next September comes his answer will be the one we seek.'

Grandma O'Leary was a tiny little woman, thin as a lath and bright as a button. In her youth she had been an intrepid rider on the hunting field, and as the size of the stud increased she had regularly ridden out with the lads at morning exercise. Too old to do so now she still visited the horses regularly, taking each one a sugar lump, a carrot or an apple and talking lovingly to them as the long, hopeful faces emerged over their half-doors.

But despite her age she was still a power in the land so far as the staff were concerned, and now she showed that she was awake to the difficulties of the choice her grandson had promised to make. She smiled at her husband, patted her daughter-in-law on the shoulder and then turned to Andy. 'When you were a little lad all you thought about was aircraft and learnin' to fly, so it was,' she said quietly. 'I know you, young Andy; if there's a war you'll be off to join the Royal Air Force and nothing we say will keep you at home. Patriotism is an old-fashioned word these days but I can't see you abandonin' your country in her hour of need. Besides, old 'uns like me and Gramps can remember the last one. You'll be called up in age order, the youngest first, and if you wait till conscription you won't have any choice of trade. The forces are famous for puttin' round pegs into square holes, so you go in as a volunteer just as soon as war is declared and get your choice of trade, Andy O'Leary. What do you say to that?'

Andy opened his mouth to answer but Gramps got in first. 'He'll do as he says he will; as he wishes, in fact,' the old man said fiercely, glaring at his tiny wife as she helped herself to a couple of sausages and a fried egg and took her place at the table. 'And now where's me fine son? Keepin' well clear; that sounds like young Bran.' Andy grinned. His father was past forty, and a very sober citizen indeed.

But right now Christmas was beginning to make itself felt. The family would soon be preparing to leave for church, and Andy was still clad in jodhpurs and sweater, whilst his grandmother was wearing a navy dress with white lace at the throat and Gramps was in his Sunday suit and old school tie. He made his excuses to the assembled company and jumped up from his place, casting a wistful eye over the thick rounds of Grandma's loaf waiting to be toasted as he did so.

'Save me a slice or two and I'll have them later,' he begged. 'I'd forgotten the time, but don't worry: I'll be respectable well before the trap is at the door.'

Gramps and Grandma had a perfectly good Morris Minor which they used pretty well on a daily basis for fetching and carrying from the village, but they never went to church in it, preferring to stick to the pony and trap. Gramps always gave Dolly a carrot when she arrived and the pony would neigh her thanks, so, Andy thought, if I hear Dolly neighing that will give me about two minutes to get down the stairs, through the kitchen and out into the stable yard. He glanced at himself in the mirror, sprinkled water on his hair, flattened it with both hands, and began to heave himself out of his jodhpurs. A couple of minutes later he checked his appearance in the mirror, straightened his tie and picked up his navy blue greatcoat. Then, hearing the clatter of hooves, he hurried down the stairs.

Later, when everyone had enjoyed a good hot lunch, he slipped out of the house and made for the stable, for he felt he had a lot of thinking to do. The talk round the dining table had mostly revolved around the future of the stud, and Andy was only just beginning to realise how, if he accepted Gramps's offer, his life would have to alter. He would have to spend all his holidays at the stud, and though he enjoyed the horses and the life his grandparents lived he was starting to see how restricted such a life would be. Yet if he refused the offer, what then? But by now he had reached the stable, so he went into Domino's stall and found that Liam had anticipated his wishes, for the gelding was already tacked up and eager to go.

'Thanks, Liam. Are you coming with me?' he asked, but found that he was glad when the manager shook his head.

'I've got to get back to that mare. She's not been well and needs lookin' after,' he said.

'You're right, of course. I'll be off then . . . if you wouldn't mind opening the gate for me?'

Liam complied, and Andy, having thanked him, rode out into the gentle countryside which, even in December, was beautiful and welcoming. He sat easily on Domino's broad back, letting the reins lie slack on his neck, for the gelding knew the way they usually took as well as Andy himself.

Presently they left the lane and descended a gently sloping meadow which ended at a pebble-bedded stream. The narrow track beside the stream was known as the hazel path, for in the autumn the cobnuts crunched beneath one's feet, but right now, with the hazel branches bare, it was simply a quiet and lovely ride for a person riding alone to enjoy.

Andy felt himself begin to relax as he rode, though the problems confronting him were still there. If he accepted Gramps's offer this would effectively become his home. He could not expect people to come all the way over to Ireland to see him, and if he came to live here his friends both at school and at home would be lost to him.

Then there was Cassie. The two had lived next door to one another for as long as either could remember and Andy realised, with a stab of surprise, that he could not bear to think he would never see Cassie again. His brow wrinkled in deep thought. He told himself there was no romantic attachment between the two of them, yet the thought of Cassie's getting on with her life without him upset him possibly even more than the idea of losing Derek, whom he had known since prep school and who was still his bezzie, as his Liverpudlian friends would say.

As the track left the brook Domino's smooth walk became a slow trot, and presently Andy saw another rider ahead of him. Hastily, before the other became aware that he was being followed, Andy pulled Domino to a halt and edged him very gently under overhanging tree branches so that if the rider ahead happened to glance back he would not be aware of their presence.

But in this respect he was unlucky, for just as Domino began to investigate the roots of an enormous beech tree – and the mast which clustered thickly on the ground around them – he must have sensed the presence of the other horse for he lifted his head and called, a nickering whinny which was immediately echoed by the horse ahead. The other rider had heard too – Andy could see now that it was a girl – and she wheeled her mount round and came towards him at a sedate trot. Andy felt a blush warm his cheeks; she was a very pretty girl, probably no more than fifteen or sixteen, with dark hair tied up in bunches on either side of her face. Andy would have sworn he had never seen her in his life before. He thought she was a little like Cassie and he saw that she was riding bareback, a neat black pony with a splash of white on its forehead which was probably how it had come by its name, for even as rider and horse drew level with the beech tree the girl spoke.

'Star saw you before I did,' she said. 'You'll be Mr O'Leary's grandson, the feller who's going to take over the stud one of these fine days.' She looked him up and down and Andy found himself bristling; she might be a very pretty girl, but that did not give her the right to look him over so critically. However, before he had decided how to put her in her place she spoke again. 'Sorry I am to disturb your nice quiet ride, but I didn't know it was you behind me,' she explained. 'I t'ought it might be Liam; he comes this way quite often, and I wanted a word with him so I did. I s'pose you've guessed who I am?' She had been staring at him critically, or so he had thought, but now her eyes warmed into friendship and he saw again how very pretty she was. Prettier than Cassie, he thought, and immediately felt ashamed, for was not Cassie his best friend after Derek? But then the girl raised her brows at him. 'Did Liam not tell you how his cousin from Dublin is spending a couple of weeks at the stud to give a hand while one of the stable lads is sick? I've done it before, and Mr O'Leary trusts me now to exercise his mounts.'

She slipped off Star's back, picked up a handful of beech mast and offered it to the pony with a little smile, whereupon Star blew impatiently into her palm with the air of one who considered beech mast to be inedible rubbish. The girl laughed.

'Sure and if I wait for you to ask me what's me name I'll likely wait all day,' she said cheerfully. 'I know you're Andy O'Leary, for you're the very spit of your grandda, so you are, but you don't know me; I'm Clare O'Hara.' She held out a hand and somehow it seemed only polite for Andy to slip off Domino's back in order to shake it.

'Hello, Miss O'Hara, or may I call you Clare?' Andy said, then added: 'Though considering you called me Andy I suppose first names can be taken for granted.'

She cocked an eyebrow. 'Of course you can call me Clare; it's me name! Are you turning back now? If so we can ride together. Surprised I am that you didn't recognise Star, if not me. Though when I think about it, she's only here to be schooled, so you've probably not seen her before.'

'I thought I didn't recognise her,' Andy said as they trotted back the way they had come. 'But then we're usually only over for a couple of weeks in the summer, so the chances are there's been a complete change of horseflesh every time we visit.'

The girl nodded. 'It's right you are, of course. And now let's put our best foot forward, or hoof rather, or we'll be late for evening stables.'

*

105

In bed that night Andy thought about Clare O'Hara. When he had told himself that coming to live in Ireland would mean losing all his friends, he had not taken into account the possibility of making new ones. He would miss Cassie, of course, but he realised now, a trifle guiltily, that Cassie wasn't the only female on the planet; there would be other girls, girls as pretty and self-confident as Clare. If he decided in favour of the stud, he could still have a perfectly good social life.

Satisfied on this score Andy slept at last, and if he dreamed of a teasing tanned face or Cassie's dark blue eyes, by morning both were gone, though neither was forgotten.

Chapter Seven

September 1939

April opened her eyes on the fourth of September and for a moment she could not think what was special about today. Then, with a jolt, she remembered. War! She and May had discussed the war the previous day, after that horrible old man had read his message to the British people, and decided they wanted no part of it. Mam and Grandma had cried and talked about something called evacuation. They had gone up the stairs together, saying they must pack, and this was ridiculous because the Clarkes never went anywhere. Yet there they stood, two bulging satchels, one at the foot of each bed, and next to them the hateful boxes which contained those horrible gas masks which May and April had twice tried to dump without success, since they informed their relatives that the things smelt horrid and they would never wear them.

'You might be glad of them, because mustard gas stinks a lot worse than the perishin' masks do,'

Grandma had said. 'Do stop makin' such a fuss, twins.'

May had asked whether they should get their little bathing suits out of what Rosheen called 'the summer drawer', but though Rosheen had shaken her head, Grandma had started crying all over again. She had muttered about mud, trenches and Uncle George's war wound, but the twins simply thought she'd gone barmy at last and took no notice.

'If it's anything like the last lot all food will be rationed and what isn't rationed will disappear off the shelves before you can say knife,' she had told them later, scrubbing her eyes with the back of her hands until they were scarlet and her cheeks dirt-daubed. Just before bedtime she had made them sit down and tried to explain what was going to happen in the morning, but as April and May could have told her, in their short lives they had perfected the art of only hearing what they wanted to hear and this was no exception. There was talk of printing out address labels to be pinned to their coats, and of writing to their mams as soon as they reached their new homes. Grandma spoke of train journeys, of staying with their teacher, of doing as they were told (ha ha, April had said bitterly), and said they were supposed to arrive at the school gates by eight o'clock in the morning before going on to Lime Street Station. Eight o'clock! That was rubbish. School started at nine, not eight, and if they were off on a school trip they might meet earlier than usual, but not a whole hour!

April sat up in bed and twitched back the curtain. It was no longer dark out there so she leaned over and gave May's shoulder a gentle – fairly gentle – punch. 'Wake up!' she hissed. 'Wharra we doin' today, May?' She giggled. 'That's a poem. Wharra we doin' today, May?' she repeated.

May giggled. 'We're goin' to gerrus an egg, Meg,' she said. 'And don't you tell me your name ain't Meg, 'cos it were the only rhyme I could think of. What's the time?'

'Too early for gettin' up,' April said. 'Only I reckon we'd better – get up, I mean – because last night someone said something about having to go to the school early, like as if we were off on a trip. We don't want to miss nothin' what's fun, does we, May?'

May shook her head. 'No we doesn't. Whose turn is it to go downstairs to fetch up some hot water?'

'Yours,' April said quickly. 'But didn't we have a wash last night? Didn't Mam say it would give us more time in the mornin'?'

May appeared to search her memory and then got out of bed and looked at the clothes which had been laid on the foot of it. 'I think you're right,' she said rather reluctantly. 'Well, we'd better get dressed then.'

It was the work of a moment for the twins to

dress and in less time than it takes to tell they were both downstairs, only to be sent straight back up again to collect their satchels and the hated gas masks. Grandma was making porridge, Mam was pouring milk into two mugs and on the table there were two packets of sandwiches, two apples and a couple of mint humbugs. Mam settled them in their places whilst Grandma served the porridge, and April thought there was something downright sinister in the way that Rosheen and Mrs Clarke kept nervously glancing at the clock on the mantel. It was almost as if they knew that something was about to happen, something not nice at all, to do with the horrible wailing noise which had occurred just after the prime minister's declaration the previous day.

April settled herself comfortably and began spooning porridge; it was lovely porridge and today Grandma had sprinkled coarse brown sugar over both twins' helpings, which usually only happened on birthdays or at Christmas.

'We've got to get you to the school gates for eight o'clock,' Rosheen said. 'Finish your milk. I've made some cold tea for you, though from what Miss O'Brien told us you'll be given something to drink two or three times on the train.'

April shot May a significant glance, drained her mug and got to her feet. 'We want the privy before we go anywhere,' she announced. 'Where's we goin', Mam? It's a school trip, ain't it? Well, it must be, because you're not goin' to come with us, are you?' April stared straight at her mother as she spoke and saw Rosheen's eyes fill with tears, saw them trickle down her cheeks.

'No, chuck, I can't go with you; I've work to do here. But if you do as you're told and stick together with your teacher and each other, you'll be fine. Some of the kids being evacuated don't have brothers or sisters so it's a lot harder for them. I telled your teacher they mustn't part you or there might be a bit of bother and she said she understood. Now go along to the lavvy and don't sit out there for ages chattin'.'

'All right, Mammy,' April said. She grabbed her sister's hand. 'Come along. You know what these school trips are like: they won't let you stop for a widdle no matter how you plead. Why's you puttin' on your coat, Grandma? Mam'll come wi' us. You ought to stay here and toast a round or two of bread, 'cos all the porridge has gone and Mam hasn't had no breakfast yet.'

Once outside in the privy, however, April addressed her sister in an urgent undertone. 'There's suffin' goin' on,' she hissed. 'Grandma *never* comes to see us off on a school trip. Shall we cut and run now, May, or shall we wait and see what it's all about?'

Heaving her knickers back into place, May gave a whimper. 'I don't like it,' she wailed. 'D'you remember the pantomime Mam took us to see last year? I feel like them babes what were took to the woods and abandoned by the wicked landlord. Oh, April, I'm that frightened.'

April, not usually demonstrative, hauled up her own drawers and put an arm round her sister's shaking shoulders. 'I know exactly what you mean, 'cos I feel just the same,' she admitted. 'Tell you what, twin, we'll do as they say and go ahead just as though we wanted to do wharrever they tell us. But trains have to stop to let people get on or off, and if we decide this here journey ain't what we want, they'll be two kids short when they gets goin' again.'

'And then can we come home?' May said, brightening. 'You don't *have* to go. Mary Louise in Standard Three ain't goin' at all. I heard her tellin' Sukie Watson that her mam don't believe in vacuation. She said she's more afraid of cows and country – I think she meant foxes and rats and things – than she is of any old German. So you see they can't *make* you go, though they pretend as how they can.'

'Oh, but …' April was beginning when their mother rattled on the door of the privy, causing both her daughters to jump guiltily.

'What did I say?' Rosheen bawled, throwing the door open. 'I said you weren't to sit there chattering away while time marched on. Are you respectable? Done all you need to do? Then it's off with the four of us and if you ask Grandma why she's comin' as well she'll probably start cryin' again and we don't want that, do we? Other mums and grandmas may feel like cryin' but they're too proud to do it.'

'They were all wailin' yesterday, so what does it matter if she cries again?' April demanded. 'She needn't come; we don't want her to come, do we May? So just you tell her what she tells us all the time: to save her breath to cool her porridge. And tell her we'll be back home before the cat can lick her ear.'

As they entered the kitchen May gave her sister a puzzled glance. 'But we don't have a cat, not since Fudge ran away,' she said. She knew that Fudge had been run over when trying to cross the Scotland Road on market day, but did not want her mother and grandmother to start crying all over again, so she reached up for their best coats, handed April hers and then struggled into her own. Grandma, she noticed, was already in her coat and hat, as was Rosheen, so it was not many moments before the small company left the house, locking the door behind them, and headed for the school gates.

'Let's have a bit of a singsong,' Grandma suggested as they saw the teachers marshalling the children into long lines in the playground ahead of them.

April pulled a face. 'Now we shall be last. Why haven't the school told us to go straight to Lime

113

Street Station?' she whispered to May. But it soon became obvious that there was a good reason. The teachers moved slowly along the lines, checking that each child had everything they were supposed to have and handing out postcards, not pretty ones but the plain sort. May turned hers over. There was nothing written on the message side save for their names, but on the other side in Miss O'Brien's neat copperplate was *Mrs Rosheen Clarke, No. 3 King Edward Court.*

April opened her mouth to ask May what she thought, because it was beginning to look as though they were not expected to be home tonight. Well, that might be what the school thought, it might even be what Rosheen thought, but it was not at all what her children had in mind. So instead of remarking on the postcards April shoved hers into the pocket of her coat and nudged May with a sharp elbow.

'I reckon we'd already guessed this school trip must mean at least one night away from home, since Mam packed clean clothes in our satchels,' she whispered. 'Does you mind that, May? If so we'll skedaddle the first time the train stops. But if it seems like fun we'll leave it a day or two. After all, it looks like Miss Rogers is comin' too, though it's Witchy O'Brien who's handin' out the postcards.' She glanced towards Rosheen and Mrs Clarke, who had stopped singing lustily and were once more snuffling into their handkerchiefs, then leaned across and jerked Rosheen's hand. 'Mammy, how long will this here vacuation last? S'pose we don't like it? Will Miss Rogers send us home? Or shall we have to make our own way?'

Rosheen's eyes widened. 'Don't you *dare* try to find your way home!' she said in a threatening undertone. 'You are a naughty girl, April, and May isn't much better. Grandma and I spent all last evenin' explainin' about the evacuation and how it was to save you from the dangers of a busy port in wartime. I can't tell you how long it will be before Liverpool is safe again so just you do as Miss Rogers and Miss O'Brien tell you and try to be good. I'm warnin' you, April, you'll get no welcome if you come home. And there'll be no school, because all the teachers are bein' evacuated with their classes, so I 'spect they're turnin' the schools into air raid shelters or somethin'. Oh, April, why will you never *listen*?'

April was about to reply that no school sounded just fine when someone gave an order and the lines of children began to file out through the gates, heading, April assumed, for Lime Street Station. She opened her mouth to ask a few more questions but this time Rosheen ignored the tug on her sleeve and started to sing again in a rather quavery voice. April and May grinned at each other and began to sing as well. '*Somewhere over the rainbow . . .*' they carolled,

'Blue birds fly, birds fly over the rainbow, why o-oh why can't I?'

When they arrived at Lime Street Station it soon became obvious why they had been told to assemble first at their own school gates. Concourse and platforms seethed with children, most in school uniform but many without, and for a moment even self-confident April looked a little taken aback. But presently it became clear that what seemed like a mass of undirected children was in fact being shepherded, class by class, into the waiting carriages. A man with a megaphone in one hand and a list in the other was walking the length of the train calling out the names of the schools and which classes were next to be entrained. April had thought that, because they had been late arriving, they would have to wait a considerable time before being packed on board, but she was wrong. Within moments, it seemed, the man with the megaphone bawled, 'St Michael's Junior, Standard Two, follow me.' May would have hung back, and April could see that her twin was both frightened and confused, so she seized her hand, towed her to the indicated carriage door and tumbled her into the train. Together they squeezed into a corner seat and only then did they notice that their mother had also climbed aboard, though Grandma was still on the platform, sniffling into a large handkerchief.

The atmosphere in the carriage was excited rather than apprehensive; other pupils seemed to regard the whole business as an event not to be missed and April found herself quite looking forward to finding out from their conversations where they were actually going. Would it be the seaside or somewhere deep in the country? Once, long ago, Rosheen had taken her and May to a little village in the Welsh hills – Betwys-y-Coed – and she remembered a river and a huge waterfall. It would not do, though, to question her fellow passengers as to their destination, for that would reveal that she knew even less than they did.

By now Rosheen had fought her way through to the compartment where the twins were seated. 'Aren't you goin' to give your mam a goodbye kiss?' she wailed. 'Oh twins, I'm doin' it for the best. I'm doin' it 'cos I love you, so just you be good little girls and stay safe. Remember, it's for your own good ...'

April felt her cheeks burn with embarrassment; trust her mammy to make her look a fool in front of half her class. And now a man with a green flag was coming along the train slamming doors and warning those who were not passengers to stand clear, so April allowed her mother to give her a kiss on the cheek and then pushed her towards the door.

'Gerroff, Mam, or you'll be took to the seaside wi' us,' she said impatiently. Rosheen looked taken aback.

'Anyone would think I weren't your mam,' she

said, turning to give May a hug, but May just gave her a quick peck on the cheek and then pushed her away.

'April's right. If you come wi' us by mistake they'll blame us and it ain't our fault,' she said, her tone scarcely warmer than her sister's had been. 'Go on, Mam, gerroff.'

Rosheen climbed down from the train with a heavy heart. It was her fault that the twins had rejected her so decisively. She should have known they had not bothered to listen to her careful explanation of what was going to happen to them; when did they listen to anything she said? Oh, they paid attention to teachers, but that was different. They respected teachers, and Rosheen was all too aware that they did not respect her. Indeed, she almost found herself wishing that they might find themselves billeted with someone really strict, even nasty, who would be a salutary contrast to the mother they had left behind. But this was no time for vengeful thoughts; now all she could do was stand back and wave violently as the train pulled out.

When the forest of waving hands had disappeared down the track, Rosheen turned to her mother. 'All them kids want is their own way,' Mrs Clarke remarked as they headed for the bakery.

Rosheen nodded miserably. 'You'll say I've spoiled 'em, Mam, but the honest truth is they've got no room in their hearts for anyone but each other,' she said. 'Mebbe all twins is the same, I don't know, but April and May might have been hatched out of an egg for all the affection they show to anyone else. Of course I hate them goin' away wi'out me, but if it changes the way they feel it'll be a good thing for us all.' She wiped the palms of her hands across her tear-wet eyes and then, despite her misery, she gave a little chuckle. 'Just let them wait till the first time they're refused a second helpin',' she said, and her tone was almost hopeful. 'If they was at home they'd nick summat out of the pantry the moment our backs was turned, but in a stranger's house it'll be different. Mebbe they'll begin to appreciate us at last!'

Before they had been travelling for twenty minutes the twins had silently agreed to skip off the train at the first stop, but they had reckoned without the tight organisation which had gone into the evacuation scheme. Instead of staying with Standard Two they had got off the train in company with a number of younger children and headed across the platform, meaning to slip away unnoticed, but this had proved impossible. The eagle-eyed Miss O'Brien had spotted them immediately, and when May had squeaked that they needed to visit the privy she had accompanied them there and remained outside the door until they emerged. Knowing the twins of old, she then led them inexorably back to the train, ignoring their protests.

'Get back into your carriage,' she ordered brusquely. 'Your class will be called when you are to leave the train and don't you dare stir out of your seats until then.' She bundled them back into their places and April pulled a very rude face indeed at her retreating back.

'Miserable old bat,' she said wrathfully. 'What does she want to interfere for?' At the next stop their class was called and they were told to get on to a bus, and by the time they disembarked once more April had given up all thought of running away home. She had no idea where they were, and no money for a return ticket back to where they wanted to be. Instead, she and May lined up with the other children on the pavement – not nearly so many now – and marched with them into the small town of Bryncwnin, where they waited in what appeared to be the church hall to be claimed. Several of the friendly-looking women who came went away with more than one child, but for some reason which April could not fathom nobody seemed to want twins. When most of the other children had been collected, the ones who remained were given jam sandwiches and weak tea and left, as April morosely put it, to see what fate had in store for them. May nudged her sister.

'I'd be ashamed if we were the last kids to be took

up,' she whispered. 'Who's been tellin' tales, d'you s'pose? Someone must have warned 'em we could get up to all sorts. Oh, April, if no one comes for us can we go home?'

April pretended to consider, and May had opened her mouth to ask again when a small, pink-cheeked woman crossed the hall and came to stand before them. She smiled and held out her hand.

'You'll be April and May Clarke, the twins from Liverpool,' she said. 'I'm Mrs Reynold and you are going to live with me in my flat above the bakery where I work. I hope we'll rub along comfortably – if we don't it won't be my fault. The billeting officer put you with me because I've got twins of my own.'

'Really? Are they boys or girls?' April asked, plainly intrigued. 'We don't know any other twins, do we, May?'

May shook her head, but Mrs Reynold laughed comfortably. 'And I'm afraid you won't meet mine either, because they're both in the Royal Air Force,' she said. 'But just remember, I know all the tricks which twins can play on a body. Believe me, I'll soon learn to tell you apart.'

By the end of the week April and May had realised they had fallen on their feet. Because of the influx of evacuees school hours changed every few days, but to their great joy the teacher in charge of the old-fashioned little schoolhouse was Miss Rogers, who found the mixed ages of her class no bar to her methods. As soon as the children were settled she began to talk of a nativity play, then of a concert to raise money for the war effort. All down one side of the room was a nature table and the twins immediately began to find things to put on it: a ripe acorn, a cream and brown striped snail's shell, and even a bird's nest, though the occupants had long flown. Very soon Miss Rogers put them in charge of the project, and she gave them leading parts in the nativity play. She took the children to the Saturday cinema in the nearest town and did not object to their noisy appreciation of the show. In short, when it was suggested that the evacuees should go home to their parents for Christmas April and May were horrified.

'We don't want to go home,' May wailed when they were told that parents could apply for rail tickets for their children if they wished to. 'Can't we stay here, Mrs Reynold? You said your twins weren't comin' home for Christmas, so we wouldn't want to leave you all by yourself. Miss Rogers is stayin', and the other children – the ones who can't go home – mean to sing carols to earn money for the war effort. Does our mam want us back? I s'pose we could go for a couple of days but we don't see why we should miss all the fun, do we, April?'

April agreed that a return for a couple of days would be possible, but in the event it did not happen.

Rosheen wrote to Mrs Reynold saying she feared that once back in King Edward Court her daughters would refuse to return to their foster home, and Mrs Reynold agreed that if the billeting officer chose to fill the twins' place meanwhile there would be nothing she could do about it.

So although the twins pretended sorrow when they wrote their weekly letters home, they exchanged wicked looks as they did so. Once more they had got their own way.

Chapter Eight

January 1940

Frank Valentine turned the corner into Knowsley Avenue, a broad grin pinned to his face. They were going to be so surprised when he gave them his news, for he had been careful never to give them even the slightest clue of what his intentions were. His wife, he thought, would be particularly pleased, though surely not as delighted as Cassandra.

His daughter had been talking rather wildly of late, though mostly nonsense, he thought complacently, swerving to avoid a large puddle. The trouble was she and that pal of hers, Rebecca, talked all sorts of rubbish; they watched too many motion pictures and dreamed themselves into believing that war was romantic. He, of course, knew better; he had fought in the last lot, mud and trenches, but you couldn't tell the young anything these days because they knew it all, or thought they did. Everyone else he knew had been outraged when places of entertainment had been closed the previous year, but he had thought it an excellent idea and had regretted the government's decision to reopen such places no more than a matter of weeks after that first, panicky closure.

Head down against the rain, he scarcely heeded when somebody called his name, but when a hand jerked his sleeve he was forced to slow his pace and saw Mr O'Leary at his elbow.

'What's your hurry, Valentine?' he said. 'I know it's raining, but . . .' He broke off and looked more closely at his neighbour's face. 'Man, you look as though you've lost a sixpence and found half a crown. Have you had some good news?'

Frank hesitated, but eventually he couldn't keep quiet any longer and he told his neighbour just what he had done for Cassie. Andy's father was flatteringly impressed, and when they reached home and parted ways Frank was almost bubbling over at the thought of the pleasure and excitement with which his wife and daughter would greet the news. When he went into the kitchen, lamplit and warm, he was almost tempted to tell them right away, just to see their faces light up.

Cassie and her mother were seated at the kitchen table. Cassie seemed to be doing homework – at least, there was a pile of books by her elbow – and her mother had just withdrawn from the oven a steak and kidney pie whose delicious aroma had met him even as he opened the back door. Both women looked up and smiled and his wife got to her feet.

'Let me help you out of your coat, love,' she said, as she said every working night. 'My, you've timed it well! The pie is just cooked, and by the time you've washed your hands and hung up your hat the potatoes will be done to a turn.'

Frank rubbed his hands and smiled at his daughter. 'Working hard at your books?' he said jovially. 'Well, I've got some news that will please you.'

Mary Valentine got the warmed plates out of the oven. 'Have you, dear?' she asked absently. 'I dare say it will keep until we've said grace. Cassie dear, you've got ink on your forefinger, so you can't have washed very carefully.'

Sighing, Cassie picked up her books and transferred them to the Welsh dresser, then rinsed her hands under the tap and dried them on the roller towel which was hung on the back of the door before returning to her seat at the table.

Her husband snorted. 'It *won't* keep …' he began, then changed his mind. 'Oh, all right, grace first and news second. Everyone sitting comfortably? Cassie, you can say grace.'

Cassie lowered her eyes. 'For what we're about to receive may the Lord make us truly thankful,' she gabbled. 'I've got some news too, really exciting news. You go first, Daddy.'

Frank had taken his place at the head of the table and was cutting into the pie, putting two medium-sized portions for his womenfolk and one large one for himself on the three warmed plates. By the time everyone had helped themselves to vegetables his wife and daughter had begun to chatter inconsequentially, and he felt oddly disappointed, as though his news had already been pushed to one side. But it would never do to spoil his daughter's pleasure in what he had arranged for her.

'Do I have your attention?' he asked. 'Cassie, do you want to hear my news or not?' He tried to sound reasonable but somehow the words came out like bullets from a gun and he saw both his wife and his daughter flinch back and then turn round, astonished eyes upon him.

'Sorry, Daddy,' Cassie said repentantly. 'We're all ears, aren't we, Mummy?'

Frank noted with approval that his wife merely nodded and then continued to gaze at him as though she could not wait to hear what he had to say, so he cleared his throat and began.

'I've got you a very important job, Cassie my dear,' he said portentously. 'As secretary to someone in the civil service. It is a post that now, in wartime, is vital for the country.' He saw Cassie's face change, but she did not look delighted. She did not even look pleased; she looked . . . embarrassed. 'Cassie?

There's a first rate salary, you'll be able to live at home ...'

'Oh, Daddy, it's awfully good of you and it sounds a wonderful job, but I've been telling you for weeks and weeks that I mean to join up as soon as I'm old enough. I'd like to join the WAAF ... Andy's talked about the air force so much, and the uniform ...' Her voice trailed away, for her father had slammed his knife and fork down and got to his feet. He looked, and indeed was, absolutely furious.

'If I've told you once I've told you a hundred times there's nothing romantic about joining the women's air force, or whatever it's called,' he thundered. 'Besides, the job I've arranged for you will help the war effort far more effectively than marching round the countryside dressed in that silly uniform. I called it a secretarial post but in time you could be PA – that's a personal assistant – and you'd meet all sorts of important people. Cassie Valentine, you'd be mad to throw it back in my face!'

'Oh, Daddy, I don't want to disappoint you ...' Cassie began, only to be furiously interrupted.

'You aren't eighteen yet and until you are you can't join up without my permission,' her father raged. 'You know nothing about it – the sort of girls you'd be mixing with, the young men whose one idea would be to compromise you ...' He turned impulsively to his wife. '*Tell* her, Mary. Tell her what she's in for if she refuses this post.' He swung back to Cassie. 'I had to obtain copies of all your exam results, all your reports, going right back to primary school. They are very eager that the right sort of young woman gets these jobs ...'

'Then why pick on me? I'm nothing special,' Cassie said, and her tone was no longer submissive. 'You've made the job sound lovely, Daddy, but it's not what I want. I *want* to join the WAAF, as a radio operator if possible, because when I went for the interview ...'

Frank Valentine had sunk back into his chair but at these words he leapt to his feet once more. 'You've already applied! No, don't deny it, you said it in your very own words. You said "when I went for the interview!" Why, you nasty, scheming little ...'

His wife uttered a gasp of dismay whilst Cassie tried to explain that she had gone to the recruitment centre with Rebecca and had given way to impulse when the recruiting officer had taken it for granted that she, too, wished to join the forces, but her father was too angry to listen to reason. He grabbed the nearest object, which happened to be a bottle of tomato ketchup, and hurled it at Cassie, missing her by a good foot but scoring a bull's eye on a framed photograph of the Valentines' wedding day, which promptly shattered and fell with a crash to the floor.

Mary Valentine winced and Cassie opened her mouth to give her father a piece of her mind, but she was too late. Mr Valentine crossed the kitchen in a couple of strides and could be heard thundering up the stairs.

Left alone, the two women smiled guiltily at each other and began to clear up the mess. 'I'm sorry, Mummy. I didn't realise he felt quite so strongly,' Cassie murmured as they worked. 'Had he told you about this job? Apart from anything else, it sounds too good to be true.'

Mrs Valentine pulled a face. 'I'm afraid you may be right and he's gilding the lily a trifle,' she admitted. 'If I were you, Cassie dear, I'd wait until he's cooled down a bit and then apologise. Remember, you have to be eighteen to join up without his permission and you aren't there yet. But if you're nice to him and promise you'll think about it … well, I know you weren't at fault but with men it's always best to pretend they're in the right. Oh dear, a bit of flying glass must have reached your cheek. I'll get the first aid box down from the bathroom, and when he sees what he's done I can guarantee that Daddy will accept your apology.'

Andy had finished his initial training and had been granted a week's leave before being sent to the airfield where his hopes of becoming aircrew would be put to the test. He had greeted his parents cheerfully and had meant to go next door as soon as the special meal his mother had prepared was over, for he was aware that Cassie intended to volunteer for the WAAF but was a trifle doubtful whether this information would please her father. Andy knew that Mr Valentine was a loving but irascible parent and might take it either way, so he was eager to find out whether anything had been decided. He had settled down at the family's kitchen table and had started to tell his parents all about service life – or rather all he yet knew about service life – when the sound of raised voices from the Valentines' kitchen next door caused him to pause and raise his eyebrows at his mother, placidly conveying a forkful of carrots to her mouth.

'Sounds as though there's a disagreement next door ...' he was beginning when there was a tremendous crash, a shriek from Cassie and then the sound of heavy footsteps ascending the stairs two at a time. Andy and his father exchanged a glance and Andy abandoned his supper and headed across the kitchen, intent upon finding out just what had happened. His hand was actually on the back door knob when his father spoke.

'Come right back here this moment,' Mr O'Leary demanded. 'I dare say we both have an idea what the fuss is about, but it's none of our business. Likely Cassie would tell you to keep out of it too, because when all's said and done the argument is between her and her dad.'

'But I want to know what the explosion was. Damn

it, Dad, Mrs V might have dropped a saucepan or something; if it was full of boiling water they could need help. It's not that I'm nosy, but Cassie's my pal; if she's in trouble ...'

Mr O'Leary grinned. 'Well done, Andy, I'm impressed, but nevertheless you stay just where you are. If Cassie wants to confide in you she's only got to pop over here which I've no doubt she'll do as soon as the coast is clear. And now let us finish our meal like Christians.'

Andy sighed and returned to the table. Sitting down and picking up his knife and fork, he glanced across at his mother and saw that she was smiling.

'What's so amusing, Ma?' he asked, rather indignantly. 'It's true that the Valentines could be in trouble. Don't you think we ought to go round?'

Mrs O'Leary's smile broadened. 'Dad's right; never interfere in a family row,' she said decidedly. 'I dare say Cassie said something about joining the WAAF, and that would have been enough to get her father on the raw. Go round later by all means; I expect you intended to anyway. You and young Cassie have always shared secrets, so no doubt she'll spill the beans.'

'Oh, all right,' Andy said. He began to eat one of the small crunchy Yorkshire puddings which always accompanied a roast beef dinner in the O'Leary household, staring suspiciously at his father. 'I believe you know more than you've let on,' he said accusingly. 'You've got a grin like a Cheshire cat and I know you and Mr Valentine often travel together on the train back from the city. Go on, Dad, *you* spill the beans.'

Mr O'Leary, looking a trifle self-conscious, looked hopefully at the tureen in the centre of the table. 'Any chance of another couple of spuds?' he asked hopefully, but when his wife shook her head he nodded at his son. 'Yes, you're right, though goodness knows why the kerfuffle. It seems that Frank Valentine had arranged a job for Cassie in the civil service ...'

At the end of the recital Andy was grinning. 'That'll be it,' he said, nodding. 'Remember when Gramps asked me to move to Ireland with a view to taking over the stud? I said I would, but then the war started so I joined up instead.' He leaned across the table and patted his mother's hand. 'You and Dad were marvellous and backed me all the way, but I dare say there were times when you wondered if I'd made the right decision.'

His mother and father nodded simultaneously, and Mrs O'Leary turned to her husband. 'So I take it young Cassie has turned down the civil service. Ah well, these things happen in families. Andy, love, I think it might be best if you don't go round tonight. Leave her to tell you all about it in her own time.' She got to her feet as she spoke, went over to the oven and withdrew a large pie which she placed in the middle of the table. 'Have either of you got room for a slice of apple pie with custard?'

The following morning Cassie went straight round to Andy's house as soon as breakfast was over, only to find that her pal was not at home. Sighing with frustration, she told Mrs O'Leary that it was nothing important and made for the Spencers' instead, where she found Rebecca at home and very willing to listen to the tale of woe which Cassie presently poured into her ears. 'So that puts an end to any hope I might have had of joining up before I'm eighteen,' she finished bitterly. 'In fact, Dad will do his utmost to keep me out of the forces altogether. It's not that he's unpatriotic, it's just that he's managed to convince himself that I'll be sent somewhere terribly dangerous, which is nonsense, of course. But I've told him straight that I won't take a civil service job so of course he's sulking, and since he suspects Mum of being on my side he'll hardly speak to her either.' She snorted. 'Honestly, men! If women behaved like that we'd never hear the end of it, but because it's Dad it's not called sulking it's called "making my feelings plain".'

Rebecca giggled. 'So it was the sauce bottle hitting the wall that really made your father's feelings plain, was it?' she asked. She chuckled again. 'Did you ask him to give his permission for you to join one of the forces? Oh, Cassie, I can just see his face!'

Cassie gave her a friendly punch on the shoulder. 'Don't be so daft; it would be like a red rag to a bull. No, I shall have to wait until I don't need his permission. What a bore! So you'll be off before me, I bet.'

Rebecca was about to agree when she suddenly remembered something and turned impulsively to Cassie. 'One of the girls at school told me something I didn't know. You can join the Land Army much younger than you can the other forces, even without your parents' consent. This girl – it was Patty Forbes, and she wants the Land Army because her dad's a farmer and she's already experienced in that sort of work – told me something else as well. When you're old enough you can leave the Land Army for one of the other services without a lot of fuss and bother. So how about that? I suppose you'd be cocking a snook at your father but you'd also be doing something worth while; something which is not the civil service.'

The two girls were in Rebecca's bedroom, Rebecca perched on the wide windowsill and Cassie sprawled on the end of Cecilia's bed. Usually Rebecca and Cassie spent most of their time in the Valentine house but today Cassie was so furious with her father that she intended to show her disapproval by absenting herself from No. 8 Knowsley Avenue for as long as possible. Now, however, she looked broodingly at her friend.

'The Land Army,' she said. 'I dare say it would

be all very well in the summer – well, last year we had a super time at the Pinner Farm, picking plums. But Lizzie Pinner told me that winters on the farm are pretty hard work. The Pinners do something called "mixed farming", and of course they've a lot of sheep, so when they're not working with the animals they're planting cabbage seedlings, or harvesting sprouts, or opening up the potato clamp, whatever that may mean, and throwing away the bad spuds, which Lizzie says stink. So I'm not too sure about the Land Army ... I don't see myself enjoying farming in February. In fact I might even prefer the civil service!'

Rebecca shrugged. 'It's up to you,' she said, twisting round to peer out of the rain-splattered windowpane. 'What had you meant to do until you're old enough to join, anyhow?'

'Stay at school and take my Higher, I suppose,' Cassie said moodily. She got off the bed and joined her friend on the window seat to look out of the window. 'Gosh, what grim weather! But the last time I talked to Andy he said it wasn't a bad thing because although it stops our aircraft from taking off it stops the Germans as well.' She gave an excited squeak. 'I told you Andy was home on leave, didn't I? Look – he's just come round the corner.' She jumped to her feet. 'I think I'll go down and get his opinion on what to do for the best. He'll have heard Dad shouting and the sauce bottle biting the dust;

I expect he's dying to know what it was all about.' She headed for the door and turned on the landing. 'Are you coming, Becky? We can go and talk in the church porch, where at least it'll be dry. I wonder if the church hall is locked? It has a little kitchen and my mum always keeps a caddy full of tea there for emergencies, so we could put the kettle on and make ourselves a cuppa.'

Rebecca shook her head. 'Ta all the same, but no,' she said decidedly. 'No point in getting soaked to the skin just to listen to what I already know.' She glanced at her wristwatch. 'In fact, I'll come down to the kitchen with you now and give my mother a hand. It's Cessy's turn to do the shopping so Mum gave her a list and she and that gormless boy she's got in tow went off half an hour ago.'

Accordingly the two girls descended the stairs and burst into the kitchen where Mrs Spencer was placidly ironing Rebecca's best skirt. She looked up and smiled as her daughter entered the room.

'Going out?' she queried. 'You'll come in after five minutes out there like a pair of drowned rats.'

Rebecca shook her head. 'Cassie's going, I'm staying,' she said decidedly, and turned to take Cassie's navy mac from the peg on the door. 'Want to borrow a brolly? Heaven knows we've got enough of 'em.'

'No thanks; the rain won't melt me,' Cassie said gaily. She wrenched open the kitchen door and viewed the enormous puddle, which had been the Spencers' path the day before, with some apprehension. But she did not mean to change her plans so she shrieked her goodbyes and splashed along the path to the neat little gate. Then she looked in the direction of No. 8 and was gratified to see Andy, in his blue uniform, heading up the road towards her. He was grinning.

'Good morning, Miss Valentine,' he said as soon as she was within hearing. 'I've just called at your house, and your mum said you might be here.' He glanced around him. 'We can't talk here; come to the church porch. At least we'll be dry in there.' He seized Cassie's arm as he spoke and together, like contestants in a three-legged race, they hurtled through the lych gate, past the graves and into the church porch. Fortunately, the wind was blowing the rain away from the open doors, so they settled themselves on the stone seat and grinned at one another.

Cassie shook rain off her auburn hair, reflecting that the mere presence of her oldest friend was a comfort. Ever since she was old enough to share his interests she had done so, cheering him on when he indulged in his favourite sports and always being ready with sympathy when his team lost. She was sure he would be equally sympathetic when she regaled him with the tomato ketchup episode, for had he not always been on her side?

'Oh, Andy, I have missed you,' she said as soon as they were settled. 'I never thought Daddy would try to stop me joining up, but that's just what he has done. From what I can gather he went round to some pal of his in the civil service and forced him to promise me a job. I don't deny he meant it kindly, but Andy, it isn't what I want!'

Andy laughed. 'He's your father, so naturally he wants what's best for you,' he said. 'I can quite understand why he's so cross; after all, a man expects to be able to tell his daughter what she can and can't do whilst she's still living at home.'

'Yes, but there's a war on, and they're appealing for girls with good educations to join the forces. Isn't that more important than some stupid job in an office? Remember, it's my life we're talking about. Next you'll be telling me it's my father's right to choose my boyfriends!'

'So it is – or at least if your father saw you taking up with the wrong sort of men he'd have a perfect right to forbid them the house and almost a duty to see you didn't get into trouble,' Andy said after some thought. 'I'd agree with you that a father shouldn't interfere with his sons' friendships, but daughters are different. Daughters need to be protected from themselves sometimes.' They had been sitting side by side on the stone bench as far as possible from the weather, and now Andy put his arm about Cassie's shoulders and gave her a squeeze. 'Poor little pussycat,' he said. 'Diddums wanted to have a pretty uniform and lots of fellers dancing attendance on her. And now Daddy's put paid to all her hopes … cruel Daddy to foil his little kitten!'

He tried to tighten his hold on Cassie's shoulders but she elbowed him sharply in the ribs and pushed him aside. 'Don't you *dare* try to patronise me!' she said furiously. 'I'm no one's little kitten, as you should very well know.' She jumped up as Andy got to his feet, still smiling as though the whole affair was nothing but a joke, and even as he caught hold of her round the waist, perhaps to apologise, she slapped his face as hard as she could. 'Well, thank you for your support, Andy O'Leary,' she shouted. 'You're just like my father, a typical bloody male who doesn't think women are fit for anything but making meals and cleaning houses.' The fact that he was still smiling, that she could feel his amusement as his arms tightened around her waist, did not help matters, and when she found she could not escape she twisted in his grasp and dug her nails into his hand. 'Kittens have claws,' she screamed at him, and at the same moment she stamped as hard as she could on his shiny black air force shoes.

Andy uttered a howl of anguish and hopped on one foot, clutching his knuckles – she had drawn blood. 'Why, you vicious little beast!' he shouted. 'I was just trying to make you see that your father was acting in your best interests. Well, you can sort out your own troubles in future and don't come running to me.'

Even in her temper, Cassie knew she had gone too far. She wanted to say she was sorry, to explain that the attack had been meant to free her not to scar him, but one look at the blood dripping down Andy's wrist and another at the fury in his eyes told her that it would be useless, and anyway why should she apologise? The things he had said had been unforgivable; his whole attitude had been that of a superior male putting a foolish young girl in her place. Nevertheless, she might have apologised, at least for the scratch, but at that moment they heard people approaching, the woman's voice high and excited and the man's a deeper rumble. Seconds later Cassie recognised the vicar and his eldest daughter, who was planning to marry in April. Not wanting to get into conversation with the newcomers she ran down the path towards the lych gate, calling in a breathless voice 'Good morning, vicar' as she went. Behind her she caught a quick glimpse of Andy, a handkerchief clapped to his knuckles, quickly escaping before the vicar and his daughter could ask any embarrassing questions.

He caught up with her out on the road and came towards her with his hand held out, but their fight – for it had been nothing less – was too recent and too painful to allow her to meet him as a friend. Before she thought she found herself saying: 'Don't touch me! I warn you ...'

And Andy, after the merest of hesitations, said coldly: 'I wasn't going to. I don't want your claw marks on my left hand as well as my right.' Then he turned away from her and walked swiftly home through the driving rain.

Later that day Cassie went round to Rebecca's and told her all about the quarrel. 'Andy took my father's side about everything and was perfectly horrid,' she said. 'Of course he's terrible angry because I scratched him, but it wasn't very deep, and I'm sure it will heal all right. Pompous idiot! But in a way the quarrel is a good thing, because it's made me decide to join the Land Army, to get away from Andy as much as my father.'

'You shouldn't act hastily. You know what you said earlier this morning about the miseries of farm work in the winter,' Rebecca reminded her. 'And from what I've heard, once you've joined there's only one way out of the Land Army – well, two ways – and that is to go into one of the other forces when you're old enough. The other is to get yourself in the family way, and no matter how cross you are you wouldn't want that!'

Cassie agreed fervently that she most certainly would not want that, but she did not add that she had little idea of what happened between a man and a woman which could result in her being 'in the family way'. School had been vague, the teacher dwelling on rabbits rather than human beings, and neither her mother nor Rebecca's, though they had issued stern warnings, had given their daughters the least idea how this peril might be avoided.

'I tell you what, suppose we go down to the recruiting office today and get the forms and things you have to fill in?' Rebecca said at last. 'Would that be a good idea? Then you could take your time deciding exactly what you want to do.' She waited for a response, but when Cassie said nothing she added, 'Only don't you think you ought to make it up with Andy before you do anything else? He's always been your best friend, and I'm sure he was only kidding when he said he agreed with your father.'

Cassie's eyes immediately flashed. 'No I do not want to make it up with Andy,' she said coolly and distinctly. 'He said truly horrible things, which I haven't told you because I can't remember his exact words. But they were the sorts of things that no one could forgive. So far as I'm concerned, our friendship is dead and can't possibly be revived. Why, he called me a vicious little beast.'

Rebecca giggled. 'That must have been after you scratched him, and I'm not sure I altogether blame him,' she said, then shook her head as Cassie began to expostulate. 'I'm sorry, Cassie, really I am, but if you had brothers and sisters you'd know how often people who really love you can say the most horrible

143

things to you and absolutely mean them just for that moment ...'

'Oh, I know, everyone quarrels. But I'm an only child and so is Andy, and when we quarrel it's rather more serious than a brother and sister having a go at each other. I'm off Andy for life and I mean it.'

Rebecca raised her eyebrows. 'If you've finished with him I'll take him on,' she said half seriously, but Cassie merely shrugged.

'You can have him and welcome,' she said promptly. 'I can't think why I put up with him for so long. He's spoilt, selfish and pig-headed, and if he wasn't my next door neighbour I don't suppose I'd have looked at him twice.'

Rebecca sighed. 'You'll be sorry,' she prophesied. 'Come on – let's get on the next bus and talk to the people at the recruiting office. No harm in talking!'

The two girls put on their coats and left the house, Cassie unusually silent. She had adored Andy once, worshipped him almost, but now she was older and wiser. She had told him what she thought of him in no uncertain terms; it was definitely too late for regrets. But Rebecca was staring at her, a smile beginning, and hastily she began to speak.

'Maybe I over-reacted,' she said slowly. 'I'd better apologise next time we meet.'

Rebecca smiled. 'I think it would be sensible,' she admitted. 'Now, let's hurry or we'll miss the bus.'

Chapter Nine

February 1940

Rosheen and her mother, having finished their day's work at the bakery, were sitting in front of the range with the doors wide open, for it had rained pretty solidly for several days and now snowflakes were mingling with the raindrops. They had planned to spend the evening knitting, but the sock Rosheen had finished earlier had turned out to be a good six inches longer than its mate, and Mrs Clarke, who was often called upon to put right her daughter's more startling mistakes, had unpicked the offending garment and now she bundled up her work, reached across to put it on the table and sighed gustily.

'I know what you're goin' to say, Rosheen, 'cos you've said it every night since Christmas,' she said resignedly. 'You're goin' to say did we do the right thing when we agreed that the twins should stay with Mrs Reynold for the holiday? Well, I've asked around, and by and large it were only the feckless parents who hauled their kids back from safety into danger. I know there wasn't a raid on Liverpool at Christmas, but that's not the point. If we'd brought the twins home my chief worry wasn't their safety but the fact that they'd fight like tigers not to go back. Yet I'm sure they must be happy there; it's nice for them to be living above a bakery, 'cos no doubt they get their share ...'

Rosheen cut across her mother's words. 'That's another thing – we don't know whether they're happy there or not, because their letters home are sort of stiff and always so short. If they weren't so far away and we weren't both working we could visit them and find out, but I'm not sure I want to do that because if they *aren't* happy what'd we do, Mam? I won't bring 'em back here because everyone says the Luftwaffe will concentrate on destroyin' the ports once the weather improves. Oh, if only they weren't so far away.'

Mrs Clarke went over to riddle the fire and bank it down for the night, then she lifted the kettle off the hob and poured the boiling water into two mugs, adding a spoonful of cocoa powder to each. 'A nice cup of cocoa last thing will send you off to sleep like a baby,' she said. 'And one thing I do admit, Christmas was a bit flat wi' no kids in the house, and of course with a good many of the other children comin' home we missed ours all the more. Even the carols sounded kind of thin with no April and May bellowin' out the words and wakin' us at two in the mornin' to examine their stockin's.' She handed her daughter one of the mugs of cocoa and cradled the other in her hands to warm her fingers. 'Christmas isn't much if you've no children to share it with.'

Rosheen nodded and sipped her drink. In her heart of hearts she knew that the quiet Christmas with no twins to harass her had not been as lonely and miserable as she had expected. In fact, again in her heart of hearts, she admitted that she and her mother had enjoyed a quiet couple of days. They had managed to acquire most of the traditional Christmas food, for rationing had not yet been biting. Rosheen had written a long and loving letter to her daughters and posted it to their new teacher; Miss Rogers had joined the forces in some capacity or other and the children were now in the hands of a Miss Ellis. Rosheen had written to Miss Ellis as soon as Miss Rogers had told her she was leaving, and Miss Ellis had agreed to keep Rosheen informed of her children's progress since persuading them to write a letter was 'like getting blood out of a stone'. Knowing her daughters, Rosheen had no difficulty in believing this and tried very hard not to worry when the letters in answer to hers did not arrive nearly as often as they had done under Miss Rogers's benevolent rule.

But when the fine weather arrives Mam and I will go to this village and see for ourselves how the girls are gettin' on, Rosheen thought at least once every day. It will be good to meet Mrs Reynold and be able to thank her properly. It's a pity in a way that she's a baker too because I can't very well take her a present from our shop, but I'll find something suitable nearer the time.

Rosheen climbed into her bed clutching the hot water bag which her mother had filled for her earlier. She wondered if the twins had hot water bags; she thought guiltily that she could easily have included a couple in the big parcel of Christmas goodies she had sent for them, but she had been so busy in the shop … oh well, she would send Mrs Reynold a postal order the very next day and ask her to buy the twins a hot water bag each. Telling herself that Mrs Reynold must surely think her evacuees had the best of mothers, she snuggled down and closed her eyes.

However, she was no more than half asleep when a small, still voice tugged her cruelly awake. This small still voice had caused her sleepless nights before and unless she dealt with it firmly it would cause her sleepless nights again. It was, she supposed, the voice of her conscience, which had taken to saying to her, often, that giving the twins everything they demanded had not been the way a really good mother would behave. She had let them ride roughshod over her. Worse, they had been rude and spiteful to their grandmother on more than one occasion because she was more of a disciplinarian than her daughter had ever been, and now Rosheen was reaping the reward, not of being a good mother, but of giving in to their whims.

She groaned, and pushed her hot water bag further down the bed to give comfort to her chilly toes. It was at times like these that she found herself thinking how different her life would be if only the twins' father were at her side. Lee had been so kind, so *good*; she was sure he would have known how to handle them, would have tempered discipline with love, and taught them the value of respect, both given and received. Oh, Lee, where are you now? Are you happy? Are you . . . married?

Abruptly, Rosheen sat up, swung her legs out of bed and groped for her slippers. It was no use; past experience told her she would lie in her bed going over and over all the things that might have been had she not been feeling so unwell that she was unable to meet him that last day. He had not even known she was pregnant . . .

She padded across the linoleum, reached up to the hook on the door for her dressing gown, struggled into it and tied the belt. She would go downstairs and make a pot of tea; perhaps a hot drink would help her to sleep. She descended the stairs quietly, not wanting to wake her mother, but when she reached the kitchen she found that lady already ensconced with a cup of tea and a couple of broken ginger biscuits from the bakery. She looked up and smiled as her daughter entered the room.

'I know you worry, but if they weren't happy the twins would've run away by now,' she said positively. 'And if they'd run away that teacher, that Miss Ellis, would have let us know. Believe me, Rosheen, the twins would soon kick up a fuss if things weren't hunky dory.' She poured out another cup of tea and pushed it across the table to her daughter. 'Drink that and stop worrying.'

Rosheen accepted the cup with a nod of thanks but then stared accusingly at her mother. 'If you really think they're happy as Larry why are you down here in the middle of the night?' she asked bluntly. 'It's the letters what worry me the most; they're too – too polite. Mam, it's a quiet time of year, war or no war. D'you think Mr Roberts would let us have a couple of days off? If we could just see the twins face to face and satisfy ourselves that all's well I could stop worrying, and we could both sleep at night.'

Mrs Clarke nodded and the anxious look left her face. 'You're right, queen; there's only one way to be sure April and May are happy and that's to visit 'em,' she said. 'We'll make the arrangements to leave as soon as Mr Roberts can spare us.'

March had arrived with its promise of spring delights but so far the weather had remained unkind. 'Shove up, April Clarke. The wind's blowin' bits of snow on me. Go on, move over!' The twins were in hiding, having no desire to attend whichever lesson Miss Ellis was holding in the cold and draughty school room. Their beloved Miss Rogers had joined the ATS and her replacement was an elderly spinster and strict disciplinarian who refused to let the children leave her classroom no matter how great their need. The nature table had gone, and the children spent a great deal of time copying whatever Miss Ellis had written on the board and then learning it by heart. April and May were bright, but Miss Ellis refused to believe that her methods bored them to tears. On the very first day of her rule she had labelled them 'difficult' and treated them accordingly. She would ask a question to which both twins knew the answer but would ignore their frantically waving hands, preferring to pick on a child who she knew perfectly well was out of their depth. Trips into town stopped happening, the picture shows saw them no more and the idea of giving concerts to aid the war effort was forgotten. Most of the villagers were aware that progress in their evacuees' lessons had stopped short with Miss Rogers's departure, but it seemed they were not particularly worried.

'As soon as the finer weather starts there'll be work on the farms even for kids like you,' the twins heard villagers say consolingly. 'I had Miss Rogers when I were a kid and I'll say one thing for her: I knows my tables right up to twelve times twelve and I can still remember that little poem thing what tells you how many days each month has got.'

The little school was surrounded by woods and the twins had spent both time and ingenuity converting an abandoned shed into a den, a sort of safe house to which they could retreat when they wanted to be alone. This had rarely happened during Miss Rogers's gentle reign, but Miss Ellis was too fond of using the cane for the twins' liking and so the den came into its own. Now, crouching miserably in the doubtful shelter of their little shed, April and May stared accusingly at each other. After a few moments May sighed, and said aloud what she knew her twin was thinking.

'When do we take off for home? I know Mam said we couldn't because there wouldn't be any school, but we hardly go to any of Miss Ellis's lessons anyway so it wouldn't be that different. But how can we get home with no money?'

April had been listening to the villagers, and now was the moment, she decided, to tell May what she had overheard. 'Mr Wallis who runs the pub in the village has a son what's in the army,' she said, 'and I heard him tell someone that this Wally, I think his name is, had got a whole week's leave. But he's up at somewhere called Wick in Scotland and he weren't given no travel warrant, so he's goin' to have to hitchhike.' With satisfaction, she observed the puzzlement in her small sister's face, and allowed a note of contemptuous pity to enter her voice. 'Don't you know what hitchhikin' is? It means you put up your thumb and waggle it up and down when a car comes. It's – it's a sort of secret sign that people drivin' cars and lorries understand. They stop and lean down and say, "Where did you want to go?" And if'n they's goin' in the same direction as you they say "In you hop", and that's what you does, you hops in.'

May looked at her sister suspiciously. 'How d'you know all that?' she asked. 'Don't say you asked the landlord, 'cos I don't believe it.'

April gave a muffled snort. ''Course I didn't. He'd have wondered why I wanted to know, and told Mrs Reynold. Didn't you notice I were late comin' to bed last night? I waited outside the pub till the fellers from the army camp started driftin' in and asked one of them to explain what hitchhikin' meant. He told me all that lot – said before the war he travelled all over Britain thumbin' lifts. Now are you satisfied? And what's more you don't have to pay anyone a penny, you just say "Thanks ever so" and off you go. I can't believe we never heard of it before.' She peered closely at her twin. 'Why aren't you smilin'? I reckon we could be home by tomorrer teatime.'

May, however, was less sanguine. 'This hitchin' might be all right for grownups, but I can't see drivers stoppin' for a couple o' kids,' she observed. 'They'd guess we was runnin' away 'cos what other reason could we have for bein' on the road without our mam? I reckon the first driver who stopped for us – if anyone did – would hand us in at the nearest police station and then we'd be for it.'

April took a deep breath and blew out her cheeks, exhaling on a long whistle. 'Honest to God, May, you don't *deserve* to have a clever twin like me. First off we say we missed the bus and could they take us to the nearest town. We give 'em an imaginary address and if they seem like nice trustable people we tell 'em the truth once we've got goin'.' Once more she peered closely into her sister's face. 'Satisfied? It may take us longer if we have to do a lot of little hitchhikes instead of one big one, but it's free, don't you understand? Free!'

Grandma Clarke emerged from Mr Roberts's office with a wall to wall smile. Rosheen scarcely had to put the question, for the answer was obvious.

'He said yes!' Mrs Clarke announced triumphantly. 'He even said we can take a big bag of broken biscuits 'cos everyone tells you how unreliable the rail service has become and we may be glad of a bite. He says there's bound to be a pub in the village which will let us book a room for a couple of nights, and once we've sorted out any problems the children may have it will be almost like a little holiday. If you like we could leave it for a couple of weeks and hope the weather improves.'

Rosheen shook her head. 'We can't do that,' she said decidedly. 'It wouldn't be fair on Mr Roberts, for a start. No, we've got tomorrer to pack and the followin' day we'll be on our way!'

April and May were in assembly, well to the back so that they did not draw attention to themselves, for the Administrator – which the girls thought was just a word to describe Mr Ford, who had been a headmaster in happier days – had gathered the whole school together to tell them that today Miss Grandmager would be coming to teach them a new song. She was a young music student, full of ideas to engage the attention of her pupils, and toured all the schools in the area on her rusty old bicycle, often singing one of her favourite songs at the top of her voice as she pedalled along. She was not a 'proper' teacher in the sense that she had no definite school or class, but all the children adored her and even April agreed when May said she wanted to attend Miss Grandmager's class today instead of sticking to their original plan, which had been to skip school and go out to the neighbouring farm. The farmer's wife would be cutting sprouts, and those children who helped would be rewarded with homemade scones spread thickly with strawberry jam.

'What does "sung in parts" mean?' May asked, mystified by the Administrator's parting shot. 'But whatever it is we wouldn't want to miss it, would we, April? And if Miss Grandmager is taking the whole school to sing then horrible old Ellis will have at least the morning off, which might make her better-tempered.'

'We'll go to our den until Miss Grandmager arrives,' April decreed. She looked up at the sky, which was pale blue instead of grey. 'I think spring's on its way, don't you? I thought winter would never end … No, don't march straight out of the school gates. Someone's bound to see you. Go round the coke pile in the corner of the playground, like we usually do, and squiggle through the hole in the railings. Come on, follow me!'

May sighed but obeyed. It was she who had discovered that they could get out of the playground without being spotted if they crept behind the coke pile, and although the pile had shrunk as winter refused to leave, meaning that the children had to crouch lower and lower to reach the safety of the wood, it still hid their activities from any watching eyes. Seconds later they were in the shelter of the wood, the trees stretching their protective arms over the two little runaways, and April plunged ahead until her sister reminded her that they must keep a lookout for the young music teacher.

'If we miss this new song we'll be in trouble with

Mr Fielding,' May observed. 'We'd better take turns to watch for her, don't you think?'

April chuckled, and led the way into the den. 'I don't think we need to. Miss Grandmager is quite a noisy sort of person,' she reminded her sister. 'Her bicycle is old and rattly and when she sings you can hear her a mile off. However, if it makes you happy—'

But at that point there was a totally unexpected interruption.

'So this is where you go, you wicked little truants!' Miss Ellis snatched at the potato-sack curtain the twins had hung over the low entrance, and reached in to grab May's shoulder. 'Come out of that, the pair of you. I *thought* you must have some sort of hideaway ... come on, out I say!'

Both children retreated to the far end of their den, frightened by the venom in the teacher's voice and by the look on her face, for her skin was greyish white with spots of bright colour burning on both cheeks. April began to say that they were just waiting for Miss Grandmager to arrive, and, gaining courage, added that the Administrator had dismissed them so they could jolly well do as they pleased until then.

'Jolly well? Jolly well?' the teacher screeched. To the children's eyes she looked downright frightening. 'I'll get some men from the village to tear this ramshackle shed down, and if I ever see you trying to sneak off again ...' She lunged forward as she spoke, apparently not realising that the ceiling was low, smacked her head against one of the branches with which April and May had strengthened their roof, and dropped like a stone. The twins gasped. Their immediate thought was flight, and April would have left Miss Ellis lying there had May not tugged urgently at her arm.

'April, she isn't movin' and there's blood,' she said in a high scared voice. 'We'd better help her up.' As she spoke she seized the teacher's arm and pulled. Miss Ellis did not move. Across the teacher's inanimate body the twins stared at one another.

'She can't be dead,' April said uncertainly. 'And if she is it's her own fault and nothin' to do wi' us, only it's our den and we were the only people about when she banged into the roof and hit her head.' Her bold front suddenly collapsed and she turned a white and frightened face towards her sister. 'What'll we do, May? If we leave her here and go and join the others and she really does die, we're bound to get the blame. Only I reckon she's foxin', 'cos her chest keeps movin' up and down.'

She said it hopefully, but May could tell that her sister was just as frightened as she was herself. 'No, she ain't foxin', but she ain't dead neither. Look, April, you've been talkin' for days about this hitchhikin' thing. You said we could be home in no time, and if you ask me, now's the time to go.'

April agreed. 'And the sooner the better, before

someone wonders where the old hag is,' she said. The figure on the floor gave a moan and the twins were galvanised into instant activity. With one accord they burst out of the den and headed, not for the school, but for the village, each knowing exactly what the other was thinking. They rushed back to the flat and shot into the pantry. Without having to consult one another April collected food and May unearthed two bottles of Mrs Reynold's homemade ginger beer.

'We'll wear wellies,' May said breathlessly, shoving her feet into her boots. She glanced round quickly. 'Is that the lot? Right. Then we'd best leave at once before the old dragon wakes up.'

'If she ever does,' April said in sepulchral tones, just as Mrs Reynold called up from the bakery asking if they were all right.

'Yes, Mrs Reynold, we're fine,' April gabbled, whilst May shrieked, 'Day off for music class.' And it occurred to May that for once in their lives it was she who was making most of the decisions.

Back on the pavement once more April cast an envious glance at the bakery window. Raiding the pantry had been a good idea, of course; she had taken half a loaf, a big chunk of cheese and some rather unripe apples, but the window display revealed doughnuts, sticky buns and what Mrs Reynold called "fancies".

As they hurried along towards the railway

station May tugged at her twin's arm. 'It's a pity we didn't have time to look in the cake tins,' she said wistfully. 'Why are we goin' to the station? We're goin' to hitchhike, remember? We've not got money for tickets.'

April, who was beginning to recover her confidence, heaved an exaggerated sigh. 'Oh, May, you really are stupid. As if we haven't talked and talked about how we'd fool everyone. We'll let people have a good look at us on the station platform and then we'll pretend we've just missed our train and need a lift.'

May was used to being accused of stupidity, but on this occasion the unfairness of it drove her to action. As they turned to enter the station she gave her twin a far from friendly punch in the ribs.

'I'm not stupid!' she said furiously. 'If I'd gone into the pantry first I wouldn't have taken dull old bread or mouldy cheese, I'd have gone for the cake tins.'

April, unused to having to justify her actions to her twin, stiffened. But it seemed pointless to argue over such a matter now that they had left the flat behind, so she satisfied herself by punching May in the ribs just as hard as she had been punched herself. 'Shurrup, you . . . you no-good son of a witch,' she said, quoting from one of the cowboy films she and her sister had seen.

Outraged by the insult, May grabbed a handful of April's hair and in seconds they were fighting like a couple of wild cats, apparently ignorant of the fact that they were making an exhibition of themselves. Several passers-by tried to separate them but it was not until a voice they vaguely recognised, sounded in their ears that they remembered their plan ... to sneak off quietly when no one was watching. Both twins scrambled to their feet and April smiled ingratiatingly at the local police constable.

'Sorry, Mr Judd. We had a bit of a disagreement,' she said rather breathlessly. 'Well, we'd best be goin' or we shall miss our music lesson and it's our favourite.'

The policeman nodded. He was an elderly man who knew very little about children, never having had any of his own. 'Off wi' you then,' he said jovially. 'And no more fightin', d'you understand? Else I shall have to throw you into a police cell until a judge happens to come by.' He laughed, and the children laughed too, for whilst the policeman's eyes were upon them they knew they must behave, but as soon as they were out of sight they dived off the road and began to slog across the ditch, glad of their wellies.

'We'll stick to the fields for a bit until we meet the big main road,' April said presently. 'That'll fool them.' Neither twin ever apologised to the other, so May realised that this change of subject was the nearest she would get to an admission that April had been in the wrong, and she accepted it as such.

'Right you are,' she said brightly. 'Good thing Mr Judd did come along, because the train arrived just as he was tellin' us off and all those people who had been starin' at us began to scramble for seats on the train, so none of them will remember whether we got on it or not. In fact, we couldn't have managed it better if we'd tried.'

'You're right,' April said, having thought the matter over. 'The only trouble is the mud. Folk who stop for us might not want us trekking big amounts of mud into their nice clean vehicles. But if I remember rightly there's a stream that runs between the next meadow and the main road. There's a dear little bridge ... and if we paddle in our wellingtons we could get rid of most of the dirt.'

'True,' said May. She glanced wistfully at her sister's satchel, which contained the food they had taken. 'We could have a little picnic. I'm starvin'. Fightin' always makes me hungry.'

April shook her head. 'We can't deviate from our plan,' she said firmly. 'If they've discovered Miss Ellis's body there'll be a search for us startin' any minute. I think we ought to get as far away from the school as possible before we even think about eatin'.'

May realised that she was no longer the leader of the expedition but did not regret it. She was about to agree with everything her sister had said when she held up a finger.

'Hush a minute. What can you hear?'

April obediently hushed, but then turned on May. 'What does it matter what I can hear? I can hear a cow mooing and another train comin' up the long hill, but what does it matter? We aren't goin' to try to get aboard a train 'cos we've got no money for tickets. So who cares what we can hear?'

May hugged herself; April had played right into her hands. 'I can hear children singin' a song I don't know, and if you can't you'd best go to the doctor 'cos you're goin' deaf,' she said scornfully.

Outraged, April raised a threatening hand. 'I don't see ...' she began, ready and willing to fight her corner, but May overrode her.

'I know you don't see the point,' she said triumphantly. 'But if we really had killed Miss Ellis, they wouldn't continue with a singin' lesson, would they? So what shall we do? Go back or go on?'

There was an appreciable pause before April answered. 'I won't call you a stupid girl because that would be rude,' she said coldly. 'All it means is that they've not found Miss Ellis's body yet. Now if you'd heard hounds bayin' and men shoutin' "Find the murderers" ...'

For a moment May considered giving her twin a good push and stomping her into the mud, but common sense prevailed. April was the older and considerably heftier twin, so she might as well bear the responsibility for their actions; besides, she could be right. Instead of arguing – which had been her first impulse – May nodded meekly. 'Then we go,' she said.

Mrs Clarke was always the first one down to the kitchen of No. 3 King Edward Court, but today Rosheen was ahead of her. They greeted one another with sparkling eyes, for today was a break from their routine.

'Mornin', Mam,' Rosheen said cheerfully. 'I've had my breakfast but I've put you out a nice helpin' of porridge and there's a spoonful of honey left in the jar. Oh, Mam, I'm that excited; imagine how much more excited the twins will be when they see us.' She heaved an ecstatic sigh. 'And now that the day has arrived I'm more sure than ever that we were right not to tell them we were comin'. I thought we'd take 'em out for tea so that they won't be afraid to tell us what's wrong, if anything is of course. If only their letters weren't so short! I got the whole lot out last night – and there weren't that many – and read them through real careful. Mam, those letters told me virtually nothin'. Sometimes what they had for dinner, sometimes a new song they'd sung in their music class, sometimes how they hated the miserable weather. They never wrote anythin' – anythin' *personal*, if you know what I mean.'

Mrs Clarke, spooning porridge, raised grizzled eyebrows. 'They told you they liked Mrs Reynold,' she objected. 'Ain't that enough for you, girl? And one letter said they wanted Miss Rogers back because that Miss Ellis didn't seem to like 'em much.' She chuckled. 'And why should she? Your twins cause more trouble than a cartload of monkeys when someone says somethin' to annoy 'em, so don't pretend they're two little angels, 'cos they ain't. As for the letters bein' short, what kid likes letter-writin'? Why, when I were a girl I had to write to my grandmother twice a year and thank her for the postal orders she sent for Christmas and birthdays and I used to beg my mother to tell her to keep the money so's I wouldn't have to write the letter.'

Rosheen laughed. 'And to think I wonder some-times where the twins get their devilment from,' she said. 'So you think they really are just bein' difficult, do you? Well, if you're right we'll give 'em a good talkin' to and then they can have a choice: King Edward Court empty of kids or stayin' in the village until it's safe to come home again.'

Grandma Clarke scraped her porridge bowl clean, heaved herself to her feet and went over to the sink to begin washing up. 'This won't take five minutes,' she informed her daughter, who was beginning to suggest that the pots would be fine left in a sink of water for a couple of days. 'You fetch our coats and hats and when you've done that I'll be ready to leave.'

Rosheen would have liked to argue, to say that they must get to the station as early as possible in order to get seats on the train, but saw that her mother was already reaching for the tea towel and held her peace. And the older woman was right. She and Rosheen arrived at the station with time to spare.

They bought their tickets and showed them at the barrier, and presently the train arrived, already crowded. However, they managed to get seats, thanks to a well brought up young member of the air force who gave up his own place to Rosheen. Rosheen sighed: it would have been nice to sit next to her mother, but at least they were both seated; she must be content with that.

The journey was not a long one, but today it seemed to Rosheen, eager to reach their destination, that the train stopped at every tiny station, and several times it pulled into a siding to let an express roar past.

'It's probably troop movements,' the young officer told her, and then, as the train drew into a small station: 'Hooray, there's a trolley with a tea urn. Do you want me to fetch you … and your mother, is it? … a cup?'

Rosheen agreed that this would be nice, and was soon sipping her drink. She had bought a copy of *Woman's Own* to read on the train, and as soon as she'd finished her tea she produced the magazine and bent her head over a knitting pattern. If only she was clever with her needles, like her mother! She could just do with one of those lacy jumpers which kept you warm but looked so glamorous! She was leaning across to point it out to Mrs Clarke when two things happened at once: the train jerked, lurched and began its slow progress once more, and the older woman gave an exclamation and jumped to her feet.

'Rosheen!' she squeaked. 'Isn't that . . . wasn't that . . . D'you see that gap in the fence? That child ... Rosheen, it were April, I'd stake my life on it.'

Rosheen stood up and peered in the direction her mother was pointing. She saw a few adults on the opposite platform clearly awaiting the next train and a neat garden surrounded by a white-painted wooden fence, but no sign of either April or May. She was not surprised – they were nowhere near the village where the twins were billeted, and besides it was still only just after noon so the girls, whether they liked it or not, would be still in school. She sank back into her seat, shaking her head, but decided to be tactful.

'I can't see anyone. Was May with her? You know those two, they're never far apart.'

'I dare say, but I only saw April,' Mrs Clarke said impatiently. 'Rosheen, we've gorra gerroff this train, else we'll miss 'em!'

Rosheen sighed. 'Talk sense, Mam,' she said wearily. 'We can't get off the train, not unless it stops again, and it actually seems to be pickin' up speed a bit. And even if we could there'd be no point, 'cos

167

we're in the middle of nowhere by the looks of it. Are you absolutely certain it was April you saw?'

'Well, no,' Mrs Clarke admitted. 'And you're right about May, 'cos of course the twins don't like bein' separated and I didn't see May. But I really do believe it was April!'

Rosheen smiled encouragingly at her mother. 'You probably saw someone who looked very like them; I do it all the time. Now, would you like to have a read of my *Woman's Own*? It'd stop you feelin' bored.'

Mrs Clarke took the magazine, muttering beneath her breath. 'You mean it will stop me imaginin' things. Oh, that's a real pretty jumper. If only we had the wool, I could knit it up for you in a trice; you could do with some new clothes.'

Rosheen sank back in her seat and turned her attention to the scene passing outside. Meadows, fields and copses were just discernible through the little bit of dirty window. She was sure her mother was mistaken but she knew it would not do to say so. Instead, she rooted round inside her bag, pulled out the packet of sandwiches she had made earlier and held it out. Mrs Clarke gave her a strange look.

'Hopin' to turn me up sweet?' she demanded irascibly. 'Well, just you wait until we reach this here school and find our girls are off on some trip or other. Then you'll be sorry!'

*

April had nipped out through a weak patch in the fence to take a look at the train which was just drawing in, for they had not had much luck with hitchhiking. As May had gloomily foretold, the drivers of lorries and cars did not so much as look at two children, the black felt hats they had taken from the flat pulled down over their eyes and their navy mackintoshes muddied round the hem. What was more, she had rammed the half loaf into her satchel alongside the chunk of rather unappetising cheese and the six sour little apples without considering that they had no knife to cut either the bread or the cheese, and now the twins were hungry. When they had seen the station master's tidy and productive garden it had seemed like a good idea to nick a few carrots which they could crunch as they walked, but the carrots had proved to be no such thing; they were some sort of flower with perfectly normal roots. April was no gardener, but she knew a carrot when she saw one, and the miserable little bunch of wavering roots which came up when she heaved were nothing like any carrot she had ever met. Luckily no one on the platform had been watching when she pulled them, but when she re-joined May she was conscious of her twin's critical stare.

'Them's not carrots,' May pointed out accusingly, gazing at the handful of what looked like perfectly normal weeds. 'Couldn't you find anything else? Oh, I'm so hungry!'

April could have screamed and slapped her twin, but in her heart she knew it was not May's fault so instead she gave the younger girl her most conciliatory smile.

'No, I know they aren't carrots; in fact I think they may be weeds,' she admitted. 'Apparently the station master don't grow nice veggies; what sort of war effort is that? I'm hungry as well, May, but the trouble is I forgot to nick a knife when I took the bread and cheese so I can't make sandwiches. I s'pose we could both bite a piece off the cheese, only the loaf needs a knife as well, so what d'you want to do?'

She thought that May would give up the idea of eating, for the time being at least, but it appeared her sister was made of sterner stuff. 'We'll hang around until the next train arrives and then we'll nip into the station master's kitchen – I seen it through the winder – and steal a knife,' May said, and there was determination in her tone. 'I say "steal" 'cos that's what they'll think, but I really mean borrow, 'cos we'll give it back as soon as we've cut the loaf into slices. Would that be all right, April? Only we's goin' to be in enough trouble when they find the body wi'out bein' accused of thievin'.'

April pretended to consider, though in fact she had already made up her mind. 'I think we'll have to make do with chunks of the loaf and bites of the cheese,' she said rather regretfully. 'You're right for once, May. With the sort of luck we're havin' today, we'd certainly be caught, and even if they didn't throw us in a police cell, like Mr Judd said, they'd be bound to get nasty. And they'd send us straight back to school no matter how we pleaded. So we'll walk on a bit further, eat some bread and cheese and drink some of the ginger beer ...'

May, whose satchel contained the ginger beer, pulled a face. 'It's tedious heavy; let's drink the lot before we move on,' she said. 'Unless you want to put the ginger beer bottles into *your* satchel, because as you keep sayin' you're older and stronger than me.'

By the time Rosheen and her mother reached the village it was starting to snow, though the flakes were mixed with raindrops. Mrs Clarke led the way into a pleasant-looking pub called the Green Man, paid a deposit for a room, explained that they had come to visit two of the evacuees and asked for directions to the school. The landlord gave them explicit instructions and noted down that four of them would be having a late tea.

'No point in feedin' them early, 'cos we've ate our sandwiches and the kids'll have had their school dinners. It'll be a bit of a treat for them to go out for a meal,' Grandma explained. 'They's city kids, you know, used to shops an' that. I dare say they'll

171

be happy to have a bit of an outin'. Kids get into mischief when they're bored, as you know.'

The landlord bristled. 'There's more to do in a village and the country round it than in any city,' he said haughtily. 'Why, most of the kids is as happy as Larry. D'you know how many went home at Christmas? Well, I ain't sure of the exact number but it weren't many, I'm tellin' you. We held carol concerts every night in aid of the war effort and some of the boys from the RAF station put on a spoof play about Hitler and his goose steppin' army … eh, it were a laugh. Then the kids did the nativity play … but I mustn't keep you.'

'Ta-ra till later then,' Rosheen said chirpily. As they headed for the lane which led to the school she stopped short. 'Bless me, if I didn't forget we meant to visit Mrs Reynold to thank her for lookin' after April and May. Oh well, we can do that when we come back. Look, that's the school! Ain't it small, though? That'll be why the village children and the evacuees take it in turns to use the classrooms.' Rosheen began to walk quickly. 'Oh, Mam, I can't wait to see their little faces!'

Having made up their minds not to give anyone a clue as to their whereabouts, the twins ate their unsatisfactory picnic seated on a fallen log which they afterwards discovered to house a great many inhabitants; it was the spiders that caused the girls to vacate their seat rather abruptly. They soon found that their choice of bread, cheese and apples left much to be desired as well. The bread was very fresh and difficult to divide when all you had was icy cold hands, and the cheese was so strong that it stung your tongue. As for the apples … April took one bite and hurled the rest of her share at the trees, scoring direct hits on a leafless oak and knocking down several acorns and an oak apple. Then she advised her sister not to waste her teeth on the apples and dusted down her coat, making sure that no small inhabitants had decided to accept a lift.

'We'd better get a move on,' she said, eyeing the bread and cheese with distaste. 'Let's scatter this lot – somethin' will eat it, but it won't be us.'

May looked wistfully at her apples, but she trusted her twin's judgement and hurled them away in disgust. If only they hadn't rushed off in such a hurry. But it was too late now to regret what was past. The girls set off.

Chapter Ten

When Rosheen and Grandma arrived at the school playground it did not occur to them that there were a great many children running hither and thither in considerable excitement, for their attention was fixed on the teacher who approached them, eyebrows rising. The woman was probably in her early sixties and wore a piece of sticking plaster on her forehead; she was dressed in an ancient tweed skirt and a loopy grey twinset. In fact, she looked just how Rosheen had imagined Miss Ellis to look, apart from the sticking plaster. Remembering that the twins did not like Miss Ellis, Rosheen gave her mother's hand a squeeze to warn her before she spoke.

'I think you must be Miss Ellis? I'm Rosheen Clarke, and this is my mother. We've come to visit April and May; we thought we'd take them out for the afternoon, if that's all right with you?' As she spoke Rosheen was eyeing the children milling about, hoping to see the twins. 'Are they here?' she said. 'I don't want to interrupt your routine but we really would like to see them as soon as possible.'

The teacher took a deep breath. 'And so would we like to see them,' she said grimly. 'The Administrator is coordinating the search for them. You'd better speak to him, though when we find them there are several people who will want a word.' She tapped the sticking plaster on her forehead significantly. 'Do you see that? One of your daughters, I couldn't say which one, inflicted this.'

Rosheen and her mother both stared. 'It would have been April,' Rosheen said automatically. 'But I don't see ... neither of the twins has ever been violent ...'

Miss Ellis snorted. 'Are you sure we're talking about the same children?' she said icily. 'They fight like wildcats between themselves and are a byword with the other children. D'you want to hear now how I got this wound, or would you rather hear it from the Administrator?'

'You'd better tell us now,' Rosheen reflected that hitting a teacher had been unknown in her own school days. 'But honestly, Miss Ellis, I can't believe either of the twins would become violent, unless of course they had cause.'

'Cause?' Miss Ellis's voice rose to something akin to a shriek. 'Mrs Clarke, your daughters are not just difficult, they're impossible. They skip classes whenever they get the opportunity and on this occasion, since I was not teaching myself, I decided to follow them and see just where they went. I knew it was not back into the village because Mrs Reynold would soon have put a stop to that sort of behaviour, so as I said I followed them out of the playground and into the woods. They had made themselves a sort of shelter out of broken branches, bits of plank and an old hay bale, and when I tore down the sacking curtain they used for a door one of the twins picked up a branch and hit me as hard as she could on the head. When I came to myself the twins had gone and I could feel blood trickling down my face.'

Rosheen was horrified. The woman must be lying. She knew the twins could be naughty but she had never known them to use violence except to one another and, very occasionally, to another child who had hit them first. She looked hard at the teacher and saw the older woman's eyes flicker. 'I'm sorry to doubt your word, Miss Ellis,' she said slowly, 'but honest to God I do know my own kids. They wouldn't dare hit a teacher, no matter what.'

Miss Ellis's cheeks flew twin scarlet flags, but she did not reply. 'Follow me,' she said briefly.

Halfway along the corridor which must lead to the school office it occurred to Rosheen that Miss Ellis had seemed to imply that the twins were not on the premises. No wonder, if they had seen someone hit their teacher on the head. An irate parent? One of the older pupils? Whoever had hit Miss Ellis,

Rosheen was sure it could not have been the twins. But she would need all her wits about her, for Miss Ellis was tapping on the door and ushering the two women into a small room containing a large man, a large desk, a filing cabinet fairly bulging with files and a narrow window overlooking the playground.

Rosheen held out her hand. 'How d'you do? I'm Rosheen Clarke, mother of April and May, and this is their grandmother. I'm so sorry, but I don't know your name, only your title ...' she smiled disarmingly, 'and I'm afraid I don't know what administrator means.'

'It means that I'm in nominal charge of the half dozen primary schools in this area, Mrs Clarke, and my name is Mr Fielding. I expect Miss Ellis has told you what happened?'

'I told them I'd been knocked down and concussed by one of her children,' Miss Ellis began angrily, but the Administrator got up from behind his desk, came round and held open the door.

'Thank you, Miss Ellis,' he said firmly, ushering her out and closing the door behind her. He turned to Rosheen. 'English law, and I'm sure Welsh law too, says that one is innocent until proved guilty,' he said gently. 'I've had very little to do with the twins, Mrs Clarke, but they have never struck me as being capable of hitting a teacher on the head.'

Mrs Clarke had been silent so far, her gaze going from face to face, but now she spoke. 'The twins are monkeys, real little tearaways, and no doubt Miss Ellis has caned them more than once, but you're right: it ain't like them, I'll tell you straight. A frog in a desk or a plague of slugs is more their style. So why does Miss Ellis think it was them what hit her?

Mr Fielding gave a little cough. 'We might have taken Miss Ellis's story with a pinch of salt, knowing that she finds the twins difficult, but I'm afraid they gave her every reason to suspect it was they who struck her down. You see, they've disappeared. We've searched everywhere we can think of, and some of the senior boys went to the shed in the woods which April and May have been using as their headquarters. The twins were nowhere to be seen. I went straight down to talk to Mrs Reynold, and she said she had heard them in the flat this morning, but they had gone again by the time she had her break and could go upstairs to check. You might like to know they took some bread and cheese and their mackintoshes with them. But did the twins know you were going to visit today? If so, they'll no doubt be back with us shortly. Then we shall hear their version of the story.'

Rosheen gave a gasp. 'We didn't tell 'em; it was goin' to be a surprise,' she said, turning to her mother. 'Oh, what have we done? It's taken us hours and hours to get here and now we'll have to go straight home, because that's where the children will be heading.'

Mr Fielding shook his head. 'Are you sure that's where they'll go? What will they do when they arrive and you're not there?'

'We don't have to guess, we *know* they're goin' home, 'cos I saw 'em from the train at one of the stations ,' Mrs Clarke told him.

'Oh, Mam, and I didn't believe you, but you were right,' Rosheen said. 'It must have been April.'

Mr Fielding frowned. 'Where was it? Can you remember?'

Mrs Clarke shook her head. 'No. But they'll know we're here 'cos we told the neighbours we was comin'. They can sleep tonight in their own beds and hop on a train tomorrer and be with us by teatime. Then we'll find out what really happened this mornin'.'

'They can't nip on a train,' Rosheen said unhappily. 'If they'd had the money they could have caught one this morning, and we know they didn't.'

'No, love, you're not thinkin' straight. If they fetch the spare key from under the mat and let themselves in, which they will do, they can borrow the house-keepin' money from the teapot on the mantel.' She stared challengingly at the Administrator. 'Our kids may be naughty – well, we know they are – but they wouldn't steal, no matter what. They wouldn't consider it stealin' to take the housekeepin' money 'cos they know we wouldn't mind.'

'Good. Now I must tell you, Mrs Clarke, that

179

I'd like the police informed. You never know what might happen to two little girls on the loose in a big city like Liverpool. I'm not saying that anyone would do them a mischief, but there's always a chance that they could get into some sort of bother. Our local constable will put the word around and before we know it the twins will be here and we'll learn the truth – or otherwise – of Miss Ellis's bang on the head.'

'Wait on a minute, April Clarke! Remember I'm your little sister with shorter legs than you.'

April sighed, but slowed. 'Now remember what I told you. Next time a big old army lorry comes past you're to turn round and face him so's he can see you're just a little girl, and the minute he slows down don't wait to ask where he's goin', just gerrin. We can argue later.'

The twins had had almost no luck with hitch-hiking. One lift had taken them in totally the wrong direction and had wasted at least an hour, and now it was growing dark. It had started to snow, too, and though the flakes were mixed with rain it was still extremely unpleasant. Their feet in their wellingtons were like blocks of ice, and their fingers in their woolly gloves felt the same. Even their mackintoshes were no help against the biting wind and had the opportunity arisen to change their minds and return to the village they both knew that they would have grasped at it eagerly. Indeed, April was about to suggest that they cross the road and flag down a vehicle going in the opposite direction when the longed-for lorry could be heard thundering up the road behind them, the engine getting louder as it grew closer.

'I'm scared,' May whimpered. 'I don't like hitch-hiking. I want to go home.'

'Me too,' April admitted. 'I wish I'd never heard of hitchhiking. And I'm sure we haven't killed Miss Ellis or there would've been a man hunt with us as the quarry and they'd have found us by now.'

As the lorry came up behind them, May, desperately trying to remember April's words, jumped into the road. Fortunately the driver had been slowing down and now he brought his great vehicle to a halt with much squealing of brakes and skidding of tyres. In the dim light from the snow-laden clouds overhead he moved across to the passenger seat of the lorry and began to yell at her.

'You bloody little fool! Don't you heed nothin'? The government's been tellin' everyone to wear a white coat or a band of white material, and here you are, just a silly kid, in a navy mac and next to invisible, what with lorries not bein' allowed to use a proper light no more ...'

'I'm sorry, I'm sorry ...' May sobbed, forgetting entirely April's injunction that she was to jump aboard any vehicle which stopped. But April pushed her ahead of her into the passenger seat and followed quickly. 'Where're you goin', mister?' she asked breathlessly. 'We want to go to Liverpool.' She looked hard at the driver. He was a youngish man and probably quite pleasant-looking except that just now his face was set in a terrible scowl. 'Will you be goin' along the Scottie? If so you can give us a lift.'

'Not allowed,' the young man said briefly. 'Can't give civilians lifts, and even if I lent you my fore and aft no one would believe you were army, or any other member of the forces for that matter, so out you hop.'

May would have obeyed but April shook her head. 'It may have escaped your notice but it's snowin' cats and dogs,' she said. 'If you ain't goin' near our home then drop us off somewhere close by. But we shan't get out of your cab till we see the Liver Birds.'

Despite the driver's protests April, peering out of the sleet-lashed windscreen, soon began to recognise familiar landmarks and hugged herself gleefully. They would be late, certainly, but not too late; Mam and Grandma would be sitting over the stove drinking cups of tea and probably discussing the day's doings. April imagined the delight with which she and May would be greeted, and as they crossed the Bank Hall bridge, she nudged May.

'We're almost home; at least I think we are. I think

we're just headin' down Stanley Road, so as soon as I see the court I'll give a shout and the feller 'll stop … oh!'

She looked across at the driver, who grinned sardonically. 'She's been asleep this past half hour,' he said. 'If we're gettin' near your home you'd best give a holler in plenty of time, else you'll find yerselves pushed out of the cab and sittin' in a puddle, and I don't mean a puddle of your own makin' 'cos you wouldn't stop at the lavvy in Crosby. I mean the sort you get when the drains can't cope with the downpour.'

'I was just about to wake her,' April said with dignity. 'And there's no need to be rude; we didn't need the privy then.' As she spoke she dug a sharp elbow into May's ribs. 'Wake up, you stupid girl,' she said in a hissing whisper. 'I don't want him drivin' right up to the court; better us have a bit of a walk, just in case, like. He's only give us a lift 'cos I nagged him, so he might tell on us given half a chance.'

May groaned. 'Is it time to get up?' she said in a sleep-drugged voice. 'Come and give me a cuddle, April, 'cos I'm freezin' cold, so I am.'

The driver laughed hoarsely and stopped his lorry. 'Out you gets,' he said. 'I can't take a pair of kids into the docks; my sergeant would have my guts for garters if I tried, so gerra move on before I cut me engine and give you a good shove outta my cab.'

April grabbed May by the scruff of the neck and

heaved her onto the pavement, whereupon May promptly fell into a puddle so that water cascaded everywhere, including, apparently, down the inside of May's boots. The driver put his vehicle in gear and April was only just in time to snatch her satchel from the cab before the lorry was off, its hooded lamps reflecting in the watery road surface. May was still sitting in the puddle, complaining that her boots were full of water and she was wet to her knickers. April grabbed her once more and heaved her to her feet.

'It's been a horrible day and you, May Clarke, are the horriblest part of it,' she shouted. 'You're useless and a cry baby and I wish you weren't my twin, and now for God's sake pull yerself together! If we step out we can be home in twenty minutes. Oh, May, do stop drizzlin' and whinin' and start makin' the best of things instead of the worst. I don't believe it's terribly late, so Mam and Grandma should still be up. Come *on*, you stupid girl! Just tell yerself there'll be a hot drink and a piece of shortbread or some broken biscuits when we arrive in King Edward Court, but not if you just stand there cryin'.'

'I hate you, April Clarke. You're the nastiest girl in the world and *I* wish you weren't *my* twin,' May said drearily. But she followed her sister's example and began to splash along the pavement in the direction of the court.

April blinked; this was the worm turning indeed.

She had grown accustomed to calling her sister many insulting names, but she was not accustomed to May's fighting back and was not at all certain that she approved. She turned to look back at the small figure. May's boots squelched with every step, her nose was running unheeded and her face, April realised, was wet not only with rain but also with tears. A sudden compassion filled her. May couldn't help being smaller and weaker than her twin, could not help breaking down when things went wrong. April stopped walking and, when May caught up, put a comforting arm round her sister's slender shoulders.

'Sorry I were angry,' she said penitently, 'but I'm just as cold and wet as you are and it makes me cross.' As she spoke they were turning into the court and heading towards No. 3. Before they reached it, however, May stopped short.

'They ain't shut the blackout blinds,' she whispered. 'Everyone else has. It must be later'n we thought.'

'Perhaps they've gone to bed,' April said, but even to herself her voice sounded uncertain. Usually with even the best of blackouts there was a pinprick of light somewhere. Other houses showed tiny chinks, but not No. 3. She approached the house and felt along the letterbox; no string. She frowned, then stooped and turned over the mat. Yes! There was the key where it always was when it was not dangling on its string. With a squeak of triumph she fitted it into the lock, opened the door and stood for a moment totally bewildered, just as the moon, which had been hidden behind scudding clouds, suddenly reappeared and lit up the empty room, the cold grate, the unoccupied chairs.

May was the first to speak. 'They aren't here,' she whispered. 'They've been and gone and left us 'cos we've been so bad.' She turned desperately to her sister. 'D'you think they're upstairs in bed? I don't. Grandma or Mam always banks down the fire so's they can boil the kettle quickly when they get up next day. Oh, April, I'm scared!'

April was still looking round the room when the moon dived into a bank of cloud once more, leaving the court in darkness. 'I don't think we ought to light the lamp, because Mam is always very strict about us not playin' with fire, but you stay here, May, and I'll just nip upstairs and see if there's anyone in Mam's room.' She set off towards the stairs but May grabbed her.

'I'm comin' too,' she said in a wavering voice. 'I won't be left here alone, I won't, I won't! But I'm tellin' you now, April Clarke, they aren't here. They've heard as how we killed Miss Ellis and they're so cross that they've been and gone and left us. Oh, April, I wish I were dead, and I wish you were dead too. And I'm so wet and cold and hungry and I hate our mam for runnin' away from us.'

April felt inclined to join her sister in her misery but knew that if she did so May would collapse completely, so she heaved an exaggerated sigh, crossed the kitchen and stared at the clock, willing it to read midnight. But the clock persisted in showing that it was only a quarter past nine, so the two girls crept up the stairs, feeling that they had no real rights in this suddenly alien house, to check that no one slept in their mam's or Grandma's room, or indeed their own. Satisfied on this point, April would have led them straight down again save that May had started undressing. April had no chance to ask her what she was doing before May made it clear. She left her clothing in a sodden heap on the floor and went to her section in the large and battered chest of drawers, from which she extracted an ancient jumper, the torn skirt – on the tight side now – and some well-worn socks. As she began to put them on she gave April a timid smile.

'They aren't here but it's still our house,' she said through chattering teeth. 'And I don't want to die of cold or starvation, so now I'm warmer, and more or less dry, I mean to raid the cake tins. Then I shall go to sleep in my own bed and when I wake up we'll ask the neighbours where Mam and Grandma've gone.'

By the time the affair had been sorted out and the twins cleared of assaulting a teacher almost two weeks had passed, and Rosheen tried to have them sent back to the village and Mrs Reynold's. To her dismay, however, permission was not granted, for Mrs Reynold had been visited by the billeting officer in the interim and had accepted responsibility for two sisters in their place. So the twins remained in King Edward Court, though their presence worried Rosheen more than she liked to admit, despite the fact that the court was filling up again with children whose parents were opposed to the continued evacuation. As one irate mother put it, the children had been sent away from the cities to save them from the war, not to estrange them from their parents, which seemed, to some mothers at least, to be what was happening in their families.

'Well, if they really can't go back to Mrs Reynold I s'pose we could send 'em to the cousins in southern Ireland,' Rosheen said doubtfully. 'They're not in the war, and there'd be a stretch of the Irish Sea between us and the twins. I shouldn't think they'd run away from there, would you?'

Grandma shrugged. 'With them perishin' girls you can never be certain,' she pointed out. 'But it's too far, Rosheen, because you wouldn't be able to visit them and it was not seein' them face to face what sparked off the trouble we've only just managed to get them out of.'

'I suppose you're right, but I want them away from Liverpool,' Rosheen said. 'The fact is, Mam,

I'm thinkin' of volunteerin' for the WAAF, if they don't get round to conscriptin' me first. I love workin' with you in the bakery, of course I do, but what with the rationin' getting stricter all the time I don't reckon Mr Roberts will need the two of us for much longer, and I know he'd rather keep you on than me. Besides, I want to feel I'm doing my bit. I haven't done anything about it yet, but it's one of the reasons I want the twins settled. I'm goin' to take a tram into the city tomorrer and talk to the billetin' people.'

The authorities were understanding, sympathetic even; they said they would look for somewhere suitable.

The twins, however, were quite content to leave things as they were and very soon they were up to their old tricks. They bunked off school whenever the opportunity occurred, they scraped through their homework, and they blamed poor Rosheen for their having to leave both Mrs Reynold's flat and the village school.

'We were happy there,' May was apt to wail on an almost daily basis. 'Miss Rogers said we could go far.'

In vain Rosheen reminded them that Miss Rogers had left, presumably taking her nature table with her. She reminded them also that they had voluntarily run away from Mrs Reynold's friendly and easy-going home. But the twins cared nothing for truth or logic when those virtues got in the way of their own desires, and get in the way they certainly did on the day that Rosheen came home from yet another interview with the evacuation authorities. The twins were helping Grandma in the kitchen, peeling apples for a pie, and looked up fearfully when their mother announced that their problem was solved.

'You're goin' to a farm in Wales. There used to be a bus, but because of the war it only runs twice a week to take farmers or their wives to the nearest town. And don't start wailin', 'cos you always said you wanted to live on a farm.'

The wails immediately turned to roars. 'But not Wales,' April shouted between noisy sobs. 'It's got big mountains and it's muddy and the wind cuts like a knife; I know 'cos Miss Rogers taught us a poem and we all shivered and shook. If you send us there we shall know for sure you hate us and we'll hate you too, won't we, May?'

May stopped roaring for a moment and looked tearfully from her sister's furious face to Rosheen's miserable one. 'It ain't only Mam's fault – there's them wicked, evil people in the billetin' office too,' she wailed. 'How far is it from Liverpool? Oh, Mam, I bet it's hundreds of miles away. You won't be able to come and see us like you tried to do when we was with Mrs Reynold.'

Their grandmother had been listening without

comment, but now she spoke. 'You've give up any right to choose where you go, and it's no good blamin' your poor mam or expectin' to get special treatment,' she said grimly. 'And I'm tellin' you straight, girls, that if you run away and come back to King Edward Court you won't find your mam here. She's going to join the WAAF and could be sent to any part of the country. And if you consider runnin' to me you can think again, 'cos I certainly don't mean to take on the responsibility for the pair of you and I'll see that your next stop will be John o' Groats – or Dartmoor prison.'

The twins stared at her with loathing but it was clear to both that they knew their grandmother would live up to her promise. They looked at one another; this was worse than their wildest imaginings and in a moment of true sisterly affection they flew into each other's arms. Then April spoke, her voice cold and hard.

'We's only children when all's said and done, but if you go ahead and send us away we'll never forgive you. We shan't write letters, norreven the one to gi' you our new address, and we'll be as naughty as we can be, and that's a promise!'

Chapter Eleven

July 1940

Cassie and Rebecca, clad in their fawn issue overalls and wellington boots, had just finished work for the day and were making their way back to the farm kitchen where Mrs Bird would be waiting, they hoped, with a sustaining meal for her land girls.

When the weather had been dreadful Cassie had often felt guilty, for had it not been for her Rebecca would probably have been wearing the blue-grey uniform of a Waaf doing war work in warm offices at HQ. But in the end, friendship had caught them out. They had gone to the recruiting office together, and Cassie explained to the sergeant on the desk that she was too young to join any of the forces except for the Land Army, which could take sixteen-year-olds without parental permission. The sergeant had looked from one to the other and had leapt to the conclusion that both girls were applying. Of course it would have been easy for Rebecca to point out the understandable mistake, but she had decided to stay with Cassie and they had signed on together.

Because the land girls were scattered throughout the country their uniforms had been sent to their home addresses, and by the time Mr Valentine discovered that his daughter had enlisted it was too late to do anything about it. The box of uniform arrived on a Friday morning and on the Saturday she had donned the yellow shirt, green jumper, baggy breeches and long boots and walked demurely into the kitchen, holding the slouch hat in one hand. She had sat down at the table, clapped the hat on her head and regarded Mr Valentine with a jaundiced eye.

'Don't get in a bate, please, Daddy,' she had said, casting a wary look at the table so that she might dodge anything throwable. But Mr Valentine was so astonished that he sat and goggled at her for a full minute before he spoke, and when he did, it had been plaintively.

'What's all this about?'

'Oh, Daddy, don't say you don't recognise the uniform!' Cassie had said in an exasperated voice. 'I am now officially a land girl, and when I get my marching orders, which they say will be within a week, I can use my rail pass to get to the station nearest to the farm where I'll be working. They haven't said anything about the location yet; it'll come along with my orders.'

There was a long pause, during which nobody spoke, but then Mr Valentine broke the silence. 'You've signed up for the Land Army?' he said incredulously. 'But when you turned down the job with the ministry I assumed you were going to head for university. My dearest Cassie, what have you done?' He had risen in order to look his daughter up and down. 'Well, you can just run upstairs and change into something decent. I absolutely forbid it.'

All this while Mrs Valentine had been sitting at the table, her eyes going from her daughter's face to her husband's like someone watching a tennis match. Now, moving carefully, she reached out for the marmalade pot and took it into safe keeping. Cassie had smiled; she couldn't help it. Her mother was the most placid of women, rarely expressing an opinion which did not coincide with that of her husband, but today, it seemed, she was going to put herself in the firing line.

'Frank, dear, did you not hear what Cassie said? She's *joined* the Land Army, which means they have accepted her and nothing can get her out of it unless she chooses to join one of the other forces. Only she can't do that, without your permission, until she's older.'

Mr Valentine had sunk back in his chair again. 'I don't understand,' he had said heavily. 'As head of this household I forbid you to do anything so foolish, Cassandra. As for that uniform, it's downright dreadful. A daughter of mine in trousers? I won't have it, I tell you.'

Mrs Valentine was a small plump woman with softly curling light chestnut hair and a great look of Cassie, but it appeared she was also about to air her own independence. 'Don't you listen, Frank?' she had enquired gently. 'The die is cast; Cassie is committed and there's nothing you, or anyone else, can do about it.'

As though her quiet words had been a signal, Frank Valentine jumped to his feet. He looked round wildly, and both his wife and daughter knew from past experience that he was looking for something to throw. Cassie placed her hands firmly on her cereal bowl and her mother snatched up the butter dish, and then, much to their surprise, her father began to laugh, though she thought he still eyed her cereal bowl rather wistfully.

'If I'd known you intended to join the Land Army I might have signed the forms for the Women's Auxiliary Air Force as soon as you were old enough,' he had said grumpily. 'I don't see why I have to be put in the wrong. If only you'd asked, my dear ...'

Inside Cassie a little voice said: 'Like hell you would!' but she said nothing out loud. She just hoped that when her mother admitted to him that she herself had volunteered to staff the NAAFI three days a week he would simply accept that this was voluntary work, on a par with the WI, and not start hurling the china about because he had not been consulted.

'Cassie?' Rebecca's voice brought Cassie back to the present. 'Didn't you hear what I said? There's a dance at the village hall tonight in aid of the troops who were brought home from Dunkirk.'

Cassie grimaced. 'I do believe that seeing those poor fellows taught us more about war than all the government lectures in the world. So if we can help them in any way, you can count me in.'

Rebecca's eyebrows shot up. 'Are you seriously telling me you really will come this time? Only since we arrived in Charing Basset there must've been at least half a dozen dances and you've made some excuse not to come to any of them. And don't tell me it's just because this one is in aid of the troops, because one or two other events have been for the same cause and you didn't come to any of them.'

'I did; I went to the very first one, don't you remember? The hall was full of glamorous Waafs and Ats in their Number Ones and there we were clumping round in bloody brogues and baggy breeches ... heavens, the alliteration! But if you recall the only men who asked us to dance were farm workers like us and I must say it put me off. If only we could wear civvies it wouldn't be so bad, but we're not allowed to shed these blessed breeches, and I believe these beastly brogues have put me off dancing for life.'

Rebecca chuckled. 'And the weather's been so foul that only a masochist would want to walk three miles to the village just in order to have a NAAFI bun and a cup of weak tea, and watch other people dancing,' she agreed. 'So what's changed your mind?'

Cassie shrugged. 'Boredom,' she said frankly. 'We work late and at the end of the day all I want to do is get to bed. And besides, you've been to them on your own and you always say it was fun, so I reckon I'll give it a go. Are any of the other land girls going, do you know?'

'Bound to be,' Rebecca said, crossing her fingers behind her back. 'But what does it matter who else is going? One thing I can guarantee: there'll be more men than women because of all the airfields around here, though I imagine Spitfire pilots may be too busy kicking the Luftwaffe out of the sky to come to a village hop.'

Cassie nodded. 'Right. We'd better get a move on if we're going to have something to eat before we leave. I wonder what's for supper.' She was opening the back door as she spoke and entered the kitchen to find the two other land girls, Maisie and Jen, already seated at the table whilst Mrs Bird handed round plates of corned beef and her husband nursed a tureen of boiled potatoes and some rather weary-looking sprouts.

Mrs Bird smiled at them and gestured to the table. 'Sit yourselves down and get outside of your supper,' she instructed. 'You'll be goin' to this here hop at the village hall, I expect, so you'll want to get a move on. That's a fair old walk from here to Charing Basset.'

By the time the girls were purchasing their tickets from the elderly man on the door the dance was already in full swing. Couples were twirling merrily around, occasionally bumping into one another, and as Cassie had expected most of the women on the floor were in uniform. The walls of the hall were lined with cheap bentwood chairs and tables though these all seemed to be occupied, mainly, as Rebecca had foretold, by air force uniforms.

'I'll bag a table and some chairs,' Cassie said, seeing their fellow land girls in the queue for refreshments. Tea or fruit squash and Marie biscuits were on offer when one produced the ticket which had been bought at the door. Looking round as she slid into her seat, Cassie recognised Bob Bird and was pleased when he acknowledged her with a friendly grin and came over, holding out a hand.

'Are you goin' to give me the pleasure of this dance?' he asked, adding hastily, 'so long as it in't a foxtrot. I can waltz with the best of 'em but the foxtrot's got me beat. I dunno why they play 'em.'

Cassie jumped to her feet; it was nice to be asked

for a dance within minutes of entering the hall. He was an attractive young man in his early twenties with dancing brown eyes and a friendly grin. And though she suspected that her hosts' son had only asked her to dance to make her feel at home, it was nevertheless a kindly action.

'Thanks, Bob, I'd love to,' Cassie said gratefully as he slid an arm around her waist. 'Though if you had to wear the kind of brogues they give us the pair of us might as well be nailed to the floor ... oh.'

Bob followed her gaze and laughed. 'You're lookin' at my clodhoppers,' he said. 'We in't allowed to wear civvy shoes even if we've got 'em, which most of us ha'n't,' Bob admitted. 'I spotted you sittin' all alone, though – where's the gal Becky then?'

'She went for refreshments, though why we bother when your mother feeds us so well, I can't imagine,' Cassie said. She was reflecting that Bob was another man who had been bowled over by Rebecca's golden good looks and had probably only asked Cassie to dance in the hope of getting to know her friend better, but of course it would not do to say so. Instead she told him that Rebecca, having put the biscuits and tea on the little table which Cassie had bagged for their small group, had been whisked into the dance – a quickstep – by a tall dark-haired air force officer. Typical, Cassie thought resignedly; I get the farmer's boy – no offence to Bob – and Becky walks off with the best looking fellow here. Not that

I got a good look at him, but I expect she'll bring him back to our table. After all, with crowds of pretty women in skirts it's quite a triumph to see someone in baggy breeches chosen by the handsome officer.

The record ended and Bob gallantly returned her to the girls' table. He was still standing by her chair, chatting to Maisie and Jen, when Rebecca led her partner over to join them, and recognising a superior officer he held out his hand.

'Good evenin',' he said cordially. 'I'm Aircraftman Bob Bird. And you are?'

Cassie stumbled to her feet. 'Andy!' she gasped. 'What the devil are you doing here?'

Andy's grin was rather fixed and seemed to hold very little amusement. 'Pilot Officer Andy O'Leary.' He turned to Cassie. 'What am I doing here?' he asked. 'Hasn't Rebecca told you? At present I'm stationed at Buckingham Airfield, four or five miles up the road.' He held out a hand. 'Going to give me the pleasure of the next dance? I'm sure Becky will understand that we need to talk.' He addressed himself to Bob. 'Sorry to interrupt, old boy, but your partner and I are old friends.' As he spoke he was pulling her, none to gently, into his arms.

'You came over here to dance with Becky, knowing full well she's my best friend,' Cassie said furiously. 'Why you would want to dance with me I don't know, because you're the last person in the world *I* want to dance with . . .'

By now they were edging on to the dance floor and Andy's cool brown eyes met her hot dark ones. 'Who's a cross little puss, then?' he said softly, and his arm around her waist was like a steel bar. 'I can ask anyone I like to dance, Miss Valentine; all you have to do is tell me you're already promised to someone else. Only who would want to dance with a tigress if they could tread the light fantastic with her beautiful friend?'

'How *dare* you!' Cassie said, her voice trembling. 'Well, you're right about one thing. No one can make me dance with you!' and with that she stamped on his foot, her brogue catching him across the instep so that for a moment he was off his guard, and in that moment Cassie whipped out of his hold and fairly ran across the dance floor to where an open-mouthed Rebecca was waiting. She shot into a chair and turned to see Andy, flushed and frowning, coming after her. He was clearly in no pleasant mood when he reached her side and sank on to the nearest chair.

'You nasty little beast,' he said through clenched teeth. 'Well, that's the last time I shall ask you to dance!' He got to his feet and jerked his head at Rebecca in a manner as brusque as it was arbitrary, and to make matters worse Rebecca smiled sweetly and jumped to her feet at once.

'What was all that about?' Jen asked as Rebecca slid into Andy's arms. Cassie was about to reply that it was a personal matter when a tall ginger-haired man came to a stop by her chair and smiled engagingly down at her.

'I don't know what Mr Wonderful said to upset you, but if you'd like to tell me you can do so as we dance,' he said a minute or two later as they took to the floor. 'O'Leary and I share a room so we're pretty good friends.' He looked quizzically down at her, a smile quirking his lips. 'Does that make it better or worse?'

'Better – no, worse,' Cassie said. 'Andy and I are next door neighbours at home. We had a disagreement – I can scarcely remember what it was, now – and I swore I'd never speak to him again.' She looked up at him. He was as tall as Andy and almost as attractive, but he had not as yet even told her his name. She pointed this out and he responded at once, letting go of her hand for a moment in order to hit his forehead.

'Oh Lor', I'll forget my own name next,' he said with a comical grimace. 'I'm Pilot Officer Trelawney, Colin to my friends. And you?'

'Cassandra Valentine, Cassie to *my* friends,' Cassie said promptly. She squeezed the hand which held hers. 'How strange, to exchange names on the dance floor!'

They had reached the corner of the room and executed several twirls, making Cassie think wistfully of her old dance dress and how it would have billowed out round her legs, making her feel both attractive and feminine. Sadly, nothing of the sort could happen to land girls' breeches, so she contented herself with telling Colin how much she appreciated his asking her to dance.

'I almost didn't come this evening, because last time I attended a village hop I really learned the meaning of the word "wallflower",' she explained. 'You can understand a chap's reluctance to dance with a woman in trousers, but we're not allowed to wear civvies even if we had any handy, which we don't.'

Colin laughed. 'You must be a very good dancer just to get round the floor in those shoes,' he admitted. 'But you *are* a very good dancer; Andy said you were.'

For the life of her Cassie could not stop stiffening a little. So they had been discussing her, had they? And she had thought it was her beautiful dark blue eyes, or her neat figure in the hated breeches, which had brought Pilot Officer Trelawney over to her table. The young pilot officer seemed conscious of her slight withdrawal and the arm around her waist tightened.

'Sorry, sorry,' he said contritely. 'It's true that Andy did suggest that we might make up a foursome when we all happened to get leave at the same moment. How would you feel about that? I take it Rebecca is a pal of yours – well I know she is – so we might have a bit of a jolly, don't you think? Only according to Andy you girls work very hard and can only get away when there's no work on the farm awaiting your attention. Still, when you *are* free, Andy and I are in a syndicate, a sort of car share, so we don't have to find our amusements on the spot. Have you ever visited Norwich?'

Cassie shook her head. 'No, I haven't. Rebecca, Andy and I all come from a village on the Wirral about ten miles from Liverpool. Why? Are you suggesting a trip into the city? But what about the seaside? It's ages since I had a paddle.'

Her companion laughed, but shook his head regretfully. 'Almost all the beaches in the whole of East Anglia are sown with mines and fenced off with barbed wire. Fear of invasion, you know, though most of them have one section where you can crowd on to a small strip of sand to let the kids make castles or paddle, or so I'm told. It's usually by the lifeboat launching slipway. We might trundle off in the old jalopy when we've all got leave – the four of us, I mean – and from what I've heard the farmer's wife you work for is a generous soul and might be persuaded, if you ask ever so nicely, to pack you up a picnic.'

As the music ended he took her hand to guide her through the crowd of uniformed men and women leaving the dance floor. 'But when will *you* be likely to get leave? There seem to be dogfights going on all the time, ever since Dunkirk,' Cassie said. She sighed deeply as she sank into the small chair, pointedly ignoring Andy and Rebecca who were coming towards them. Colin took the seat beside her. 'Becky and I often say we feel out of it because land girls work at least as hard as the girls in the regular forces – I suspect even harder – yet we don't get the recognition. I've talked to Waafs who work in offices and seem to do nothing but flirt with the aircrews, and they think our life consists of haymaking, apple harvesting and learning to milk a cow, but it isn't like that at all, worse luck. If you can imagine a ten acre field of sprouts when there's been a sharp frost in the night and we are cutting the sticks and stripping the sprouts off with our bare hands, that's just one of the winter jobs we soon learn to hate. By December the main topic of conversation will be how to cure chilblains, or how to keep warm in bed at night because we're in an attic directly under the roof with no possibility of any sort of heating.'

'What about hot water bottles?' Colin asked. He turned to grin at Andy, who was listening to their conversation with a curling lip. 'We're discussing the possibility of a day out; the trouble is we can't even think about asking for leave whilst the Luftwaffe are attacking our airfields, and if we leave it too late winter will be upon us.'

Andy glanced up at the clock. 'Time we were shifting,' he said. 'Our transport leaves in ten minutes and I don't fancy having to walk back to the station.' He leaned over and punched Colin on the shoulder. 'You coming? Then say goodnight to your oh so charming partner and we'll be on our way.' He was still holding Rebecca's hand and Cassie watched with considerable annoyance as he towed her friend out of the dance hall.

Colin grinned at her. 'They'll be going out for a smooch,' he said cheerfully. 'Care to join them?'

'No thank you,' Cassie said coolly. 'Two's company, three's a crowd.'

'No? You aren't tempted by my manly beauty into even one small chaste kiss?' Colin said dolefully. 'Oh well, just my luck to have picked on an ice maiden; I must be more careful next time!'

Cassie stifled a giggle. 'Never allow a ginger-haired man to take liberties,' she said, keeping her mouth prim. 'Give them an inch and they'll take a mile.'

'Ginger hair? I'm fair, with just a touch of Plantagenet gold, and no red whatsoever,' Colin said indignantly. 'And if there's a dance here next month will you come along? Then I can prove what a gentleman I really am.'

Cassie began to reply jokingly, then stopped short. Through the open door she could see Andy and Rebecca, locked in each other's arms. Fury, pure and violent, surged through her. How dare Becky behave in such a wanton manner with Andy

O'Leary! She, Cassie, might no longer want him herself, but that did not mean that Rebecca could have him.

'Cassie? What's the matter?' Her companion's eyes followed the direction of her own and he tutted gently. 'I told you they'd gone out for a smooch. Care to change your mind and—'

He got no further. Still hot with fury Cassie grabbed his hand and almost dragged him out of the hall. She would show Mr Clever O'Leary, pilot officer or no, that he was not the only one who could behave badly. As they drew level with the other couple Rebecca made a soft little purring sound which only increased Cassie's rage, so that when Colin reached down and kissed Cassie's cheek she responded fiercely, hoping that Andy was watching, knowing it was unlikely.

The toot of one of the gharries was enough to have the men clapping their caps on their heads and straightening their uniforms. The transport would not wait for them, Andy had said so, and the driver must be growing impatient, for everyone knew that dances at the village hall stopped at ten thirty.

Cassie disengaged herself from Colin Trelawney's arms and smiled rather mischievously up into his face. 'Thank you for a delightful evening, Mr Trelawney,' she said demurely. 'But I don't think a foursome with Rebecca and Andy would be a very good idea, do you?'

'If the mere sight of my old pal Andy kissing your old pal Rebecca is enough to drive you into my arms, then I think it would be a *very* good idea,' Colin said frankly. 'My goodness, and I called you an ice maiden! Ah well, we live and learn. These dances are held once a month but it would be nice to meet again before then. Tell you what, we could catch a bus into the city, see a flick, have a fish and chip supper and get to know one another better. What d'you say to that?'

'It sounds fun ...' Cassie was beginning when the driver of the first lorry in line revved his engine impatiently. Colin jammed his cap more firmly on his head and gave Cassie's cheek a pat.

'I'll be in touch. I know the Birds' farm, so as soon as I'm free I'll let you know,' he said quickly. 'You're a grand girl, Cassie Valentine, but next time I kiss you – and you kiss me back – I'd like it to be for affection and not revenge. All right?'

Cassie was saved the necessity of replying by the warning honk of the last transport drawing up outside the hall doors. There was a mad scramble for places and then they drove off into the night, leaving Cassie feeling rather ashamed of herself. Colin was a nice bloke and didn't deserve to be used, and now, looking back on her behaviour, she realised that she would never have dreamed of kissing a virtual stranger had it not been for Andy and Rebecca. Feeling rather depressed, she returned to the village hall to pick up her green issue jersey just as Rebecca came out with both their jumpers draped over her arm.

She grinned at Cassie, apparently unaware of any ill feeling. 'I brought your woolly; you'll need it before we get back to the farm,' she said cheerfully. 'My goodness, that Andy knows how to smooch. I'm astonished you could bear to part from him. I mean, he kisses really nicely ...'

Cassie snorted. Andy was her next door neighbour and had been her friend for as long as she could remember, but they had never exchanged any but the most fleeting of embraces. However, she had no intention of admitting as much, and instead said haughtily: 'I'm afraid I'm not interested in Andy's carryings-on. In fact I'm astonished at you, Becky! Andy must believe he's on to a good thing.' She gave a mirthless laugh. 'I'm sure on your next date – *if* you've agreed to another date – he'll expect far more for his money than a mere kiss or two.'

Rebecca stiffened, and even by the pale light of the moon overhead Cassie saw her friend's cheeks darken at the implied insult. 'How *dare* you!' Rebecca said, her voice trembling. 'If you think I arranged to meet Andy this evening you're totally mistaken. And as for allowing any man to take liberties, don't judge my behaviour by your own. So put that in your pipe and smoke it, Cassandra Valentine! You're just jealous because you snubbed Andy and he turned to me.'

Cassie was about to assure her that she had never thought of Andy as anything more than a friend, but she was not granted the opportunity to do so. Bob and the two land girls, Jen and Maisie, emerged from the village hall and Cassie realised with a stab of shame that they had stayed behind to help clear the hall, pack up the refreshments and so on. She turned away from Rebecca and began to apologise to Bob, who assured her at once that the work had been done in a trice.

'I bet you waited in the hope of a lift back to the farm,' he said. Cassie thought she heard a note of awkwardness in his voice and guessed that he must have heard the raised voices as he pulled aside the blackout curtain and emerged from the hall. 'I've room for you both if you don't mind sitting on someone's lap.'

'Oh, thanks Bob, but I'd just as soon walk,' Cassie said rather stiffly. She turned to Rebecca. 'You go with Bob; I'd prefer to walk.'

Maisie giggled. She was a plump, easy-going girl engaged to a soldier who was on an ack-ack battery down south, and though she must have worried over the intensity of the German bombardment against the cinq ports she seldom mentioned such fears. Now she smiled at the two combatants.

'If we squeeze up …' she began, but Rebecca and Cassie shook their heads simultaneously, both insisting that they would prefer to walk.

'We came on foot so we might as well walk back,' Rebecca said. She laughed shortly. 'We probably won't arrive far behind you, overloaded as you are.'

Cassie saw Maisie and Jen exchange glances and realised that they too must have heard the row between her and Rebecca. She thought ruefully that they had probably both said more than they meant, but the damage was done now. All she could do was try to make it up on the walk home, and hope that the quarrel would be forgotten and life would return to normal.

Bob put the big old car into first gear and began to creep forward, and Cassie and Rebecca set off in its wake at a fast walk. Cassie turned and looked at Rebecca's face in the cold moonlight.

'Look, I'm sorry I said what I did,' she said awkwardly. 'It was just that I've never thought of Andy as anything but a friend, and a neighbour of course. Can we forget the whole thing?'

There was a brief pause, but when Rebecca spoke it was angrily.

'You insinuated that I was easy, and that I'd plotted to meet Andy at the dance,' she said, her voice shaking with fury. 'And you did it in front of everyone. Maisie, Jen and Bob will think you wouldn't have said it if it hadn't been true. You're just a jealous cat!'

'*Jealous*?' Cassie infused the word with as much incredulity as possible. 'Jealous of you? You've got a very high opinion of yourself, my girl. Just tell me truthfully that you didn't arrange to meet Andy tonight to put me on the spot and maybe, just maybe, I'll believe you.'

'*Believe* me?' Rebecca's tone mimicked Cassie's. 'I don't care whether you believe me or not, and as for Andy, he's a very attractive fellow and he's shown good taste by preferring me to you.'

Cassie began to retort, then realised the futility of it, and for the rest of the walk home the girls preserved an icy silence.

They reached the farmhouse and found Mrs Bird dispensing mugs of hot cocoa and her homemade shortbread fingers. Bob had already left, or so Cassie assumed, and their appearance in the kitchen seemed to be enough to send Maisie and Jen off to bed, carrying their mugs of cocoa with them, but when Cassie and Rebecca would have followed Mrs Bird shook a chiding head.

'Little birds in their nests should agree, in't that so?' she asked the two girls. 'We don't want no squabblin', particularly over a young man, which I gather from Jen and Maisie was the root of the trouble. I hoped you might come in havin' made up your differences, but one look at your faces was enough to tell me I were mistaken. I dunno which of you started the trouble but I'm tellin' you here and now to shake hands and cry pax. We can't have arguments; agreed?'

The girls shook hands and mumbled apologies, then made their way up to their attic bedroom. Once there Cassie began at once to undress and don her issue pyjamas, but Rebecca sat down on her bed and spoke to Maisie and Jen, both of whom were feigning sleep.

'Don't be so daft, you two,' she said peremptorily. 'I know you're awake, and you both know that Cassie and I had a bit of a falling out. It was over a feller, needless to say, but it was just a tiff, like. We've made it up and we want you to forget that we ever fell out. Can you do that, do you think?'

Maisie giggled and propped herself up on one elbow. 'You'd better explain just what it was all about, so we can forget it properly,' she said. 'We can't forget something we only heard half of, can we, Jen?'

Jen followed her friend's example and sat up as well. 'We think you both want the same feller, someone called Andy,' she said. 'Maisie thinks he used to be your boyfriend, Cassie, but for some reason you swapped. Were we right?'

Rebecca and Cassie exchanged glances. Both, Cassie realised, would have liked to say m.y.o.b. – mind your own business – but realised this would only make things worse. She sighed. 'It was something like that,' she said. 'But we've agreed to forget it and you two can jolly well do the same. Mrs Bird won't have disagreements amongst her girls, she said as much after you two had come up to bed, so we shook hands on it. Satisfied?'

'No, but if you're pals again that's good,' Jen said. 'We'll forget it, won't we, Maise? And now let's go to sleep or those bloody cockerels will start up their dawn chorus and we'll be like wet rags tomorrow morning. Last one in draws back the blackout blinds. Goodnight, everyone.'

Very soon silence reigned in the long attic, but Cassie, pulling the sheet defensively up over an uncovered shoulder, thought that things would never be quite the same, either between her and Rebecca, or between her and Andy. Not that it really mattered, she told herself. If Andy just wanted a pretty blonde then he could have Rebecca and welcome. If, however, he wanted a girl with character and brains...

But what young man cared about character or brains when he could have Rebecca's looks and charm, she thought bitterly. Oh, to hell with Andy O'Leary! The words of a popular song began to drift through her head. *Let him go, let him tarry, let him sink or let him swim, he doesn't care for me and I don't care for him ...*

Only, alas, she realised as she felt sleep claim her,

he was her feller by right of – of something or other. Oh Andy, Andy, you may have feet of clay, you may go for Rebecca's blonde prettiness instead of my sterling worth, but we'll always be friends, and that isn't to be sneezed at.

She slept at last as the first cock began his serenade to the dawn.

Andy awoke next morning when the summer sunshine crept through a gap in the blackout blind. For a moment he simply lay there, wondering why he felt vaguely dissatisfied with life. Then he remembered; that wretched dance! What on earth had made him behave so badly? He had known Cassie almost all her life and knew full well that she'd always been envious of Rebecca's golden good looks. In the normal course of events this would not have mattered, the two girls being such good friends, but to taunt her as he had had been an act so unwise, he now considered, that he had been lucky to escape with nothing worse than a bruised foot. To compare the two of them had been like waving a red rag at a bull, when he had actually meant to apologise for their previous quarrel instead of making things worse.

In the bed opposite Colin stirred and opened a sleepy eye. 'Morning, old chap. Reveille gone yet?' he asked groggily.

'Not yet, but any minute now,' Andy told him.

'I'm going for a shower in the hope that the other bods haven't already run off the hot water.' He paused. 'Tell me, Colin, you seemed to be getting on pretty well with Cassie Valentine. Was she still mad at me? I can't think what made me behave the way I did. She and I have always been friends but last night ... oh, I don't know, I just wanted to rattle her cage, if you know what I mean!'

Colin gave a sleepy chuckle. 'You did that all right,' he observed. 'If you ask me, you'll have to tread carefully for a bit.' He grinned. 'Can we do a swap? You can have Miss Valentine and I'll content myself with Miss Spencer; how's that for a solution?'

Andy chuckled. 'We'll go to the dance next month and I'll tell her how sorry I am,' he said. 'If I can make her laugh she'll forgive me. I know I don't deserve it after the way I behaved last night, but she's a really generous person and if I go slap up to her and apologise I'm sure she'll let me off.'

Cassie awoke to find that her mind had been made up for her. Staying on the farm would mean she had no choice but to work alongside Rebecca, and as Rebecca's friendship with Andy developed things would become more and more difficult. Best to get away before matters came to a head. Due to some clerical error she had been sent application forms for the services a few days earlier, just as she turned seventeen. She and Rebecca had laughed together over the blunder, but now she would put it to good use. She would escape from the farm, and from Rebecca, and join the Women's Auxiliary Air Force, which was what she had always wanted anyway.

Downstairs she could hear preparations for the day ahead already beginning. It was not her turn for milking, so she would show Mrs Bird the papers and tell her what she meant to do. More and more women were volunteering all the time and being eagerly accepted, she knew, so she did not anticipate any difficulty over her own application, even without her father's consent.

She slipped out of bed and padded over to the washstand. As she began to deploy soap and water, flinching at the icy chill of it, she thought hopefully that perhaps Waafs were provided with hot water for washing. Well, it looked as though she was about to find out.

Chapter Twelve

Rosheen suspected that Mr and Mrs Sidney Wright might find the twins too much. The billeting officer had told her that Mr Wright had been chief cowman on the Nidds' farm but had retired from his position a couple of years previously. However, when some of the younger men volunteered for the services he had returned to his old job and his wife helped out up at the farmhouse, for they lived in a tied cottage and were happy enough to be earning and not having to dip into their savings. Rosheen would have liked to visit the Wrights herself, taking the twins with her, but the twins had flatly refused to consider the idea.

'I'm tellin' you,' April had said, her very tone expressing impatience. 'I'm tellin' you we'll run away and I mean it. We'll probably stay one night and then come home, 'cos now we know about hitchhikin' and don't need money for fares we can go anywhere we like.'

When Rosheen told her mother what April had said Mrs Clarke nodded her head with an air of finality. 'I told you what would happen if you let those varmints get the upper hand,' she reminded her daughter. 'Well, they've got to learn to do as they're told. You go ahead and join up, love, and we'll tell them I'm going to stay in Bootle with George. They can write to me there, and George will see that I get the letters.' She had patted her daughter's cheek. 'Don't look so glum, chuck. It'll be the makin' of the twins, if you ask me. You've spoiled 'em rotten, but though they're wilful and selfish there's good in 'em somewhere. I tell you, it'll be the makin' of 'em!'

So the arrangements were made, the twins' clothing and small personal effects packed into two cardboard cases, and when the train which would take them part of the way to their eventual destination had drawn in to Central Station, May had flung her arms round her mother's neck and wept all down the front of Rosheen's best cardigan. April had regarded her sister's tears with disgust, but when they had actually been bundled into a carriage and given the packets of sandwiches Rosheen had prepared, her own defiance had cracked at last.

'I love you, too, Mammy,' she had said, sniffing. 'Don't leave us. We'll be real good if you promise not to join the air force. Mams don't join the air force anyway – me and May have asked everyone and they say it's only for dads, or brothers.'

Rosheen had smiled but shaken her head. 'I'm afraid it's too late to change my mind,' she had said.

'A letter came this very mornin'. I'm to report to the trainin' centre in three days' time. And there'll be lots of other mams there, don't you worry.'

She had remained on the platform, waving, until the train was out of sight, then returned to the court and begun to help her mother with the preparations for her own imminent departure.

'I'll miss you, Rosheen, but I shan't miss those varmints,' Mrs Clarke said as they made their way to bed that night. 'When you said goodbye to them did you point out that you would've taken them to the Wrights' place yourself if they hadn't threatened to run away?'

Rosheen shook her head. 'No, because they called me Mammy and promised to be good if only I wouldn't join the WAAF,' she said ruefully. 'Oh, I hope they'll love the Wrights and be happy there, but if they're really miserable, you won't desert my girls? You'll let me know and I'll get leave and come home … I'll do somethin' …'

Mrs Clarke stopped outside her bedroom door and tutted. 'If you love your girls, and I know you do, then sendin' them away from Liverpool is just about the best thing you could possibly do,' she said. 'So for goodness' sake stop imagining snags and look on the bright side. The countryside is the best place for kids in war, you've said so yourself a hundred times. Now go to bed and don't worry, because what's done is done.'

Rosheen sighed but obeyed her mother, pulling back the blackout blind as soon as she was ready to slip into bed. Then she began to wonder whether the twins were sitting up in their beds at Cragside Cottage longing for their mammy. For a moment tears formed in her eyes, but with an enormous effort she banished them. You know your daughters better than anyone else, she reminded herself. I can't remember one instance when they didn't come out on top. If I feel sorry for anyone it ought to be for the Wrights. This made her chuckle, remembering some of the twins' more inventive exploits, and presently, rather to her surprise, she fell asleep.

The twins had arrived at Cragside Cottage wearing their most demure expressions. They had held a secret parley whilst the official who had accompanied them was in the lavatory and had decided that they should look meek and heartbroken. It was annoying that they had to put on an act, because they were longing to explore what might be their new home for a time at least, but they wanted to make a good impression on Mr and Mrs Wright, and thought that demureness would be more welcome to an old couple than curiosity.

The official told the taxi which had brought them from the village to wait and knocked on the door, and when it was answered by a tall, grey-haired woman, she introduced herself and the twins.

'Their mam has packed their cases so they should have everything they'll need,' she had said briskly, 'but you'd best show them round anyway.'

Mrs Wright smiled grimly. 'There ain't much to show,' she said, ushering them into a short hallway. She jerked her thumb to the door on the right and opened it a short way. 'Parlour; don't use it much,' she said briefly. 'Kitchen's straight ahead. Our bedroom's the door on the left, but that won't concern the girls.' She gestured to a flight of wooden stairs. 'Up the stairs with you, I'm not climbin' them again.'

The twins hesitated until it was clear that the official did not intend to climb the stairs either, and then they hurriedly mounted the flight to find themselves in a large bare room, sparsely furnished with an ancient chest of drawers, a big brass bedstead, a washstand and a solitary chair. They exchanged astonished looks, and April pulled back the thin and much patched quilt to reveal a sheet yellowed with age and two pillows stuffed with what looked like hay, and indeed was just that. She sat down on the bed, hearing the springs twang, then opened her small case, stood up and pulled out the top drawer of the chest.

'This one's mine; you can have the second drawer,' she announced. 'I say, May, there's no blackout blind. We'd better tell the woman what brought us here. Mebbe she'll say we can't stay in a room with no blackout.'

The two girls descended the stairs and were ushered into the kitchen. One end of the room was almost entirely taken up with a range which, despite the fact it was a warm day, had a cheerful fire burning. The floor was flagged, the walls were whitewashed, and various unmatched pieces of crockery were set carelessly down on a large and ancient Welsh dresser. The lady of the house was stirring a blackened pot over the flames and looked round as the twins entered the room.

'Dinner won't be long,' she said, and April nudged her sister and pointed to the scrubbed wooden table already set for four people. The twins had eaten their sandwiches long since and now perked up at the thought of another meal, but May, remembering the absence of blackout curtains, jerked the official's sleeve and informed her of this fact.

Mrs Wright turned back from the range. 'You'll be goin' to bed and gettin' up in daylight at this time o' year,' she said. 'I've got an old sewin' machine, and I'll run curtings up before winter, don't you worry.'

'Very good. Anything else, girls?' the official asked. 'You're a fair way from the village but you'll be wanting to go there for your schooling.' She turned to Mrs Wright. 'Have you a bicycle they might borrow?'

'No. They'll ha' to walk, same as the rest of us,' Mrs Wright said. She glanced at the clock on the wall. 'Are you stayin' for dinner? Only I got no warnin' ...'

The official hastily denied any wish to remain for the meal, which smelled like a stew of some description, and said her goodbyes. The twins expected to sit down at once but their hostess explained they would wait for her husband's return, and even as she spoke a gaunt man entered the cottage, ducking under the lintel of the back door, and grinning shyly at his visitors.

'Mornin', young ladies,' he said gruffly. 'I dare say you're hungry, like what I am, so I'll just wash and then we'll see what Mrs Wright has got for us.' He began to wash his hands with great thoroughness, and while he wiped them on the roller towel he turned once more to the twins. 'Which is which?' he asked. 'Can't have guests with no names.'

The twins giggled. 'I'm April because I were born first and she's May,' April said.

'Oh aye, 'cos she weren't,' Mr Wright said. He took his place at the table, closed his eyes, clasped his hands and said a rather lengthy grace, during which his wife stood in what April afterwards described as 'a prayerful attitude' until he had finished, whereupon she thrust large spoonfuls of vegetables and gravy on to the four waiting plates.

'Dig in,' Mr Wright said hospitably. 'Don't you wait to be asked, maidies, because my old lady is a woman of few words.'

The stew was accompanied by big floury potatoes, half each for the twins and two for the adults, and followed by stewed apple and custard, the milk for which had been provided by Mr Nidd.

'He'm good to us and he'll be good to you,' Mr Wright explained. 'He'm a rough and ready feller like meself, but generous. You may not have fancy grub at Cragside Cottage but you won't never go hungry.' He turned to April, who was following his example and wiping a slice of bread round the remaining gravy in her dish. 'Enjoy that, did you?' he asked, picking up the now empty dishes and carrying them across to the sink. 'Now, when dinner's finished my good lady here has a bit of a snooze and so does I, but when we wakes up I'll tek you up to Marigold Farm and show you around. Happy wi' that?'

The twins did not even bother to glance at each other before agreeing with this suggestion. They had already decided they liked Cragside Cottage and the Wrights, even though April said later that she thought there must have been at least a pound of turnips in her dinner that day.

'There's a war on,' May reminded her. 'Ever so many things is rationed. And anyway, you said we were goin' to run away.'

The two girls were in their bedroom changing their neat school clothing for worn old garments and boots. April snorted. 'You are *so* stupid, May Clarke,' she said, but even to her own ears the words sounded half-hearted. 'I said if we didn't like

Cragside Cottage we'd run away, but so far – apart from the turnip – we do like it.'

May gave a little snort of amusement. 'And where would we run to, Miss Clevercloggs?' she asked derisively. 'Mam won't be at home and nor will Grandma, and I don't fancy tryin' to explain to Uncle George that we'd run away a second time, do you?'

'No-oo,' April said after some thought. 'To tell the truth I dunno what to think, but I believe, twin, that we may have landed on our feet. The old people aren't likely to interfere with us; I reckon we'll be left to our own devices. But we'll give it a week and see how we feel then.'

They gave it a week and discovered that their reading of the situation had been more or less right, the only real snag being that their hostess was an indifferent cook. Porridge appeared for breakfast, stew – usually meatless, except when Mr Wright had acquired a rabbit to add to the big black stew pot – at midday, and jam sandwiches at teatime. The twins realised that Mrs Wright was doing her best and only suggested once or twice a day that she might vary the turnip stew, a criticism which she took in good part without feeling the need to change her routine in the slightest. The children liked both her and her husband, although in one matter they were not allowed to get their own way. Either Mr or Mrs Wright accompanied them to school or met them when classes were over until they had impressed upon the teacher that the twins must not be allowed to neglect their studies.

'Summer's different,' Mrs Wright informed them. 'In summer it's all hands to the pump as they say. Haymaking and such means the farmer needs all the help he can get; even youngsters like you can be useful. But in the winter you'll go to school every day or you'll answer to me and Mr Wright; understood?'

It was understood, and when the Wrights told them that they must give their word not to sag off school they complied.

'Only I don't want to be here for Christmas, 'cos turnip stew on Christmas Day is a cert,' April said. She sighed reminiscently. 'Grandma's a good cook, too. If we can just have Christmas at Uncle George's we can tell Grandma we want food parcels instead of Christmas presents. Likely she'll give us enough grub to last us till Easter. What d'you say to that idea, sis?'

May beamed. 'It's the best idea you've had in your whole life,' she said enthusiastically. 'I know Grandma is living with Uncle George but everyone's going home for Christmas. All the kids in the village school, at any rate, so I don't see why we should be different.'

Chapter Thirteen

April 1941

'Rosheen!'

Standing in the breakfast queue, Rosheen saw her friend Cassie waving from a table for two with a bowl of lumpy porridge, a mug of weak tea and two regulation slices of toast spread out on the table before her. She waved back, even as her own bowl of porridge with the toast balanced on top was thrust into her hands by a member of the cookhouse staff.

'There you are, chuck,' the woman said cheerfully. 'Get outside of that.'

Rosheen thanked her and hurried across to take her place opposite Cassie. The two girls had met again in the uniform queue at the training centre the year before. Rosheen had been looking around, hoping to see a face she recognised, when her eyes had rested on a tall, dark-haired girl she was sure she remembered from somewhere. The girl was smiling tentatively back at her and Rosheen moved down the queue to stand beside her.

'Remind me,' she said in a low tone. 'I'm afraid I can't remember your name, but the minute I set eyes on you ...'

The recollection of where she had seen her came back with the suddenness of a flash of lightning as the tall girl began to speak. 'I *knew* you looked familiar, though it was a long time ago. You're the mother of those twins who got into a fight outside the bakery – you gave us all penny buns, as I recall. Isn't it odd that we should meet again like this? I was just thinking I didn't know a soul here, and to tell you the truth I was feeling more than a bit lost ... but what about the twins? How are they? Who's looking after them?'

Rosheen had smiled. 'They've been evacuated to Wales and they're very happy, which is my main concern.'

'Oh, I see. My name's Cassandra Valentine, Cassie to my pals, and you are ...'

'Rosheen Clarke, and you can't be happier than I am to have found a friend,' Rosheen had admitted. 'Is it all right by you if we stick together, Cassie?'

The other girl had nodded. 'It suits me just fine,' she said. 'Shake on it.' They had shaken hands firmly and then they had reached the head of the queue and the corporal in charge had begun to talk of measurements, and shoe sizes, so the conversation was temporarily abandoned.

Now Cassie and Rosheen were on the same station

229

working in the typing pool, and, Rosheen reflected as she spooned lumpy porridge, she had seldom been happier. Despite the difference in their ages Cassie and she had remained firm friends, though Rosheen had very soon realised that she would have to change certain things if she wished to continue to work in the offices. Carefully, hoping no one would notice, she began to imitate the way Cassie spoke, and to take care with her grammar when typing letters. It had never occurred to her that she was a mimic, but very soon people started saying that she and Cassie sounded like sisters. Yes, Rosheen loved it all, and woke when reveille sounded with a pleasant feeling that she would enjoy the day ahead no matter what it might bring.

At first she had felt guilty, because once she was a uniformed Waaf she knew she was in for the duration, twins or no twins, and the weight of responsibility for April and May simply rolled off her back. If they had been unhappy, of course, she would have been unhappy too, but though they grumbled – it was a matter of pride with them to find something to grumble about – she could tell from their letters that they had settled very well with Mr and Mrs Wright. The only thing they really minded was the food, and her mother had promised to try to dispatch food parcels once a month.

The girls were grateful and said so, though they still constantly asked for permission to return to

Liverpool. Oh, not for too long, because they wanted to be in the Welsh countryside for the summer, but they would have liked to return to the city during the winter months. Rosheen was guiltily aware that she had felt almost relieved when Liverpool had been a target for the Luftwaffe at Christmas, because the news that their old school was now nothing but a pile of rubble had definitely made the twins think twice. No one can have everything, and it seemed to Rosheen that the girls liked their new life almost as much as Rosheen liked hers.

Mrs Clarke had never revealed to the twins that she was still in King Edward Court. She was doing her bit for the war effort, working in the NAAFI, fire watching and giving an eye to any neighbour who had more children at home than she could cope with.

'Rosheen? Are you thinking of those twins again? There's a couple of letters for you on the bulletin board, so we'll pick them up on our way to work and then you can relax.'

Rosheen nodded. She had never confessed to anyone, not even Cassie, that worrying about the twins was something she seldom did. It seemed awful not to worry about your children, but it was such a relief not to have to deal with their naughtiness every day! Her only worry, in fact, was that April and May would sag off school during the winter months and get into such trouble that the Wrights, albeit reluctantly, would refuse to house them any longer.

But she had failed to take the Wrights' determination into account, because when the snow had made travel next to impossible Mr Wright had got out his old sledge and pulled the girls into the village every day. This had not endeared him to her daughters, and she had received an indignant letter from April which had been so funny that she had given it to Cassie to read, although the final sentence had given her a tiny heartache.

The letter had started off abruptly, which Rosheen had recognised as April's way of expressing her annoyance over Rosheen's perceived failings as a parent.

Mam, Mr Wright is not our mother. Sometimes we hate him and his bleedin sledge. If you was a good mother you would take us away from here in the winter cos its mortal cold and the food is horrid. Mrs Wright aint so bad as him but she dont know how to cook. She throws everythin into a big pot of boilin water and cooks it until its all sloppy, then she calls it stew and makes us eat it. We want you to act like a good mother should and take our ration books away from her. Grandma can teach us how to boil eggs and fry bacon and that. Its no use askin Mrs Wright to show us how to cook cos she dont know, so dont forget our ration books. If you wont do this when your children are starvin and thin as rakes then you dont love us. April Clarke.

PS we asked Mr Wright why he didnt have no children and he said they married late. We didnt know you could only have children if you were married.

Now, the two girls finished their breakfast, picked up their post and went to the offices. Cassie ran an experienced eye over her own mail and then over Rosheen's. 'One for me from my mum, one for you from your mum and … gracious, one from April. You are honoured,' she said. She glanced at her wristwatch. 'We should have time to read them before we start work if we hurry.'

The girls signed in then settled on a couple of rather hard wooden chairs to open their letters. Mrs Clarke wrote that the twins were still pestering to come home, for a brief period at least, and would give no particular reason for this sudden urge.

It's not as though they'd be seeing you, love. Knowing them it's more that whatever it is they're after is something they're afraid one of us might disapprove of. And in a way, I do see their point. If you could get a few days' leave I suppose you might visit the Wrights, but from what I can gather there's some special magic in a return to Liverpool,

233

don't ask me what! So what are the chances of your coming home, just for a couple of days? You see, I'm afraid if we don't fall in with their plans they'll simply come back home anyway, and if that happens the Lord alone knows what we'll do next. What do you say? Can you get a few days' leave? I'd sort it out if I could, but a grandma is no substitute for a mother.

Think it over, queen; it'd be real grand to see you.

Rosheen put the letter aside and picked up the one from April. It was like most of the twins' letters, brief and to the point.

Dear Mam,

May says its no use being cross with you 'cos you wouldnt let us come home, even for a few days. Mam, we MUST come home, well splain when we see you. If you wont let us well run away again, but we dont want to do that, summers coming. Mrs Wright thinks youre a bad mother what wont visit her children. We mean it. Remember its our birthday in a couple of weeks. Oh Mam please please please! Youll regret it for ever if you dont let us come home and meet us there.

From April and May

Silently, Rosheen handed the second letter over to

Cassie, who scanned April's scrawl and then raised her eyebrows.

'Well? They're up to something, clearly, only she doesn't even hint at what it is. Do you have any idea?'

Rosheen shook her head. 'It's plain you don't know them,' she said ruefully. 'I suppose I could go to Liverpool, only it would be so complicated! Mam's taken in a family whose house was destroyed in the raids, and anyway we daren't let the twins know Mam's still in the court or we'd never get them to leave; and I can't impose on Uncle George. I wonder, if I offered to go to the farm ... what d'you think, Cassie? Any ideas?'

'Yes. Look, we're both due for some leave now we've completed our training. Our house at home has three good big bedrooms, so if the twins can top and tail in our spare room and you and I do the same in my old bedroom that's night-times taken care of. If that suits you we'll fix our leave, and then you can send a telegram to the Wrights giving them dates and so on. What do you think?'

'Oh, Cassie, thank you ever so much,' Rosheen said gratefully. 'But are you sure your mother won't mind? And what about your dad? From what you've told me, he might not relish the thought of three strangers invading his house.'

Cassie laughed. 'Flying ketchup bottles, you mean?' she said. 'Fancy you remembering that. But

I promise you, Dad would never do such a thing whilst there were guests in the house. So shall we do it? I must admit I'm really looking forward to meeting your twins officially.'

'Yes please,' Rosheen said fervently. She grabbed her friend's arm and jerked a thumb at the window by which they were sitting. 'Look, there's our Section Officer. Why don't we tackle her now about getting leave? And you know we were talking the other day about re-mustering? They say women are needed urgently in transport units and I've always wanted to learn to drive. Perhaps we could arrange that to begin when we get back. Come on; let's catch her before she starts work.'

April and May had agonised over the letters to their grandma and Rosheen. The trouble was they were afraid that if they admitted the reason for wanting to return to Liverpool, permission would not be granted. Mam would say bicycles were far too expensive, adding that since neither girl could ride one yet she would certainly not allow them to jeopardise their own lives and other people's by whizzing along the little lanes which were the only sort of roads around Mr Nidd's farm.

For the twins, though perfectly capable of walking three miles into the village and three miles back, soon discovered that the evacuees who had the best lives were the ones who lived in the village itself or were the possessors of bicycles. 'If we had bicycles we could ride them to school and not bother the Wrights at all,' April had told May. 'It'd be our duty as well as fun.'

'But our mam might worry that we'd cycle on the main roads and end up squashed flat as a pancake by some soldier driving an army lorry,' May pointed out. 'Because whatever you say, April, our mam is a good mam. Besides,' she added, 'I heard Mrs Tedd at the King's Arms say that even old bicycles are like gold dust these days.'

April flung up her hands. 'We *must* have bicycles. Stop whining, May Clarke, and think how to persuade Mam to buy us even one old and rusty machine between two of us. We could take turns to sit on the carrier if she can only get hold of one, but the important thing is to have transport. It ain't just gettin' into the village; there's all sorts of reasons for wantin' a bike ...'

'What?' May said suddenly. 'What reasons?'

April goggled at her twin for a moment and then hit her briskly in the stomach, and in no time they were fighting like cat and dog. They were in their bedroom, getting dressed to start their school day, but stopped fighting abruptly as they heard someone coming up the stairs. Mrs Wright rarely did so, which meant that it would be Mr Wright, and he believed a sharp slap stopped most bad behaviour. Accordingly they parted, April to seize a hairbrush

237

and begin brushing her locks whilst May grabbed the damp flannel and blotted a scratched cheek.

Mr Wright reached the top of the stairs, grabbed the brush from April and applied it hard to the seat of her cotton dress, despite a screech of protest from his victim.

'How many times do I have to tell you, fightin' ain't allowed?' he asked patiently. 'No, I don't want to hear why you fought; git down them stairs or you'll get no breakfast, and that's a promise.'

When the twins received a letter from their mother saying she would join them in Liverpool for a few days they were delighted. The period she mentioned would include their birthdays and, as April immediately said, it would give them time to search out at least one second-hand machine which could be their birthday present. They knit their brows over the inclusion of a friend of Mam's, LACW Valentine, but then they realised that they could not object. They knew it cost a great deal to go to a boarding house, so the offer of a free night or two must be eagerly grasped. The money saved could go towards their birthday bicycle. Not that Mam knew about that yet; the twins did not mean to lose the surprise element of their plan.

'April! April Clarke, *will* you wake up! Happy birthday! Today's the day we catch the train and meet our mam at Central Station. She was supposed to arrive in Liverpool yesterday and she said if something went wrong and she couldn't meet the train we were to go to Uncle George's place, only we don't want to do that, so for goodness' sake wake up.'

April groaned and sat up, blinking. 'Get up yourself, you stupid girl,' she snarled. 'I was having the loveliest dream and now you've spoilt it, like you spoil everything. In my dream Mam had bought us two brand new bicycles … oh, I hate you, May Clarke.'

May sighed resignedly. 'Don't call me stupid and spoil the day before it even starts. Mrs Wright came up ten or fifteen minutes ago and lit our candle. You know we're goin' to catch the milk train, and Mr Nidd is drivin' us to the station in the pony trap. Well, he will be if you're ready in time, so do get a move on.'

April groaned again, but pushed back the covers and headed for the washstand. May had already washed and was in her underwear, and April, glancing towards the window, realised that it was a very good thing May had persisted in waking her. Dawn was breaking, and though she had no means of telling the time she knew that the milk train left very early indeed and it would not do to miss it.

Mrs Wright, although she could not cook, could iron beautifully, and she had advised them to wear their nicest dresses and jackets. 'You've not seen your mam or your Grandma for months and months,' she had pointed out, 'so you'll want to look your best.' Accordingly April scrambled into vest, liberty bodice and the blue checked cotton dress which was a bit tight for her under the arms. 'Tell your mam to see if she can get you something a bit bigger from that Paddy's market I've heard so much about,' Mrs Wright had suggested. 'There'll be a jumble sale in the village at the beginning of the summer term but you won't have as much choice there as in Liverpool. Might as well make the most of your little holiday.'

May fastened the buttons on her best shoes, grabbed her jacket and headed for the stairs. 'Porridge is on the table,' she shouted back as she entered the kitchen. 'Mr Nidd will be here before we know it.'

Cassie had not realised how much she missed her parents until she and Rosheen had arrived home the evening before the arranged meeting. Mrs Valentine, not normally a demonstrative woman, had had tears in her eyes as she gave her daughter a hug.

'Oh, Cassie darling, Father and I have missed you so much,' she said. 'Over and over we've talked about arranging a meeting, but we're all so busy!' She broke away from Cassie's embrace and held out her hand to Rosheen. 'You must be Rosheen Clarke,' she said, smiling warmly, although tears were still wet on her cheeks. She shook the younger woman's hand then leaned forward and planted an airy kiss on her cheek. 'Why should we be formal?' she said gaily. 'I understand you both mean to re-muster to the transport unit. I've heard they're more generous with their leave so perhaps we shall be seeing more of you and your children.'

Rosheen returned the smile, though with twinkling eyes. 'You've not met my children yet, Mrs Valentine, and I'm afraid when you do you may change your mind,' she said. 'It's not that they're naughty exactly, they're just extremely ingenious about getting their own way. However, I dare say Cassie has told you they'll be nine tomorrow – well, April will – and I do believe they're beginning to try to think of others instead of concentrating on their own desires.'

Mrs Valentine looked a trifle startled. 'Oh well, so long as they're happy,' she said vaguely. She turned to her daughter. 'But here we are talking in the hall when I've just taken a batch of scones out of the oven. I'll put the kettle on and we can have civilised afternoon tea in the back garden, since it's such a lovely day.'

When they had demolished their civilised afternoon tea – neat little cucumber sandwiches and Mrs Valentine's scones – Cassie took Rosheen for a tour of the neighbourhood.

'As you can see, our house is semi-detached.

Have you ever heard me mention the O'Learys? They have one son, Andy, who's a couple of years older than I am. We used to be good friends, but then he fell for a girl who lives a couple of houses further along Knowsley Avenue.' She pointed to the Spencers' house. 'Becky is in the Land Army now but we used to be best friends, so I'll pop in and see her parents before we go back. Oh, and that reminds me. Remember the first time we met?'

'In the uniform queue?' Rosheen said, after a moment's thought. 'Yes, I remember. What about it?'

Cassie chuckled. 'No, not then, idiot. Don't you remember those kids fighting outside a bakery whilst their mother was inside buying penny buns? Well, the girl with me, the one with the gorgeous blonde hair, was Becky, so you have met her, even though you may not remember it.'

Rosheen, however, admitted that she only had the vaguest memory of a pretty blonde who had helped to separate her feuding daughters, and said as much.

Cassie laughed. 'Fancy you not remembering Rebecca; she's much more striking than I am. But anyway, you aren't likely to see her on this occasion because both of us getting leave at the same time would be too much of a coincidence.'

'It would, wouldn't it?' Rosheen said vaguely. She was staring at the little shrub-bordered path which led down the side of the Spencers' house. 'You did say she was in the Land Army, didn't you? Only there's someone coming down that overgrown little path in ATS uniform and she's waving at us.' She turned an enquiring look on her friend. 'What's the matter? Cat got your tongue? You look as if you've just seen a ghost!'

Cassie began to smile and then to laugh, and as the girl in ATS uniform came up to them she said, 'Rebecca! Is this a flying visit, or are you on leave like my friend and me? But Becky, last time I saw you you were in the Land Army. What happened? Did they chuck you out?'

Rebecca stiffened. 'So were you. In the Land Army, I mean,' she said coolly. 'But I'd always really wanted either the ATS or the Wrens, so when you disappeared I put in a request for a transfer and got taken on. What happened to you?'

'Oh, I thought it was time to move on,' Cassie said airily. 'This is my friend Rosheen Clarke, by the way. Rosheen, this is Rebecca Spencer.'

The two girls smiled at each other and shook hands, but the conversation remained rather stilted until Cassie mentioned that she and Rosheen were hoping to re-muster to a transport unit.

'Oh, you lucky things,' Rebecca exclaimed impulsively. 'I've always wanted to learn to drive and the air force teach you, don't they? I'm hoping to get on to the ack-ack batteries myself. It would be hard work, but very interesting.' She suddenly seemed to recollect her grievance and gave Cassie a defiant look. 'The uniform may not be as glamorous as yours, but I don't care about that. They'll only be taking the best applicants – you have to be really good at maths, for one thing, which would keep you out, if you don't mind my saying so.'

Cassie felt her cheeks burn and was about to refute the suggestion that she could not add two and two when the justice of Rebecca's remark came home.

'No, I never was any good at arithmetic,' she admitted wryly. Suddenly, formality deserted her and she leaned forward and tweaked one of Rebecca's bubbly curls, peeping out from beneath her peaked cap. 'Look, Becky, the truth is that I was in a flaming temper after that row at the dance, and next day I went straight down to the recruiting office and signed the papers. I'm not sorry I did it, because now I'm in a job I love, but I am sorry you and I never made it up. And look what happened – we're in different forces as a result and quite possibly won't meet again till this wretched war is over. I'm really sorry for the awful things I said, so please can we put it behind us and start again?'

Rebecca's whole face changed and became, Cassie thought, once more the face of her best friend. 'Oh, do let's, Cassie,' she said warmly. 'Unfortunately my leave finishes tomorrow so I'll be off at the crack of dawn, but even if we don't see each other again for years we can exchange letters, can't we?' She sighed. 'Sometimes I seem to spend my life writing letters.' She bent her head and examined her well-polished brogues for a moment then looked up, meeting Cassie's eyes directly. 'But look, I might as well make a clean breast of it. I'm seeing quite a lot of Andy. We met up again quite by chance and we've been writing to each other ever since.' She gave a rueful smile. 'Do you mind, Cassie? Only it would look very odd – and most awfully mean – if I stopped writing to him.'

Cassie felt the familiar stab, which she supposed was jealousy, that struck her whenever she thought of Andy and Rebecca together, but she pinned a smile to her lips and answered as cheerfully as she could.

'Mind? Of course not! When Andy and I next see each other I shall apologise to him for the way I behaved and tell him I'm delighted my two best friends get on so well.' She tucked her left hand into the crook of Rosheen's elbow and her right into Rebecca's. 'Well, since we're all headed for the village we might as well go together.'

There wasn't a lot to do in the village, the shops bearing notices in their windows explaining what they didn't have, but the weather was fine and the path by the river inviting, so the three girls set off to walk along it to a little café which Rebecca assured Rosheen would offer them a cup of tea and a bun.

'The lady who runs the café bakes her own cakes, and they're delicious,' Cassie added. 'Mum would say "You'll spoil your supper", but we shan't, of course. And on the way home, Becky, you can tell me what Andy's doing now. He and I haven't been in touch since the row, but if you'll let me know his address I'll apologise for my behaviour by letter. It'll be easier that way, don't you think?'

Rebecca agreed, and the three girls drank their tea and ate their buns in perfect amity. But later, when Rebecca had left Cassie and Rosheen at the Valentines' garden gate – a garden which had once been bright with flowers and now boasted neat rows of peas, beans and carrots – Cassie remembered something. The O'Learys, too, had put their flowerbeds and lawn down to vegetables, and she was just saying 'When I write I shall have to mention that his parents are turning into market gardeners ...' when she clapped her hand to her mouth. 'Oh, damn, I forgot to get Andy's address from Rebecca, and she said she's leaving at crack of dawn tomorrow. Never mind – I'll ask her for it when I write.'

Rosheen gave a little snort, whether of amusement or derision, Cassie did not know. She looked enquiringly at her friend.

'Sorry. I shouldn't have laughed, and no doubt you know your friend better than I do,' Rosheen said, 'but I'd bet my next month's pay that she doesn't send you your Andy's address.'

They had been sauntering towards the house, but at these words Cassie stopped short. 'Not send me the address? But why ever not? After all, I apologised, and anyway, I'm not nailed to the ground. I can pop next door tomorrow … oh!'

Rosheen grinned wickedly. 'And are you prepared to admit to Andy's parents that you don't know his address?'

Despite herself, Cassie laughed. 'Oh, well. I'll let a few weeks elapse and then I'll get my mother to go round to the O'Learys and say I've lost it. But I still don't see why you think Becky won't tell me.'

Rosheen's smile widened. 'Do you have her address? Did you give her yours? Honest to God, if you really want that feller's address you'd better go round this evening and shake it out of her, otherwise the war will be over before you know the name of his station!'

'Hey, Andy! Are you off after lunch? If so we might go into town on the liberty truck and see if we can buy some razor blades. Actually, there are several things which I might get in the big city. Going to come with me?

Andy was in the cookhouse queue for what looked like slabs of some greyish meat swimming in a sea of gravy, but turned at the sound of Colin's voice. The two men had done their stint on single-engined kites and along with a great many other pilots had come to Welford RAF station to learn how to fly Lancaster bombers and Wellingtons, commonly known as Wimpys after J. Wellington Wimpy, the popular Popeye cartoon character. Already Andy was sure that it was better to have a crew with you in the aircraft, all experts in their own field. In some of the big crates you even had a second pilot, in his case Colin Trelawney, so now he grinned at Colin and indicated that his friend should join him in the queue.

'Yes, good idea,' he said. He looked with distaste at the mess of protein – he supposed – which the cook had just slammed on to his tin plate. 'Shall we bother with this, or see if we can get something to eat in Norwich?'

Colin pulled a face, then glared at the fat little Waaf who was sloshing potatoes and carrots about and indicated his friend's plate. 'What *is* that?' he asked suspiciously, and then, when the Waaf shrugged, said that he would stick to potatoes and carrots. 'I'm a vegetarian, you see,' he said untruthfully. The woman stared.

'What's one of them?' she asked, then bridled when Colin and Andy both laughed. 'It's meat ... or mebbe fish ... but they can't make you eat it.'

'Right,' Andy said, and scraped the contents of his plate into the pig bin. He dipped his irons into the cooling water and raised his eyebrows. 'Pudding?'

The corporal at the end of the line shot him a

darkling glance. 'Rice,' he said briefly, 'and marrow jam.'

Andy sighed. The rice pudding was unsweetened, so someone had had the bright idea of adding a spoonful of disgusting jam to each helping. Still, he thought, as he received his portion and made for an empty table, it would keep the wolf from the door until they reached the city.

He had taken his place and was watching, with some amusement, the faces of other diners as they began to eat when Colin joined him and plonked his food down on the table whilst he fished in his pocket and produced a letter. Sitting down and picking up his fork, he passed the envelope to Andy. 'It's that popsy of yours,' he said through a mouthful of mashed potato. 'Does she write every day?' He laughed. 'She doesn't mean to let you forget her, does she?'

Andy jammed the letter into the pocket of his flying jacket. 'I'll read it later,' he began, but when he saw Colin begin to frown he remembered that when one is in constant danger superstitions abound and hastily withdrew the envelope, slit it open and began to read.

Dear Andy,

It was awful arriving home and passing your house, knowing you weren't there. If you could have just got a forty-eight it would have been something, but no such luck. Mum is now working in the NAAFI so she fed me there a couple of times. She is a good cook and manages to make first rate meals despite rationing. I didn't realise they now keep chickens which lay pretty well every day at this time of year, though Mum says not in the winter. I saw your friend Ferdy, and he asked me to go to a village hop. I didn't think you'd mind so I went along with him, but halfway through the evening I realised I was just too tired for dancing and went home.

Don't think I have any other news. Take care, my darling. I think of you all the time. Will telephone Sunday morning as usual.

All my love, Rebecca.

Andy stared hard at the letter; something was missing, though he could not put his finger on exactly what it was. Shrugging, he thrust it back into his pocket and took a mouthful of rice, then pulled a face, pushed back his chair and went over to the pig bin. 'Lucky little porkers. I wonder how many of them turn their snouts up when they smell marrow jam?' he said to Colin, who was also scraping a large plateful of rejected vegetables into the pig bin. 'I reckon we ought to get an extra bacon ration, because I'm sure we must feed a whole flock – or is it a herd? – of pigs on the Welford leftovers.'

Colin grinned. 'Marrow jam flavoured bacon,'

he said thoughtfully. 'The mind boggles, doesn't it? Now let's get a move on or we'll miss the liberty truck.'

They were actually in the truck, heading for Norwich, when Andy realised why Rebecca's letter had seemed odd. He had received one from his mother the previous day in which she had mentioned that Cassie, too, had had some leave at last. She had not elaborated but, subconsciously, he had expected Rebecca to repeat the information. He had not forgotten the row, but if the two girls had been on leave at the same time surely Rebecca should have mentioned the fact? After all, for as long as he could remember the Valentines and the Spencers had been as thick as thieves. What, after all, was one little falling out between such old friends? I suppose I ought to write to Cassie and apologise for all the nasty things I said, he told himself, but knew he probably would not; they were sure to meet again sometime and then they would pick up their friendship just as if the fight had never happened.

Right now, however, both young men were intent on shopping and were very pleased with themselves when they managed to acquire razor blades and a bar of soap each. After that they went to the cinema and saw a showing of *Gone With The Wind* and enjoyed a meal at the cinema restaurant. It was only sausage and chips but it was a good deal better than what was on offer at the cookhouse.

It was not until they were back in their quarters and getting ready for bed that Andy's mind reverted to the two girls. He told himself he was fond of them both but had no intention of getting heavy with either of them. For the time being a long-distance flirtation with Rebecca suited him very well, but it was a pity, after all, that he was not in touch with Cassie too. For a few minutes he tried to imagine the letter he would compose if he *did* write to apologise, but before he had worked out how to begin his eyes had closed and he was asleep.

Once Rosheen and Grandma had grasped the absolute necessity of acquiring a bicycle for the twins they promised to do their best, though Rosheen warned them that it would probably be old and needing attention. Then she outlined her plans for the day.

'Grandma and I thought we'd go for a nice lunch in Lewis's restaurant, then do a bit of shopping and finish with a visit to the picture house to see a film – preferably a comedy – before going back to the Valentine house.' She smiled anxiously at her daughters. 'You're going to be good, aren't you? The Valentines are being awfully kind to put us up.'

The twins smiled as though they had never in their lives been difficult. 'We'll be angels, honest to God we will, Mam,' April said virtuously. 'We'll even help with washing up and making our beds.'

May giggled. 'Bed, you mean,' she pointed out.

'But what about our bicycle, Mam? You did say we could have one.'

Rosheen shook her head chidingly. 'I said if we saw one for sale at a price we could afford, your grandma and I would buy it for you,' she corrected her younger daughter. 'But I don't intend to start searching the city now. We'll get the *Liverpool Echo* and look through the ads this evening after tea. If there's one advertised we can chase it up tomorrow.'

'My birthday!' May squeaked. 'If we find a bicycle on my birthday I can have first go; that would be fair, Mam, wouldn't you say?'

Rosheen hesitated, knowing how April resented any challenge to her authority, but April was nodding, clearly seeing the justice of her twin's remark.

'Right,' Rosheen said decisively. 'We'll grab an *Echo* and follow up any adverts for bicycles; are we agreed?'

Both twins nodded vigorously, as did Mrs Clarke. 'That's a very good idea,' she approved. She smiled at her daughter and smacked her lips. 'Now if Lewis's have got shepherd's pie on the menu that's what I'm having.'

Chapter Fourteen

May opened her eyes when the shaft of sunlight fell across her face. She lay curled up against her twin's back, wondering vaguely why they were sharing a bed. They often did so in the winter, of course, for warmth mainly, but it was not winter. And furthermore she was neither in the Wrights' cottage nor her own little bed at No. 3. A moment's thought supplied the answer: she was in the Valentine house, cuddled up close to her twin.

May sat up cautiously, in order not to wake April, who could get very nasty if she was disturbed early. And yesterday had been pretty tiring, one way and another. They had enjoyed an excellent lunch in Lewis's restaurant – shepherd's pie followed by strawberry jelly. The grown ups had finished up with coffee and the twins had opted for cherryade, giggling when it fizzed up their noses. After that they did a spot of shopping around the city centre before enjoying the promised visit to the picture house, where they had seen *High Gang*, and finishing up with tea in the cinema restaurant.

'I told Mrs Valentine we'd get a bite to eat in the city to save her having to cook for us,' Rosheen had explained. 'And Grandma and I can check the *Echo* as we eat.'

May wriggled under the bedclothes again. No need to hurry, because they were on holiday, or as good as. Unfortunately the *Echo* had not been able to supply a bicycle in its advertisement columns, but you never knew: today's edition might offer a choice of several machines and they would be able to take their pick. There was even a slight chance that, if they were cheap enough, Mam and Grandma might buy the girls a bicycle each. And even if the paper failed to oblige, April had had one of her bright ideas. She said she had noticed postcards stuck in the corners of several of the smaller shops, advertising various things for sale. Before giving up they could check out the cards and follow up any that mentioned a bicycle. And just in case none did, Mam had promised a ride on the ferry or a trip on the overhead railway instead, whichever the twins preferred. Remembering all these treats in store, May decided that the sooner she got up and dressed the sooner her exciting day could begin. She began to tickle her twin's neck.

'Wake up, April,' she whispered. 'Don't you remember where we are? Mrs Valentine said we can have the bacon Mrs Nidd gave her to thank her for looking after us for our breakfast. Oh, April, will you wake up! It's a lovely sunny day and you're wasting it. And s'pose there's a bicycle for sale, which would you rather give up? A ride on the overhead railway or a trip on the ferry to Woodside?'

Mrs Nidd's present was appreciated by every member of the Valentine family as well as by Rosheen and the twins. Mrs Valentine, a notable cook, delighted the girls by telling them to help themselves to her homemade tomato ketchup, and though they had no idea why this invitation set their mother and Cassie off into giggles they very much enjoyed the treat. After breakfast they collected a bucketful of poultry meal and scraps and fed the chickens, chatting to them as they did so and telling them of the delightful day to come, but April had something on her mind and later asked her hostess why she did not boil up potato peelings, pea pods and other such things for the hen, as Mrs Wright did. Mrs Valentine was at the sink washing up the breakfast pots and she turned and smiled at April, her eyes twinkling over spectacles perched on the tip of her nose.

'But I do,' she said. 'Only I do it in Mr Valentine's little woodshed because he doesn't like the smell.'

April snorted. 'I bet Mr Wright doesn't like the smell either,' she said and then, remembering her manners, added: 'But we're going to the city today in search of the bicycle which me and May mean to share. Is there anything you would like us to get you whilst we're there? We're going to Paddy's market to look for a new summer frock for me to wear, because mine's too tight under the arms.'

'What a nice child you are,' Mrs Valentine said, smiling. 'Tell your mother that I'm quite handy with my needle – I even have an old treadle sewing machine – so if you find something that just needs a small alteration I'd be happy to do it for you.'

April flushed with pleasure. 'That would be lovely,' she said eagerly. 'Mam used to make us dress alike, bein' twins an' all you know, so we're glad of anything different now. But is there something you'd like us to pick up for you, Mrs Valentine?'

'I could do with some toothpaste,' her hostess said thoughtfully. 'And I don't s'pose you'll see any bath salts but a packet of those would be a real treat. Only I know you're going to be pretty busy, so don't search specially for my stuff. After all, when I'm not working in the NAAFI or fire watching I can always manage a quick trip into Liverpool, so just you enjoy your day, my dear, and let's hope you come home this evening with a nice new bicycle.'

When breakfast was over Rosheen insisted that Cassie should come into the city with them. 'You may not want to take the ferry to Woodside or buy a ticket for the overhead railway, but I'm sure you'd like a good snoop round all the shops,' she said. 'It's your leave as well as mine, don't forget.'

Cassie agreed that this was so but pointed out that she had never met Mrs Clarke, who might object to finding their family party increased by someone who was not even a relative.

Rosheen shook her head. 'Mam's spending the day doing some baking for Uncle George. And we're goin' to go to the Scottie to examine the postcards in the windows of the small shops first, see if we can find a bike for sale. Then we'll go to Paddy's market to buy cotton frocks for the girls, and I know you've never been to Paddy's market, so that will be a new experience for you.'

'Well, if you're sure …' Cassie began and was promptly included in the day's doings. 'If Paddy's market is as good as you say I might pick up a dance frock,' she said dreamily as they got ready. 'Wouldn't it be lovely to arrive at one of the village hops in a proper dress instead of uniform!'

Rosheen thought, privately, that a serving member of the forces would not be allowed to wear civilian dress to a village hop, but did not say so. Instead, as soon as the small party reached Liverpool she and Cassie organised a cycle hunt and sooner than Rosheen believed possible they found a small flower shop with the longed-for postcard in the window. *BICYCLE FOR SALE*, it said in wobbly capitals. *GOOD CONDITION. APPLY WITHIN.* The four females stared at one another, almost unable to believe their luck.

'Good condition,' April breathed. She turned to her mother. 'Why haven't they given a price? It probably costs pounds and pounds, almost as much as a new one.'

May stared at her twin. 'If they see we're just a couple of kids mebbe they'll charge less; that's why there's no price on the card, stupid.'

April whirled round, her fists shooting out in a workmanlike manner, but then she caught Cassie's eye and lowered her hand. 'There's only one way to find out ...' she began, but May was already in the shop and waiting eagerly at the counter for a customer who was buying red roses to depart, for it was plain that an interruption in the middle of a sale would not help their cause. As soon as the young man had paid for his roses, however, Rosheen gestured to the children to say nothing and approached the counter herself.

'There's a postcard in your window ...' she began, and the middle-aged woman in the floral overall glanced towards the card in the window and tutted.

'The bicycle, you mean?' she said. 'It ain't here yet – I'm sellin' it for a friend of mine and she can't bring it round till tomorrer mornin' first thing. There's bin one or two folks askin' about it already, so I've told 'em all to come back tomorrer and it'll be first come, first served.' She smiled kindly at the twins' crestfallen expressions. 'Was the bicycle for you, young ladies?'.

The twins nodded dumbly, unable to speak for disappointment, but Cassie spoke for them. 'Look, if we come in again tomorrow, and no one else has got here before us, can we buy it? We'll have the money all ready by then.'

The woman smiled. 'Well, of course you can, queen. First come, first served, as I said.'

Rosheen looked at her friend with gratitude as they left the shop and turned their footsteps towards Paddy's market. 'When you said we'd have the money ready tomorrow, did you mean . . .'

'Yes, of course I'll lend you anything you need,' Cassie said briskly. 'You'll be able to pay me back in no time once we've re-mustered.'

'Oh, I will,' Rosheen agreed happily, all doubt vanishing from her face. 'Girls, I've a feeling we shall get that bicycle.'

April, however, was uneasy. 'S'pose we arrive at the shop just after someone else buys it,' she whispered to her twin as they browsed amongst the stalls. 'S'pose someone comes early, gets the bike and cycles off?'

May clucked impatiently. 'The shop opens at nine so I reckon if we arrive at ten to nine and wait outside until the lady unlocks the door the bicycle's ours, am I right? The shop lady was awful keen to sell it so that she could give her friend the money, wasn't she?

Only how are we to make sure we get there early? The thing is we have quite a long journey what with buses, trains and trams, so anyone who lives in the city will win hands down. You don't s'pose we could persuade Grandma to go to the shop for us?'

'It's a thought,' April said, then shook her head. 'But Grandma doesn't know the shop and she'd probably try and haggle the price down and lose it. I've had a better idea – why don't we persuade Mam to let us spend just this one night on the couch in No. 3's kitchen? It might not be very comfortable but at least we could be outside the flower shop when the owner comes to unlock. If we work on Mam and make all the usual promises to be good as gold why should she object? It's not as though it's winter or wet and rainy. In fact, May, you could ask for a night on our own in Liverpool as a birthday present. Mam's a real softy over birthdays and she knows how badly we want that bicycle.'

At that point Rosheen looked over her shoulder and smiled at the two girls behind her. 'Aren't we lucky with our weather?' she said gaily. 'I think we should buy some buns or a sandwich or something from the nearest bakery and take it to St John's Gardens. It's such a lovely warm day that I'm sure the cherry trees will be in blossom. After that we'll get a copy of the *Echo* and see if there are any more bicycles for sale in the adverts column, just in case this one goes. How does that suit you?'

The girls said it suited them fine and worked on their mother all afternoon, trying to persuade her to let them stay in Liverpool just for the one night so that they might be outside the flower shop as soon as it opened.

Rosheen, however, was adamant. 'I didn't bring you up from the country in order to risk your lives in the city centre,' she said firmly, and then, when April opened her mouth to object, 'No, love, don't try to persuade me because my mind is made up. We'll catch the earliest train we can manage tomorrow and go straight to the flower shop. Do you agree?'

April, always the spokesperson, nodded solemnly. 'Oh all right, Mam. Let's hope there's another machine advertised in the *Echo*, then.' She looked at her sister, caught May's eye and winked, then pretended an interest in a window display of ladies' corsetry and drew her back behind the others, pulling her close so that she could whisper in her ear. 'Mam will be sorry when we don't get on the train this evening,' she hissed. 'But I've got a feeling about this bicycle; if we don't get it we'll never find another one. We'll wait until we're at the station and then we'll disappear. I'd sleep on the platform all night if it meant we could get that bike.'

May was doubtful. 'We'll be in awful trouble,' she said uneasily. 'Mam will never trust us again, because we did say we'd be good.' She looked straight at April. 'I'm not sure any bicycle is worth all the trouble we'll be in.'

April cast her eyes up to the sky. 'What a stupid girl you are! Mam's forgiven us for every single bad thing we've done so why should running away just for one night be any different? Tell you what: as soon as the last train to the Valentines' village has gone we'll go round to number three, fish the key out from under the mat and let ourselves in. I bet the housekeeping money is still in that teapot on the mantel, so we'll be able to pay the shop lady.' She scowled at her sister. 'Don't you see, May? If we don't get this bicycle we shan't have another chance.'

May sighed. April was so sure she was right, always certain of getting her own way, and when it was something she particularly wanted no one, least of all May, could change her mind. She was like a hound on the scent, head down, eyes fixed, and until she got whatever it was she wanted, talking to her was useless. She would follow the trail as a hound would, until she reached the end, and it was just bad luck for anyone who got in her way.

But running away, after Mam and her friend Cassie had gone to such lengths to give them a good time! May wished she had the courage to defy April and make sure she got on that train, but she knew she would not. April was the leader, the one who took decisions, and May knew that she herself was a follower. But to follow April into the sort of defiance which her sister had planned was really asking more than she had ever done before.

As they ran toothpaste and bath salts to earth, bought two quite nice cotton frocks at Paddy's market, and had tea and sticky buns in a little café on Scotland Road, May berated herself for not having the courage to reveal her sister's plan. When it all came out, which it would, they would both be in the most awful trouble. Everyone would be disgusted by their behaviour. In fact, now she thought about it, even the Wrights would say they had behaved shabbily. And what if the key were not under the mat, or the money in the teapot? She put these questions to her sister as they lagged behind the adults, and rather to her surprise April listened.

'I thought of that too, and I've had an even better idea,' she said. 'Remember that big air raid shelter opposite the entrance to King Edward Court? Grandma said it's got bunks and food and all sorts in it. We can spend the night there, and in the morning we can go to the shop and hold on to the bicycle until Mam and her friend come with the money.'

For the first time since April had suggested her plan, May smiled. 'Perhaps there'll be a raid and then we'll be doing the right thing,' she said. 'I do hope there's a raid!'

'Phew, what a day,' Cassie said as they boarded the train and sank into a couple of empty seats. 'What do you mean to do if the bicycle's gone by the time we reach the flower shop tomorrow morning? Your girls will be furious and probably blame me for living out of town, but I don't see what we can do apart from hope for the best.' She half stood up to peer through the window. 'Where are the little monkeys, anyway? I thought they were with us ... well, they were when we stopped for a cup of tea and a bun. Goodness, don't say we've lost them!'

Rosheen, too, got to her feet and pressed her face against the window. The platform was crowded but there was no sign of the twins. Still, the train was not due to leave for another few minutes, which ought to give April and May time to reach the barrier, have their tickets punched and get on board. She was saying as much to Cassie when she suddenly stopped short, a hand flying to her mouth.

'That's done it!' she exclaimed. 'I've got their tickets! They can be so woolly-headed that I thought I'd best hang on to their returns; I never thought we might get separated. Oh, damn, damn, damn, whatever shall we do now?'

Cassie sighed. 'We'd best get off the train before it starts,' she said resignedly. 'I expect they're up by the barrier arguing with the guard right now. It's a nuisance, because if we miss this train it's an hour and a quarter before the next one. Still, that's one of the penalties of having children, I suppose. Oh, but I've thought of something else; what if they're already on the train? I know they don't have their tickets but they strike me as a very ingenious couple, and I shouldn't be at all surprised if they've wheedled their way past the guard. D'you think we should split up? I could go to the barrier and explain to the official whilst you search the ... oh, damn!'

The train had begun to move, and out of the window both girls saw the guard warning folk to stand clear as he slammed the last door.

'Too late,' Cassie said resignedly, sitting down once more. They had the carriage to themselves apart from a couple of women with large shopping baskets and a small man with a little grey moustache who twitched every time he caught their eyes. 'Now what can we do about the twins? It isn't a corridor train so we can't search it now it's moving. Tell you what though, when we get off we'll explain to the station master that we got separated from the children and ask him to telephone Central Station. I'm sure the authorities will agree to send them after us when they know we've got their tickets. It's the only solution I can think of.'

Rosheen agreed that this was a good idea, but after a few minutes she turned a worried face to her friend.

'I've just had a thought,' she said slowly. 'The girls wanted to spend the night in the city ...'

Cassie stared at her, her eyes rounding with astonishment. 'Rosheen! You can't mean you think

266

that they got left behind on purpose! Where would they spend the night? D'you mean you think they'd go out to Bootle and sleep on your uncle's sofa just in order to be at the flower shop early?' She shook her head, beginning to smile. 'No children of their age could think up a plan like that! And both Mother and Father have been saying how good the girls have been and how polite and helpful.'

Rosheen chuckled grimly. 'They're always on their best behaviour when they want to impress,' she assured her friend. 'But I won't judge them until we've heard their story. Knowing April, if they did get left behind deliberately, she'll have concocted some tale or other to account for their absence from the station. But I know what will have happened: they'll have gone to King Edward Court. Well, all I can say is they're in for a big surprise.'

When the knock came on the door Mrs Clarke was sitting comfortably in an old basket chair drinking a lovely hot cup of tea and planning to have a boiled egg and two rounds of bread and marge before seeking her bed. She had had a good day with her brother George, and had almost enjoyed coming home to find her lodgers already in bed. Now she heaved herself to her feet, retaining her grip on the enamel mug of tea, crossed the kitchen and opened the front door. Evening was well advanced and because she expected her visitor to be an adult she looked straight out at head height and thought for a moment that someone was playing a trick on her. Then a small and reedy voice reached her ears.

'Grandma! Grandma, what are you doin' here? We thought you was livin' with Uncle George. It's us, April and May. Oh, Grandma, we've been so worried! We thought the house was empty and then we see'd a chink of light under the door and thought it was burglars, but we had nowhere else to go because we lost our mam and her friend Cassie when they was too busy chattin' to notice we'd took a wrong turn, and when we reached the station we couldn't find our tickets 'cos Mam must've kept them. Oh, can we come in? We's been so upset and it's not our fault. Oh, Grandma, we's so unhappy. Can we come in?'

Without waiting for a reply both children slipped past her and entered the warm kitchen, flinging them-selves on to two of the elderly chairs and watching their grandmother apprehensively. Even April could tell that she wasn't at all pleased to see them.

'What the devil have you been up to now, the pair of you?' Mrs Clarke said crossly. 'And don't you give me no sob story 'cos you know I shan't believe it. Your mother must be half mad with worry.'

April rubbed her eyes, smearing dirt all over her tear-stained face. 'No she ain't. We got the guard to send a message to the Valentines' station, saying we'd missed the train and reminding Mam she'd kept our tickets,' she said. 'We meant to go out to Bootle and get you to buy us a couple more tickets so we could get the next train but it were too far for our little legs and—'

Mrs Clarke snorted. 'A likely story,' she said contemptuously. 'I've known you since you were a couple of red-faced babies howling for your bottles so you can't fool me easy. Why did you fancy staying here all night?'

The twins stared at her in wide-eyed astonishment. April began to speak but was promptly told to hold her tongue.

'I know you're up to something, even if I don't know what,' Mrs Clarke interrupted her. 'And come to think of it, I don't want to know. You must be well aware that I can't turn you out but I don't intend to lose any sleep over your carryings on. You can kip down on the old sofa in the parlour. What time is the first train back to the Valentines' village?'

April looked thunderstruck and Mrs Clarke reflected, with some satisfaction, that it had never occurred to her granddaughter that she might be thwarted. Then April began to sob, giving little hiccups and rubbing her eyes once more. 'If you send us back before we've done our shopping you'll be the cruellest woman in the world,' she wailed. 'We'll run away from you as well as from Mam because there's this bicycle ...'

The story of the bicycle caused Mrs Clarke to

pretend to busy herself getting some biscuits out of the pantry so the twins didn't see her twitching lip. Trust those little devils to get their own way! But May, who had been silently listening to the flood of words from her sister, suddenly abandoned her chair and flung herself on to her grandmother's lap.

'I'm sorry, I'm sorry, I knew it were a naughty thing to do,' she cried, burying her hot tear-wet cheek against Mrs Clarke's neck. 'Only you see we want a bicycle desperate bad ... oh, Grandma, we're so sorry!'

'And so you should be,' Mrs Clarke said, but May's tears had softened her, for she knew the smaller twin had probably argued against the deception. She jerked her thumb at the parlour door. 'It's time you were in bed, or at least curled up on the old sofa. And don't you let me hear a squeak out of either of you until it's time for breakfast. There's a blanket in the cupboard under the stairs; you can cover yourselves with that. And if Moaning Minnie sounds off get in the air raid shelter pronto. Understood?'

Once the twins had settled Mrs Clarke went into the parlour and gave each child a goodnight kiss. May was her usual loving self, but April was clearly grateful to find herself forgiven.

'I really am sorry, Grandma,' she muttered, putting her arms round the older woman's neck in a rare gesture of affection. 'Once we've got the bicycle we'll be good for ever and ever, amen.'

Despite herself, Mrs Clarke chuckled. 'Until the next time,' she said wryly. 'And don't forget, if you hear Moaning Minnie start to wail, grab your blankets and go straight to the big air raid shelter. But I shouldn't think there'll be a raid tonight; the Luftwaffe have been targeting poor old Barrow, though they overfly Liverpool on their way.'

May was already asleep, but April nodded dreamily. 'Shan't forget, Grandma,' she said. 'Goodness, what plane makes all that much noise?'

Mrs Clarke looked uneasy. 'I dunno, but don't you worry your head about it. And now I'm off to my bed, because I'm sure today has lasted forty hours instead of the usual number.'

The raid started before Mrs Clarke had been in bed twenty minutes and the twins shot up on the sofa simultaneously, faces white and eyes dilated.

'What was that bang?' May squeaked. Safely tucked away in the green hills of Wales she had heard the thrum of the engines overhead but not the shriek of the dive bombers or the *crrrump* as the bombs fell.

'Shelter,' April shouted. 'Come on, May, you heard what Grandma said. We've got to get to that shelter.'

Grandma's last act before she left them earlier had been to pull back the blackout curtains, and now through the window it looked as though the entire city was on fire. Flames shot into the sky from the dock area and noise battered their ear drums. To add to the twins' confusion, there were shrieks and shouts from within the house as the Burrell family headed for safety, but before they could investigate Mrs Clarke was beside the twins and urging them to hurry.

'The big shelter is built of strong concrete and it's deep,' she said. 'Come along, you two, this is no night to be dillydallying.'

It was not far from the court to the shelter but even in the couple of minutes it took the twins and their grandmother to reach safety, time seemed to stand still or last for ever. April, looking fearfully up, realised she could see the underbellies of the huge aircraft, see the doors open to let fall their fearsome cargo on the poor little houses and shops below. She opened her mouth to inform her grandmother of this interesting fact and found herself hustled down a number of concrete steps out of the worst of the noise and lights.

'Shut up and grab your sister,' Mrs Clarke shouted, seeing that May was actually trying to hang back in order to watch the terrifying attack. 'The sooner we're under ground, the better. Come *along*, May Clarke, or I'll give you a clack across the ear that you won't forget in a hurry. Oh, trust the pair of you to turn up during the worst raid of the perishin' war so far!'

*

Rosheen was awoken by the heavy drone of aircraft overhead and realised at once that the Luftwaffe were heading for Liverpool. She sat up in her borrowed bed and leaned over to poke Cassie in the back. 'Wake up,' she said urgently. 'The message from the twins said they were going to find their grandmother, which might mean anything; as far as they knew she would have been in Bootle, but what if they intended to go to the court after all? Oh, I hope to goodness they've found that big air raid shelter on the Scottie, because judging from the noise, this is a really heavy raid. I wish I knew for certain where they were!'

Cassie groaned and sat up. 'Judging from what I've seen of them, those twins always fall on their feet,' she remarked. 'But your mother will take good care of them, I'm sure.'

Rosheen nodded, trying to stay calm. 'No need to panic, but I think you and I should either get into the nearest shelter or crawl into that Morrison thing you say you keep under the stairs. I'm sure we ought to take some action, anyway.'

Cassie, slinging her dressing gown round her shoulders, was already on her way out of the room. 'You're right. Let's get moving. Mum and Dad will be fire watching, or chivvying folk into the shelters, so there's just us two.'

Another enormous explosion occurred just as they were about to cross the road, and both girls were knocked over by the force of the blast. Rosheen scrambled to her feet first and seized her friend's hands, hauling her bodily upright. 'Are you hurt?' she asked breathlessly. 'No, don't answer that; we'll get into the shelter first. It's only at the end of the road, we can reach it in half a minute. Can you run? Only the Luftwaffe seem to be targeting the Wirral, whether on purpose or by accident! The kids are probably safer down by the docks than they would have been here. Are you ready? Then run for it, kiddo!'

April looked around her from the relative safety of the little bunk into which she and May were tucked, on a rather small wooden shelf. The place was crammed and there were several children, mostly of her own age or younger. Even as she stared at them, however, she remembered her mother saying that some parents had insisted on bringing their children home, claiming they had hated being evacuated. What strange children they must be, to prefer this to the beautiful country, she thought. And how did they ever sleep? How could they stand the continual bombardment of noise, the way the entire shelter would suddenly light up as the blast blew the curtain aside and allowed the brilliant glow to illumine every corner before the shelter warden twitched it impatiently back into its former position.

April turned round to speak to her twin and

274

frowned. May was asleep again – lucky old May – and would not be grateful to be brought back, even for a moment, to this horrible place. It smelled of damp concrete, cat pee, rubber boots and ... yes, cheesy feet, as well as something she could not identify, a horrible smell that she supposed must have come from the aircraft overhead. She sighed, and addressed her grandmother. 'Grandma, do we have to stay here much longer? I'm getting cramp in my bum because this shelf is so narrow. I'm not like May; she could sleep on a clothes line.'

Mrs Clarke shook her head. 'No one will leave here until the all clear sounds, so don't you think you can sneak off if I close my eyes for a moment, because the warden isn't just there for decoration, you know, he's there to see that everyone – and that means you too, April – toes the line. Just remember that you wouldn't be here at all, but on the Wirral with your mam and her friend and safe as houses, no doubt, if you hadn't missed that train on purpose.'

'It wasn't our fault ...' April began indignantly, but her voice faded into silence as she met her grandmother's accusing eyes. 'Oh, all right, I s'pose it was our fault in a way, but can I get off my shelf please? There's somethin' goin' on at the far end – a lady tellin' stories and handin' round toffees. Can I go up there please, Grandma?'

Mrs Clarke followed April's gaze and realised that the child was right. Some civic-minded person had opened a large story book and was reading to a group of children, though how they could concentrate on the tale when their ears must be filled with the noise of the raid she could not imagine. Still, if it stopped April from pestering her it had to be a good thing, so instead of insisting that the girl made the best of her uncomfortable perch she nodded with assumed reluctance and warned her not to wake her sister. At least if April joined the other children she herself need not scruple to nod off for a few minutes. Everyone in the shelter would combine to keep the child safe under ground.

April had never been shy, but she would have felt happier approaching a group of children all of whom knew each other, she assumed, had May been able to accompany her. Indeed, for a moment she toyed with the idea of waiting until Grandma closed her eyes and then giving May a nudge, but dismissed it. With her luck May would wake with a start, perhaps even a shout, and Grandma would guess at once that she, April, had deliberately ignored her wishes. So she slid off her uncomfortable little shelf and joined the group around the reader, and in a very few minutes had introduced herself and settled comfortably on a blanket spread out on the floor, informing the assembled children that she was April Clarke, that her sister, May, was asleep on a bunk at the other end of the shelter and that she was fed up with being shut away down here.

'We're staying with our grandma in King Edward Court,' she confided in the little girl who sat next to her. 'We used to live there ourselves, till we were vacuated. Now we live in a cottage on the Nidds' farm. We feed the poultry and sometimes carry out the grub for the pigs, and Mr Wright is goin' to teach us to milk a cow. D'you like animals?'

The little girl, who had said her name was Kate – she could not have been more than six or seven – smiled shyly and admitted that she loved animals. She had been cuddling what April had assumed to be a teddy bear, half covered in a piece of old blanket, but now she lifted the blanket to reveal a very large black cat whose yellow eyes stared balefully up at April.

'His name is Scat,' her new friend informed her. 'My mam called him that because she says when he was a kitten I called him Katescat. But I have to keep him what the warden calls under control, because some people say it ain't right to bring animals into the shelters in case they does a wee-wee on the floor.'

April chuckled. 'I wish I had a cat,' she said wistfully. 'A cat would be company and wouldn't take up much room. Besides, Mrs Wright says cats are clean and even when they are small kittens they know better than to do a dirty in the house.' She eyed her companion curiously. 'Where d'you live?'

The small girl began to say that she and her mother – as well as Scat the cat – lived in a flat above a greengrocer's on Scotland Road when there was a loud bang so close at hand that April felt the reverberation through every bone in her body. Kate cried out and April was just about to try to comfort her when the younger girl jumped to her feet.

'Scat's gone!' she shrieked. 'He doesn't like the bangs and that one was so big . . . he's scratched all down my arm 'cos he was in such a hurry to gerraway.'

April was on her feet in an instant. 'Where will he go?' she shouted. 'Don't worry, Kate, I'll find him for you.' And with that she pushed passed the heavy curtain and ran up the steps so fast that the warden, lumbering after her, had no chance of foiling her escape.

Once in the open, a quick glance round by the light of the fires now burning briskly from bombed buildings revealed Scat the cat at once. He was legging it as fast as he could towards the courts and April realised that pursuit was useless. She would never catch up with him in the maze of little streets, and even if she did the creature would almost certainly resist arrest. She had turned to go back to the shelter, meaning to apologise nicely to the warden and explain that she had been hoping to find her friend's cat, when there was another tremendous explosion and something hit her in the chest, taking her breath away for several paralysing moments. She found she was lying on something very hard, and fog, greasy, foul-smelling and thick, obscured her view of anything but the . . . paving stones? Yes, they were paving stones.

For a moment she simply lay there, terror nailing her to the spot. Am I dead, she asked herself? Where's everyone gone? Oh, I'm so frightened. But the bombing must have stopped – I can't hear a thing, not even voices. How odd! Then she touched her ear and felt something wet and slippery. It must be blood, she thought. Insensibly this gave her hope, and courage too. She remembered, now, stories she had heard of people temporarily deafened by blast. It had clearly happened to her, though where the fog had come from, or whether it was a consequence of the explosion, she could not have said.

Her exploring fingers found a cut, and when it began to sting as she tried to gauge its length, that cheered her, too. It was after all, only a cut. Trembling in every limb, she began to scramble to her feet, meaning to find the steps so that she could return to Grandma and May, but as she stood up she realised that the fog only reached as high as her waist and was not a fog at all, but brick and stone dust from the ruined buildings around her. As she stared round a lamppost loomed out of the dust and she grabbed it, grateful to have something to hold even though it had not cast a light since the war had started. But it was solid and ordinary and she remembered now that it had stood quite near the stairs down which she would have to go to find Grandma and May.

She took a couple of tottering steps, letting go of the lamppost with reluctance, then blinked, puzzled. Where the stairs should have been there were huge blocks of masonry, and in the light from the sky overhead, which was gradually getting stronger, she could see nothing but destruction. The school had gone, the little greengrocer's, the confectionery shop where, in happier days, the twins had bought sweeties. April frowned; she simply could not understand what had happened. The shelter was safety, everyone had kept telling her that. If you went to a shelter and stayed below ground you might find it uncomfortable, boring, perhaps even frightening, but you would be safe. That meant that somewhere beneath the pile of rubble May, Grandma, and probably even the warden would be waiting for someone to come along and clear the steps. But why did they not cry out? Or had she simply not heard them, still being deaf from the blast? She supposed that must be the answer, but who was to move the fallen buildings in order to get at the shelter's many inhabitants? For the first time in her life, April longed for someone – anyone – to tell her what to do.

When, presently, someone grabbed her arm she was so frightened she gave a little shriek, and it was as though the shriek had cleared her ears for she could suddenly hear again, albeit through a sort of muffling curtain. It was an ARP warden and she turned towards him, relief flooding over her. A grown up – someone who knew what she should do! But for some reason he was cross with her, scolding her for being out on the streets before the all clear had gone.

He spoke normally, she supposed, but she could not make out the words and this seemed to annoy him for he gave her a shake. 'Where's your mam?' he bawled, red-faced. 'You ought to be in the shelter, not walkin' the streets when there may be enemy planes gettin' rid of their bombs before flyin' off home, the bastards.'

Her hearing still seemed patchy but for some reason these words came clear and strong; perhaps it was indignation at his brusque tone, but whatever the explanation she had managed to recognise both what he said and the note of accusation in his voice.

'Well? Where's your mam? Or was you with your grandma or an aunt or some such? All I know is you're a kid what ought to be in an adult's charge, not wanderin' the streets. So where is they?'

April opened her mouth to reply and suddenly it was all too much. She gulped on a sob. 'They's down there,' she said, jerking a thumb at the pile of rubble which had so recently been an air raid shelter. An air raid shelter, furthermore, full of lively chattering humanity, reading stories, having singsongs, passing flasks of hot tea to anyone who fancied a cup.

The man stared at her. 'And you're expectin' me to believe that that was a shelter and you got out of it with no more than one little cut above your ear and your clothes half tore off your back? You can tell that to the marines.' He laughed coarsely. 'I'm new in this district but I'm too old to believe in fairy stories. No one's comin' out of that little lot alive, and since you ain't thin enough to get between those lumps of masonry, wherever you come from it weren't there. You're just tellin' bald-faced lies.'

The unfairness of this remark made April stare at him disbelievingly. Did he honestly think she would pretend to have come out of a bombed building? He must be mad as a hatter. She looked around her and saw devastation on every side. The warden still had hold of her shoulder but now she released herself from his grip and stared up into his fat, unfriendly face.

'I came out before the explosion. I was tryin' to catch my friend's cat,' she said quietly. 'And if you don't get proper wardens to help me immediately I shall tell everyone you're a murderer, because my grandma and my sister – and the air raid warden – were all in the shelter when I left and if you're right ...' here her voice began to wobble but she fought for self-control, 'if you're right, and they're still all down there, every moment you waste ...'

Her first words had wiped the smirk clean off his face and when he next spoke he did so remorsefully.

'Sorry, chuck, sorry; I ought to have realised ... Come wi' me. I'll fetch the fellers what have the heavy liftin' equipment and we'll soon have them out. And I'm sorry for what I said. Your grandma's under there, you say, and your sister? Well, you come along wi' me and we'll have that rubble moved in a trice.'

But April, freed from his grasp, sat down on a large lump of masonry and shook her head. 'No!' she said. 'I'm not leavin' here until my sister and my grandma are safe. You said no one could make it out of there alive; well, you're wrong, I know you're wrong, but I'm goin' to make absolutely certain that they're safe before I leave this spot.'

'If you go round tellin' people wharr I said ...' the man began, and then, looking at the small figure perched on the rubble before him, he seemed to change his mind. 'I'm rare sorry, queen,' he said. 'I shouldn't have said none of them things. But earlier in the night my street took a pastin' and I reckon it threw me off track more'n a trifle. If you come wi' me to the warden's post they'll give you a couple of butties and a hot drink while everyone I can fetch to help will start diggin', I promise you.'

Chapter Fifteen

May awoke to total blackness. She tried to move but something was holding her down. She tried to speak, but her voice seemed to get lost in the echoing darkness and all that emerged from her lips was the tiniest of squeaks. Trying to move even a tiddy bit was such an effort that, having made it, she decided not to bother again until she had regained more strength. One of her hands was free from the iron grip of whatever was holding her down, though, and she moved that hand cautiously because the rest of her had made it plain that she was to stay exactly where she was on pain of ... well, of pain. Her head was resting most uncomfortably on a pile of what felt like bricks or cement blocks and she could not feel April anywhere near her, nor Grandma for that matter. She moved her head and immediately emitted a tiny whimper because something rough and large had scratched her cheek. She had decided that this grip on her body was one of April's practical jokes and thought about begging April either to stop or to fetch Grandma, but presently she must have slept again.

Later, though she had no means of telling how much time had passed, her memory of the night's events began to come back and for a moment sheer terror grabbed her. She remembered the shelter, the narrow little shelf upon which she had been trying to sleep, and her twin rushing off towards the exit, apparently chasing somebody's cat. Then there had been an explosion louder and more frightening than any of the bangs and crashes which had preceded it. She had flown off the little shelf like a bird and landed in a burst of stars, pain and darkness. It was useless trying to remember what had happened after that. Oh, but she was cold! Away from this terrible place, this place which was supposed to keep children safe, she thought that the sun had come up and life was continuing. Now that she strained her ears she could hear sounds. People speaking, advising one another, occasionally even laughing, someone calling out to anyone 'down there' – down where? – that rescue was on its way, that they must not despair. As the sun came up more people with something called 'lifting equipment' would be arriving, she heard, yet still she lay in darkness. Where was April? April was the leader, the strong one. She'll rescue me, take me back to Cragside Cottage, May thought. We'll never run away again. If I could just call out, let them know I'm here … but she could not. When she opened her mouth she was aware of the gritty taste of brick dust, and later the foul smell which she had noticed when they first entered the air raid shelter became more pronounced. She heard someone say 'bodies' and tried to call out, then remembered an old trick that she and April had sometimes used. Deep in their minds, she thought, there had always been a link between herself and her sister. Now was the time to use it. She lay very still, summoning up all her power of thought to channel it into a message which her twin would understand.

April, where are we? she thought desperately. *I think the air raid shelter and the school above have fallen in. You are lying on my chest, holding me down. Can you gerroff, please?*

April sat on the lump of masonry in an old jersey which belonged to one of the ladies in the WVS, with a mug of hot tea held between her filthy, trembling hands. She had been here for eight hours and many were the people who had tried to insist that she must leave, have a hot bath, find some clothing more suitable to her age and size than the WVS jersey. But every time the persuader thought she had been successful and held out a hand to accompany the child to the nearest assembly point, April would hesitate and then shake her head.

'You don't believe, any of you, that there's anyone left alive down there,' she said, almost apologetically, 'but I know you're wrong. While I stay here I can tell May what's happening, tell her not to give up. She's weak, my sister May, but I can give her strength. While I'm here she knows there's two of us fighting to get her out. If I go she'll give up, I know she will.'

The woman had smiled and sighed. 'But you need to get some rest …' she had begun. 'And how will your sister know you've left, especially if you only do so for a couple of hours?'

April had looked at her as though she was an imbecile. 'We're *twins*,' she said, as though everyone knew that that explained everything. 'I don't know how it works, but I do know that she's alive and knows I'm here, near at hand, near enough to pass on any messages she might have for the diggin' men. I tell you, I know what May's thinkin' and feelin', and I know that while I'm here she won't give up. Can't you understand that?'

The would-be rescuer was old and plump, her face creased now with worry. 'But, my dear child, you'll make yourself ill and that won't help your sister,' she said at length. A sudden thought struck her. 'If you can pass her some sort of message, surely you could tell her that you were leaving her just for a couple of hours in order to get some sleep? My dear, you *need* rest …'

'So does May,' April said rather grimly. 'Oh, so does poor old May!'

*

287

The next time May woke up it was still to total darkness but also to the sound of voices; real voices, not the tiny thread-like sound, small as the buzzing of a weak mosquito, which came to her from her twin. Someone was stirring and crying out, the cry ending in a muffled groan. May opened her eyes, which she had been keeping firmly closed, and for the first time looked around her. April was still near, she could sense that much, but though she strained her eyes into the dark, at first she could see nothing. Then she thought she saw a line of lighter grey; if she moved her head a little she became certain of it. It was just a crack of light, but it gave her hope, and she thought urgently into her twin's receptive mind.

April, there's a crack! I can see grey. It's not proper light but it's something. She hesitated for a moment, but then decided she might as well ask the question which hovered in her head. *Will it be long now? Before they rescue us, I mean. You say I mustn't give in, but I can't help myself. I've never liked the dark … oh, April, will it be long? Has Mam come yet? Does she know I'm under here? And where is Grandma?*

There was a pause, during which May heard an odd sort of dripping noise and then another groan, but when April contacted her again her thoughts were cheerful.

No, it won't be long now, and don't worry about Grandma. She's there with you, and someone called Katie. They're trying to get everyone out, so they have to be very careful. Mam's coming as fast as she can. And now you rest, May Clarke, and get strong, or you aren't the girl I think you are. Just you hang on in there, May. I've told everyone how brave you are so don't go letting me down ...

But the rest of April's homily was lost; May turned her head into her cruelly uncomfortable concrete pillow and let sleep – or something very like it – claim her.

Rosheen and Cassie spent a terrible night in the dank chill of the shelter, accompanied by an elderly couple who lived a little further up Knowsley Avenue. Rosheen was frantic with worry for the twins, knowing how they would fret over being confined in a shelter – and she dared not let herself imagine that they were *not* so confined – and when the raid seemed to have passed the Wirral and the reverberating crunch of falling bombs came less frequently, she announced that danger or no danger she would simply have to go and look for them.

'They'll be waiting for me,' she said tearfully. 'I've got to get to them, come hell or high water ...'

She had jumped to her feet, but Cassie put out a restraining hand. 'There'll be no public transport running until they sort themselves out, and even then it will be in chaos,' she said sensibly. 'Look, Rosheen, if the children and their grandmother managed to get to a shelter they'll probably be back in the court by now, making breakfast and worrying about you. As soon as the buses start running we'll catch one to the city centre, but until then you'll have to possess your soul in patience.' She had smiled lovingly into Rosheen's pink and worried face. 'Look, sweetie, the Luftwaffe gave the city a good pasting at Christmas and I was worried sick for Mum and Dad because I was miles away and unable to check the lists. But everyone was fine, and even when you get to Liverpool there won't be much you can do, so let's go home and you can help me to prepare some breakfast for when my parents get back. They'll have had a rough night, and though they're usually provided with cups of tea, porridge is a lot more filling and comforting somehow.' They had climbed out of the shelter as she spoke, and now started walking quickly along Knowsley Avenue. 'Rosheen, do you understand what I'm saying? You can't do anything until we can catch a bus into the city. I'm sure the railway won't be running – I heard one of the wardens say Lime Street Station had been hit.'

Rosheen's eyes widened with horror. 'King Edward Court isn't all that far from Lime Street,' she quavered. 'If only my mother managed to get them into a shelter! Oh, Cassie, if they're safe I'll never grumble at their wild ways again!' She turned to her companion as they entered the house. 'It's a lot to ask, I know, but could you possibly ...'

Cassie smiled reassuringly. 'Of course I'll come

with you, you silly dope,' she said affectionately, answering the unvoiced question. 'As if I'd leave you at such a moment! Mum and Dad won't be home for ages – they'll be helping with the clear-up – so I've nothing to stay at home for anyway. Now who'll make the porridge, you or me?'

'I'll make it, but I'm certain I won't be able to eat it,' Rosheen said, choking back a sob. 'How I wish I was the sort of mother that my own mam was. I've given the twins too much leeway, put up with the trouble they've sometimes got me into. If only they're safe, I'll make them do as they're told in future instead of letting them get their own way over everything.' She had been stirring the porridge as she spoke, and now she began to spoon it into the dishes which her friend had set out on the kitchen table. 'If I'd insisted on their staying close to us when we were coming home yesterday – and I could have, you know – then they wouldn't have spent the night in such danger.' She swung round and plunked into a chair at the kitchen table, then automatically dipped her spoon into the bowl before her and began to eat hungrily. 'Oh, Cassie, if only I'd been a better mother!'

Cassie went round the table and gave her a hug. 'You have two wilful children, but I'm sure their hearts are in the right place,' she said, crossing her fingers behind her back, for not being a parent herself she found it difficult to forgive April and May for their disobedience and complete indifference to the worry they had caused. 'So finish your porridge whilst I make some toast, because if we're going to search Liverpool you'll feel a lot better with something inside you.'

Although Rosheen hadn't believed her friend, she soon realised that Cassie had spoken the truth. Fortified with porridge, toast and tea, and the knowledge blossoming within that her mother would never have abandoned the twins, she set off with Cassie.

'We'll go straight to King Edward Court,' she said decisively. 'It's always been a hotbed of gossip, and if the twins went in there at any point someone must have seen them. So, plan A is to get off when the bus stops on the Scottie and cross-question anyone we meet.'

As luck would have it, however, they did not have to search very far. They got off the bus just past King Edward Court and Rosheen gasped with horror. Most of the small shops which had lined the streets at this point were gone; and then, as she turned towards where the shelter had been, she saw a tiny figure perched on a block of masonry, her clothes filthy and torn, her small face white with exhaustion, and recognised her elder daughter.

Rosheen uttered a sound between a groan and a scream and seconds later April was in her arms, letting the tears which she had held back pour out of her eyes and down her cheeks. But as soon as Rosheen released her she pointed a quivering finger at the terrible mound.

'Oh, Mam, May's down there and so's Grandma, only poor Grandma can't answer when I call her,' she said, her tone suddenly high and frightened. 'But Mam, I can hear May, although nobody else can, and I know she's not dead. Only the men with the heavy moving equipment are very slow and I don't believe they understand how I know May's still alive. But she won't be, Mam, if they don't get a move on. Every time we talk in our heads her thoughts are weaker. I ordered her to hang on but she's getting so she can't do as I tell her.' She turned a worried, dirt-streaked face up to her mother's. 'What'll I do if May dies, Mam? Who'll look after me, if she dies?'

Rosheen stroked the curls on her daughter's head. 'I'm still here, and anyway you are the one who looks after May, who decides what you're both going to do,' she pointed out. 'I'm sure she will be all right, but if by some terrible mischance she does need you, I know you'll stand by her, the way you always have.'

April looked at her mother, her eyes rounding with disbelief. 'But Mam, May is the one who looks after *me*,' she said, clearly astonished by her mother's ignorance. 'Oh, I know I'm always calling her names, but that doesn't mean anything. May's the sensible one, honest to God she is. She's always looked after me; if she wasn't there I wouldn't know what to do.'

As April had expected, the rescuers took far more notice of what she told them when Rosheen backed her up, and in her dark and pain-filled prison May continued to send her thoughts winging upwards whenever she felt able to do so. There were times, of course, when she was close to despair, but April's orders, peremptorily delivered, kept her going, forbade the surrender she craved. April told her, with devastating frankness, that she must not dare to die, she must always be there to support her, because that was the only way April could be strong enough to ensure that help reached her in her underground prison. Rosheen and Cassie took it in turns to stay with April, and by lunchtime May too had had a visitor. She became suddenly aware that someone or something was moving towards her; a pair of eyes, moon-wide and golden as the sun, were coming closer.

For a moment May panicked; the eyes seemed to have no body, no legs or arms, and for a moment she flung up her arm to ward them off, but even as she did so she heard a deep, resonating purr. It was a cat, big, black and white-whiskered. It must have forced its way through a crack or a crevice in the rubble and come to tell her help was at hand. Feebly, May stroked the cat between his big pricked ears.

'Are you Scat?' she asked as the creature began to rub its feather-soft fur against her cheek. 'Oh, Scat, you're so brave, but can you get out again, having got in? If so, you might go out again and show them the way you came, just in case a very small, very skinny girl might get out that way too. And once I was out I could tell them how to rescue Grandma.'

And so, in the end, it proved. April ordered her twin in no uncertain terms to persuade the cat to leave her so that they could watch its return to the upper world, and May followed her twin's advice as she had always done. It was hard, though, to repulse the cat when it purred so loudly and stretched its neck to lick a salty tear from her cheek, but she knew in her heart – as usual – that April was right. She wanted more than anything else on earth to escape from her prison, and if the cat could lead her to safety then she must do her best to follow him.

Even with the help of the big black cat, however, it was the next day before May was gently hauled out of her dark hole and saw her grandmother being loaded into an ambulance. 'Grandma,' she whispered feebly. 'Oh, Grandma, you're all right! I thought – I thought you were dead. Why didn't you speak to me when we were both under all that rubble?'

Rosheen gently smoothed her daughter's cheek. 'She can't answer you, darling, because she's in what they call an induced sleep, but the nurse who reached her first says she'll be fine.' She smiled reassuringly, though in truth her mother had looked dreadful and Rosheen's heart was wrung with pain. Still, it was no wonder Mrs Clarke's face was grey, after such an ordeal. Rosheen could hardly bear to imagine what her mother and daughter had gone through, trapped underground for more than twenty-four hours not knowing whether rescue would ever come. But it had, thank goodness, and come in time too; but Rosheen did not think she would ever forget how close she had come to losing them.

Chapter Sixteen

It was a fine day in early June and Rosheen and Cassie, their kit bags over their shoulders, crossed the parade ground to where a large lorry stood. Cassie hailed a small Waaf who was just about to climb aboard.

'Excuse me; are you the intake for the MT division?' she called. 'We were told a gharry would be arriving at ten o'clock, but it's only quarter to ...'

The Waaf turned and grinned at them. She had wildy curling red hair beneath her uniform cap, and a great many freckles. 'Yes, that's right; and the driver says he won't start until he's got his full complement of passengers,' she said cheerfully. 'But everyone has arrived early and it's a fair old journey, so if you'll just hop aboard ...'

The girls did so, and greeted the Waafs already ensconced on the tin benches. Then Cassie turned to the redhead. 'You say we've got a long journey ahead of us, but for goodness' sake, how do you know? I thought the Royal Air Force were so security conscious that they never told us anything; this "need to know" business and all that.'

The redheaded Waaf grinned delightedly. 'Well, the driver needs to know ... and he's my boyfriend.' My name's Cherry Bates, by the way.'

Rosheen and Cassie grinned back. 'So do you know where we're going, as well?' Rosheen asked.

'I do indeed – it's a village in the mountains of Snowdonia; it's called Llandegfan.'

'Gosh,' Rosheen said, rather inadequately. 'That's a good way off. How long will it take us, do you reckon?'

Cherry Bates grinned again. 'A couple of hours with my Jimmy driving; four hours with anyone else,' she said. 'Though once we get into the mountains I've been told the roads are more like tracks, which may slow him down a bit.'

'Snowdonia!' Cassie said suddenly. 'We had a holiday there before the war, in the most beautiful little village; I think it was called Betwys-y-Coed. There was a cake shop which sold ice creams as well as the most delicious buns and gingerbread.' She glanced hopefully at Cherry's freckled face. 'Did your boyfriend say anything about Ty Bwty café? I'd give a week's pay to visit that place again!'

Everyone laughed, but Cherry shrugged. 'Dunno, but I dare say we'll find out soon enough. We're bound to get some time off, because apparently this village is very remote indeed and with the best will in the world no one can work twenty-four hours out of the twenty-four, not even us Waafs.' She turned her cheerful smile upon the two girls. 'What were you doin' before you re-mustered?'

'Clerical work. Typing, filing, filling out work sheets … boring stuff,' Cassie admitted.

At this point a young leading aircraftman addressed them from the back of the gharry. 'All set?' he said, raising an eyebrow. 'Everyone got their cookhouse issue of sandwiches for the journey? Right then, we're off.'

They stopped for their comfort break in a pretty little village, and Cherry's boyfriend led them to an inn where he was obviously well known. Everyone was glad to get out of the gharry and stretch their legs and then to sit down in the small garden at the rear of the building to eat the sandwiches provided by the cookhouse. Cassie was folding her greaseproof paper around the last sandwich when she remembered the letter from her mother that was nestling in her kitbag. She had collected it from the bulletin board on her way out to the gharry, but had not been able to read it in the swaying, jolting vehicle. Now was her chance, so she fished the envelope out of her kitbag, reminding Rosheen that she, too, had received a letter that day.

'Better get them read before we climb back into the gharry,' she advised. 'Good thing we've neither of us got sensitive stomachs ... and according to Cherry these are the good roads!'

Rosheen laughed, but agreed that Cassie's reasoning was sound. Her letter was from Mrs Clarke, and she tore it open, hoping for news of May. She found it in the very first paragraph.

Mrs Clarke had not wasted words.

Dear Rosheen,

I thought you'd like to know that I've just come home from visiting May. She's quite her old self and anxious to leave the convalescent home and return to Cragside Cottage. Her awful experience is rapidly becoming a part of the past and personally I think she is coping with the trauma better than I did myself. Why, within minutes of our arrival she and April were bickering over nothing at all; just like old times! Both twins are delighted to hear that the air force are teaching you to drive and no doubt will pester for someone to give them a car!! So don't worry about either of them; I wouldn't lie to you and I tell you they are fine. Folk think the Blitzkrieg is over; let's hope they're right. Your Uncle Eamonn turned up the other evening. He's in corvettes and he said that as his ship came into Liverpool Bay the city looked as though a giant had landed on it from a great height, wrecking the familiar buildings until it could have been anywhere. So I reckon the

Luftwaffe thinks we're finished and won't waste time on us in future.

You'll guess from what he says that every house – every corner of every house – is bulging at the seams with people desperate for a roof over their heads. But I'm one of the lucky ones; dear old No. 3 is still standing and as soon as stuff's available I shall start making it weatherproof and that. This war can't last for ever.

Yours affec., Mam.

Meanwhile, Cassie had opened her own envelope and unfolded the sheets within, which were covered in her mother's neat hand. The first few paragraphs were all concerned with the war and the efforts her parents were putting into their various jobs – her father was considering a post at the War Office – but as she turned to the second sheet she saw the name *Andy* and began to read more closely, a worried crease between her brows.

Andy's stationed quite near the city of Lincoln, so of course I suggested he should visit my cousin Martha; do you remember her? I believe he has done so at least twice. He dropped me a postcard saying she was good company despite her age – she's eighty-four – and on the second visit she gave him a bar of chocolate! I suspect it was a pre-war hoarding, but none the less welcome for all that.

Cassie frowned. Lincolnshire! That was miles away, she thought. As for her mother's cousin Martha, she had no recollection of her whatsoever. Sighing, she returned her attention to her mother's letter.

And isn't it lucky for Andy that Rebecca has been posted to Feldenfield, which is quite near his station? It'd be nice for the two of them to meet up from time to time. Of course I like to think that when your posting comes through you'll end up in the same area, but I don't suppose it's possible.

Cassie felt a rich tide of warmth invade her face. Only a few weeks before she had assured Rebecca that she felt nothing for Andy but friendship, that she was even pleased that her two best friends were getting on so well. But now she felt the familiar stab of what she could no longer deny was jealousy, just as the driver hailed them.

'Come along, girls; time to get back on the road,' he commanded, and seeing Cassie pushing her letter back into her kitbag added: 'You'll have plenty of time to answer that once we reach Llandegfan. In fact, you'll be glad of it, for there's literally nothing else to do.'

For the rest of the journey, Cassie tried to sort out her real feelings about Andy and Rebecca. She – Cassie – and Andy had been close all their lives; even as teenagers they had stuck together, until that stupid quarrel in the church porch, and then that wretched dance where they had both behaved so badly. In the year since then their ways had parted – she felt a pang at the thought – and if he and Rebecca were romantically involved it was none of her business any longer, except as a friend of both parties. So why did she feel so bereft? It was time she took herself in hand and began to act her age. She nudged Rosheen, sitting on the bench beside her.

'I just heard Cherry say another ten minutes and we'll be at our destination; from what I've seen we're in the most beautiful countryside. I believe I'm really going to enjoy every minute of our course.'

The six weeks' training had flown by, and as the girls climbed back into the gharry Cassie joked that one of them should be driving, as everyone had passed the course. But Fred, the official driver, said laughingly that he did not intend to risk his life by letting an over-enthusiastic Waaf take over his vehicle. So Cassie and Rosheen settled down and watched through the gap in the canvas as the village disappeared into the great forest on the slopes of the mountain.

'Well, girls, what did you think of that?' Cherry said, settling herself near the back of the vehicle to get a better view of the country they were leaving behind. 'We're all fully qualified MT drivers now, and Fred says when we get back to our home base our postings will already be on the board. You're also asked to rate your course on a scale of one to ten, one being the worst, obviously.'

Cassie, watching as the outside world rounded another corner, thought about the last six weeks. They had arrived mid-afternoon and been dropped off at their billets in a tiny hamlet, and within days most of the intake were lining up to complain about food and conditions in the mean little houses which lined the village street. The inhabitants wanted the money – and the extra ration cards – which the air force provided, but had no intention of either welcoming the Waafs or providing them with anything but the most meagre fare. The girls soon discovered that breakfast would consist of thin gruel-like porridge, without milk or sweetener. If you complained, your hostess immediately became a Welsh speaker without a word of English, and this talent extended to ignoring complaints about the rickety bunks – two thin blankets and one dirty pillow – with which the girls were provided. High in the mountains the weather was sometimes cold despite the time of year, but when it was warm the girls would have appreciated an open window in their crammed little attic rooms. However, when they tried to force the tiny panes apart, they discovered that these had been nailed to the frame.

Complaints were looked into, of course, and

things improved a little, but Cassie thought that had it not been for the fact that their instructors drove them into Betwys-y-Coed whenever they were free to do so, they really might have starved. But the café she had remembered was still there, run by a cheerful rosy-cheeked Welsh woman and her teenage daughter, so they were able to enjoy tea and cakes, cheese sandwiches and other delights once their working day was over. It enabled them to keep going on the watery vegetable stews – no meat, no potatoes, no carrots – which their unwilling hostesses provided, and Rosheen told Cassie she just hoped that none of the Waafs would think the villagers were typical of the Welsh, most of whom, like the Nidds and the Wrights, were friendly and generous people.

Aside from their billets, however, all the girls agreed that it had been an unforgettable experience. In their free time, which was limited, they had explored the countryside, even climbing some of the high peaks which surrounded the training centre.

The higher you climbed the more dramatic the views and the more dramatic the views, Cassie and Rosheen agreed, the clearer became the mountain air. There were birch woods as you descended into the valleys, as well as mossy gorges, tumbling waterfalls and pools in which the grey trout lurked. Both girls knew they would never forget the beauties of the place, and when Cassie found an old postcard

305

depicting the Swallow Falls she sent it to her mother, suggesting that they should once more have a holiday in this glorious countryside.

Despite the many difficulties of driving through such harsh terrain they all did well, and when they had passed the course the instructors had thrown a party for them which included a great many fancy cakes and well-filled sandwiches as well as cups of hot strong tea and homemade ginger beer.

During her time in the remote little village, Cassie had received a letter from Rebecca, which she read with mixed feelings.

Andy re-mustered on bombers because he had grown to hate the loneliness which is all part of piloting Spitfires. We see a lot of each other now we're not based so far apart, but I don't think either of us is serious. Tomorrow is too uncertain for anything but friendship. Of course I have no idea when you will get a posting, but please be kind and contact Andy. He's at RAF Rigby, near Lincoln. I'm sure he's happier flying his beloved Lanc with his crew around him than he was in his Spit, but I'm also sure a word from you would be truly welcome. Life's too short for grudges and he regrets your quarrel as much as I do, which is saying a good deal.

Dear me, I sound like Peter Pan – 'clap your hands if you believe in fairies' – but honestly,

Cassie, it would please him so much. Your old friend, Becky.

Thinking back to the letter, Cassie was unable to stop the unreasoning annoyance returning. What right had Rebecca Spencer to tell *her*, Cassie Valentine, to eat humble pie over a childish little quarrel for which Andy had been largely responsible? In her heart she suspected that she was being both wrong and silly and she knew that if she met Andy tomorrow she would want to tell him she had forgotten their differences. She knew it would be easier to do it by letter, particularly now that she had his address, but something – she thought it was pride – held her back. But it was no use poring over Rebecca's letter and wondering how best to reply. She ought to grit her teeth, push her reservations aside, tell Andy she was sorry for the quarrel and await his reaction ...

'Cassie?' Rosheen peered into her friend's face. 'What's the matter? You've been scowling and fiddling with your kitbag for the last ten minutes.' She shook her head as Cassie began to reply. 'No, don't tell me; I saw you re-reading Rebecca's letter and I bet it's reminded you of the quarrel you had with that pilot officer, the one who lives near you at home – the Irish fellow. Why on earth you don't simply write to him as if nothing has happened I really can't imagine.'

Cassie stared at Rosheen, thunderstruck. Her friend was so practical, and so sensible, too. Despite her enjoyment of the course and the glorious countryside she, Cassie, had been unable to stop fretting about Rebecca's letter, and now Rosheen had shown her the best path: a nice friendly letter to Andy, telling him all about what she was doing now, without a word of apology because it was simply unnecessary. She heaved a great sigh of relief and turned to smile gratefully at Rosheen.

'You are a genius,' she said. 'Why didn't I think of that? It's the obvious solution and will enable me to start my new life with a clear conscience.'

Rosheen looked startled, then gratified. 'So now will you stop making mountains out of molehills and start planning this new life of yours?' she said severely. 'When I think of my worries over the twins and my mother, yours do seem rather trivial. To be honest, my biggest worry at present is how to get enough leave to visit April and May now they're back at the Wrights' place.' She looked anxiously at Cassie. 'They won't try to make us take the driving course as leave, will they?'

Cassie giggled. 'I'd like to see them dare,' she said cheerfully, and Rosheen thought to herself that it was the first time Cassie had laughed since they had got into the gharry. 'In fact, from what my instructor told me, we ought to get leave before being posted to our new station, so you needn't worry; Fred's been in the Royal Air Force for fifteen years and knows *everything.'*

'Well, that's a weight off my mind.' Rosheen leaned forward to peer at the other inhabitants of the gharry. 'What does everyone else think? No, not about the billets but about the course. Wish we could grade the billets one to ten but the RAF are only interested in our driving capabilities. I bet some of you crushed your first matchbox, unlike me.' She pretended to hook her thumbs behind imaginary lapels. 'My matchbox was still whole after climbing the worst hill of the lot.' There was general laughter, for the trick most valued by the instructors was to place a matchbox behind the rear wheel of the vehicle which would be crushed if the gharry slipped so much as a quarter of an inch back when the order was given to 'get into first and climb this bleedin' hill'.

Cassie and Rosheen joined in the laughter and then settled back to watch the scenery, for even the redoubtable Fred could not hurry either up or down these precipitous mountain roads.

And when they arrived at their station and said goodbye to the friends they had made on the course they found that Fred's promise of postings was no idle boast. They reported to their Section Officer, went to the cookhouse for a cup of tea and a wad, and then rushed to the mess where the first thing they saw on the bulletin board was the longed-for list.

'A whole week's leave!' Rosheen said, drawing an ecstatic breath. 'I'll be able to visit the twins, and my mother. What about you, Cass?' She laughed. 'I'm not sure where Albercroft is, but it's somewhere in Lincolnshire. You could visit Andy and apologise in person.'

For a moment Cassie just glared at Rosheen, but then she saw the humour of it and laughed as well. 'We're probably miles away,' she said airily. 'And remember that at your instigation I'm going to write a lovely friendly letter which will get me off the hook. Oh, and I've been meaning to ask you: your mother's family came from southern Ireland, didn't they? Is it anything like Snowdonia? Because if so I wouldn't mind spending a holiday there when the war's over.'

Rosheen smiled dreamily. 'My mother says Ireland is every bit as beautiful,' she said. 'But you should know that. Doesn't Andy whatshisname have relatives there?'

'Well, yes, but I've never met them,' Cassie said. 'And as things stand at the moment I probably never shall.'

Rosheen dug a sharp elbow into her ribs. 'You're going to make it up with Andy, don't you remember? When this perishing war's over, you'll probably marry the bloke.'

Cassie stiffened. 'I shall *not* …' she began, then started to giggle. 'What a ridiculous conversation,' she said cheerfully. 'Honestly, Rosheen, how could I possibly marry Andy? He brings out the worst in me. And I've decided not to write immediately because I want to be able to describe the station to which I'm being posted and the work I shall be doing. Perhaps I should send him a card instead – you know, one of those ones where you tick boxes. What do you think?'

Rosheen looked shocked. 'You can't do that. It's tantamount to an insult, and I thought this whole exercise was meant to show him you want to be friends again,' she said. 'If you send him one of those tick box postcards he'll never forgive you; take my word for it.

Cassie was about to reply when the door of the mess flew open and two of their fellow trainees burst into the room.

'Hello, you two,' the first girl said. 'Have you looked at the bulletin board? We're off to Lincolnshire, where most of the bombers fly from, but first of all we get a whole week's leave. What d'you think of that?'

Chapter Seventeen

October 1942

Andy walked down the fuselage of *B for Betsy* and out into a white mist which came up from the ground almost to waist level. He breathed deeply of the autumn air and looked east to where the greyness of dawn was already giving way to the first tentative rays of sunshine. It looked like being a fine day; dew spangled the grass and the birds were up and pouring out their joys and sorrows in song. Once he would have thought it a perfect day to take one of his grandfather's horses out on the gallops, but he knew that was just wishful thinking. He would have loved to go back to the O'Leary stud, but was in general too busy – and too tired – to face the journey. He thought, with wry humour, how silly he'd look if he, the birdman, were to end up a drowned corpse in the Irish Sea.

Now, though, he should have felt pleased with himself because the raid had been successful. *B for Betsy*, under his now considerably experienced hands, had managed to dodge both the flak from below and tracer from the attacking Messerschmitts. They had been formation flying, of course, keeping their height for as long as possible.

As always after a heavy raid, however, he was exhausted. Keeping the big kites on course was hard on your leg muscles, but at least this time he could get a meal and then go to bed as soon as they came out of the debriefing. He might even sleep; sometimes exhaustion allowed it but more often it jerked him awake, reliving moments he would far rather forget. Yet this had not been a bad sortie, in fact quite the opposite. On a previous visit to Augsburg they had been well peppered, the bullets only just missing his friend Colin, who was now his navigator. After the training course it had come to the notice of the authorities that Colin was a sufferer from something Andy had never heard of, a sort of super headache accompanied by bright lights and vomiting and a tendency to lose track of time. Migraines such attacks were called, and if there's one thing one does not want when piloting an aircraft it is a migraine.

Colin's condition was kept from the crew members for as long as possible, but when Andy, as skipper, realised that such an affliction could cost the whole crew their lives he and his squadron leader had a long talk which ended in Colin's becoming Andy's navigator and emergency second pilot, and

Colin proved to be one of the best navigators in the squadron.

Now, Colin, bringing up the rear, was already through the exit door and down on the concrete. The two men went through their routine on what Andy thought of as automatic pilot, as they headed towards the Waaf who would drive them to the debriefing hut. The crew piled in, Andy, as skipper, seeing them all settled before going round to the front of the vehicle and addressing the driver through the open window.

'Lovely day for it, Jinny. No bullet holes this time, so I'm hoping I can drop off for a couple of hours. Anything happen whilst we've been away?'

The girl shook her head. 'No, Skip, nothing unusual,' she said as she revved the engine, getting into first gear and pulling away slowly so that Andy could jump into the vehicle without her having to stop. As he climbed aboard his crew looked at him expectantly.

'What d'you reckon's for dinner, Skip – or brekker I should say?'

Andy shrugged. 'The usual,' he said laconically. 'God bless dried egg. What would the cooks do without it?'

Half an hour later, debriefed and fed, he and Colin made their way to the Mess to check the bulletin board as they did every morning. Andy scanned the board and began to take down his mail. One from his mother, one from Rebecca – he grinned; the one from Rebecca had S.W.A.L.K. neatly printed across the back – and one from someone whose writing he did not immediately recognise. He looked around. Colin was already absorbed in his own mail, so he joined him at a small table for two, bought a KitKat and a cup of tea and opened his mother's letter first. Despite being Irish his mother had thrown herself into the war effort on behalf of Great Britain with tremendous enthusiasm. She and Mrs Valentine had always been pals and now they took on any work which needed help from their capable hands. Andy scanned the letter, which was full of the usual chatter until he came to a PS which made his heart beat faster. *PS Rebecca had a forty-eight and came home, but only popped in for five minutes. She's looking well. I expect her mum was pleased to see her because it's been a while since she got leave. Take care of yourself, son. No heroics please! Your loving mother.*

Andy smiled. So Rebecca had been home, had she? He knew her ack-ack battery was simply ordered to wherever one was needed. He opened the letter, scanned it quickly, and put it down on the table with a grimace. She was not a good correspondent, but who was he to complain? He hated writing letters, and when at last he was forced to do so kept such missives short. Feeling guilty, he pulled the letter forward again.

Darling Andy,

I do miss you most horribly. Went into Ely in the liberty truck, because most of us had never seen the cathedral, very dramatic. Climbed the tower and at the top could see miles and miles of what they call the fen country. Very boring but there was a tea shop which sold your favourite doughnuts. Wish you were here!

All my love, Rebecca.

Andy pushed the two letters he had read into his pocket and stared curiously at the third; then, with an impatient gesture, he tore it open. And it was from Cassie. For a moment he could only stare at the unfamiliar writing. He had known Cassie all his life, but, he now realised, they had never before exchanged letters. Now he saw that her writing was similar to Rebecca's – same school, he supposed – but the content was very different. It was a long letter, telling him all about her life, mentioning that she could now drive, which made him suppose she was referring to the MT.

'Christ, has someone written a novel, and if so why are they sending it to you?' That was Colin, peering intently at the first and last flimsy sheets. 'Don't say Rebecca's got it into her head to send you pages from her diary!'

Before Andy could stop him Colin had grabbed the last page of the letter. *Hope you are well and enjoying your new job*, it ended. *I meant to write to you when I came off the driving course, but somehow I was always too busy. I'm in Lincolnshire now, though, so who knows? We might meet one of these days, you never know. Yours sincerely, Cassie. PS Seen much of Rebecca lately?*

Colin ran a finger along the signature. 'Cassie, Cassie. One of your many popsies?' He frowned, his sandy eyebrows drawing together. Then his face cleared. 'I *knew* I'd heard that name before! The ice maiden at the dance. You had some sort of row ... I can't remember the details but I do recall asking her to go to the flicks. She said she would but then we all moved on ...' He grinned down at his friend, still sitting at the small table. 'How odd! I haven't thought of her once in all this time and I don't believe you've heard from her either, have you?'

'No I have not, and I'll thank you not to go poking your nose in where it's not wanted,' Andy said angrily, snatching the last page out of Colin's hand and jamming the whole letter into the pocket of his flying jacket. He got to his feet and jerked his head towards the Mess door. 'Can't stand chattering all day just because some girl's written to me,' he said. 'Let's get some shut-eye, or it'll be evening before we know it. We can come in later to see who's on the Battle Order.'

As Andy had suspected, it was turning into a lovely day as he and Colin reached their billet. They were preparing for a big raid on Germany but had

317

not yet received the Battle Order, so for once they should have time to relax and get a proper sleep. Yet when they climbed into their beds Andy knew he would not be able to drop off. Apart from the fact that he ached with weariness there was 'the letter'.

After the ill-fated dance at Charing Basset, he remembered, he had been quite eager to avoid her. She was a pretty girl all right, but where on earth had she got the idea that she owned him? He had been determined not to get in touch with her but to wait until she contacted him. It would be untrue to say he had watched the mail, but as the weeks and then the months passed he had grown impatient. He knew of her doings, of course, because his mother and hers had always been friends, and now they belonged to a group which called themselves 'Busy Bees' and met on Thursday afternoons to knit socks, turn sheets, sew shirts, and swap news about their offspring. Then, of course, when their children returned home on leave, such interesting titbits as there were would be passed on. Between Rebecca and his mother, Andy reckoned, there was not much he wasn't told about Miss Cassie Valentine's activities.

Lying in his comfortable bed, he scowled at the ceiling. Oh, her letter had been friendly enough, but it had contained no hint of apology, nor any indication that she was longing to see him again. What on earth was the matter with the girl? Was she still annoyed because he had taken up with Rebecca? Well, if so she could jolly well snap out of it. Piloting his beloved Lanc was his work, a matter of life and death, nothing to do with a petty quarrel which had happened over two years ago. He tried to remember exactly what had been said but the details would not fall neatly into place. Rebecca and Cassie had both been land girls then, but after that they had both quit the service – he grinned – in order to escape one another's company. A fat lot of good that had done them. Oh, they had ended up in different forces to be sure, Rebecca in the ATS and Cassie in the WAAF, but they had soon resumed their former closeness.

Andy glanced at the bed opposite his own, expecting to find Colin already in the land of Nod, but instead he met the other man's blue-grey eyes staring straight back at him.

Colin grinned. 'Worried what the fair Rebecca will say when she discovers you're two-timing her?' he asked. 'Don't tell me she won't care, because I've seen the backs of her envelopes, even if I'm not privy to the contents of same. Miss Spencer is getting her feet under the table; you won't escape easily, my son.'

Andy sat up on one elbow. 'She can think what she likes,' he said firmly. 'She doesn't own me and nor does any other woman, and that includes Cassie. Damn it, man, we had a silly little quarrel before the war and an even sillier one not long after it started. She's borne a grudge because I kissed her friend and now she thinks a chatty letter will put all to rights. Well, she's bloody well wrong.'

'Oh well, if that's the way you feel you won't object if I get to know your Cassie better. No, I'm not trying to annoy you, I genuinely liked the girl. Where's your Rebecca now? A foursome might be the very thing to sort the matter out.'

Andy, who was beginning to realise he was on the very verge of sleep, gave a martyred sigh. 'That'll be the day,' he said drowsily. 'And now for God's sake stop nattering and go to *sleep*.'

Colin chuckled. 'I met Badger before I went into the cookhouse,' he observed. Badger was their mid-turret gunner. 'He says the Battle Order for good old *Betsy* doesn't come into force for another three days, so if we have a quick zizz now we can have a proper sleep tonight. Oh, bless our squaddie for his kind heart.'

Andy felt as though an enormous weight had been lifted from his shoulders. He would have plenty of time to consider what reply, if any, he should make to Cassie's letter. She had said she was at an airfield close to his, so perhaps they really could get together. Rebecca, he knew, was on an island off the west coast of Wales so she was unlikely to be able to rendezvous with her childhood friends. But we'll arrange something, Andy told himself contentedly, burrowing his head into the pillow. Yes, something can be arranged. It would be too ridiculous to break up what was a good friendship just for the sake of one's pride.

Soon, he slept.

Despite her intentions to write to Andy, it had been some considerable while before Cassie actually did so. For one thing she was extremely busy and for another she had been put forward as possible officer material, which meant courses and examinations, although in the end she had withdrawn her application, giving as her reason a desire to remain with her flight as acting corporal.

After finally writing to Andy, Cassie had waited for a response and was disappointed when after a couple of weeks no letter had arrived. Her station was not far from his and she was easily able to ascertain that nothing had happened to him, but when she returned to her Mess one evening after a hectic day ferrying an officer from one important meeting to another she was hailed at once by a fellow Waaf, who told her that there had been a phone call for her earlier.

'It was a feller; nice voice, no particular accent. He left a number for you to ring back. I've written it down, though no doubt you know it by heart.' She handed Cassie a scrap of paper with a telephone number written neatly across it and Cassie went to the counter, glancing at the clock on the wall as she did so. She had arranged to meet Rosheen in the Mess when she got back from her trip, but not for another half hour, so she ordered a sandwich and a cup of tea to fill the chinks until she could have a proper meal.

She wasn't sure what to do about the telephone call; contacting someone by telephone when you did not know his name was a hazardous business. The number might or might not be answered by the person who had tried to contact her, and to make matters worse the operator saw to it that calls were short, sometimes breaking into the middle of a conversation to remind both parties that there was a war on. Fortunately, the decision was taken out of her hands when the telephone rang again and she saw the young LAC who answered it look round the room as if searching for someone. Cassie jumped to her feet like a greyhound released from the trap, abandoning her almost cold cup of tea and the crusts of her sandwich.

'Is it for me?' she asked eagerly. 'I'm ACW Valentine; I'm waiting for a call.'

The young aircraftman looked relieved. 'It's a Pilot Officer O'Leary,' he said, then walked off to sit at a nearby table so that her conversation could be private.

Cassie approached the telephone. Suddenly she found that her heart was beating faster and her mouth felt dry. 'Hello. Is that you, Andy?' she whispered into the receiver. 'It's Cassie.'

'Well of course. Who else?' Andy's voice came over the wires just as she remembered it, but also quite different. Deeper and with a tinge of impatience as though he thought she could not have doubted who he was. 'Thanks for your letter. Sorry I've been so long in replying but we're pretty busy.' He gave a rather strange laugh. 'Germany's a long way off. I take it you know I retrained on bombers? Lancs? The best kites in the business, as it happens, and *B for Betsy* and her crew are tops.'

'Mm-hmm,' Cassie said vaguely. Typical Andy: even if it wasn't true he would claim that everything he touched was the best. She infused her voice with just a trace of sarcasm. 'But remember, Andy, you telephoned me, not vice versa. What did you want to say? I don't want to box you into a corner, but if it's just a telephone call to let me know you were still in the land of the living—'

He cut across her, his voice suddenly sharp with anxiety. 'Don't say that. Life's too short to take its name in vain.'

Suddenly Cassie remembered the many little superstitions that kept the fliers in the air. After all, she had been one of the Waafs, fetching crews from a successful sortie when they had been strafed by a Messerschmitt diving from clouds and ripping up the runway with tracer bullets. She had been lucky;

323

the Messerschmitt had been shot down but his fire had killed an ambulance driver and a member of the cookhouse staff, both ambling along to get their evening meal. After that, she had always put her gharry into gear as soon as an aeroplane landed, and opened the door of the debriefing hut with her right hand. Later, she heard without surprise that since that evening the pilot of the kite which had been the focus of the Messerschmitt attack had always put his right boot on first and worn an old medal which had belonged to his grandfather pinned to the inside of his flying jacket. Foolish superstitions perhaps, but if you believed they kept you safe …

'Sorry. I forgot for a moment. Oh, it *is* nice to hear your voice, Andy. Can we go back past all those silly quarrels and pick up our friendship where we left off before the war? I dare say we've both done a lot of growing up since then.'

Andy's voice was a little stiff. 'I think perhaps we'd better make a definite date and not leave things to chance. I see a lot of Becky and would suggest a foursome, but she's somewhere off Wales with her ack-ack battery, miles away from Lincolnshire. Have you got a friend you'd like to bring along? I share a billet with my navigator. You met him at that wretched dance when you were still a land girl, clodhopping round in breeks and wellies. Do you remember him? He remembers you.'

Cassie thought of Rosheen, of her rosy face and

frank speech. But she had sometimes suspected that Andy was a bit of a snob, and if she brought Rosheen along to the meeting it was just possible that he would not recognise her friend's true worth. And if he did not … well, that would be the end of her regard for him.

Just then a voice spoke sharply in her ear. 'Your time is up, caller. Please hang up.'

Needless to say, it was the operator. 'Oh, oh, wait,' Cassie squeaked, other considerations vanishing beneath the fear of being cut off before they had arranged a date. 'Are you free tomorrow? I can get somebody else to answer any calls for me provided I arrange it in time.'

'The Saracen's Head at noon? Can you manage that?' Even as Cassie said quickly that she could manage it very well, they were cut off.

She hung up the receiver and moved away from the telephone, her mind suddenly finding something else to worry about. Why had he suggested a foursome? It was almost as though he wanted to prove that he had a great many friends and she was no longer necessary to him. And why had she not had the courage to say she would bring Rosheen along? For all she knew the two might have a great deal in common, since they both felt so strongly about their Irish heritage. I could still take her with me, Cassie thought, leaving the Mess and heading across the parade ground to her Nissen hut. I could, but I shan't. This is one of the moments when my service and civilian lives can jolly well remain separate. I'll meet Andy, tell him I'm sorry for the stupid rows and take it from there.

Andy came out of the Mess, skirted the queue still waiting for the telephone and shouted to Colin. They were not on ops tonight because rumour had it a big raid was planned in forty-eight hours, and the men had been advised to get as much sleep as they could before take-off at 2100 hours. He was still wondering why he had suggested a foursome when he reached his billet: a farmhand's earthen-floored cottage with a coke-fired stove, a couple of bunk beds and nothing much else. Once, the airfield had been adjacent to a small village, a hamlet so tiny that the authorities had not hesitated to move the villagers out and take over the half dozen or so cottages it comprised. Andy and Colin were billeted in the end cottage, the one furthest from the outbuildings, thanks to John Rogers, their squadron leader. That good man had already flown thirty-five sorties over Germany, bringing his crew back undamaged each time, but his care for them did not stop after they came in to land. He knew Colin could have slept on a clothes line and Andy needed quiet and dark, and because the two men had always messed together he had given them the best accommodation he could.

As Andy entered the kitchen, Colin, who had been stirring a pan over the stove, looked round and grinned. 'We're in luck; Mr Haisby who used to live here shot a rabbit and Mrs Haisby made a stew. They've given us half, so I gave them that tinned sponge pudding you've been saving for a special occasion. Is that all right?'

Andy grunted. He was already beginning to question the impulse which had made him suggest a date with Cassie. However, it was too late now, and anyway in his heart he was curious to see Cassie again after so long. She would have changed, he was pretty sure of that. Had he not changed himself? But Colin was staring at him, eyebrows lifting.

'Andy? Still thinking about that old flame of yours? I saw you on the telephone as I was coming out of the Mess but thought you might be some while. Was it Cassie whatshername ... Nightingale, was it?'

Andy laughed. He was being ridiculous; she was just a girl like any other Waaf, and they had been firm friends once and could be so again. But he would make it clear that he wanted no romantic attachments: getting too close to anyone was unwise – even unfair – in time of war. Most of the fellows with whom he came in contact were bomber pilots and crew, and though they never spoke of it they knew their chances of survival were slim. He had seen too many times the devastation and misery which the loss of a loved one caused to those dear to them, and he did not wish to inflict such suffering on any girl. So his many flirtations – even the one with Rebecca – fell short of full commitment. Life was too uncertain to make promises he might not be able to keep.

He crossed the kitchen and peered into the bubbling pot, sniffing at the steam rising from it. 'Not Nightingale, you fool. Valentine,' he said easily. 'I say, that stew smells good. And yes, it was Cassie on the line and we're going to meet tomorrow in the Saracen's Head at noon.'

Colin raised his brows. 'The Saracen's Head? With everyone in a blue uniform flooding in for beer and sandwiches around lunchtime? They'll all realise you're meeting some girl or other. Give us your plate and I'll start serving up.'

Andy whistled beneath his breath. 'Damn – I never thought of that. I wonder if she's still in her Mess? If I ring back at once I can change the rendezvous to somewhere a little less public. What do you think of the Leopard and Child? Or I suppose we could simply meet there and then move on.'

'Have your stew first,' Colin advised. 'I thought you were going to suggest a foursome?'

'I did,' Andy said ruefully. 'Fortunately, the operator put a stop to that. It's weird enough to be meeting Cassie again after all these years without two strangers looking on.'

'I'm not a stranger,' Colin observed, setting down the plates of stew. 'Go on, be a sport. Let me at least come with you so I can see if the delightful Cassie remembers me.'

Andy, slipping into his seat and lifting his spoon, thought it over and decided he would leave it to his friend to decide whether to come or not. He said as much as they ate their meal and, as he had known he would, Colin laughed and denied any particular interest in the pilot's love life.

'Like the rest of us, you fight shy of too much involvement, which is kinder for all concerned and simply common sense,' he said airily. 'I'll come with you on the liberty truck. Lincoln's a grand city; an afternoon wandering those ancient streets – and popping into the cathedral if I'm up to climbing the hill – is never time wasted. And on the homeward journey we can discuss how you and Cassie got on.'

When the stew was no more than a pleasant memory, Andy and Colin sauntered up to the NAAFI. As usual, Andy's crew had settled themselves comfortably in one corner, a small pile of coins in the centre of the table and cards spread pretty loosely around. There was a haze of cigarette smoke in the air and a general feeling of relaxation after a hard day's work. Andy greeted them, then went over to chat to the ground crew. Samson, his flight engineer, slapped his own hand of cards down on the table top.

'I'm out,' he announced cheerfully. 'I may have had a worse hand in my life, but if so I've forgotten it. Want to take my place, Skip, or perhaps come with me on a trip to the cinema? There's a good film showing at Clasketgate.'

Andy shook his head. 'I'm off to Lincoln tomorrow to meet a friend. I just popped in for a beer before going to bed. You know what Groupie said: "Rest while you can". Are you coming, Colin?'

They went over to the counter and bought drinks, then Andy returned to peer at the cards on the flight crew's table. Chimp, the rear gunner, slapped a hand protectively over the cards he had fanned out. He was nineteen years old and already an excellent gunner, for he held his fire in the coolest fashion until the enemy was practically upon them, then fired his tracers where they could do most damage.

'Don't look at my cards, Skip,' he commanded. 'I'm taking these chaps to the cleaners. When we do the checks next I'll tell you how I done it.'

Colin and Andy laughed and moved to a table at which another couple of crew members were sitting, drinking cocoa and reading the latest edition of a motorcycle magazine, for both men had been despatch riders at the start of the war. Colin pretended to nudge the table, causing outraged cries from Taffy the bomb aimer. Andy laughed again and slapped the man on the back.

'Don't worry. We just popped in for a quick beer,

then we're going to catch some shut-eye,' he said, raising his voice as someone started to sing a well-known and irreverent corruption of 'Old King Cole'. Andy sighed. 'Thank God for Groupie,' he muttered into Colin's ear, jerking his head at the singing men. '"Old King Cole" goes on for ever, but we shan't hear so much as a whisper of it once we're back in our billet.'

'Got any Brylcreem? I've used the last of mine.' Andy tried to sound nonchalant, as though it didn't matter. Not that it *did* matter, of course; he was meeting a friend, not a prospective lover, not someone who was liable to make inroads into his personal life. He had just come out of the ablutions where he had had an almost hot shower, and that in itself augured well for the meeting, for hot showers at RAF Rigby were rare and wonderful events. Usually one dived, shivering, into the little shower cubicle, pulled the dangling cord to release the water and presently emerged, soaked through and shivering, to hurry back to one's billet, which might have seemed chilly that morning but felt positively hot compared with the ablutions.

'Help yourself. I bought some last time we were in Lincoln,' Colin said generously. He peered at his friend. 'You could do with a haircut, old fellow, but I dare say it will stop your wig flapping around in the wind.'

He held out the desired pot and Andy took a fingerful to rub into his scalp. Then he picked up his comb, made a parting, and turned to grin at the other man.

'All done and dusted and ready to go,' he said, trying to infuse his tone with enthusiasm. 'If I decide to take the wench out for lunch, is it to the Leopard and Child or to the Lyons Corner House? I think the Corner House is probably the best bet – my recollection is that Cassie was fond of her grub.'

'The Corner House it is, then,' Colin observed. He combed his hair, clapped his cap on the ginger waves and gave his companion a shove. 'Stop preening, you self-satisfied oick, or the liberty truck will leave without us. You wouldn't want to stand her up, would you?'

The drive into town was not a long one, and the talk was general. Most of the men aboard would be on ops the following night yet there was little talk of the war. Andy was almost silent, listening to others and occasionally nodding or shaking his head, but Colin was in good form. The last time Andy had visited Mrs Valentine's cousin Colin had accompanied him, and now he kept his fellow passengers in fits describing how the old lady had insisted upon her guests partaking of a large trifle, not realising that the mock cream with which she had decorated this treat had gone off. His impression of Andy's efforts to pretend enjoyment whilst swallowing sour cream brought howls of laughter from the men, some of whom remembered similar incidents, and very soon Colin thought Andy was in a much more relaxed frame of mind. For Andy, though he would have denied it angrily, was a sensitive soul over some things.

When the gharry drew up outside the Saracen's Head the men began to climb down, and Colin followed the rest. Everyone knew that the sandwiches at the Saracen were amongst the best to be found in Lincoln, so it was no surprise when the entire contingent filed into the big, noisy pub. Colin hesitated. Should he go on to one of the many other pubs in the city, leaving Andy to meet his old friend in comparative anonymity? But it was too tempting; he eased himself into the crowd pushing his way in through the doors and stared around him. He saw several Waafs but only one, sitting quietly by herself on a banquette, was actually staring at the men as though trying to recognise one in particular. She was a pretty girl, trim in her immaculate uniform, and he was sure he recognised Cassie Valentine, even surer when Andy broke away from the pack and approached her. For one moment Colin thought her eyes were going to slide past his friend, but then she jumped to her feet, skirted the little table behind which she had been sitting and held out her hands. It was an odd gesture. Colin found he could not tell whether she was repelling Andy's advance or welcoming it. But of course they were both in uniform; to kiss a senior officer in a public place was probably a court-martial offence. And then the girl smiled and her whole face underwent a change. She had large dark blue eyes which filled with warmth when they fell on Andy and a soft kissable mouth ...

Abruptly, Colin felt like an intruder, a spy almost. Because of the way Andy had talked about Cassie he had felt no guilt over watching them, but now, suddenly, everything was different. As quietly as possible he detached himself from the men surrounding him and made for the door. Andy had implied that Cassie was nothing to him; perhaps he had honestly believed it. Perhaps it was even true. But the girl was a different matter; the look in those big dark eyes spoke volumes. Andy might say she was nothing to him but a friend – well, that was *his* story. But Colin, out of the pub now and pushing his way through the crowds on the pavement, thought he knew better.

That morning Rosheen and Cassie had gone straight to the bulletin board after drill. Recently Cassie had been upgraded to temporary corporal and then to full corporal, which meant that she took drill almost every morning, though in fact the job really belonged to their sergeant, a fat and easy-going man who regularly overslept and was content to leave the task in Cassie's capable hands. Not that Cassie minded;

there was something almost hypnotically soothing in a well-trained team of girls, each one moving in time with the others, so that on one memorable occasion it had been her flight which had performed their drill on the parade ground in front of a very distinguished visitor: the Queen.

'Hasn't she got the most beautiful smile?' Rosheen had said when the momentous occasion was over. 'It makes you proud to be British, especially when you think that she and the princesses have been right at the heart of the bombing ever since the war started.'

'Yes, and when she heard that Buckingham Palace had been bombed she said she was glad it had happened because now she could look the East End in the face,' Cassie said. 'And she really admired our drill. She spoke to every single one of us personally.'

But that had been a long time ago and now the war was becoming concentrated on the nightly raids from the big bombers. America had come in at the end of 1941, and their contribution was massive, as was their pursuit of girls. Presents of nylons, chocolate and various other commodities rained down upon the female staff in factories, shops and cafés, but the Waafs, Cassie told herself, held themselves aloof from such tempting gifts.

'British boys are good enough for us, and if they can't scatter nylons and chocolates because they're too busy fighting the enemy then good for them,' she had said.

Rosheen had blown a raspberry. 'What rubbish!' she remarked. 'It's just that our station's pretty remote and the only Yanks we get to see are when we go on the liberty truck to Lincoln.' She giggled. 'By the time we get there the Yanks have run out of everything except chewing gum and those mints with the hole in the middle, so it's not that we're too high-minded to accept stuff, it's that we come on the scene too late.'

Right now, though, Cassie was brushing a minute speck of dust from the shoulders of her best uniform. All morning she had been fussing over her appearance, thinking how shameful it would be if Andy failed to recognise her. But she knew war changed people; she had seen boys of eighteen look forty after an exhausting night raid, until youthfulness had been restored by a game of High Cockalorum in the Mess.

'Cassie, I need your advice.' Rosheen's voice broke into her thoughts. 'I've not seen the twins since May left the convalescent home and they moved back to the Wrights'. They're growing up, and growing away from me, and though my mother does her best to keep her eye on them she finds it difficult now they're back in Wales. Do you think our Section Officer would grant me a spot of leave?'

Cassie considered, though they both knew what her answer would be. 'I'm sure you'd get at least a week, if you asked,' she said. 'In fact, why haven't you asked before? I know we're stretched in the motor pool, but the fact that you have children should make you priority.'

Rosheen sighed. 'I don't like to ask for special favours, especially when I know the twins are being so well looked after,' she said. 'Everyone wants leave; look at your poor friend Becky. She's not been home for absolutely ages, you told me so the other day. But the truth is I've had a letter from my mum and she's a bit worried about May.'

'I'm not surprised – I know it's over a year since the bombing but a little kid doesn't get over something like that in a hurry,' Cassie said at once. 'Just you tell the Section Officer that you need to go home for a few days and I'm sure it will be all right. Look, would you like me to come with you to see her? We've got time before the liberty truck leaves …' she grinned, 'especially as I'm driving it today.'

'Would you?' Rosheen said gratefully. 'I'll bring my mother's letter just in case she makes a fuss. And once we've got my leave settled you'll be able to concentrate on lover boy.'

Once her liberty truck had dropped its passengers off Cassie went straight to the Saracen's Head, even though it would be almost an hour before her rendezvous with Andy. She peeped into the bar, which was more or less deserted, then made her way to the Ladies where she combed her hair, dabbed powder on her nose and checked that the seams of her very best silk stockings were straight. Then she decided to have a look at the shops. She found a chemist which stocked various beauty preparations, including a package of rather faded baths salts which she bought for Rosheen, for their Section Officer had not hesitated to grant her leave and she would be off in a couple of days, armed with a travel warrant which allowed her to reach Liverpool and Cragside Cottage within the specified time.

Usually Cassie enjoyed shopping, even though the shortages meant one's foray might be unsuccessful, but today she was too nervous to relax. Everywhere she looked there were young men in air force blue, any one of whom could have been Andy, and eventually roaming the streets with a thumping heart became too nerve-racking and she returned to the pub, where already men were lining up at the bar. She wondered whether to buy a drink – it would be the natural thing to do – then decided against it. Andy, damn his arrogant eyes, could do the honours so far as drinks were concerned.

She had chosen to sit on a banquette in the corner so she could examine the crowd without having to crane her neck, yet it was still a surprise when a voice said: 'Cassie Valentine! I'd have known you anywhere.' She looked up quickly and it was Andy.

She had meant to be cool, calm and collected but was none of those things. She jumped to her feet and held out both hands, half warding him off, half inviting him close, and the minute their hands touched a jolt like an electric shock froze her in position, looking up into his face, half smiling, half tearful.

'Andy!' she said, unable to keep the pleasure out of her voice. 'Oh, Andy, you've grown.'

They both laughed and Andy dropped her hands and caught her elbow. 'Let's get out of here; find somewhere less public and have a spot of lunch,' he said urgently. 'D'you fancy Lyons Corner House? The only thing is it'll be crammed with air force bods as well ...'

'I don't mind,' Cassie said dreamily. The sheer pleasure of being with Andy once more still had her in its grip. 'Or we could go to that little café on Silver Street? They've got a couple of tables and they do nice sandwiches. It's a bit old ladyish, but very quiet.'

'Right, you're the boss,' Andy said cheerfully, leading her out of the pub. 'You know I'm on bombers now, and I know you're in the motor pool, so let's hope we can chat over our meal without referring to the dangerous subject of our past disagreements.'

They emerged on to High Street and turned towards their destination. 'Oh, that; I trust neither of us wants to dig that up. In fact I've even forgotten what it was about,' Cassie lied, whilst an image of Rebecca, golden-haired and blue-eyed, danced tauntingly before her. 'Tell me about your crew.'

He was still holding her arm, but the sight of an officer heading towards them reminded them both of the perils of their situation. Cassie had put on her cap – as had Andy – as they emerged from the pub, and now they both saluted the officer smartly, keeping a good six inches between each other as he passed. Then they went under the stone bow and headed for Silver Street. As Cassie had predicted, the little café was quiet and the sandwiches – cheese and pickle and Spam salad – were good, so whilst they ate conversation was at a minimum. Cassie smiled at him every time their eyes met but presently it occurred to her that Andy's smile was a little forced, as though he were thinking of something else. Rebecca? Come to think of it, Rebecca had not mentioned Andy in her recent letters. She had told Cassie that her ack-ack battery was constantly on the move and had advised her friend to address her letters to Mrs Spencer, who would then redirect them.

It's a wretched nuisance, because it means my mail arrives several days or even weeks after the sender has written it, she had written.

But I love getting letters – everyone does – so please, dear Cassie, don't stop writing. You don't know how I envy you, working mostly in daylight and with people your own age. The men I work with are in their fifties and resent the fact that we girls are every bit as efficient as they are themselves, if not more so. Possibly I chose the ATS for the wrong reasons but now I'm stuck with it, so keep on writing, love, and next time we get leave perhaps we'll meet.

'Cassie?' Andy said. He laughed. 'You always were a complete dream. Good job you're not in my flight – you can't go off into another world when you're flying God knows how many tons of *B for Betsy*. When you get to know your kite you form a very special relationship with her and the other members of the crew ...'

He went on for some time on this theme whilst Cassie gazed at him across the small table and tried to trace the changes. She thought that the gravity of war showed on his face, but told herself that when it was all over and forgotten he would be, once more, the Andy she knew and, she was now beginning to suspect, loved. They finished their meal and Andy paid the bill and escorted her out on to Silver Street. Cassie realised she was waiting for an invitation, a suggestion ... call it what you will, it was Andy's move now. A wander down the river to Brayford's Pool? A bus trip to some little known beauty spot? A quiet hotel room ... she shivered ... with a big soft bed; she would have agreed, she thought now, to any one of them, but the suggestion when it came was unexpected.

'Want to see a flick?' Andy's tone was casual. 'There's a good show at the theatre on Clasketgate, or so the chaps tell me.'

After Cassie's romantic imaginings this remark had the effect of a bucket of cold water; she actually gasped before she was able to pull herself together and say, submissively, that they would do whatever he wanted.

'We'll go to the flicks then,' Andy said, and to her annoyance Cassie heard relief in his voice. 'It's a comedy, Laurel and Hardy. You'll enjoy that.'

Cassie toyed with the idea of informing him, crossly, that she would prefer a romance, but knew she would not do it. She had realised, even as they ate their sandwich lunch, that Andy had anticipated this meeting with quite as much apprehension as she had felt. For her, however, the touch of his hand on hers and that once loved lopsided grin had been enough to change her back into the starry-eyed little girl who had worshipped her big, handsome next door neighbour. She had valued their friendship more than she had realised, but now she must accept that the warmer feelings which had sprung to life at his touch were one-sided to say the least. As they made their way towards the Theatre Royal she told herself that Andy was the sensible one; that she had only felt as she had because she had had a crush on him as a child. Nevertheless, as they entered the cinema foyer and Andy paid for two seats in the stalls she remembered one of the Waafs in her hut commenting that she was going into Lincoln to get sixpenn'orth of dark.

'What did she mean by that?' Cassie had asked Rosheen as they walked across to the ablutions together. 'What an odd expression!'

Rosheen had laughed. 'She and her feller are going to the flicks,' she had explained. 'They'll get seats in the back row and canoodle. If you ask her what the film was like you'll probably find she's scarcely had time to glance at the screen, especially if he's got wandering hands and she isn't in the mood.'

Cassie had been astonished at the time and now she waited, half apprehensively, to see whether Andy intended to concentrate on the film or on herself. The answer was not long in coming. He bought her a small bag of toffees, which made her choke over a remembered comment: 'Give her toffees so she's chewing instead of expecting to be kissed,' she thought, half insulted, half amused. When the show was over and he suggested having a quick meal at the Saracen's Head before parting, however, she was easily able to thank him politely but say that since she was driving the liberty truck she must not risk being late.

Together they walked through the city to the

parking area, where a line of gharries awaited them. But when Andy would have shaken hands, as though they were no more than casual acquaintances, Cassie rebelled. She refused to hold out her hand and instead reached up and kissed him firmly just below his ear.

'Thanks for a lovely day, Andy,' she said, trying to sound nothing but practical. 'Next time we meet – if we do – it'll be my treat. Only I expect you'll be too busy, now you've discovered that we've both changed a lot since joining up. Good night; sweet dreams.'

Andy reached out as though to prevent her leaving, but Cassie's pride had received a battering and she had no desire to prolong the moment of parting. If at any point during the day he had made one attempt to draw a little closer she would have responded gladly, but he had made no such attempt and she was afraid her self-esteem would not survive another snub. So she ran round the gharry, jumped into the driver's seat and turned to the girl already sitting on the passenger side. She began an animated conversation and then realised that there was no need. Andy had disappeared.

Back at the station Colin looked up as Andy entered the mess. He was grinning. 'Well?' he asked. 'I saw you meet her, but then I made myself scarce. What happened? Give!'

344

Andy came over and sank into a chair alongside Colin. 'Had lunch, went to the flicks, came home,' he said laconically. 'Anything else you'd like to know, Mr Give?'

Colin chuckled. 'I want to know everything that happened, right down to the last kiss,' he said. 'Where did you have lunch? What film did you see – only I bet you didn't see much of anything – and when's your next date?'

Andy sighed. 'She's not a bad kid, but she's not really my type,' he said. 'If you'd like an introduction I'll happily give you one, because I got the distinct feeling that she was waiting for me to suggest something a good deal warmer than a seat at the cinema.'

'You conceited brute,' Colin said, staring at his friend. 'What makes you think you're irresistible?' Even as he heard his voice saying the words, however, he remembered the moment that Cassie and Andy had met, remembered the love – had it been love? – shining out of those big dark eyes. He said curiously: 'Was there really nothing stronger than an old friendship between the pair of you? I got the impression—'

Andy cut across him. 'Oh, that! That was years ago, when I didn't know one end of a woman from the other. We've been neighbours for ever, you see, and Cassie, who's an only child like me, just fell into the habit of treating me like an older brother.

In fact, to be honest, she had a crush on me. She used to follow me around like a little pet lamb, but of course that sort of thing ends as you get older. Now, I hope, we can just be friends and forget all that other business.'

'Didn't you hold her hand in the flicks? Didn't you kiss her goodnight? You stood a good chance of getting your end away and didn't take it?' Colin said reproachfully. 'I'm ashamed of you, O'Leary.'

Andy snorted. 'You know we've always said we'd steer clear of romantic entanglements, which is what Cassie would speedily become if I let her. I agree we go back a long way, and maybe after the war ... but right now the kite and the crew are what matters. I've no time to add even the most tempting popsy to the list.' He grinned at Colin. 'The offer of an introduction still stands. How about it?'

Colin pulled a face. 'How generous you are,' he said mockingly. 'Here's me with a queue of women wanting my attention and you offer me your leavings? I've got my eye on that pretty little RT operator, the one with black hair and blue eyes, so thanks for the offer, but no thanks.'

Andy shrugged. 'Please yourself,' he said casually. 'She refused my generous offer of a meal, by the way, so shall we amble along to the cookhouse and see what tempting delights are in store for our supper?'

Chapter Eighteen

Despite only having a couple of days to arrange things, Rosheen soon found herself on the train, heading for home. Because of the shortage of any sort of accommodation following the May blitz, she knew that No. 3 King Edward Court was now shared by a number of those who had lost their own homes, so she did not walk straight into the house as she would once have done. Instead she knocked politely, waited a moment, and actually had her hand on the doorknob when it shot open and there was Mrs Clarke, beaming and ushering her daughter into the kitchen, where Mrs Plevin was standing by the table. Rosheen knew from her mother's letters that the two women had joined forces, two very good cooks who could make a meal out of almost nothing, and had actually started a sort of cookery school in the court to pass their skills on to others.

'It was my daughter, just as I thought, Mrs P,' Mrs Clarke told her neighbour, before turning back to Rosheen. 'Are you hungry, love? I made scones earlier.' She laughed. 'Fruitless, eggless, sugarless, butterless scones, but even using dried milk and chopped up bits of carrot they fill the chinks. Want one?'

Rosheen knew a cue when she heard one. Her mother was rightly proud of her abilities as a cook and would take it for granted that her daughter would accept the offer, and presently the three of them were seated round the kitchen table, a butterless, fruitless, eggless scone in one hand and a cup of tea in the other. Rosheen finished her scone first.

'That was delicious, Mam,' she said truthfully. 'And now tell me – how are the girls?'

Mrs Clarke smiled. 'They're doing well in school and now that May's come out of her shell they're making friends, which they've never bothered to do before, being a law unto themselves as you might say. They wanted to come up to Liverpool and travel back to the Wrights' with you tomorrow, but I told them it wasn't on. I know you have a travel warrant, but I never heard of an evacuee being given one, and I don't know what the rail fare would be, so I put a stop to that little plan. I can't remember – when did you see them last?' She saw an apprehensive look in her daughter's face and added quickly, 'Don't think I blame you. It was made perfectly clear when you joined the WAAF that your work there must come first. And you had plenty of time off whilst May was in hospital. But it must be at least six months, maybe longer, since you saw them.'

'It's more like a year,' Rosheen said ruefully. 'You see, I felt that they were happy with the Wrights, and with you popping over from time to time to check that all was well … oh, Mam, have I been a neglectful mother? Honest to God, I've done my best, but when you're in the services and there's a war on you can't just up sticks and leave unless it's for a real emergency, like the May blitz.'

Mrs Clarke wagged a reproachful head. 'Did I insinuate that anyone was in the wrong?' she asked and then, turning to her friend: 'Have I ever said a word against my daughter, Mrs P?' And upon Mrs Plevin's assuring Rosheen that this was not the case Mrs Clarke turned back to Rosheen. 'The twins are happy and useful, their manners have improved more than I ever thought possible, and they treat the Wrights with love and respect,' she said.

Rosheen had to force her mouth, which had dropped open in astonishment, to resume its normal shape. 'You mean there's been no talk of running away for more than a year? I can hardly believe it. Are you sure?'

Mrs Clarke chuckled. 'Run away? It's the last thing on their minds,' she said firmly. 'And anyway, they're over the moon at the thought of seeing you again after so long. Honest to God, Rosheen, they've made all sorts of plans for your visit, but even if they hadn't known you were coming I can promise you that they'll stick to Cragside Cottage – and the Wrights – like glue. The only thing is, May's not quite as lively as I could wish. Sometimes she doesn't sound like herself at all. But when you get to the village I'm sure she'll perk up and put our minds at rest.' She beamed at her daughter. 'Another of my Woolton scones?

Rosheen smiled back. 'I don't like to take your food, because the air force feed us pretty well, actually,' she said. 'But if you insist . . .' She took the proffered scone.

Mrs Clarke smiled. 'What would you like to do this evening?' she asked. 'There's a good film on at the Forum.'

Rosheen had not expected an ecstatic welcome when she arrived at Cragside Cottage, but that was what she received. She pushed open the little wooden gate and walked up the path, reaching the front door just as it shot open and the twins hurtled out. She gathered them in a warm embrace, conscious of both surprise and exhilaration, for her daughters had never been demonstrative, had always behaved as though a show of affection were some sort of weakness. But today, it seemed, was different. And they'd grown! They were almost as tall as Rosheen herself. They were kissing and hugging her, not afraid to show their delight, and presently they tugged her through the front door and into the cottage kitchen where the Wrights stood with welcoming smiles.

'Mornin', love,' Mr Wright said. 'I expect you're wondering why these here turrible girls ain't in school. Don't you worry, m'dear. They've got permission to stay home until you have to leave us, though knowin' them they'll probably want to give a hand with the apple harvest while they're here. And now how about a nice cup of tea and a bit of apple cake?'

'That would be lovely,' Rosheen said happily. She gazed at April and May, looking suddenly so different, then thanked Mrs Wright for the cup of tea she had placed on the table before her. 'Goodness, I can't believe how tall the girls are; nearly as tall as me! And how pretty!'

April and May had sat themselves down one on each side of Rosheen, and now April spoke. 'We're not identical any more, are we, Mam? And our teacher thinks we'll get more and more different as we get older.'

'Ah well, all young things change as time passes,' Mrs Wright said comfortably. 'You'll learn to 'preciate bein' different, same as you 'preciated bein' the same. And them as loves you – like your mam here – won't have to worry when they can't buy identical clothes.'

Rosheen laughed. 'They've not been dressed alike for many a long year,' she said. 'Now what's all this talk about harvesting apples? Am I allowed to help as well, or had you other plans?'

'Well, I expect it would be polite to go up to the farmhouse to see Mr and Mrs Nidd,' May said thoughtfully. She eyed her mother's trimly uniformed figure. 'I say, Mam, we aren't the only ones who've changed; you've got a figure like a fillum star, and I like the way you're doin' your hair. We'll be rare proud of you, April and me, when we goes up to the farm!'

Rosheen had booked herself a room in the Llew Coch in the village – Red Lion in English – and they went up to the farm to call on Mrs Nidd as soon as Rosheen had confirmed her booking. The landlady of the inn was a comfortable soul, plump and smiling, and she agreed to provide Rosheen with bed, breakfast and an evening meal for fifteen shillings and sixpence a night. She had asked hopefully if Rosheen would be staying the whole week, saying this would reduce the bill, but Rosheen could only shake her head.

'It's just for the four days,' she said regretfully. 'And if the weather turns nasty I'll maybe beg your permission to entertain my daughters in my room. However, the forecast is good so maybe we'll be up at the farm helping with their apple harvest most of the time, which it seems the twins would prefer to more organised outings.'

Rosheen thoroughly enjoyed her sojourn in

the village. To her mind the twins were becoming the children she had dreamed of mothering. They were loving towards her and the Wrights, polite to their teachers, and friendly with other children, and Rosheen could not help thinking that most of the improvement had come about since the May blitz. To be sure, April had changed very little from the rosy-cheeked, self-willed child who had stayed by her sister throughout that terrible day, but May's traumatic experience seemed to have turned her from a rather whiny, heedless child into a responsible young woman. Nevertheless, Rosheen thought she could see why her mother had been so worried. Despite May's stout insistence that she was perfectly well her skin had a translucent look, and even when she was laughing it seemed to Rosheen that her eyes were serious. May has suffered, she thought with a pang, and it shows on her poor little face. But when she had tried to cross question her younger daughter about the state of her health, May had been dismissive.

'I've healed fine, absolutely fine,' she told her mother. 'Nothing hurts any more – well, not very much – and I'm getting stronger every day.'

On Rosheen's last full day in the village the fine weather broke at last, so Mrs Nidd set the three of them to work in the big barn grading Bramley cooking apples. Presently she summoned them back to the farmhouse kitchen and suggested that one of the twins might like to help her take a big basket containing various edibles down to the workers whilst the other helped Rosheen make the tea. She looked thoughtfully at the girls. 'April, you come with me; give May's leg a bit of a rest.' She bustled off, leaning heavily to port with the weight of one handle while April struggled manfully with the other. Rosheen was still staring after them, reflecting that not so long ago April would have objected long and loud to being given such an order, when she heard her elder daughter's voice behind her.

'She's forgotten her mac. If ever there was a stupid girl, her name is April Clarke.'

Rosheen whipped round. It was May all right, grinning across the kitchen at her mother with April's waterproof in her hand, but the voice which had issued from her lips was unquestionably April's.

That evening, helping Rosheen pack her kitbag in her room at the Llew Coch, April explained.

'May started it,' she said, 'but I wish I'd thought of it first, because it's a really good idea. You see, it's a sort of game to make us forget that May is different from me because of the blitz. She's only got to walk across the room, or try to pick up something too heavy for her, and a total stranger can tell us apart at once. Even people who used to think we were identical never mix us up any more, so we thought –

well, May did – that if we practised talking like each other we could fool them anyway.'

Rosheen couldn't help herself; she began to laugh until the tears ran down her cheeks, and the twins joined in. Finally, however, Rosheen wiped her eyes and addressed her daughters in as stern a voice as she could manage. 'All right, I do understand, and you mustn't try to trick people because you'll find it really does upset them.'

'The kids at school don't mind; they think it's funny,' April mumbled, but Rosheen shook her head. 'I said no and I mean no,' she told them. 'It's all right to play tricks on kids of your own age but don't you dare involve adults, or you'll have me to reckon with. I'm going to tell Grandma exactly what you've been up to, and you must promise her, as well as me, that you won't do it any more.'

Mrs Clarke greeted her daughter's return with enthusiasm, and thought the swapping of voices hilarious. 'The little devils!' she exclaimed after Rosheen had put her in the picture. 'I must be the least observant person in the world, because I'm sure they probably did it every time we met. No wonder I thought May wasn't quite herself!'

Rosheen giggled. 'Was I mischievous as a child?' she asked. 'Sometimes I wonder about their father; he must have been a real hellion, though it wasn't apparent.'

Mrs Clarke stared. 'You haven't mentioned him for years; not even when we thought we might lose our little May when she was first brought out of the shelter. Do you still think about him?'

Rosheen had blushed to the roots of her hair, but now she shook her head. 'He never crosses my mind,' she said firmly. 'Why, I can't even remember his face.'

Chapter Nineteen

October 1944

'Wakey wakey!' Andy's rear gunner's voice scarcely penetrated his sleep-drugged ears, but the hand on his shoulder, shaking impatiently, ensured that he woke. Andy opened an eye and blinked around, then uttered a soft moan. He was in the Nissen hut at RAF Rigby and earlier in the evening had read the Battle Order which told him that take-off would be 22.00 hours. He gave another groan. His fortnight's leave had been great, but because his mother had wanted him to return to Ireland to see his grandfather it had not been very restful. And the return journey to his base had been the worst he had ever experienced. Connections had been late or had simply not arrived, and when a train did pull in it was usually already so crowded that he had been unable to board it. The result was that he had arrived at RAF Rigby with no time to do more than sit down on his bed and get into his flying gear before going to the Mess for dinner.

He remembered sitting down on his bed all right – some kind person had made it up for him – but he had no recollection of getting between the sheets, although he had obviously done so. And now here was Chimp shaking his shoulder and reminding him that they had a great deal of work to do before *B for Betsy* could take off on her night's task: a bombing raid on the Ruhr, he could not remember where.

'Skip? Don't you go back to sleep, you lazy blighter! Everyone else is just about ready to catch the bus.'

Andy moaned softly beneath his breath. If a fortnight's leave left you in this sort of state he hoped he would never get another. But Chimp was looking at him enquiringly and he blinked and grinned, getting to his feet and reaching for his boots.

'Sorry, Chimp. I had one hell of a good leave, but it was all go. And Christ, the journey back here from my grandfather's place was every sort of hell. Missed connections, overcrowded trains – a couple of times we were shunted into sidings so that a more important train might go through – and of course the inevitable breakdown. So I missed dinner in the Mess and came straight here; must have fallen asleep by mistake.' He was putting his boots on as he talked.

Chimp nodded impatiently. 'All right, we've all just come back off leave but if there's one person *B for Betsy* can't manage without it's you, Skip. So let's get a move on, shall we? The crew bus is waiting; I told them you wouldn't be more than ten minutes at the outside.'

Andy glanced quickly round his bed area, checking that he had donned the necessary clothing, for though down here it might seem mild, as the Lancaster reached its cruising speed of twenty thousand feet it became exceedingly cold. Sometimes the gremlins who rejoiced in making life difficult actually managed to freeze some piece of equipment, but it was part of every bomber pilot's duty, and that of his crew, to check constantly, even when over the target with enemy fighters attacking from every angle and the flak coming up from the German ack-ack batteries just, as Andy remarked, to make life a little more exciting.

But right now, having checked that everything was as it should be, he thanked Chimp for waking him and walked out with him to join the rest of the crew in the bus, which was driven by a pretty little Waaf with shining chestnut hair who reminded him of Cassie.

Once in their seats the crew exchanged chat about their leaves, waiting for the moment when they would be given the exact time of take off. When it came, everyone was relieved; there was nothing more irritating and enervating than waiting in the dark for a call which did not come. At the marshalling point Andy brought the great black Lancaster to a halt and spoke to the crew.

'Rightyho, let's start the checks. Throttles?'

'Set on a thousand, Skip.'

'Trims, elevators two notches, nose down?'

'Yessir.'

'Supercharger?'

'M gear.'

'Pitch?'

'Fully fine and locked.'

The checks went on, and at the exact time he had been given Andy released the brakes and the great black aircraft surged into the sky. He grinned to himself. Now all they had to face for a few hours was the cold and the mind-numbing boredom. Radio silence would be complete until they were over Germany, when it might be necessary for the crew to warn their pilot of approaching danger. But for now he could relax, and immediately his mind went back to his leave and to Cassie. He had not seen the girl for months, yet from the moment he had set foot in his own home in the small village on the Wirral she was all he could think about. They had been such good friends! Of course, when she had been small she had driven him to distraction by following him around, worshipful eyes fixed on his face whenever he left the house. But that had soon been forgotten when he discovered that the girl next door was an intelligent and lively companion. But the war had interrupted all that, and the subsequent intrusion of other girls into his life had made his friendship with Cassie seem almost irrelevant. Almost.

Andy shifted uneasily in his seat. He had encouraged Colin Trelawney to get together with Cassie, and now he wondered why on earth he had done such a thing. Cassie was his property, he felt, and if he chose to throw her at Colin's feet that was his business, but nevertheless it annoyed him that Cassie had so willingly accepted Colin as a substitute for himself. And now Colin had left him to become a navigator on Halifaxes on the same airfield as Cassie, and it was even possible that by now the couple might have ...

Andy wrenched his mind away from the mental image of Colin and Cassie entwined in a lovers' embrace and scowled into the darkness ahead of him. Surely she would not, could not, let her friendship with Colin go further than her friendship with himself?

In the seat beside him Samson, the flight engineer, made tiny adjustments to the instrument panel. Behind him at the little green-curtained navigator's table, newcomer Robbie traced their progress, and as the great kite reached its cruising altitude Andy's inner eye formed a picture of Cassie as he had last seen her. She had removed her cap and her smooth dark auburn hair had gleamed in the sunshine whilst her large blue eyes had sparkled with pleasure at seeing her old friend. They had met as usual in the Saracen's Head, where Cassie had told him that she was being posted along with her friend, an Irish girl by the name of Rosheen, to the same airfield in Yorkshire as Colin, and had come to say t.t.f.n., though not, she hoped, for long. Andy's eyebrows had climbed at the mention of her new airfield. She would be working in the motor pool and would doubtless come into contact with Colin on an almost daily basis. He had felt the familiar stab of jealousy, but had dismissed it at once as indigestion. After all, he had told himself many times that getting attached to any woman whilst the war raged on was not a good idea. Now he could prove it.

Cassie had given him her sweet three-cornered smile. 'I'll be sorry to be moving even further away from Lincoln,' she had said, 'but you and I haven't seen much of each other despite being so close.'

If it was a reproach, he deserved it. They had met three or four times since their original reunion in this very pub, but always at her suggestion, never his, and even this meeting had been Cassie's idea – her farewell to both Lincoln and himself, he realised.

Knowing it was likely to be the last time he saw her before the end of the war, Andy had half expected her to suggest a meal, a walk down to Brayford's Pool or even a visit to the cinema, but she did not. Having told him that she was on the move she simply got to her feet and held out a hand. Then she had twinkled at him.

'Well, nice to have met you, Andy. You never know, I might get another posting in the months to come and find myself at Rigby. Dear me, don't go pale, it'll probably never happen.'

Andy had grasped her hand, tried to pull her close – such old friends should surely not part on a handshake? – but she had resisted, laughing but firm.

'Don't be daft, you can't go kissing Waafs in a public bar. I'll write.'

And with that she had turned her neatly uniformed back and walked swiftly out of the pub, not giving him a chance to follow her; not that he had tried because at that very moment he had been hailed by one of his crew.

'Fancy a beer, sport? Johnny's in the chair.'

'Overflying the coast, Skip.' The navigator's voice brought Andy back to the present, to the steady drone of the Merlin engines and the everlasting dark. Presently he would be glad of the dark, when they reached the target and were dodging enemy aircraft and the inevitable white and yellow flak coming up from the German ack-ack batteries. That reminded him of Rebecca and he caught himself wondering whether, down below, he would presently be raining bombs down on pretty girls just like Rebecca – just like Cassie.

But it didn't do to think like that. He remembered someone telling him years ago that the Brits were trained to concentrate on bringing the enemy kites down, whereas the Germans were told to aim for the crews. Perhaps it was propaganda – there was a lot of it about – but he knew that he and all his fellow fliers concentrated on offloading their bombs in the right places and downing as many enemy crates as they could. They seldom thought of the airmen at all. Andy and *B for Betsy* flew on.

Cassie swung herself into the driver's seat, wound down the window and looked out at the men who were loading the truck for her journey up to Scotland. They were going in convoy, half a dozen of the big heavy lorries, and would probably take the entire day to reach their destination, which was fine by Cassie since it meant she ought to be back by the time she and Colin had arranged to meet, three days from now. The trouble was, though Cassie had become very fond of Colin, she had still not decided on a total commitment. She and Rosheen had talked it over endlessly – chewing the fat, Rosheen called it – yet despite, or perhaps because of, Rosheen's worldly experience Cassie simply could not make up her mind. She was extremely fond of Colin, who was generous, loving and humorous, but her old friendship with Andy was always in the back of her mind, even though, certainly on Andy's side,

Cassie thought, not a lot remained of their pre-war relationship. Yet somehow whenever she thought of taking Colin home, of accepting his repeatedly urgent suggestions that they should become lovers, she could never quite escape from the feeling that she was Andy's girl and would be until the end.

The sergeant in charge of the convoy shouted something and Cassie engaged first gear, gently eased her foot off the clutch and began to move forward. In the big lorry behind her she knew Rosheen would be doing the same thing, and once they were off the base and crawling at a steady twenty miles an hour along the village street she was able to let her mind return to Colin. He had many good points, most of which were missing in her old friend Andy. She had mentioned his name to her mother and that understanding person had replied immediately that she should bring Colin home so that she and Daddy might see for themselves what sort of man he was.

Not that we doubt your judgement, darling, her mother's letter had gone on, *but we have seen so many mistakes that have come about due to the war and we don't want you to be one of that number.*

Perhaps she had Rosheen in mind, but Rosheen's mistake had come about well before the war, and since hostilities had started Rosheen had never so much as glanced at a man to Cassie's knowledge, let alone had a boyfriend. And it was not that she did not attract men, because she most certainly did; they loved her bubbly personality, the Irish brogue she could assume when requested, the sense of humour which turned solemn occasions into humorous ones. Cassie had wondered whether at some point her friend would try to find a substitute father for the twins, but it had soon become apparent that she had no such intention. The two of them often made up a foursome with Colin and one of his crew, but Rosheen always made it plain that she was not in the market for a casual affair, or indeed any affair.

'I'm a married woman,' she had untruthfully explained when one of Colin's crew had asked her for a date. 'My husband's six foot two and a boxing champion, so just you mind your manners because one word from me and you'll find yourself backed into a corner and swearing you'll never touch a woman again.'

Cassie, concentrating on driving and keeping her distance from the lorry in front, thought that she and Rosheen were the sensible ones.

The war was gradually drawing to a close, though the bombers still droned on their way to rain their cargo on the industrial cities and particularly along the Ruhr. They saw few German bombers now, though the flak continued relentlessly, but that was because the doodlebugs and V2 rockets did not need pilots and the damage they could create, without the loss of one German life, was tremendous. And that's why we're attacking the Ruhr, because the doodlebugs and rockets are being launched from there, Cassie reminded herself, but surely the war has to be nearly over. Colin had told her when he came back from a raid that though there were still pockets of resistance it was nothing to the fight put up the previous year.

'We lay our eggs – Johnny's a first rate bomb aimer – circle a couple of times so we can tell them at the debriefing just what we hit, and then we make for home,' he had explained. 'Of course there are still the Junkers and the Messerschmitts but even they are few and far between. In fact, what with the success of Operation Overlord, it simply can't last much longer. Thank God for the Yanks and their flying fortresses.'

'Thank God for them,' Cassie had agreed. 'And now let's stop talking about the war. There's a dance on at the village hall tomorrow. Want to come?'

'All right, Skip? We should be making landfall at RAF Corby in the next thirty minutes.' Colin leaned closer, reading the instrument panel over the pilot's shoulder but everything looked as it should and he relaxed. He had successfully steered them to the target and now he had plotted their course home. Very soon now, he told himself, he would be able to contact Cassie, who he knew was driving to Scotland.

In his mind a vision of her rose: the thick hair

glossy as a chestnut just out of its husk, the big dark blue eyes and the softly kissable mouth. He loved her helplessly and grieved when she made it plain she did not return his feelings. Oh, she liked him very much, he knew that. After all, she enjoyed his company, sought him out, had actually suggested that next time they both had leave he might accompany her to her parents' home and meet them for the first time. She was a complete enigma, loving and giving one moment, the next withdrawing from him as if even the touch of his hand might in some way compromise her. He had discussed the situation with Toby, the turret gunner, and Toby had suggested the possibility that she might still be holding a torch for Colin's friend Andy.

Colin had considered the possibility but after some thought had shaken his head. 'No, it can't be that. It's true she was pretty hot on him a couple of years ago, but when she mentions him now, which isn't often, she more or less dismisses him. I don't believe they even exchange letters. I know she gets all his news, because their mums are thick as thieves, but that's very different from holding a torch, wouldn't you say?'

Toby had shrugged. 'Women are funny creatures, difficult for us poor blokes to understand,' he had said. 'Why not ask her? I mean, she's obviously not a gold digger, because you're always strapped for cash, and she's not short of friends. Pretty girls like your Cassie could have half a dozen men eager to take her about. Why don't you suggest a naughty weekend, and get her reaction?'

'She'd slap my face and march out of my life for ever,' Colin had said, laughing. 'Oh, well, I keep telling myself that no girl asks a feller home to meet her folk unless she's serious. Wouldn't you say that's true?'

Toby had shrugged. 'Dunno; sheilas are a closed book to me,' he had said, borrowing from their Australian rear gunner's vocabulary. They were in the sergeants' Mess, having just finished their pre-raid meal, and now they got to their feet, glancing anxiously at their wristwatches, but the crew bus which would take them to their kite had not yet arrived. 'I don't know that I've been much help to you,' Toby had added apologetically. He was older than the other six members of the crew and because he had a steady girlfriend back home he was deemed to be experienced, particularly by Skip, who was just nineteen, and the rear gunner, Paul, who was even younger.

'It has been a help just to talk about it,' Colin had admitted as they walked. 'I know the crew, or most of them, think that Cassie and I are serious, and I reckon her friend Rosheen thinks the same. It was that invitation to meet her parents which made me hope, but I suppose it's possible she was just being kind.' He had glanced under his brows at Toby, but that experienced young man – he was twenty-seven – had shaken his head.

'As I said, I don't know much more than the rest of you about women, but I do know one thing. No intelligent woman would consider it "kind" to blow hot and cold on you, the way your Cassie sometimes seems to do. If I were you I'd ask her why the invitation to meet her parents. You may feel as though you're driving her into a corner – well, in a way you will be – but it's my belief she'll play fair. She'll tell you to your face whether you've got a chance with her or not.'

'Oh, but—'

'I know – you're afraid she'll tell you that you've not got a chance and that'll put an end not just to your hopes but to all the other things. Trips to the cinema, a drink at the pub, a walk in the woods. But at least you'd know where you stand.'

'I know you're right really and it's time I chanced my arm,' Colin had said after a long pause for thought. 'But it's like putting all your eggs in one basket and then tripping up and smashing the lot.'

Toby had laughed. 'Or putting all your chips on the black of the roulette wheel and seeing the ball land on red,' he said. 'Honestly, Colin, I can't really advise you because I'm one of the lucky ones. Jill's a darling, and she loves me too. But in your case – if it were me I think I'd have to speak out. Damn it, man, you and she have been on the best of terms ever since I came to RAF Corby. I can't believe she'd want to cut you out of her life just because you asked her to clarify the situation. Tell you what, we've got our fifteenth op soon; that's halfway through our tour. Think about it between now and then and make up your mind.'

But now, as he looked out of the window and saw the landing lights beckoning, he spotted a kite above them. He just had time to wonder what a mozzie was doing so close to the runway – surely it was too high to attempt a landing – before the rear gunner's urgent voice rang out.

'Angels one five, Skip, coming in fast.'

Colin heard the crash of an explosion as the enemy aircraft approached at a crazy speed, spraying tracer bullets along the length of the fuselage. He remembered the Japanese kamikaze pilots and for a confused moment thought that this must be one of them. Then he heard a crew member give a grunt of pain and knew the lad had been hit.

Paul's frantic voice rose above the engine's roar. 'The bastard! He must have followed us home and—'

And Colin's world exploded into coloured lights and blackness.

Chapter Twenty

Cassie and her convoy stopped for breakfast at a dingy roadside café where they were supplied with hot tea and the ubiquitous bacon sandwich. They were allowed a twenty minute break here so all the drivers took it in turns to visit the lavatory whilst someone else watched over their precious cargo. As soon as she had finished her sandwich Cassie got to her feet.

'I'm just going to give the station a ring,' she said, trying to make her voice sound indifferent. 'Make sure Colin got home safe and sound, though he's been pretty lucky so far.'

One of the other drivers, a skinny lank-haired girl called Mabel, clicked her fingers to get Cassie's attention and spoke rapidly.

'Say, Valentine, do me a favour. If you get through ask if Tommy Dutton is okay. I don't need to talk to him, I just want to know he's safe.' She shrugged, giving Cassie a gap-toothed grin. 'It's different when they're working in the motor pool or driving the blood wagon or the crew bus. I never worry then.'

'Tommy Dutton? Is he the short feller with very blond hair and white eyelashes? His kite took off just after Colin's.' Cassie headed across the café to where there was already a short queue to use the telephone. However, the girl on the exchange dealt with each call incredibly swiftly and soon Cassie was returning to her table, a worry line etched between her soft brows.

'I spoke to the Squadron Leader. Your Tommy's fine, Mabel,' she said, and then turned to Rosheen and lowered her voice. 'Groupie said they were all down safely, but when I asked about Colin there was a bit of a pause before he repeated that all the kites had landed safely. I have a nasty sort of feeling that Colin may have sustained an injury of some description, but I didn't ask to speak to him now because you know the programme as well as I do: debriefing, after-flight meal and bed. It would be sheer selfishness to mess up their routine.'

As they walked back to their lorries Rosheen seized Cassie's arm and gave it a little shake. 'Why won't you come clean and admit you're really fond of Colin?' she asked. 'He's a nice bloke, one of the best. If it was me he wanted I'd have said "I do" a long time ago.'

'Oh, Rosheen, you've always said you're not interested in forming any sort of relationship with a man,' Cassie reminded her as they reached their vehicles. 'I've always thought it was once bitten twice shy, and the number of times you've said you don't need any help with bringing up the twins while you've got your mum must be at least a hundred. Has Colin added you to his list of conquests?'

Rosheen climbed into the driver's seat and wound down the window. 'That was what they call a rhetorical remark,' she informed Cassie with dignity. 'I like Colin very much, everyone does, but I was talking for you, so to speak. You haven't cried off men, not if I read the signs correctly anyway. You're just waiting for the war to end so you can make Andy O'Leary the happiest man on earth.' She was silent for a few moments, and Cassie thought she looked as though she was thinking of something – or someone – else entirely, but then she said briskly, 'Though why you care about a man who doesn't even bother to come and see you when he has leave I can't imagine. Look, goose, you must care about Colin or you wouldn't have flown to the telephone to make sure he got down safely.'

Cassie heaved a sigh and reached into the cab of her own lorry for the starting handle to crank the engine into life. Back at the station there would have been a strong young member of the motor pool to do it for them, but on the road one did the work oneself. Accordingly Cassie went along the row starting engines and exchanging pithy comments with the drivers before returning to her own cab and climbing aboard. Then the sergeant gave the signal and the lorries started off once more, taking advantage of the fact that no civilian liked to get caught in the middle of a convoy and so allowed them on to the main road in a long line, waiting to follow with what patience they could muster until the last lorry drew out.

'Sister!' Cassie had meant her voice to be calm and collected – Colin was only a good friend, after all – but it came out high and anxious. She had lost her bearings in the maze of corridors and seeing the navy blue dress and starched white cap in front of her had been unable to prevent herself from running after the sister and seizing her arm. 'I'm here to see Sergeant Trelawney. They told me at the airfield that he was here, and the nurse on reception showed me the way to his ward, but—'

The sister raised her eyebrows. 'Are you a relative?' she asked doubtfully. 'I expect you know he was badly injured just before he came in to land and we're restricting visitors to close friends and family.'

'Badly injured! I thought . . . I hoped . . . Groupie said the kite came down all right, so I imagined . . . But I don't think Colin has any relatives near enough to visit. He comes from a tiny village on the coast of Sutherland, in Scotland. But I'm a close friend. I'm sure it would do him good to see me.'

The sister stiffened slightly. 'We have a routine we follow with every admission to the hospital,' she said rather coldly. 'I don't know whether Mr Trelawney's parents are on the telephone but if not the local constable will take a message. However, since you say his relatives can't visit I'll speak to Matron and I'm sure she'll agree you can see the young man, so if you'll just wait in here ...' she crossed the hall in a couple of strides and pushed open the door clearly labelled *Waiting Room*, '... I'll see what I can do. As you will realise, the hospital is bulging at the seams and we're all run off our feet, so I've not actually seen Mr Trelawney yet and it's too soon for his case notes to have been written up. But if Matron agrees ...' she left the sentence unfinished and Cassie sat down in the empty waiting room. She had barely been seated a minute, however, before the door was pushed open and a woman in her fifties came in. She wore a dark dress with a voluminous white apron over it, and when Cassie jumped to her feet and opened her mouth to speak she raised an imperious hand.

'Are you Mr Trelawney's young lady?' she asked. 'If so ...'

'I'm a good friend,' Cassie said again, truthfully. 'We've known each other pretty well for a couple of years now, so I'm sure a visit from me would help rather than hinder his recovery.'

Matron looked doubtful. 'He's not yet regained

consciousness,' she said. 'However, you can see him for five minutes.' Her formidably large figure had hitherto completely blocked the doorway but now she moved to one side and beckoned Cassie to follow her. 'His crew have visited,' she said as she led the way towards a flight of stairs. 'Nice lads, all very concerned. Here we are.' As she spoke they reached the head of the stairs and she ushered Cassie into a large and airy ward, indicating the second bed on the right. Cassie crept forward, horrified by what she saw. She would have described Colin as pleasant-looking, but now his face was almost frightening. On the right side purple bruising and bandages hid everything bar the corner of his mouth and one eye. And on the left stitches in long lines made him almost unrecognisable. One of Colin's legs had a cage over it, presumably to keep the bedding off some sort of wound, and the rest of him seemed to be largely connected to tubes leading in and out of bandages. In short, he looked far worse than Cassie's worst imaginings. Going closer to the bed she looked for a hand to hold, wishing with all her might that she could somehow convey her affection and sympathy, but Matron guessed her intention and stopped her.

'Time's up,' she said briskly. 'If, as I infer, you are stationed at Corby, you're only a bus ride away and can visit again when your friend regains consciousness.'

'Oh! But I thought it would help to know someone was near by,' Cassie said.

Matron, however, was shepherding her out of the ward and back down the stairs. In the wide reception hall she pointed to a board which detailed visiting times. 'The rule is only two visitors to a bed,' she said briskly. 'You'd better liaise with his crew. In my experience these lads are closer than brothers and support each other in every way, so it might be best if you arrange to see your friend at times when they cannot.'

They were actually at the revolving doors which led to the outside world when a question occurred to Cassie. 'Matron, why was there a cage over Colin's leg?' she asked, and saw a guarded look cross that otherwise serene countenance.

'His foot has been badly damaged; possibly beyond repair,' Matron said after a moment. 'He does not know yet, but amputation may be our only course. His captain has been told, and no doubt he passed the information to the rest of the crew, but Mr Trelawney himself must be kept in ignorance until he is stronger.'

Back at Corby, Cassie was lucky enough to spot Toby Belcher crossing the parade ground as soon as she walked through the tall gates in the fencing. He had not seen her and did not hear her shout, so she broke into a run and caught his arm.

'Toby! I've just come from the hospital. Poor old

Colin. But Matron told me there was a possibility he might lose his foot. Oh Toby, isn't it a pity?'

Toby stared at her, a curious expression on his face. 'He loves you,' he said coldly. 'When you saw him in that bed with his face all cut about and a cage over his leg, what did *you* feel? Glad that it was Colin and not that Andy of yours? A fellow who doesn't even try to spend part of his leave with you? Colin's like that saying: *true blue and will never stain.* Can't you appreciate that? And if you can't you should back off and let some more discerning girl get close to him. Personally, I think you should back off anyway. If you wanted Colin and meant to stop blowing hot and cold then I'd be behind you all the way, but you don't, do you? He's just someone to take you around and buy you the odd meal. Listen to yourself: you've just come from the hospital, after seeing the sort of state Colin's in, and all you can find to say is *isn't it a pity*! Well, Miss Valentine. Colin's too good a man to waste his time on a girl who doesn't know her own mind, so why don't you just leave him alone!'

Cassie was shocked. No one had ever spoken to her in such terms before, and she didn't like it. She longed to refute Toby's words and say that Colin had no expectation of their ever being anything but good friends, but in her heart she knew that he was right. Colin did love her, and she did not love him. Yet because she enjoyed his company she had let people assume that they were, if not lovers, at least seriously attached. And now Toby's words had blown the careful façade of closeness apart and she saw her attitude through other, more critical eyes than her own.

She looked helplessly at Toby. 'I'm so sorry, and I do understand what you mean,' she said. 'But to hurt him now when he's beset by so many troubles would be unpardonable. Later, as soon as he's fit, I'll do as you say and back off.' She was smitten by a sudden thought. 'You've met my friend Rosheen, haven't you? She's in the motor pool with me – a dark-haired Irish girl, a bit older than the rest of us? She likes Colin very much – she said the other day that if he was keen on her she'd grab him. Suppose I bring her to the hospital—'

She was interrupted. 'You'll do no such thing,' Toby Belcher said wrathfully, so fierce an expression on his face that Cassie actually took a step back. 'Haven't you done enough damage? The last thing Colin wants is some woman he doesn't know seeing him the way he is. Or hadn't that occurred to you? Do you think he's going to come out of this looking like he did before? If so, all I can say is you're a true optimist. He's got a broken nose and a split cheekbone, to say nothing of enough stitches to start a tailor's shop. Girls care about such things, I believe.'

'I don't; looks don't matter to me,' Cassie

mumbled, close to tears. 'If Andy was in Colin's position it wouldn't affect the way I feel about him—'

Toby gave a harsh exclamation. 'There you go again,' he said furiously. 'Grow up, Cassie Valentine, and don't you *dare* take anyone into the hospital unless Colin asks you to.'

Chapter Twenty-one

May 1945

As luck would have it Rosheen was visiting the Wrights when the momentous news that the war had ended came over their tinny little wireless set. The accumulator was about to expire and the twins were poised to carry it into the village to get it topped up when the familiar voice of Alvar Lidell came over the airwaves, tiny but still distinct, informing the nation that Mr Churchill was about to speak. There was to be an official holiday – Victory in Europe day – when everyone would have a holiday before they began the serious work of becoming, once more, a nation at peace.

May whirled round in a circle, making a buzzing noise and holding her satchel out at shoulder height. 'Everyone will have a day off, including us,' she announced in ringing tones, nudging her sister in the ribs. 'They've been planning this for ages. There's going to be a big party on the village green with all sorts of lovely cakes and things. Mrs Nidd's made a victory cake; she said she's been saving a bag of icing sugar ever since 1939, and she's going to colour it with powder paint from the school cupboard. If it'd been a couple of weeks later we could have had strawberries and cream.' She turned to her mother. 'Even strawberries without the cream would be a treat.'

Rosheen, who had been listening with an indulgent smile, now admitted that the Gladstone bag she had brought down from her RAF station contained goodies which she too had been saving for this very occasion. 'And after the party is over we'll have to think about what to do next. I shall be one of the first to be demobbed, because women with children are going to get preferential treatment,' she observed. 'We've been pretty lucky. Number three wasn't bombed, though your gran says there's not a pane of glass left in any of the windows, and the secondary school where you'll be going in September wasn't bombed either. But an awful lot of people in Liverpool don't even have homes to go back to.'

April pulled a face, and May swung on her mother's hand, gazing appealingly into her face. 'Must we go back to King Edward Court?' she wheedled. 'You know we'd rather stay here, and Mr Churchill said we must all work like anything to bring England back to what it was before.' She looked from her mother's face to Mrs Wright's.

'What was it before?' she asked plaintively. 'April and I don't remember before the war.'

'Oh, girls, I must have told you at least a hundred times that your teachers think that if you stay on at school you could pass your school certificates and perhaps even go to university,' Rosheen said longingly. 'Imagine that, twins! You would be the first people in the Clarke family to go, and if you chose Liverpool University then you could still live at home.'

Both twins pulled a disgusted face and for a moment the old resemblance was there and anyone watching would have known they were twins. 'But we want to leave school and work on the land,' April said. 'Mr Nidd said he would employ us as soon as we were fourteen.'

Rosheen laughed but shook her head. 'One thing at a time, girls,' she said gaily. 'May I remind you that you won't even be fourteen for another whole year!'

April sighed philosophically. 'Well, if we go back to school and work very hard can we spend the holidays with the Wrights?' she said. 'It's not as though we're young kids any more – we pull our weight, both Mrs Wright and Mrs Nidd say we do.'

Rosheen smiled. 'If Mrs Wright and Mrs Nidd agree, I dare say you could stay here until the end of August,' she said. 'And if you want to prove how helpful you are . . .' She picked up the accumulator and waggled it meaningfully.

The twins were about to depart through the back door when it opened and Mr Nidd came into the kitchen in his stockinged feet. 'There's going to be a victory parade of all the troops who can attend,' he told them. 'I doubt it'll be much of a parade round here 'cos most of the farm workers volunteered at the beginning of the war and ain't come home yet, but if you kids would like to see the spectacle in town – and that'll be grand – you want to come with us on the milk train and find yourselves a good position overlooking the route.' He eyed the accumulator. 'Get a move on, girls; we don't want to miss the one o'clock news.'

Rosheen had been granted a forty-eight, along with practically everyone else, but so disorganised was the system that she overstayed her leave by a whole week and felt, during that time, that she got closer to her children than she had ever been. It seemed to her that the twins were not only maturing nicely, like cheese, but were showing a side to their characters which she was sure had been absent before the May blitz. The girls were far less self-absorbed and actually considered the effects of what they had planned before taking action. They were helpful, too, not waiting to be asked but voluntarily coming forward to wash the pots, or feed the hens, or simply run upstairs and fetch Mr Wright's spectacles so that he could read the newspaper which Mr Nidd passed on to him at the end of each day.

And it was nice, Rosheen thought, to be consulted by her daughters before they did something which might not be popular. Once, they actually asked her advice.

April started it. 'Mam, I'm pretty sure you don't realise, but we've missed an awful lot of school. You see, once we got strong enough to be truly helpful, the Nidds and the Wrights were happy enough for us to work on the farm. Old Mr Blenkinsop did his very best to take the place of Mr Nidd's sons, but for the last couple of years his arthur-itis has made him unable to get out of his bed some days. So May and I pop up to see him before going off to work and he tells us what we should be doing, and then we go and do it.'

Rosheen raised her eyebrows. 'So? I believe it's been happening all over the country, what with schools having to take in evacuees and lessons being changed or postponed. Why should you be any different?'

May heaved a sigh. 'No one else talks about exams or universities,' she pointed out. 'All our friends here will leave school next year and work in shops or factories – the clever ones may even work in offices – but they won't be taking exams. You want us to go to senior school in Liverpool, but we can't help thinking we'll probably not even understand half the lessons.'

Rosheen sighed. 'Watch my lips,' she commanded, parroting one of her sergeants who was fond of the phrase. 'Every schoolchild in England has had their education interrupted by the war. If it turns out that you've missed some essential points you can simply tell your teachers and they'll arrange for you to go to evening classes. There's a place on Stanley Road where one can take them, I know.'

May looked relieved, but April, who had plainly been hoping for a get out, did not. 'I've had enough of lessons,' she grumbled. 'All right, I admit we must have one more year in school, but after that I want a job so I can earn money of my own.' She scowled at Rosheen. 'We'll soon be old enough to work in a factory, and when we do we'll want lipsticks and face powder and pretty clothes for when we're not at work … oh, Mam, can't you understand?'

Rosheen cast her mind back to those far off days when she had been fancy free and childless. If her mother had suggested that she stayed in school she would have been horrified. Probably she would have run away; perhaps she might even have run to the twins' father, though that would have been difficult since America was a big country and she had no idea where he was. But the last thing she wanted was for the twins to follow her own particular path, so she shook her head chidingly. 'Girls, listen. If you could just pass all your exams and go on to university you would be able to get really good jobs and earn big salaries, more than anything a factory would pay you. But there's no point in talking about it yet. Just work as hard as you can for the next year, and we'll discuss the matter again.'

As Cassie neared her home excitement gripped her. The war was over! Her father was still in London but her mother had promised to be home, but Cassie had always been closer to Mrs Valentine than to her rather domineering father and now delighted anticipation gripped her as she walked up the garden path. Like Rosheen – and everybody else – she had been given a forty-eight, but unlike Rosheen had no intention of staying over her appointed time. She loved her work and was actually toying with the idea of remaining in the air force. She had not been home for longer than she cared to admit, and as she approached the house she felt her muscles tighten. How much would it have changed? She knew it had not been bombed, but there would surely be other, more subtle differences. Indeed, she spotted one as soon as her home came into view. The garden, with its once well-tended rows of vegetables, was waist high in weeds, and when presently she flung the back door open and the good smell of cooking assailed her nostrils she realised that the changes which had taken place were more profound than she had supposed. Her mother was still neat as a new pin, but her face was drawn and weary and her beautiful hair, which had been the same deep auburn as Cassie's, was white as snow. Six years of war, Cassie reflected, could not be eradicated overnight.

As she entered the kitchen Mrs Valentine gave a little chirruping cry and cast herself into Cassie's arms.

'Darling, it seems a lifetime since I saw you last,' she said.

Cassie kissed her mother's soft cheek. 'It's marvellous to be home,' she said warmly. 'Oh, Mummy, it's wonderful to see you again, but why the weeds in the vegetable beds? I thought growing food was of the upmost importance.'

'So it is,' Mrs Valentine assured her. 'And I'll get round to clearing the mess just as soon as I've got a moment. But Daddy and I have been pretty busy at weekends so it may have to wait.' She cast her daughter a mischievous look. 'Unless you and Andy would like to give us a hand? Did you know Andy's coming home today? Home for a couple of weeks, what's more. Though he certainly deserves a break – the bomber boys have had it pretty hard what with the night raids and so on.' She stood back, holding her daughter at arm's length and letting her eyes wander approvingly over Cassie's uniformed figure. 'My, you are smart! And I see you're wearing your corporal stripes. Oh, Cassie, I'm so proud of you! Your father has made arrangements for us to go to the London victory parades; will you be there? And what's happened to that young man you were going to bring home to meet us? I know he's just a friend, but ...'

Cassie had forgotten the invitation. She had made it before Colin's accident because she had been so frustrated by Andy's continuing silence – although according to Rebecca Andy didn't write to her either, not since she had started dating the sergeant in command of her ack-ack battery – but now she felt ashamed, knowing that she had been using Colin as a sort of stalking horse, hoping to make Andy jealous. But her mother's blue eyes were fixed on her face, so she broke into hasty speech. 'Oh, you mean Colin Trelawney. He's a navigator on our station, but he was badly injured when his plane was shot up by a German fighter and he's still in hospital. As for the victory parades, I simply don't know whether I'll be wanted or can take leave instead, but whichever way it goes I shan't be bringing Colin to meet you just yet.' She smiled at her mother, trying to keep the excitement out of her eyes. Andy was coming home! She wondered whether, when he saw her again, he would ask her to marry him, but she had no intention of becoming a wife just yet. Besides, she was not sure what changes the last couple of years of separation might have made to their feelings for each other. They would have to get to know one another all over again before she could consider his proposal – always assuming that he made one, of course. But her mother was still speaking; with an effort, Cassie turned her attention to what she was saying.

'. . . Andy's such a good son; he either wrote or telephoned at least once a week to assure his mother he was safe and well.' Mrs Valentine looked up into her daughter's bright face and Cassie noticed yet another change. Her mother had once been the same height as she was, perhaps even a little taller. Now she had shrunk.

She opened her mouth to reply, then closed it again. She did not wish to admit to her mother that she and Andy had barely exchanged a word for more than two years; indeed, she only knew he was still in the land of the living because Mrs Valentine mentioned him in her letters. But it would not do to say so.

'I'll get out of my uniform and into my old clothes and start weeding as soon as we've had whatever it is I can smell in the oven,' she said instead. 'Shall I have a guess at what you've been cooking?'

Her mother gave a cry of dismay and hurried over to the Aga, flinging open the oven door and producing a large and delicious-looking object from its depths. 'It's your favourite, egg and bacon pie,' she said triumphantly, 'though it's going to be supper, not lunch, because Daddy's coming home tonight and he likes it too. The hens have been laying beautifully, so I put three eggs in a brown paper bag and took them down to Mr Hughes, the butcher in the village, and asked him to do a swap for some nice lean bacon. He was quite willing – they don't keep hens – so that was easy. But I suppose you'll want to go next door first and see whether Andy's arrived yet?'

'I'll go and get changed and after lunch we can tackle the weeds together,' Cassie repeated. 'You have to remember, Mummy, Rigby and Corby are a fair way apart, so I've not seen all that much of Andy and I'm sure we've both changed a lot in six years.'

Her mother nodded understandingly. 'Then we'll wait lunch until you've been round to the O'Learys',' she said. 'He might have made arrangements which I know nothing about, and since your letter said you would only be having two days' leave you might as well make the best use of what time you have.'

Cassie, feeling rather foolish, went round to the O'Learys' and knocked politely on the back door before opening it and walking into the comfortable, untidy kitchen she remembered so well. Andy's mother was seated at the kitchen table making a pile of sandwiches which, judging from the look of them, contained roast pork and apple sauce. Cassie remembered that the O'Learys could come and go as they liked across the Irish Sea, and however much she might – and did – disapprove of the black market she could not blame them for bringing back food whenever they visited their erstwhile home. Apart from anything else, the O'Learys were generous souls and she knew her own parents had benefited more than once from their open-handedness.

Mrs O'Leary had looked up as the back door opened, and now she beamed at her visitor. 'Hello, alanna. How well you look, to be sure. I'd invite you to help yourself to a sandwich but it's sure I am that it's not food you're wanting but me darling Andy. He's only been home ten minutes and has gone up to his room to dump his kitbag – ah, I hear him coming.' She twisted round to look at the kitchen door and Cassie heard the thunder of Andy's feet as he descended the stairs in his usual impetuous fashion.

For one awful moment she actually considered flight but she was given no opportunity. Andy burst into the room, saw her, grinned, and the next moment she was in his arms and he was telling her that she was his best girl and seeing her was the nicest moment of all the VE day celebrations.

Shocked, Cassie pulled herself out of his arms and addressed him with some heat. 'What's got into you, Andy O'Leary? It's all very well to call me your best girl, but that wasn't how you treated me the last time we met, or have you forgotten? After all, it was a long time ago.'

Andy pulled a face. 'I swore I wouldn't get entangled with *any* woman whilst the crew of good old *Betsy* needed their skipper to be single-minded,' he said. 'But I thought about you all the time, knowing you'd be waiting for me when it was all over.'

Mrs O'Leary had left the room as soon as Andy had seized Cassie in his arms, so they had the kitchen to themselves. Cassie raised her eyebrows. 'Thought about me all the time?' she echoed. 'Well you've a damned funny way of showing it! And what makes you think I'd be waiting for you, anyway? After two years of silence I'd have been a fool to give you more than a passing thought.'

Andy took her back into his arms and began to trace kisses down the side of her face and into the soft nape of her neck. 'Come on, Cassie. Admit you were saving yourself for your one true love; me!'

'Well, you conceited pig!' Cassie said, only half teasingly. Firmly, she detached herself from his embrace a second time and moved away, shaking her head when he would have followed her. 'Honestly, Andy, you've got a nerve. Let me assure you that we've got a lot of hard work in front of us before I will so much as accept a box of chocolates from you. Can't you *see*, you stupid man, that as far as I'm concerned you built a brick wall around yourself and it's not going to be easy to bring it down.'

'Oh, but I thought you'd understand,' Andy said. 'It's not as though we'd not known each other well before the war. All I'm trying to do is pick up our peacetime relationship where it left off.' He looked appealingly into Cassie's eyes. 'What's wrong with that? I'm sure other members of the forces coming home are saying exactly the same things to their wives and girlfriends.'

He tried to catch her hand, but once more Cassie eluded him. 'I can only speak for myself, but I'm telling you, Andy, that for the last few years it hasn't felt as though you were treating me like a friend.' She stared at him, trying to read something in his expression, though she could not have said exactly what. 'And it isn't only me who has found your attitude strange, to say the least. After Colin was so badly wounded and they had to amputate his right foot you visited him twice. Andy, I was at that hospital almost every day and I wasn't the only one. Oh, I know you were busy fighting the war, but so were others. The boys from his kite had a sort of rota so that Colin was never without visitors despite not having any family close by. And he was your best friend!'

Andy looked hunted and Cassie saw with some satisfaction a flush creep up his neck and darken his cheeks. 'Colin and I had grown apart,' he said gruffly. 'But I did write, you know. Remember, I wasn't within shouting distance of Corby. I could only visit when I had at least a forty-eight and at first I thought Colin was too ill to want people coming

395

into the hospital at odd hours.' He pulled a face. 'But how did Colin sneak into this conversation? I thought it was *our* relationship – yours and mine – which was under scrutiny.'

Cassie shook her head. 'No, it's your whole attitude which I'm finding it difficult to understand. And it's that which you and I have got to work at if we're ever going to regain our former friendship. It's all very well to say you didn't want to get entangled with any woman, but I'm *not* any woman, or wasn't. When we met to say goodbye at the Saracen's Head I expected you to follow me, but you didn't and I was so upset that I decided then and there that our old friendship was dead. Before the war we'd both taken it for granted that we were more than friends. During the war you proved over and over that even friendship was not something you wanted. Now you think you can walk back into my life and take up where we left off. Well, Mr Perfect, you've got a lot of proving to do before we can even call ourselves bezzies, as they say in Liverpool. And frankly, Andy, I'm not sure I want to bother.' She grinned at him.

Whilst they talked she had kept the kitchen table between them, but now Andy walked round it and took her hands, lifting them one by one to his mouth and kissing her knuckles. 'You're right, darling Cassie; I behaved very badly and deserve everything you've just thrown at me. And the one thing I've not said is the most important: I love you with all my heart, Cassie Valentine, and I want to marry you and whisk you off to Ireland. You've never seen the wonderful old house I shall one day inherit, nor my grandfather's stud. How about taking a bit of a holiday there so that we can start our relationship and our new lives at the same time? Would you like that? Ireland is beautiful and Grandpa would welcome you warmly both as a visitor and as the girl I'm going to marry.' He looked hopefully at her. 'What do you say?'

For a moment he could see that Cassie was wavering. As a young girl she had been a keen horsewoman and the thought of a few days in the Ireland which he had described so lyrically was clearly tempting but not, it seemed, tempting enough, for the next moment she was shaking her head. 'No, Andy. I've got two days' leave and then I must go back to Corby. Apart from anything else I want to see Colin. He's been a good friend to me, and even if I can't love him I like him very much. I had a phone call from him just before I left to come home. They're going to send him to a convalescent home in Blackpool where they'll teach him how to cope with his artificial foot. It was a very jolly phone call, all things considered, but that's Colin all over. He's already planning what he'll do when he's demobbed – oh, and he said to tell you all the best, and that he hopes to see you some time in the near future.'

'Blackpool's quite a way from here, but I suppose, if it pleases you, I could get there,' Andy said doubtfully. 'We could go together; there's a big training centre at Blackpool and drivers for the air force have a course going at Weeton so we should be able to cadge a lift.' He ducked his head and looked at Cassie through his lashes; a naughty little boy look. 'If you won't come to Ireland until we've sorted ourselves out then going on a spree to Blackpool might be the next best thing.'

Cassie could have screamed. She knew very well that he had not really taken in how she felt. She took a deep breath. 'Andy, you are trying to undo the harm six years of war has dealt our relationship in a couple of weeks. I know we didn't always agree – remember the fight in the church porch, and that dreadful dance? – but I think those were the worst quarrels we ever had.' A frown creased her brow. 'But marriage – even getting engaged – would put our relationship on a quite different footing. When we were children my mum used to call us Mr and Mrs Kiss and Scratch, remember? What sort of start to a relationship is a nickname like that?'

Andy laughed. 'We were just a couple of kids then; six years have made big changes to us both,' he pointed out. 'And if you expect us to spend another six years sorting ourselves out you must be stark, staring, raving mad. I'll give it my best go whilst I'm still in the air force, and if you're not convinced by the time I re-enter civvy street then I'll stage a kidnapping and carry you off to Gretna Green.' He held out a hand. 'Is it a bargain? It'll be a while before I'm demobbed – no wife, no kids – so that should give us time to realise we were made for each other.'

VJ day came after the explosion of the second atom bomb had spread its great mushroom cloud across the sky. Andy and Cassie went to the cinema and saw the terrible pictures of Hiroshima; screaming women, their hair and clothing alight, ran through the streets and for once Emperor Hirohito inter-vened and announced to the nation that Japan had surrendered.

By now Mrs O'Leary was talking constantly of the glories of the O'Leary family stud in Ireland and doing her best to persuade her friend Mrs Valentine to look kindly on a marriage between their children.

'Sure and haven't we expected them to make a match of it ever since they were old enough to toddle,' she had said, her eyes swimming with emotion. 'Andy's eager for the match because not only does he love Cassie to distraction but doesn't a feller of his age needs a wife?' She saw Mrs Valentine's sceptical look and giggled. ''Twould be a new life for the pair of them,' she assured her friend. 'Oh, I know they grew apart when they were separated by the war, but isn't all that behind us now? I was talking to Cassie the other day and

I t'ink she's ripe for a move. She's a country girl, your Cassie, and when she sees Grandpa O'Leary's stud she'll love it as Andy does.'

Mrs Valentine was of the same opinion, and it was not many days into Cassie's second spell of leave that she realised her daughter was unlikely ever to live at home again, or not by choice, for Mr Valentine had not changed. His home was his castle and his was the only voice allowed to be heard when it came to giving and taking orders, which it did one morning at breakfast when Cassie, opening a letter which had arrived for her, gave an exclamation part of pleasure and part surprised.

'Rosheen's written to say they're sending people to Germany, to serve in the army of occupation there,' she announced. 'I've always wanted the opportunity to travel—'

She was rudely interrupted. Her father, who had appeared to be deep in his newspaper, slapped it down on the table and took Cassie's letter out of her hand without so much as a by your leave. He read it whilst his wife and daughter stared at him with incredulous dismay, then handed the missive to his wife.

'She won't go; I forbid it,' he said, his tone almost conversational. 'She's had enough of this war, and she'll take that job in the civil service I lined up for her.' He picked up his paper again. 'What will they think of next? A young girl like our Cassie in a foreign land, and a land full of Germans what's more! It won't do.'

Cassie picked up her letter with fingers that trembled. 'I don't recall asking you if you would like to read my correspondence,' she said frostily. 'If I'm posted to Germany …' she turned her sweetest smile on her father, who was peering at her over the top of his paper, 'I shall be delighted.'

Slowly, Mr Valentine lowered his paper and gazed incredulously at his daughter. 'I don't believe I heard you correctly, my dear,' he said, fixing Cassie with a basilisk glare. 'I was not merely giving an opinion, I was *telling* you that you've done your duty and will now take up civilian employment as soon as I can arrange it.'

Cassie looked across at her mother. Mrs Valentine's face wore a mixture of support and apprehension. 'What will Andy say if you go gadding off to Germany?' she asked. 'Mrs O'Leary was telling me that his grandfather has decided to retire, so he'll be taking over the stud rather sooner than they expected.' She smiled affectionately at her daughter. 'Do you remember how you used to love to ride? You always wanted a horse of your own, but of course it was quite impossible then. But if you do decide to marry Andy – and it is the wish of my heart that you should do so – you will have as many horses as you like.'

'But not if I go to Germany,' Cassie said quickly.

She managed to catch her father's eye. 'Daddy, I'm not just being awkward to defy you; I'm a member of the forces and until I'm demobbed I have to do as I'm commanded. As it happens I would like to be a part of the army of occupation. All the knowledge I've gained is thanks to the Royal Air Force; I can't just throw it away and swan off into the wide blue yonder to do my own thing. You've been working at the War Office; surely you must realise that I'm not a free agent, any more than Andy is. We obey orders, go where we are sent and thank our lucky stars that we won the war and aren't subject to the brutal rules which the enemy would have used to enslave us. So please, Daddy, don't rock the boat.'

She was watching her father's face as she spoke, and was not surprised when his next remark showed that he still thought his word was law, even when it was in direct opposition to the government's. 'I'll pull a few strings; I'm sure there are dozens of young women who are free to go to Germany. Certainly they're still recruiting as though the war had never been won.' He turned to his wife. 'Any more toast? I know the butter's run out but your homemade marmalade is delicious.'

Despite his mother's hopes, Andy was summoned back to his unit and he ws glad to be going. He thought he and Cassie had been getting on very well – a whole week had passed without even the tiniest disagreement, though Andy had been horrified when Cassie said she might be posted to Germany. It was clear that he understood much better than her father how things worked, for although Mr Valentine went confidently off to London to pull his strings he came back chastened and with what would have been, in a less self-satisfied man, his tail between his legs. 'What a pity you did so well in your German language exam at school,' was all he said.

At the end of her leave Cassie found herself by no means reluctant to return to Corby. The fact that her father still behaved more like a dictator than a parent had made her realise that she could never live under his rule again; she had been independent for too long.

A letter had arrived at breakfast time from a friend stating that Cassie's name was on the list of those to be posted to Germany, and as soon as she finished her meal she went round to the O'Learys' to show it to Andy. She had expected him to be disappointed, if not actually angry, but Andy, too, had received a letter.

'Perhaps, by the time we've served our twenty-four months, you'll realise the advantages of marrying an Irish farmer,' he said. 'And that's what I'll be as soon as I can shake the air force dust off my shoes.'

As soon as she returned to Corby, Cassie went to the Mess and found that she was confirmed as sergeant of her flight, instead of corporal. When she saw where she was to be posted her first impulse was to rush to the phone and check whether Andy was off to the same destination, but as she inched forward in the queue for the telephone she changed her mind. You haven't seen Colin for two whole weeks; you lectured Andy about his neglect yet apparently you're considering doing the same thing yourself, she thought. After all, whether or not Andy and I are together in Germany, Colin will be left behind, and I may not see him for years. I should speak to him first.

The girl in front of Cassie was lifting the receiver from its cradle on the wall when Rosheen came into the Mess. Cassie waved and Rosheen hurried over to her, beaming.

'So you're back,' she said happily. 'Have you seen the bulletin board? Just about every member of our flight – apart from married women and mums like me – is off to Germany, and your sergeant status has been confirmed.' She laughed. 'Though you've been corporal for so long that pushing us around must have become second nature. Why are you telephoning? You've only just come back off leave; didn't you say everything you wanted to say whilst you were home?'

Cassie shook her head. 'I'm not ringing home. I'm going to ring Colin and tell him the news. I feel rather awful about it, because the poor chap won't

404

be going abroad or doing anything interesting so far as I can see until his foot is sorted, but as you know he never grumbles. Oh, Rosheen, life's so unfair!'

At that moment the Waaf in front of them replaced the receiver and moved away, and Cassie took her place.

She had rung the hospital several times, and the girl on the switchboard recognised her voice. 'He's not here, Corporal Valentine,' she said. 'He left for the convalescent home in Blackpool yesterday.'

Cassie put down the receiver and turned away, surprised at the mixed emotions she was feeling. On the one hand, to go with the army of occupation into Germany would be the biggest adventure the RAF had handed her so far. On the other she would be telling Colin that their ways were parting for good far more decisively than if she were being posted within the British Isles. But she remembered how Toby Belcher had reproached her, and knew it would be for the best.

She was about to join Rosheen, who had taken two cups of coffee over to a table, when it occurred to her that if she and Andy were posted to the same place it would be the best opportunity they were ever likely to get to mend their friendship; no, to change their friendship into something stronger and more lasting, though she admitted to herself that she was not sure what. Marriage? The thought sent a delicious tingle through her whole body. But a good marriage, she knew, was not something which was simply handed to you on a plate; she had tried to explain that to Andy the last time they had discussed their relationship.

Right now, however, she had more important things on her mind. She was going abroad for the first time in her life, and in a position of some authority. Smiling to herself, she imagined her father's reaction to the news that she would be off his hands and out of his control very soon now. She would go straight to her Wing Officer, explain the situation, and ask for sufficient leave to get to Blackpool and back before she was dispatched to her new posting.

Chapter Twenty-two

Summer 1947

Dear Rosheen,

At last the day we've all waited for has come and I and the rest of my flight have been told to report to Padgate to be demobbed. I've learned a great deal since arriving in Germany, some of it best forgotten, but now I must start learning how to be a civilian. Andy is also being demobbed – lovely word – and I expect you can guess that he has proposed marriage, but I said it was too soon. Marrying Andy and moving to southern Ireland was once the height of my ambition, but a lot of water has flowed under a lot of bridges since then and I want to experience being a civilian before I tie myself up with a man of my own. Andy is very dear to me and in a way marrying him would solve a thousand problems, but I'm not sure it would be the sensible thing to do. Oh, I mean to marry him eventually, and he knows it, but not immediately.

Sometimes, the idea of marriage can seem like a prison sentence and I'm not yet ready to hear the hollow clang as the door slams behind me.

Oh, what an awful thing to say! But his rejection of me, during the war, still rankles. He says that his war was a single-minded affair, with no room for women, but somehow it doesn't ring true. Other men managed to do their work and enjoy normal relationships; why not Andy? So you see I've never really understood why he behaved the way he did.

But I shouldn't unload my worries on you, dear Rosheen, because I know full well you have worries of your own. Since your mother had to move out in order to look after her brother, you've had all the responsibility for the house, the bills and the twins themselves, and I guess it hasn't been easy. How old are they now? Coming up to sixteen? Goodness, when I was that age I was in the Land Army and poised to change to the WAAF. I was so resentful of my father's behaviour, to tell you the truth, that I would have done almost anything to annoy him. But you have double trouble; not just one teenager but two. It must have been very hard at first to stand out against the twins' desire to leave school and earn some money but you stuck to your guns and aren't you glad you did? They have proved themselves to be a lot more sensible than you and I were at their age, and I'm sure they'll pass their Matric with flying colours.

The only thing is, though, if they do go to university what'll you do then? I know you've got your old job in the bakery back but I'm sure you're wasted there. Isn't there some handsome young fellow who wants to sweep you off your feet and carry you away from King Edward Court and all its works? I know you said you're not interested in marriage but you had male friends when we were in the WAAF together, I remember it distinctly. Why don't you give romance a chance? Dear me, I'm beginning to sound just like my mother! She thinks the only respectable career for a woman is marriage. She's very tactful, but every time she writes she asks whether I've decided to make Andy a happy man which, of course, is just another way of asking if I've come to my senses!

In fact, Andy and I have scarcely seen one another despite being posted to the same country. Oh, Rosheen, I'm so confused, but I do know I want a home of my own, a loving man and eventually children. Perhaps when Andy and I actually meet again he will dismiss all my doubts and sweep me off my feet; I certainly hope so.

Have I told you about Colin? He's going steady with Rebecca – he met her again quite by chance when he was visiting Andy on one of his leaves – one of Andy's leaves, I mean – and I really do think they'll make a go of it. I must say I'm glad, because he deserves some good luck after everything he's been through. He walks absolutely normally now, though he can't run any more. Rebecca says she's always considered herself a fast walker but she has to go faster just to keep up with him!

But this letter is growing somewhat lengthy so I shall sign off. When I get home I'll write again and suggest a date in August when we can meet. It will be marvellous to see you again; I've missed you more than I can say. I've missed Colin, too, but that is a different story.

Lots of love to you all, Cassie.

*

Cassie got off the bus at the village stop feeling like a stranger, for she had just exchanged her well-worn uniform for a green skirt and matching jacket, a cream blouse and low-heeled court shoes. She had met two of the girls who had been in her flight at the demob centre, and was amused when they both saluted her, then broke down in giggles. 'Sorry, sarge. It's going to take some getting used to, this being a civilian,' the taller of the girls had said. 'It'll be hard for you as well; you were within a second of saluting back, weren't you?'

Cassie had smiled but nodded. 'You're right, I was,' she had admitted ruefully. 'But we'll get used to it, just as we got used to service life. And it'll help that so many people will be in the same boat. I say, that hat is very fetching! I'm not going to wear mine – it looks like a pudding basin.'

The other girl had pulled a face. 'It's a funny old world,' she observed sagely. 'I'm sure when my alarm clock goes off in the morning I shall jump out of bed and start doing drill. I used to resent it, but now I know it kept us fit and up to the mark. The thought of bungling out of bed and going to an office … hey up, there's the bus! Let's run, or we'll have to stand all the way to the station!'

Now, Cassie walked down Knowsley Avenue and clicked open the front gate, noticing with pleasure that the garden was neatly weeded once more, and made for the back door. She flung it open, smiled at her mother seated at the kitchen table and struck an attitude. 'Taran-tara! I'm a civilian again,' she said proudly. 'And the clothing actually fits. Oh, Mummy, it felt so strange at first, but I suppose I'll get used to it.'

Her mother had been working at the sewing machine as her daughter entered the room, but she stopped her task to clap her hands delightedly. 'What a lovely sight; I'm really proud of you, and that costume fits you a treat,' she said admiringly. 'You'll have to go round the neighbourhood showing yourself off. I must say the Royal Air Force are doing people proud; Ralph from up the road has a tweed suit which makes him look like a bank manager.'

411

She laughed. 'Well, that's what his mother says, at any rate.'

Cassie remembered the weedy boy who had occasionally sat next to her on the school bus. She giggled. 'Bank manager! Bank clerk more like,' she said. She went round the table and peered over her mother's shoulder. Clothing was still rationed but Mrs Valentine had always been clever with her needle and now she was concocting, from a generous length of parachute silk, a light summer dress for Cassie.

Cassie looked at the pattern, cut out in brown paper, which her mother was following. She whistled under her breath and gave her mother's shoulders a squeeze. 'You are a genius,' she said admiringly. 'I shall be the belle of the ball.' She looked hopefully across to where the kettle steamed gently on the hob. 'Fancy a cup of tea, Mummy? I'm parched, and if you have such a thing as a biscuit I wouldn't say no.'

Mrs Valentine finished the seam she was working on and stood up. 'You've had a long journey; just sit yourself down and I'll have tea and a buttered scone before you in a tick,' she said. 'There's a letter for you – I put it in your room, on your bedside table, so you could read it as soon as you got back.' She smiled guiltily at her daughter. 'I did *not* think Daddy would dream of opening your letters. He can't help regarding you as a child, though. That's why I think it would be a good thing if you and Andy got married and moved to Ireland.' She twinkled at her daughter. 'I expect Daddy thinks Andy would take on the role of "man who knows everything", though I'm sure Andy himself has no such intention. He's a darling, and you've been keen on him ever since you were seven or eight. You have so much in common, and to have a beautiful country house to look after, with stables, and glorious countryside ...'

Cassie wrinkled her nose. 'Andy actually suggested marriage as soon as the war was over but I never said definitely that I would. As for loving horses and having a beautiful house, that would *not* be the reason I accepted Andy's proposal. *If* I do – which is by no means certain – it will be because I've been in love with him since I was old enough to know what love is.'

As Cassie spoke her mother handed her a scone and the promised cup of tea. 'Now eat that up and drink your tea. And if you'll take my advice, darling, you'll get in touch with Andy as soon as he arrives home. And Mrs O'Leary tells me there's just a chance that Andy's friend Colin might be staying with them for a few days. I should like to meet him – Colin, I mean – because you talked about him a lot at one time.' She laughed. 'I actually thought you were considering marriage with an unknown Scot from some wild and woolly village in the Highlands. But

413

of course we always knew you and Andy were made for each other.'

'Oh, Mummy, you're so conventional,' Cassie said, taking a bite of the scone and speaking rather thickly. 'Colin is the nicest chap you could possibly meet but I've never thought of him as a possible candidate for my hand. In fact I believe he's going steady with Rebecca. However, if he does come to stay with Andy I'll bring him round and introduce him.'

Andy came home the following day. Cassie and her mother were in the kitchen, having just finished washing up after a frugal lunch, when there was a brisk tattoo on the door and Andy burst in. He crossed the room and gave Mrs Valentine a smacking kiss on the cheek, then turned and whisked Cassie up in his arms, nuzzling against her neck to make her laugh. The wireless set in the corner was playing *Family Favourites* as Cassie, giggling, freed herself from Andy's embrace. It was all very well to share a cuddle but not, she felt, with her mother present, so she tapped Andy lightly on the cheek and he stood her down just as the back door opened again and Colin came shyly in. He grinned at Cassie, then held out a hand to Mrs Valentine.

'Sorry for intruding,' he said in his soft Scottish burr. 'But I thought I'd come in and introduce myself since Andy abandoned me halfway up the garden path.' He smiled engagingly. 'I'm Colin Trelawney and it doesn't need much guesswork to tell me that you are Cassie Valentine's mother.'

Mrs Valentine laughed and took the hand Colin was holding out, shaking her head. 'No need for introductions; Cassie's talked about you a great deal. You've been a good friend to her, and any friend of Cassie's ...'

' ... is a friend of yours,' Andy finished the sentence.

'That's it,' Mrs Valentine said. 'Andy's mother told us you might be popping in ... how long will you be staying?'

'Probably for longer than you imagine; he wants to see the stud and meet my grandparents,' Andy said airily.

'From what you tell me it's a good deal more impressive than my croft,' Colin said ruefully. 'But I don't intend to become a crofter, as I have already landed rather a good job with McPherson and Fee.'

Andy whistled beneath his breath. 'Well done you,' he said admiringly. 'So will you be off to Scotland after you come back from the stud?'

Colin nodded. 'Quite soon after. I've a few loose ends to tie up here first.' He turned to Cassie. 'I've not been in uniform for a couple of years, but being a civilian was a real shock at first.'

'It *is* a shock, isn't it?' Cassie agreed. 'I feel I'm neither fish, fowl, nor good red herring. I joined the

Land Army when I was barely sixteen, so I never had a job in the ordinary sense. And now I feel I'm a real misfit.' She smiled. 'Though Mummy assures me that I'll settle comfortably soon enough.'

'We're all in the same boat,' Andy said. 'I know I'm one of the lucky ones, with a home and the work I love waiting for me, but even so there'll have been changes at the stud which I'll have to get used to, and some of them maybe not ones I'll like. Remember, I've never actually worked at the stud except under my grandfather's wing, but now the responsibility will be mine and I'm not at all sure I shall make all the right decisions.' He shot a teasing look at Cassie. 'Of course, if I had a wife by my side, someone with whom I could discuss my problems, it would be different.'

Mrs Valentine laughed. 'Hinting with my daughter will get you nowhere,' she said ruefully. 'She's as obstinate as her father in many ways.' She swung round suddenly and caught her daughter's hands. 'I've had a brilliant idea, one of my best! Why don't the three of you go over to Ireland for a bit of a break? I've not been to the Emerald Isle for many years myself, and Cassie's never been.' She gazed at the three faces. 'It would be a breathing space, time out. Andy's the only one of you who knows anything about the stud, and since his grandfather's still nominally in charge, Mrs O'Leary says, he won't need to take on the responsibilities for it yet. You could ask Rebecca to join you, make up a foursome.'

Cassie smiled. 'That's a marvellous idea Mummy. To take time out is a good plan; I'm all for it.' She turned to Andy. 'Would your grandparents mind if Rebecca and I tagged along?'

Andy shook his head. 'Not at all, they'd be delighted!' he said. 'We'll talk to Rebecca and then I'll ring Grandpa and between us we'll arrange everything.' He slipped his arm round Cassie and gave her a squeeze. 'Your mother's a genius,' he told her quietly. 'It might have been awkward with just the three of us, but if Rebecca agrees to come that's the biggest hurdle over.'

Grandpa O'Leary came to the station to pick his guests up in a pony and trap which had seen better days, but his welcome was warm and as he saw them into the trap he turned a rosy face, innocent as a child's, and scanned them keenly. 'Which one's the bride?' he asked jovially. 'Sure and can I guess now.' He pointed his whip at Rebecca. 'It'll be the lass with hair as yellow as the sun and a smile as sweet as icing on a wedding cake.'

'Wrong, wrong, wrong,' Cassie said, shaking her head and thinking that Mr O'Leary was not the only one who had backed the wrong horse. She had expected Andy's grandfather to be a tall and rangy man, admittedly in his sixties, but even so an athletic figure and still a power in the land. Instead her hand

417

was shaken by a little man, bow-legged but whippy as a willow wand, with a rosy face, bright dark eyes and a tilted smiling mouth. He reminded her strongly of a leprechaun, and when she whispered this fact to Andy he grinned.

'You wait until he gets into his stride,' he whispered back. 'His charm makes us as much money as the excellence of our stallions. I'm afraid he's my master where that's concerned. Pity – it might have helped me get on with the type of person one would not normally introduce to one's wife.' He saw Cassie's puzzled look and explained, 'They're a rum lot, horse dealers, and some of the neighbours are more than a little odd as well.'

Cassie opened her mouth to take Andy down a peg or two – he had always been arrogant – but changed her mind. He was only showing off, and she realised he had every right to do so as the trap swung through an open five-bar gate and drew to a halt before a very imposing property. The farmyard – if you could call it a farmyard – was paved with slabs of spotlessly clean stone. The house itself was partially clad in Virginia creeper, and surrounding it was a ring of horseboxes, the occupants peering as the clatter of approaching hooves warned them of an arrival. As they began to descend from the trap, the back door shot open and old Mrs O'Leary came across to greet them and give Cassie a hug. The two of them had met several times when the old lady had

418

stayed in Knowsley Avenue, and had always got on well. Now Cassie introduced Colin and Rebecca to the older woman, and then followed her hostess into a large and untidy kitchen.

'Sure and haven't you chosen a grand time to be seeing over my husband's stud?' Mrs O'Leary said. 'Most of the mares and their foals are out to grass but we've kept the best stabled until you've seen them.'

'Oh, Mrs O'Leary, I hope you don't think I'm any judge of horseflesh,' Cassie said at once. 'I love horses and I love to ride, but you could probably palm me off with a Welsh cob and tell me it was a blood stallion and I wouldn't know the difference.' She glanced round at her friends. 'And I guess Becky and Colin are no more expert than I am.' Her gaze roamed around the kitchen with its quarry-tiled floor, whitewashed walls and practical furnishings. 'What a lovely room!'

'So it is. And sure and I'll take you upstairs so you can get out of your travelling clothes,' the old lady said, addressing Cassie and Rebecca. 'Andy, Mr Trelawney is in the blue room next door to yourself, so you can do the honours, so you can.'

'Rightyho, Grandma,' Andy said, breezily. He opened a door and ushered his guests into a large square hall from which a flight of stairs led to the upper storey. 'Go on, Grandma, you lead the way.' He lowered his voice as his grandmother began to ascend the flight. 'She'll be dying to show you ladies the bathroom, which is so new I haven't even seen it myself, so don't forget to give admiring cries.'

As they followed Mrs O'Leary up the stairs Rebecca nudged Cassie. 'Isn't Andy lucky to have this lot handed to him on a plate?' she whispered. 'Of course, you and I have lived in houses with bathrooms and indoor lavatories for years, but not many country people can say the same.'

Colin, following them, had overheard the remark and gave a rueful grin. 'I don't know a single crofter who has an indoor lavatory, let alone a bathroom,' he admitted. 'It'll be a tin bath in front of the fire and a chilly run to the end of the garden to use the "wee hoosie" for me when I go home.'

Cassie was about to remind him of the conditions prevailing during the war when old Mrs O'Leary reached the head of the stairs and flung open a door. 'This is your room, lasses,' she said. 'We've plenty bedrooms but we thought you'd like to be together …' she twinkled at them, 'so you can talk about us amongst yourselves. The boys are on the upper landing next door to the bathroom. I'll show you how to work the geyser before we go downstairs, though we mustn't linger too long because I've a steak pie in the oven for youse dinners and it won't do to let it dry out.'

Cassie had not known quite what to expect, but after Andy had taken them on a tour of meadows, woodland and pastures she realised that he had not exaggerated when he had said that his grandfather had built up a fine business, a business which would need all Andy's energies to keep going.

They returned to the house and Rebecca opted for a hot bath to help her to relax, whilst Colin retired to his room to write some letters. When they had disappeared upstairs, Andy led Cassie back outside to inspect the stables. 'Grandpa's not as fit as he once was,' he said as they walked along the front of the boxes. 'But he knows what he's doing and he's said he'll teach me all the tricks of the trade. And you must meet our manager; Liam has worked here for a dozen years or more, starting at the bottom and working his way up. I told Grandpa that Liam could run the place without help from anybody else – apart from the lads, of course – but Grandpa simply said he's not family.'

'That's true, but are you sure he doesn't mind that it will be you taking over and not himself?'

Andy nodded. 'I'm sure. Grandpa's favourite saying is "The best manure for the land is the farmer's boot", and the more I see of the stud the more I realise how right he is. I can leave Liam in charge knowing he'll do a grand job, but if things did get sticky he'd go to Grandpa for advice.' He looked at her shyly. 'If – if things work out it would be an enormous help if you could oversee the office work. You've seen Grandpa's office; at present Liam looks after the wages and feed bills, orders supplies and so on, and when I've settled in I'll be sharing that with him, but the paperwork really needs a third person who could take over the responsibility. Will you think about it?' He grinned at her. 'Something else for you to think about: Rebecca and Colin are going to town tomorrow to visit a cinema and take a look at the shops. They won't be back until the evening, so we'll have the day to ourselves. What would you like to do?'

Cassie's heart gave a delighted little hop. 'Can we go for a ride?' she asked eagerly. 'Have you a nice little mare with good manners, the sort of mount a complete novice might ride?' She looked hopefully at Andy and saw pleasure bring a flush to his cheeks.

'Oh, I was hoping you'd say that! It's what I've been longing to do ever since we arrived, and of course we can find you a little mare with a kindly eye and gentle manners. But I know you're not a novice, whatever you may pretend, so we could make a day of it and take a picnic. Does that idea suit you?'

'It sounds lovely,' Cassie said. 'It's a good job Becky and Colin are in love. As things stand all four of us can have the best of both worlds. Colin and Rebecca are getting a free holiday and you and I can get to know each other all over again.'

For the first week, everything went so well that Cassie was almost tempted to accept Andy's proposal and start making plans for an autumn wedding, but then doubts began to creep in. She and Andy squabbled over the most ridiculous things. He had always been bossy, but at first she had not objected since after all the stud was going to be his one day, which gave him, she felt, the right to take decisions, but then it seemed to Cassie that everything she suggested was immediately queried until she felt that if she said 'black' Andy would say 'white' as a matter of course. In fact, he was behaving just like her father. And very soon the second week of this 'getting to know one another' break became a battleground on which the entire family was deployed. Sometimes the atmosphere could have been cut with a knife, and Cassie was not surprised when Rebecca pretended that she'd had a telephone message calling her and Colin back to the Wirral. She was beginning to wish she could come up with some similar excuse herself, and after she and Andy had waved the escapees off she went to her room, telling everyone that she had been neglecting her friends and must write to Rosheen.

'Why don't you do it down here? It seems odd to shut yourself in your bedroom just to write a letter to your girlfriend,' Andy said suspiciously. 'Why so secretive? Are you sure you're writing to Rosheen and not to some fellow you met in the MT section?'

She knew he meant it jokingly, but she had come to realise that he was jealous of any mention of those war years when they had scarcely spoken and had only met half a dozen times; which was ridiculous, she thought impatiently, when one considered why she had come to Ireland with him in the first place. She did not even answer his implied criticism but ran up the stairs, went into the bedroom she had shared with Rebecca and shut the door with a decisive snap. There was a small desk in the window embrasure and she settled down at it, wishing that Rosheen were not miles away. Her friend was so level-headed and sensible; she would understand. Cassie picked up her pen.

Dear Rosheen,

I'm in such trouble. Andy and I got along swimmingly when we first arrived at his grand-father's place but that's all changed. It sometimes seems I can't open my mouth without putting my foot in it – ha ha – and Andy's the same. He criticises everything I do so I suppose it's only natural that I should turn round and criticise everything he does, but honestly, Rosheen, it's no recipe for a happy marriage. In fact if we went on the way we have been doing we would probably be filing for divorce before you can say knife. I'll give you a 'for instance'. Andy was off to a sale of yearlings yesterday. I would have liked to go with him but when I suggested it he made every excuse under the sun ... well, not quite, because he did say 'Come if you think you'd like it but the show ring isn't covered and it looks like rain'. Rosheen, the sky was as blue as a lark's egg and there wasn't a cloud in sight. Mind you, it did rain later in the day, but that's not really the point. So anyway, being a well brought up child I stayed behind with Grandma and the pair of us had a baking afternoon. I made a batch of gingerbread from an old recipe of Andy's great-grandmother's, because Grandma said it was his favourite. When the men came home I cut the gingerbread into squares and offered Andy one. He said thank you very politely but I noticed he didn't so much as take a bite so I asked him what was wrong with it. 'Oh, nothing,' says he airily. 'But gingerbread needs at least three days in an airtight tin before it's fit to eat, didn't you know?'

I'm telling you, for two pins I'd have brained him with the bloody tin. He was deliberately making me look small in front of his grandparents. If I did what he was suggesting and put the gingerbread away he'd probably have found fault with the shortbread. Only he didn't know I'd made that; he thought it was his grandma's so he praised it to the skies, said he'd never tasted better.

Rosheen, what'll I do? I've been happy enough to accept the O'Leary hospitality but now all I want is to get away. I did mention to Grandma that I didn't seem to be able to do anything right but she only said 'pre-wedding nerves', and pointed out that I was pretty critical of Andy myself. Well, who wouldn't be, when everything I say seems to be wrong? So I think Andy and I must have a serious talk. I just wish he was more like Colin Trelawney. I used to think Colin wouldn't say boo to a goose but if it's that or quarrelling all the time, I know which I prefer.

Oh, don't listen to me, I'm still in a temper after his latest attack. Do you know, he actually had the nerve to suggest that I was writing to some fellow I'd met during the war and not to you! I know he'd say it was a joke but I don't think it was, in fact I'm beginning to think that whilst he doesn't seem to want me himself, he doesn't want anyone else to have me either. I wish you could come over to Ireland and tell me what I ought to do, but you do have the telephone number of the stud so perhaps you could phone? You've never met Andy, which means you can't possibly be biased, or not in his favour at any rate. The only trouble with telephoning is that the instrument is in the stud office so not very private. And now I come to think of it there's an extension in the hall which anyone might pick up, so perhaps phoning isn't such a good idea after all. If things get worse I shall just cut and run. So be warned, you may have an unexpected visitor. It would be awkward to go home, because of course Mummy and Daddy *and the O'Learys next door want me to marry Andy.*

I'm so sorry to burden you with my problems, but I'm in desperate need of advice and I know how practical you are. Everyone at home will say 'wedding nerves', like Grandma, but I'm sure it isn't that.

Hope you and the twins are well, see you soon, love Cassie.

PS Don't worry that I'll just turn up on your doorstep because if I do decide to cut and run I'll send you a telegram.

Cassie clattered down the stairs and crossed the hall. Like most farmhouse kitchens, the O'Learys' was the heart of the house and the room where the family spent most of their time. Andy was slouched in a chair reading the *Farmer's Weekly*, Grandpa was polishing the horse brasses and Grandma was darning socks using an orange instead of her wooden mushroom because the latter had somehow disappeared in the welter of oddments scattered around the room. Cassie smiled brightly at the assembled company.

'I've written my letter to my secret lover,' she said sarcastically. 'Now I'm going to the village to post it.' She directed a challenging look at Andy. 'I'm afraid I've already sealed it, but you're welcome to look at the address.' She turned to old Mrs O'Leary.

'You'd like my friend Rosheen, I know. She's very straightforward and honest. We were in the WAAF together, and she has twin girls, April and May.'

Andy looked up from his paper. He had ignored her remark about the letter and when he spoke it was a neutral tone. 'I'll walk down to the village with you,' he said. 'Or don't you feel like company? Would you rather go alone?'

Cassie happened to be looking at his grandfather as he spoke, and saw the look of pain which crossed his rosy face. Guilt made her feel ashamed. Grandpa O'Leary loved Andy, and was proud of him. She had not intended to hurt the old man and hastily manufactured a bright smile.

'Whatever makes you think I'd rather be alone?' She glanced out of the kitchen window, the view framed by red gingham curtains. 'It's a grand evening for a stroll – I shan't even need a coat.'

She was glad to see the pain in old Mr O'Leary's face replaced by pleasure. 'So it is, so it is,' he said enthusiastically. 'Will I be comin' wit' you? 'Tis half an hour yet before we eat the grand pie me good wife's made.'

Andy cast a quick, amused glance at Cassie and she answered it with an equally friendly look. 'Thanks, Mr O'Leary, but maybe it's time Andy and I talked about my leaving,' she said. 'I dare say there are a thousand things I ought to be doing at home.'

'Oh aye, things like buyin' a weddin' dress,' Mr O'Leary, ever the soul of tact, suggested. 'You'll be wantin' a bridesmaid or two, I dare say, so that gal you mentioned, the one with twins, could be your matron of honour if the little 'uns would like to be flower girls. You'll want to get married in your own parish, of course?'

'Do hush, you silly old fool,' Grandma said, obviously well aware of the situation. 'Just let these young 'uns sort out their own problems, for problems they undoubtedly have.'

Andy grinned at his grandmother. 'Any further delaying tactics?' he asked. 'And don't worry that we'll murder one another now there's just the two of us, because I'm a real gentleman so I am and Cassandra here is a proper little lady.'

Both grandparents laughed. 'Don't be too long now; supper will be on the table in t'irty minutes so you'd best hurry,' was old Mr O'Leary's parting shot.

The minute they were out of the stable yard Andy took Cassie's hand and got straight to the point. 'It isn't working, is it?' he said. 'Everything was grand the first week but it's been going downhill ever since. It seems to me I can't do a thing right. When we were young I used to boss you about and you took it like a lamb, but now I have to measure every word I say and if I get it wrong you go for the jugular. When we first met after the war I thought it was as though we'd stepped back in time and could start again, but it's not so, is it?'

They were halfway down the lane, avoiding puddles and ducking under overgrown hedges, for though O'Leary land was kept in pristine condition the unadopted lane that ran through it was over-grown, with untrimmed hedges and tangled verges. Cassie was so astonished that she could only stare at her companion, her eyes rounding, and she listened without interruption as Andy continued. 'I begin to suspect, Cassie, that we're neither of us very nice people,' he said ruefully. 'I lied to you about why I didn't want to get involved with women during the war. Oh, that was part of it, but mainly I felt I'd gone through a door and should shut it behind me and begin a new life – a different sort of life – with a clean slate. Do you understand?'

'I think I can see how you might feel that, but I don't understand why you had to lie about it,' Cassie said, not meeting his eyes. 'Didn't you trust me enough to tell me the truth?'

Andy caught hold of her shoulders and forced her to look at him. 'Of course I trust you. But it was agony to see you pulling away from me and leaning towards Colin, although I tried to tell myself you'd come round. You know he was in love with you, don't you?'

Cassie met his gaze at last. 'Yes, I do,' she said honestly. 'And it will be a long time before I can forgive myself for encouraging him to think I might one day feel the same about him, when all the time I was in love with you.' She smiled. 'And whilst we're confessing to our sins, I've been jealous of the way you look at Rebecca sometimes, as though – as though—'

Andy laughed delightedly and tightened his hold on Cassie's shoulders. 'I'm very fond of Rebecca, of course I am, but she's not my type. Oh, Cassie, how could you think I'd look twice at any other girl if you were around? And I've worked out what I'm doing wrong. You see, I've got too used to being skipper of a Lancaster, which is no sinecure. I've been making decisions that could have endangered the lives of my entire crew if I'd got them wrong, and when you're flying towards your target with Messerschmitts and ack-ack guns trying to stop you completing your mission you have to know that your orders will be obeyed.' He took a deep breath and pushed a lock of Cassie's hair behind her ear. 'I'm going to have to learn to talk to people again instead of commanding them. Oh, Cassie, tell me it's not too late; give me another chance?'

Cassie wound her arms around Andy's neck and kissed his cheek. 'We should have had this con-versation as soon as we reached the stud,' she said remorsefully. 'Don't forget, although I was only a sergeant I too have been giving orders and expecting instant obedience from my flight. So of course it's not too late, even if it takes time for the effects of war to wear off. And now we understand each other we can face whatever the future holds together.'

Andy beamed and gave a whoop. 'We'll start from scratch,' he said joyfully. 'We can make a go of it if we acknowledge the difficulties we face.

Cassie smiled. 'Do you realise we both actually apologised?' she said. 'And now let's go home and tell your grandparents that I'm no longer talking about going back to England.' With their arms clasped tightly round each other's waist they turned back towards the house, but after a few paces Andy pulled Cassie to a stop.

'What about your errand?' he asked. 'If you remember, my love, we were walking to the village to post a letter to your friend Rosheen.'

Cassie's hand dived into her pocket and found the letter. 'Oh, that!' she said airily. 'There's no hurry; it can wait until tomorrow,' and on the words she crumpled the letter into a ball.

Chapter Twenty-three

December 1948

Rosheen was in the kitchen, baking, when she heard the postman. She checked the clock on the wall: Mr Tomkins might appreciate a cup of tea, for it was icy cold and a bitter wind did little to add to the comfort of those unfortunate enough to have to work outside in this weather. Rosheen trotted up the hall, swooped on the mail, and opened the door. She had been right: Mr Tomkins stood on the top step, hand already reaching out to the doorknob. Rosheen smiled at him.

'Morning, Mr Tomkins,' she said. 'How about a nice cuppa? And I've a round of shortbread cooling on the windowsill. I say, it's perishin' cold today. D'you think we'll have a white Christmas? Do come in and let me shut the door.'

Mr Tomkins complied, and presently the two of them were seated on opposite sides of the big kitchen table, sipping from their respective mugs.

'You're a good lass,' Mr Tomkins said. 'There's

nothing like a hot cup of tea to warm a fellow through.' He peered inquisitively at the letters Rosheen had thrown down on the table. 'I see your mam still writes to you reg'lar; still in Bootle with that brother of hers, is she? And how're them twins? Still enjoyin' their studies?' He peered round the kitchen as though expecting to see a twin suddenly materialise. 'It'll be their Christmas holidays now, though?'

'You're right; they're not at school, but they've got holiday jobs,' Rosheen admitted. 'But we're going away for Christmas, to a wedding in Ireland. Did you ever meet my friend Cassie? We were in the WAAF together?'

Mr Tomkins scratched his head, tipping his post office cap back in order to do so. He did not employ Brylcreem on his grey thatch and Rosheen was tempted to offer to lend him a comb, but said nothing.

'Cassie?' the postman said thoughtfully. 'Would that be the little lass wi' ginger hair? I misremember her name, but as I recall she lived in Nightingale Court. Not that anyone lives there any more, because it's a part of this 'ere slum clearance what the Nazis done for us.'

'I know who you mean; Bessie Dale,' Rosheen said quickly. Given a warm fire and a cup of tea, if you didn't watch it Mr Tomkins would still be with you by teatime, so she reached across and opened the letter from Mrs Clarke. 'I'll just make sure it's nothing important,' she added, extracting a couple of sheets of thin paper from the envelope. She scanned them briefly, then got to her feet. 'But I mustn't keep you.' She fished the postman's bag out from under the table and handed it to him, pretending to stagger under its weight. 'Goodness, Mr Tomkins, it'll be night time before you get this lot delivered!'

Mr Tomkins snorted. 'Everyone's leavin' it till the last minute,' he observed. 'They never thinks of the postman. Ho no, they never considers us. And why's this pal of yours rushing into marriage when everyone else is settling in for Christmas?'

Rosheen laughed. 'I wouldn't call it rushing into marriage,' she protested. 'She and her young man got engaged last Christmas so it'll be a year by the time they tie the knot.'

'Oh aye? When I were a lad five years weren't uncommon for an engagement,' Mr Tomkins said, shouldering his bag. 'When do you leave for Ireland? If it's tomorrer like, I'll wish you seasons greetings right now and you can give me my Christmas box.'

Rosheen wagged a reproving finger, then crossed the kitchen and scooped the shortbread into a waiting bag and handed it to the postman. 'The twins' jobs finish at five o'clock tomorrow,' she told him, 'and we're leaving on the ferry the day after that. I don't expect any more post before then, so you can take the shortbread instead of the tuppence I would have given you otherwise.'

'Tuppence? You'd ha' giv' me more than that! Well, many thanks and seasons greetings,' Mr Tomkins said, pocketing the brown paper bag. 'You're a good lass, Rosheen Clarke, and you make the best shortbread of anyone in Liverpool. When's you comin' home from this Irish wedding of yourn?'

'Twenty-seventh,' Rosheen said, opening the door. 'The happy couple are having a week in London as a honeymoon so I reckon everyone will leave as soon as Boxing Day's over.'

'Ah well, see you in the New Year,' Mr Tomkins said philosophically. 'Have a good Christmas, queen, whilst you're livin' on the fat of the land which I understand the Irish does, what wi' no rationing an' all. And give the twins me best wishes when they gets home tonight.'

Mr Tomkins left and Rosheen flew to her oven, but the mince pies could do with another five minutes so she closed the door on them and returned to her mail. Two Christmas cards, one of which was from Sally Plevin – now Sally Stewart – who had married a Northumberland man and had frequently invited Rosheen to visit her, extolling the beauties of Northumberland until Rosheen quite longed to see them for herself. The other was from a neighbour who had gone to live with her married daughter and had enclosed a note reminding Rosheen a trifle wistfully of the days when she had lived in the courts and they had regularly shared a joke together.

Lastly came a missive from Cassie. She, too, wrote often about the beauties of Ireland, in particular the charms of the O'Leary stud, and Rosheen smiled at the recollection. She was going to see it for herself, and though it would have been nice had the wedding been in summer Cassie assured her friend that a further invitation to visit would be forthcoming once next summer arrived. *Oh, Rosheen, I simply can't wait to see you again. Isn't it odd that you've never met Andy in all the years we've known one another? You might say it was a treat in store ... I certainly think so!*

There wasn't much more to the letter than that, so Rosheen hastily read the last page and rushed back to the range, wrenching the oven door open and giving a whistle of relief when she saw that the mince pies were done to a turn. Despite the twins' holiday jobs money was still in short supply, and at Cassie's suggestion Rosheen's wedding present to the happy couple was a beautiful tiered cake, iced by Rosheen herself, and a couple of dozen mince pies, ostensibly from the twins – they had bought the mincemeat – to be enjoyed at the wedding breakfast.

Rosheen had not told Cassie this, but in fact she rather hoped she might be able to find a bed and breakfast place where she and the twins might put up for a few days before returning home. She was proud of her Irish heritage and hated having to tell enquirers that she had never visited the land of her birth, although in truth she had been born in Liverpool and apart from her war service had lived there all her life. She picked up one of the mince pies and took a cautious bite, then squeaked.

Serve you right, Rosheen Clarke, she scolded herself. Do you want to fit into your wedding finery or don't you? The wedding takes place the day after tomorrow so surely you can wait just another couple of days. She stood the mince pie with its missing half moon down just as the door opened and the twins came clattering down the corridor and into the kitchen.

'Ooh, mince pies,' April said. She picked up the one her mother had bitten, split it in two and handed half to her sister. 'Can't take damaged goods to a wedding,' she said through a mouthful. 'Did you know it was snowing, our Mam? It's only just started, but it's laying. Oh, Mam, s'pose the ferries stop running! I've never been a bridesmaid and judging from what Auntie Cassie says the frocks we'll be wearing are real pretty. S'pose we miss the wedding? I'll die of disappointment, and so will May.'

Horrified, Rosheen went to the window and looked out. Snow was indeed whirling past the panes and already the cobbles which paved the court were hidden. She turned back to her daughters. 'One thing we never thought of was snow,' she said gloomily. 'Oh, I know there is such a thing as a white Christmas, but it's pretty rare. Still, we've a couple of days' grace before the crossing and maybe, if the wind drops, the ferries will sail anyway. Cassie said in her last letter that we must look out for her relatives aboard the ferry because most of them will be travelling with us. You both met Mrs Valentine when we visited the Wirral, so we can ask her to introduce us to the rest. Come to think of it, they might simply put the wedding off if they realise there'll be no bridesmaids or matron of honour. But we mustn't meet troubles halfway; the weather may clear.'

Rosheen awoke on the day of the wedding and lay still for a moment, listening, then got out of bed, crossed the room and pulled back the curtains. The court was still a white-out with snow actually piling up against some of the doors, but the wind had dropped and the Christmassy scene was lit by wintry sunshine. When Rosheen tilted her head up she could see a sparkling pale blue sky. However, it was still extremely cold, so she unhooked her dressing gown from the door and pushed her feet into her slippers before she padded across the room and out on to the landing. The previous day the ferry sailings had been cancelled and the wedding party had begun to despair of making the crossing. The Valentine contingent had booked into a hotel,

439

whilst Mrs Valentine cheered everyone up by saying that snow alone would not be sufficient to cancel the sailings.

'If the wind drops we might still make the reception, even if we can't actually attend the ceremony,' she had told the assembled guests. 'Well, I'm not a woman to apportion blame but I did say I thought it was a trifle risky to be having a Christmas wedding. It's not just the snow, it's the Irish Sea. I remember, during the war ...'

'She's off,' April had whispered to her sister. 'If we just wander away we can avoid hearing the lecture all over again.' She had pulled a face. 'Well, let's hope the weather forecast is right and the ship sails first thing tomorrow.'

Rosheen opened the twins' door and was not surprised to find their beds empty. The wedding meant a lot to her daughters, she knew. They had not seen the beautiful full-length frocks which Cassie had had made for them, but to please their mother they had had their hair cut in identical styles and at first glance were immediately identifiable as twins. Their disappointment when the planned crossing had been cancelled was understandable, but looking out of the window and seeing the trees no longer lashed by a vicious wind Rosheen began to think it was quite possible that they would make the wedding after all.

The twins were already in the kitchen, May

pouring tea and April slicing the loaf, and as soon as their mother appeared she was thrust into a chair, given a cup of tea and a piece of toast and told to hurry up with her breakfast.

'We're sure the ferries will do the crossing today, because Mr McAlistair – who works on one of them – has left for work and he wouldn't do that if they'd cancelled all the sailings,' May said triumphantly. 'April and I ran out into the snow – don't fuss, Mam, we put on our wellies and overcoats – and asked him what he thought, and he's pretty sure the ferries will actually sail today, although they're almost certain to be late. He said there'd be too many disappointed passengers if they cancelled again, and when we explained about the wedding he laughed and said he knew old Mr O'Leary well and the ould feller would have a grosh of vehicles standing by when the ferry eventually docked, ready to whisk the guests to their destination.'

On the day of the wedding, Cassie hopped out of bed and ran at once to the window, jerking back the curtains with an impatient hand. Outside, the world was white; the farmyard, the range of stables and the rutted lane which led to the village were blanketed in snow. Cassie gave a moan of dismay. Everything had been going like clockwork. The O'Leary relatives had arrived the previous evening, ready to do anything they could to help though so far, Cassie reflected rather bitterly, their help had consisted of eating enormous meals, telling a great many stories and getting to know the Valentines, or at least getting to know Mr Valentine, because his wife was one of the wedding party still in Liverpool, having promised to organise things from her end.

The group had planned to leave on the first sailing, but judging by what she could see from her window, Cassie imagined that the sailing itself would be in doubt. Even if it was merely held up, what on earth would they do? Her father was here to give her away, but her mother, as well as her matron of honour and the bridesmaids, would be absent from the wedding.

'What on earth are you doing? You'll perishing well freeze ... oh, my goodness. Snow! But you'd best get back into bed, because no one wants to marry a girl with double pneumonia!'

Cassie had jumped at the sound of Rebecca's voice, but then took her advice and spoke ruefully. 'Oh, Becky, it's all going to be spoiled. I shall have one bridesmaid – that's you – but no twins and no matron of honour, let alone half the number of wedding guests we've catered for. Honestly, it seems as though Andy and I are fated not to have things easy.'

She slipped back into her bed, then spoke more hopefully. 'Of course it may not be snowing in

Liverpool, and anyway the ferries may sail despite the snow. What's the time?'

Rebecca picked up the little alarm clock from the table by her bed. 'Seven o'clock,' she announced. 'The wedding isn't till two so stop worrying and get a bit of extra sleep. Your lovely prospective mother-in-law said she wouldn't serve breakfast until nine, so you don't have to get up yet. For heaven's sake stop worrying over something which may never happen. The snow's only a very light covering, perhaps no more than half an inch.'

Cassie cuddled down as Rebecca spoke, irrationally comforted by her friend's words. What did it matter after all, if she only had one bridesmaid instead of three? Her father slumbered in a room just up the landing, ready to give her away, the church had been booked for weeks and the wedding breakfast, she knew, would be set out in plenty of time. The honeymoon might have to be delayed but that would not matter. What really mattered was that by this afternoon she and Andy would be man and wife; the very thought made her shiver with delight, for she and Andy, working together at the farm and the stud, were now in perfect harmony. Cassie sighed. It had not always been easy but they had persevered over the past year, and when they had set the wedding date they both knew they were doing the right thing. They were marrying for the right reasons, because they loved one another deeply, because Andy accepted her as his equal, and because Cassie herself knew her opinions to be valued.

She glanced at the alarm clock's small face, then sat up. It was supposed to be unlucky for the bride and groom to meet before the wedding, but she was not superstitious, and anyway, because the house was bursting at the seams, Andy was sharing a room with her father just a little further up the landing. Unlucky or not, she found she wanted reassurance from Andy himself that the snow did not matter. She glanced across to where Becky was curled up and checked that her friend was asleep, then slid out of bed and padded over to where her dressing gown hung on the door. She put it on, thrust her feet into her fluffy pink mules and opened the door, stepping out on to the landing and nearly dying of fright when strong hands seized her shoulders and drew her into a close embrace.

'Oh, Andy, you scared me stiff!' she gasped, and felt his laugh against her cheek.

'Great minds think alike,' he whispered. 'I was coming to ask you if you'd looked out of the window yet? I thought you might be worrying that the ferries wouldn't sail, but what does it matter, after all? What really matters is our marriage, and that will go ahead if it snows ink, so don't worry, my darling; you wanted a white wedding and you're getting one!'

*

When the wedding guests arrived at the terminal for the Irish ferries Rosheen found a telephone and rang the stud. Mrs O'Leary answered and assured Rosheen that all the arrangements were in hand. Because the ferry was unlikely to dock on time it had been decided that the party from England had best go straight to the church. The twins would find their dresses in the vestry, and after that things would proceed as though nothing had disturbed the plans.

And so it proved. Old Mr O'Leary, in his best suit, had commandeered every vehicle for miles around, and when the wedding guests arrived at the little station they were bundled without ceremony into the waiting convoy.

'Where's the bridesmaids?' he hollered. 'I'm to take them first and show them where to change.'

April and May waved to get Mr O'Leary's attention. 'We're here. Are we coming with you?' April said, looking around for her mother.

Mr O'Leary nodded. 'Mine's the car at the front, so we can leave straight away.'

The twins went with him whilst Rosheen travelled in an old-fashioned carriage with Mrs Valentine. When they reached the village church, they found the pews half full and people milling around everywhere. Mrs Valentine began to tell Rosheen who was who, but suddenly the younger woman clutched her arm. 'See those three fellers, all with their heads together?' she said excitedly. 'Who's the man with the pink flower in his buttonhole? The one talking to the man with dark curly hair? Well, I never did; I never thought to see *him* again.'

Mrs Valentine looked puzzled. 'They've all got a pink buttonhole. One of them's Andy, the bridegroom,' she said. 'I think one of the others is the best man, Colin Trelawney. You must know him, Rosheen. You and Cassie were on the same station as he was.' She looked curiously at her young friend. 'Haven't you met Andy? I'll introduce you … oh, where's she gone running off to?'

Rosheen caught up with the men, who were clearly heading for the church. She greeted Colin warmly, then looked up into the face of a complete stranger. For a moment Rosheen was speechless: from a distance she had been certain that the man Mrs Valentine had called Andy was well known to her. Then the third man turned to face her, and she realised her mistake. At first the man looked surprised at the sudden interruption, but then Rosheen saw recognition dawn.

'You!' he whispered. 'I can't believe it! After all this time … how long has it been?'

Rosheen smiled. 'Seventeen years, give or take. I saw you from a distance and I couldn't believe my eyes.' She pulled him over to one side, away from the crowd. 'Look, I'm not here to cause any trouble, because Cassie's a dear friend of mine, but there's something I think you should know.'

He looked into her eyes, a frown creasing his brow. 'Sure and don't I want the answer to one or two questions myself? Why did you stand me up all those years ago? Didn't I wait all day for you, desperate to catch a sight of you, to come and tell me not to go for the job at the stud, to keep looking in Liverpool? But you never showed up. I got the hint, went for the interview, and got the job.'

Rosheen looked up, stricken. 'You mean you never went to America? Oh, Lee, and all these years I've been thinking . . . so when you said you were so desperate for a job you'd go to America if need be, you were actually coming for an interview here? Oh, if only I'd known. Because I did go down to the docks to meet you as I'd promised, of course I did, but I'd been feeling so dreadful that morning – I had a terrible headache and felt awfully sick – that it was much later than we'd agreed, and the only ship sailing for New York that day had already gone.'

A look of understanding crossed his face. 'So you never stood me up?'

Rosheen shook her head. 'No, but none of that matters now. You're about to get married, and I wouldn't do anything to interfere with that.'

His eyebrows shot up. 'I am? And isn't that news to me?' He chuckled. 'Andy's the one getting married, you silly goose ...'

447

Rosheen looked puzzled. 'But Mrs Valentine pointed you out. I thought it was odd, because you told me your name was Liam.'

He smiled. 'That's because my name is Liam.' He nodded his head towards the other man now entering the church with Colin. '*That's* Andy ... he's my boss.'

Realisation dawned and Rosheen felt her cheeks grow warm. 'I've jumped to conclusions like a cock at a blackberry, haven't I? I'm so sorry.'

Liam smiled back. 'Well, I wouldn't have put it quite like that myself, but not to worry ... ah, here comes the bride. I'd best go in.'

As he spoke there was a crunch of gravel and a Rolls pulled into the churchyard. Snow had begun to fall in little flakes, drifting down like confetti, though the sun still illumined the wintry landscape. The chauffeur got out of the car, adjusted his cap, and opened the door for Cassie, a dream bride in snowy lace, holding a bouquet of Christmas roses. Mr Valentine helped his daughter out of the car, eyeing her with loving admiration.

Cassie glanced around, spotted Rosheen and felt a tide of relief wash over her. If Rosheen was here then so were her bridesmaids, as well as all the wedding guests who had come to wish her well. Ridiculously, tears filled her eyes as Rosheen ran towards her and gave her a hug.

'You made it!' Cassie said thankfully. 'When the

snow started I had awful visions of having only half a wedding, but the moment I saw you I knew everything was all right.' She glanced around the churchyard, empty now apart from Mr Valentine who had gone to wait in the porch. 'I expect Andy's already inside waiting for me to drift up the aisle like some exotic snow maiden.' A doubt seemed to shake her. 'He *is* inside isn't he? He hasn't stood me up?'

Rosheen laughed. 'I've heard of wedding nerves but yours are ridiculous,' she said. 'He's the one who may be feeling a trifle nervous. He and Liam arrived in time to help your father-in-law gather the guests together and tell everyone the way to the house, where the wedding breakfast, I suspect, is probably already set out.'

Cassie clapped her hand to her heart. 'Here's me getting in a state over Andy, when I know perfectly well that he would never let me down, and forgetting that you've never met him. Though I see you've met Liam Banks; he's our manager as well as Andy's best man. I saw you chatting as the car approached the church. Liam's nice, isn't he?'

Rosheen hid a smile. 'Very nice,' she replied gravely. And then she grabbed her friend's arm as a strain of organ music began to issue from the little grey church. 'Come on, you awful girl. I've just spotted the twins, looking unbelievably beautiful, poking their noses out of the porch, so unless you want to be in their bad books you'll get a move on.' She chuckled. 'I don't want any quarrelling over who's going to carry your train, so let's get this show on the road! Let me go in first, then I can check that the girls have their posies and so on.'

They entered the church, and Rosheen slid into the seat which Liam was clearly saving for her. Cassie reached Andy's side and he turned to look down at her, his eyes full of love. 'Darling girl, I was beginning to think you'd lost your nerve,' he whispered. 'It's a terrifying thing, this marriage business. Oh, Cassie, I love you so much!'

Cassie smiled up at him and was about to reply when the rector spoke up in his rich Irish brogue.

'Dearly beloved, we are gathered together …'

Throughout the wedding ceremony, the twins behaved as the little ladies they thought themselves to be. Though the sun shone, it was still a very cold day and the girls, dressed demurely in white organza with little fur boleros to keep them warm, regarded themselves with deep satisfaction. They knew the bride was the main attraction and were careful not to try to outshine her, but they were delighted with their dresses, the wreaths of sweet-smelling briar roses, carefully trimmed of thorns, which crowned their smoothly shining hair, and the little white satin slippers Cassie had given them. They thought they looked nicer than the chief bridesmaid –

Becky, Cassie had called her – but obeyed her every command, and when the bridal couple went into the vestry they helped Becky to straighten Cassie's train.

On the way out of the church there was a hold-up as the photographer arranged groups in the porch, and the twins exchanged quick glances and slipped back into the vestry to tuck strands of hair behind ears and rub shiny noses with the tiny powder puff May had secreted in the bodice of her dress. Then they peeped out of the vestry door, May noting with approval that Becky was holding the bride's train without assistance.

The doors of the church were narrow, and whilst photographs were being taken the crush of people prevented the twins' escape into the sunshine. Suddenly April turned to her sister. 'Did you see that?' she said in a hissing whisper. 'That feller, the one who saved a seat for our mam in the pew directly behind us, has pinched a posy of Christmas roses from the last pew and given it to her.' She sniffed. 'The cheek of it – they weren't even his to give!' She grabbed her twin's shoulder, giving it a little shake. 'Did you see it?'

May jerked her shoulder from her sister's grasp. 'Course I saw,' she said scornfully. 'I reckon we ought to catch him up as soon as we can get away from the crowd and tell him he's wasting his time makin' eyes at our mam. She ain't interested in men, never has been.'

'And if you ask me she don't know nothing about S.E.X.,' April interpolated. 'When she tried to tell us about the birds and the bees she went red as a beetroot. I'm sure as check that she don't know anywhere near as much as we do.'

May began to agree, then stopped, a frown creasing her brow. 'But April, if she's our mam – and she is – then how come she got us without knowing about S.E.X.? It don't make sense.'

'Oh, May, how can you be so stupid?' April squeaked. 'Haven't you ever heard of divine mis-conception? I s'pose it must have been that. But you're right: that feller can lay off tryin' to get round our mam because he's wasting his time; she don't like men. Hey, people are beginning to clear out of the porch. Shall we go?'

'Might as well,' May agreed. Suddenly another thought struck her and she pulled at April's arm. 'Tell you what, our April, it 'ud be a good thing if our mam did get herself a feller; it would give us a bit more freedom. Ever since Grandma went off to Bootle, Mam's been hangin' round our necks like – like the perishin' albatross in that poem: *The Ancient Mariner*, I think it's called. Mam will be lonely when we leave home, so we'd best keep our eyes peeled for a nice, handsome feller to come a-courting and take her off our hands.'

May was only half joking, but April seized on the suggestion. 'You're right, our May,' she said as they wriggled through the departing crowd. She giggled and jerked her thumb to where her mother and the stranger stood. 'Look at that! They're holdin' hands! Tell you what, May, we'll have a bet. I bet you ten bob our mam gets herself a feller before we go to university.'

'You're on, April Clarke,' May said. 'Hey, look – she's pointing at us!'

'Let's clear out before she calls us over and introduces us,' April said urgently. 'C'mon, May, don't hang around. From now on we've got our own lives to lead. I say, did you *see* the wedding cake, and all them plates of off-ration grub? I can't wait to get stuck in!'

Liam clasped his large hands round Rosheen's small ones as she raised the Christmas roses to her lips.

'Sure and isn't it too bad that I've no Christmas present for you,' he said regretfully. 'But the last thing I expected was to find you again, my lovely girl.'

Rosheen gave a purring chuckle of amusement. 'Well, I've got a gift for you,' she said. 'Two, in fact. It's going to come as quite a shock ...'